THE BEST OF TIMES

THE BEST OF TIMES

A novel by
J. Louis Yampolsky

MOUNT ROSS PRESS

The Best of Times

Published by:
Mount Ross Press
Wynnewood, Pennsylvania
mountrosspress@gmail.com

Publisher's Cataloging-In-Publication Data
(Prepared by The Donohue Group, Inc.)

Names: Yampolsky, J. Louis, 1928- author.
Title: The best of times : a novel / by J. Louis Yampolsky.
Description: [Wynnewood, Pennsylvania] : Mount Ross Press, [2022]
Identifiers: ISBN 9780578348537 (paperback) | ISBN 9780578348544 (ebook)
Subjects: LCSH: Veterans--New Jersey--History--20th century--Fiction. | Businesspeople--New Jersey--History--20th century--Fiction. | Wives--Death--Psychological aspects--Fiction. | Loss (Psychology)--Fiction. | Technological innovations--Fiction. | Mobile communication systems--Fiction.
Classification: LCC PS3625.A67225 B47 2022 (print) | LCC PS3625.A67225 (ebook) | DDC 813/.6--dc23

Paperback ISBN: 978-0-578-34853-7
eISBN: 978-0-578-34854-4

Copyediting and Proofreading: Kim Bookless
Cover and Interior Design: GKS Creative
Project Management: The Cadence Group
Photograph of J. Louis Yampolsky by Michael J. Ross

Prologue

HE STOOD QUIETLY, leaning against the signpost. Waiting. He picked at his teeth with a stained wooden toothpick.

There. There she is. Approaching . . . graceful strides, erect, so good-looking. She was smiling as though something funny had just occurred to her.

He returned the toothpick to his pocket and pushed off from the signpost. Two quick, silent steps and he had her. She gasped, recognizing him as his left hand shot out to seize her upper right arm. He clubbed her left temple with a hardened fist, knocking her unconscious.

* * *

The incident hadn't happened yet. It was almost twenty years off.

I'm Jack Laurel, and this is my story. It begins with a beautiful sunrise in December 1943.

1

Morning in the South Pacific

THAT MORNING, A song stuck in my head, repeating again and again. I could not get rid of it.

I heard it the night before on Armed Forces Radio, coming from KHJ Radio in Los Angeles. The hosts that night were Bing Crosby and Dorothy Lamour. Bing's voice came through the radio remarkably clear. That baritone voice, rich and deep.

"What's our next request, Dorothy?"

There was a smile in her response. "This one is from Corporal Wes Davis of Scottsbluff, Nebraska, Bing. He writes from somewhere in the Pacific to request "I'll Be Seeing You" and dedicating it to Harriet. His girl, maybe? Well, here it is, Wes, sung by Peggy Lee with Benny Goodman's band. For Harriet."

And the music played.

> *I'll be seeing you*
> *In all the old familiar places . . .*

This morning, the song was in my head. I didn't want it, considering what was coming, but it wouldn't go away.

* * *

I studied the horizon through my field glasses. Blue sky, bluer ocean. Diamonds dancing on the waters.

The first of the early morning sun's rays emerged from the sea to start the day. The ball of fire rising out of the east was burning off pink mist that lay along the horizon.

I scanned slowly along the horizon line from east to west. All was tranquility. Seabirds wheeled overhead, their cries filling the fresh morning air.

I'll be seeing you . . . all day through.

The binoculars made a slow sweep westward. They paused at a warship near the horizon, a heavy cruiser, then moved on. A cluster of warships came into view, closer in.

2

Attack on Cape Gloucester

December 26, 1943

THERE WERE HUNDREDS of ships. Destroyers, medium and heavy cruisers, tankers, LSTs, minesweepers, ships of every description.

At precisely five o'clock in the morning, a hundred bombers and the same number of fighter planes roared into sight, coming out of the east. The music in my head stopped abruptly. The fighters came from aircraft carriers beyond the horizon. The bombers were land-based, from bases in northern Australia. The barrage began. The day shattered.

Body blows from the boom of the warships' big guns pounded us and sucked the air out of our lungs, hammered our ears. The world was on fire, screaming with the sounds of war: the drone of a hundred bombers, the blasts of their bombs, the snarling whines of the fighter planes, and the staccato bursts of their strafing runs. Thick smoke bellowed up from the bomb blasts.

We sat on the deck of the troop transport, all eyes focused on the thin strip of land in the distance that grew bigger as the ship came closer to our rendezvous with the waiting circle of landing craft, a thousand yards offshore.

It was December 26, 1943, the twenty-fifth month of the War. I was a second lieutenant, in charge of a forty-man Marine Corps rifle platoon headed into our first combat mission. We were part of the First Marine Division's attack on the Japanese-held island of New Guinea. The Jap was fortifying the island into a base for an invasion of Australia. There was an airfield on the northwest shore of the island, at Cape Gloucester. Our objective was to capture it.

Our ship was part of the attack force. There were twenty troop transports like the one we were on, thirty patrol boats, twenty-five amphibious DUKWs that would hit the beach and continue on as land-based troop carriers and mobile artillery, and twenty LSTs—huge cargo ships that would drive up onto the beaches, giant bow doors opening to spill out their cargoes of tanks, jeeps, half-tracks, and motorized artillery.

Soon we could make out the waves rolling onto a narrow beach of black sand, a jungle beyond and a mountain range in the distance. There were at least a hundred LCIs—landing craft infantry, the smaller landing craft that ferry the troops from the transports to the beaches.

A one-mile strip of beach was the center of a boiling cauldron of war, filled with black smoke and dark fire and the explosions of thousands of shells that whistled in over our heads from the warships behind us. And the noise! It was unbearable. My ears were going to burst; my brain was going to burst. Hell must be like this.

I studied my men—mostly boys, really. They studied the island, wincing from the roaring in their heads, impassive, most of them smoking, trying to stay calm or pretending to be calm. Truthfully, we were all filled with fear—indescribable, teeth-clenching fear. No one more than me. It was our first engagement.

Our ship stopped. As it did, it began to roll from side to side. The waiting landing craft circled us. Sailors aboard the ship threw cargo nets over the side for us to climb down into the landing craft.

"Up on your feet, men!" I shouted. "The captain will signal our turn."

The rolling of the ship was having its effect. It was an effort to stand without something to hold on to. One of the men called out, weakly, "Lieutenant, I'm gonna be sick." No sooner had he said it when he vomited in great spasms onto his boots and the deck. No one moved or even looked at him. Each man was absorbed by his own thoughts and fears.

I forced myself to project calm and confidence. "Okay, men," I shouted above the noise. "We'll be climbing down the cargo net in a few minutes into the landing craft, just like we practiced. Keep calm. Sergeant Kelly and first squad will go down first, then second squad, third squad, fourth squad. I'll go down last, into the bow, and I'll be first out onto the beach. You'll follow me onto the beach and into the bush. We'll be running. Keep up with me. Ready . . . move to the rail!"

I struggled to keep my voice firm and strong. *Mustn't show worry. Gotta put on a good front.* My attitude had to project confidence. *Let's get on with it!* I knew that every man among them was contemplating his own death—or worse, some horrible maiming that would leave him alive as less than a man. I tried to crack a joke to ease the tension, "They promised me an ocean cruise!" I shouted out above the noise. A few men laughed, nervous laughter, attempts to be tough. It is fear of ridicule and contempt from the platoon that moves the men—that and the discipline we try to instill—but the need to look brave in front of the others is the strongest motivation. A coward is a pariah.

We climbed down the net from the rolling hull of the ship into the bobbing landing craft, each man with a rifle slung over his shoulder and a sixty-pound backpack of ammo and supplies. Down the cargo net we struggled. A man slipped and fell, clawing at the net as he fell but unable to catch hold. He fell with a cry between the ship's hull and the landing craft. Two sailors on the landing craft threw him a line and leaned over the side to haul him up. He tried to jam his rifle horizontally between the two hulls, but the landing craft brushed it aside and slammed against the hull of the ship, crushing him instantly. I felt rather than heard the squashing sound. The episode took less than five seconds.

"Leave him be," shouted the captain of the landing craft. "Finish loading—we ain't got all day!"

The last few men and me dropped into the boat, and we moved into a horizontal line with ten other landing craft and sped toward the beach, into that hell of noise, smoke, fire, ships beaching themselves, tanks and DUKWs driving onto the beach, soldiers running out of the LCIs, up the beach toward the jungle, some falling before they reached it, aircraft swooping low over the island on strafing runs and the big shells from the guns of the distant warships raining onto the island.

Our LCI hit the beach and lowered its ramp. "Follow me!" I shouted over my shoulder, racing down the ramp.

***

Heavy fire was coming at us from out of the jungle. The Jap was invisible in the solid green denseness of the jungle. I ran across the beach toward the line of jungle, stopping every ten yards to turn to face my men and wave them onward. "Move! Move!" I shouted, and waved my arm furiously, urging them on. I heard the *crack* of the Jap rifles and the *zip-zip-zip-zip* of a machine gun. I heard the bullets whizzing by. Three of my men fell on the beach before the platoon reached the jungle's edge. One was my aide. He was running alongside me only a couple of yards away with a walkie-talkie slung over one shoulder and the battery and antenna pouch on his back. He took a hit in his chest. *Thud!* He grunted as he fell, instantly, the last sound he ever made. I stooped over him, quickly collected the walkie-talkie, took off the battery and antenna pouch, and stopped the nearest man. "Here!" I shouted above the noise. "You're my aide. Put the pouch on your back and take the walkie-talkie. Give me your rifle." Before the campaign was over, he, too, was killed. Another man became my aide.

Our job was to take the Cape Gloucester airfield. We did. The fighting lasted only a few days. My forty-man platoon lost seven men. The company lost fifty-two, including our captain—the company commander, a seven-year veteran. He'd been in the first American offensive of the War, in August 1942. Guadalcanal. He survived six months of deadly combat on Guadalcanal while seventy-one hundred American servicemen were killed. I used to study him as if he were a superman; I studied everything about him. I wanted to capture the essence of the man, the indefinable quality that had carried him safely through the Guadalcanal campaign. Cape Gloucester was his second combat mission.

Replacements arrived, including a fresh new second lieutenant for my platoon. He was two years older than me, but he seemed only a boy. Having survived my first combat engagement, I had become a man. The first lieutenant, who had been the captain's aide, was promoted to captain. He was the new company commander. I moved up to take his place as the company's first lieutenant.

***

That was my company's first combat engagement. The next was Peleliu in September 1944. We lost fifty-six men on Peleliu, including the new captain. That's where I was promoted to captain to take his place.

3

The Pacific Strategy

AMERICA'S ENTRY INTO the War began with the Japanese attack on Pearl Harbor on December 7, 1941. The Jap swept through all of Southeast Asia in three months, including all the islands and island chains in the South Pacific. Australia was to be next, then Hawaii.

In the summer of 1942, after stopping the momentum of Japanese advances, the American strategy was to invade and retake one strategic island at a time, leaping across vast ocean stretches toward island targets, leaving Japanese garrisons behind to wither, cut off from replacements, supplies, and support. Every island we captured became a forward air base and supply depot, ever closer to the Japanese homeland. Every one of our invasions involved hundreds of ships, thousands of planes, tens of thousands of soldiers, sailors, and Marines. All told, there were eleven amphibian invasions. Each exacted its toll in thousands of American lives. Journalists referred to those deadly amphibious assaults in the Pacific—three of which I survived—as "island-hopping." It had a benign sound.

4

Okinawa

THE OKINAWA INVASION was my third, in April 1945. There were more Americans in the Okinawa invasion than in the 1944 D-Day landing on Normandy in France. And more American ships and planes. Of my original 186-man company that landed on New Guinea sixteen months earlier, fewer than one hundred of us remained. After each engagement, the replacements arrived and about half of them died in the next engagement. The War was a death machine, insatiable. It ground us up, relentlessly, and demanded more.

On Okinawa, we didn't lose a man the first day. A miracle. Maybe the Jap was gone? They fought to the death at our two previous engagements and at all the other places where my company and the First Marine Division were not in it, places like Guadalcanal, Tarawa, Kwajalein, Saipan, Eniwetok, Guam, Tinian, Iwo Jima. The Jap couldn't repulse our amphibious assaults. Every one succeeded, no matter how steep the price in American lives.

Four hours into the Okinawa attack, we thought maybe the Jap had pulled out, bringing their troops home for the ultimate battle, the invasion of Japan. Wrong.

The worst part of fighting the Jap was that he never surrendered. When he was beaten and knew it and should have surrendered, he fought on. So we continued to lose men after the fight for an island was won. The Jap fought to the last man. Yes, for real—to the last man. On Peleliu, my second invasion, the island was won in a few days, but the Jap fought on for twenty-five. The Jap lost two thousand men before the island was won then six thousand more after he was beaten and should have surrendered. We lost one thousand Marines on Peleliu to win the island and then two thousand more because the Jap never quit. Total Japanese prisoners taken on Peleliu: five, who ran out of ammo and didn't have the nerve to jump off a cliff or fall on their bayonets.

On Okinawa, we began to relax by the end of the first day. It looked like the island was ours for free, a cakewalk. On day two, as we pushed into the interior, we learned how wrong we were. The Jap was dug in, in caves and fortified bunkers. We were going to have to root him out, one cave at a time. My battalion's first objective was to take the Yontan Airfield. It took us three days and cost my company fifteen men.

I listened to Armed Forces Radio that night after we secured the airfield. There was a rebroadcast of radio station WNBC, New York: *Today, on day four of the Okinawa invasion, the battle-hardened veterans of the First Marine Division captured the Yontan Airfield after three days of fighting. Our casualties were light. Control of the airfield will permit delivery of supplies and reinforcements by air and assures our victory in the battle for Okinawa.*

We all had a grim laugh at the expression *battle-hardened veterans.* As if surviving a battle made a soldier smarter or better than the ones who bought it. *Battle-hardened veterans.* What a joke. *Lucky bastards* was more like it. And what of that other phrase, *Casualties were light*? Were the families of those who died that day comforted to know that *casualties were light*? I guess after surviving only one or two other amphibious landing operations, they were not yet *battle-hardened.*

After eighty-two days, Okinawa was secured. My company lost forty-two men; we were just one company among five hundred or so. The Jap lost one hundred thirty-seven thousand troops. We suffered twelve thousand killed and another forty thousand wounded. Doggedly, we began to reassemble for the biggest effort of all, the invasion of Japan.

5

The War

I ENLISTED THE DAY after I graduated from Atlantic City High School in June 1942. I was eighteen. I was selected for the Marine Officers' Candidate School, or OCS, on the basis of a series of physicals and IQ tests. Marine OCS usually required a minimum of one year of college, but so critical was the need for combat lieutenants that a special program was created for enlisted men: the Marine Enlisted Commission Educating Program. It started with the regular, arduous three-month OCS program to turn us into Marine officers; *ninety-day wonders,* we were called. Those of us who made it through OCS moved on to Marine Basic School for Officers at Camp Lejeune, North Carolina, a tough twenty-six-week program that force-fed combat tactics and tested us to the limit of physical endurance. We came out as second lieutenants.

I was assigned to a newly formed rifle company in the Third Infantry Regiment of the First Marine Division. I was barely nineteen, a living testament to the desperate need for combat officers.

The war was a blur of training exercises, and waiting, and boarding troop ships, and storming beaches and fighting and losing men, and then waiting and waiting, then moving on … and then the next island, and more blood and men lost.

The average combat life of an infantry second lieutenant was two and a half days. A second lieutenant who survived his first amphibian landing stood a good chance of becoming a first lieutenant for the next, and captain for the next. That's how I came to be a captain before I was even old enough to vote or be served in a bar.

***

World War II aroused a unified patriotism and national effort unlike any American war since the Revolution. Because it was a war of survival. The enemies had the military might, determination, industrial capacity, and global reach to defeat, occupy, and impose their will on us. We witnessed France, with what was supposed to be the world's best and most modern army, falling to the Germans within a few weeks, and the Philippines, Malaysia, Indo-China, and Burma all falling to the Japanese in less than a month. Our country, our very way of life, was in danger.

There was no full mobilization in our earlier wars. Our national existence was not at stake in those wars. WWII had to be won, the high level of casualties notwithstanding. It was the *Good War* because it was necessary.

The world will never see an equal to the American war effort of WWII. President Franklin D. Roosevelt asked for hundreds of warplanes monthly, along with hundreds of tanks, trucks, and jeeps. American industry gave FDR not just hundreds but thousands each month. He asked for ten new merchant marine ships per month. American industry gave him two per day and every day a warship as well. Factories, fully mobilized and reactivated after ten dreary years of the Great Depression, poured out the weapons of war and the thousands of different support items that it takes to fight a war in dozens of distant places simultaneously. It was the greatest industrial effort the world had ever seen and likely ever will again.

Time has blurred our comprehension of the immensity of that effort. Think of the impossible achievements. Think of a *thousand* bombers over a German city, with a hundred fighter planes flying cover, in a single air raid, darkening the sun and filling the skies with the droning roar of 4,000 engines; ten airmen in each bomber; 10,000 airmen in the sky on a single raid. What an effort. Average losses were 5 percent. That's fifty downed bombers, 500 airmen lost on a single raid, one raid of hundreds. More than 100,000 American airmen lost their lives in raids over Germany.

An estimated fourteen million men served in America's armed forces during the War. Almost one out of every nine citizens.

Think of an amphibious landing on a remote Pacific atoll, with 500 ships and landing craft and 1,000 warplanes, 50,000 soldiers, sailors, and airmen in one effort of many.

No spot on earth was out of reach of the American war machine. Men, ships, planes, and armies were sent anywhere in the world that the military effort wanted them. *Send them,* said the strategists: send them to Africa, England, France, Italy, Asia, India, Burma, Malaysia, Australia, New Guinea, the Philippines, Alaska, Greenland, Iceland, and a hundred islands and places with no names. And send them they did, by the thousands and the tens of thousands.

Was there another country in all of history that could wage such a war?

6

August 6, 1945

THE UNITED STATES had been at war for forty-four months. It would go on, it seemed, for years and cost the lives of several hundred thousand more American soldiers, added to the 416,000 already killed and the hundreds of thousands maimed for life. We were certain the Jap would never surrender in battle. Only invasion and conquest of Japan itself could end the War.

***

It was on this day that Air Force Colonel Paul Tibbets, flying a long-range four-engine B-29 bomber, the *Enola Gay*, dropped the first atomic bomb on Hiroshima, bringing almost total destruction to 90 percent of the city's structures and killing 70,000 people instantly. Radiation sickness killed 30,000 more by year's end and another 100,000 over the next five years. The bomb had a nickname; members of the scientific and military team that built it and planned the drop called it *Little Boy*.

Newspaper headlines screamed:

ATOMIC BOMB!

What was an atomic bomb? Nobody knew. As many as 100,000 people were involved in the Manhattan Project that created it, yet it was the best-kept secret of the war. Not even Harry Truman, who ordered the bomb dropped on Japan, knew of the project until FDR died in April, just four months earlier, and the vice president received his briefings as the nation's thirty-third president.

A second bomb, more powerful than the one that destroyed Hiroshima, fell on Nagasaki three days later. It, too, had a nickname: *Fat Boy*. It essentially wiped the city off the map, killing 40,000 people instantly and another 40,000 in the days, weeks, and years ahead.

Japan surrendered five days after Nagasaki, on August 14, 1945, ending history's most devastating war. So, at last, it was over. Surprisingly, for those of us on Okinawa, preparing for the invasion of Japan, there was little jubilation, just the exhaustion that men allow themselves after a job is done. I prayed, humble and thankful for my good luck.

7

Easy Duty

AFTER V-J DAY, Okinawa duty got to be kind of nice. All the tension was gone. The weather was good. The routine was relaxed. The barracks were improved. I drilled the company every day to keep up a semblance of discipline.

Instead of speculation about our next engagement, conversation turned toward what was happening back home, especially the baseball season. After three years of second-rate ball, the sport was exciting again with the return from military service of players like Bob Feller, back with the Cleveland Indians, Charlie Keller at the Yankees, Hank Greenberg and Hal Newhouser back with the Detroit Tigers, and Eddie Stanky at Brooklyn. Ted Williams was headed back to the Boston Red Sox and Joe DiMaggio to the Yankees. A new kid returned from the War, Red Schoendienst, was looking real good with the St. Louis Cardinals.

You can imagine the quality of wartime baseball when you think that a one-armed outfielder named Pete Gray was in the St. Louis Browns starting lineup. And how about this: there was a rumor that Branch Rickey, general manager of the Brooklyn Dodgers, signed a Negro ballplayer, name of Jackie Robinson. Can you believe it? A Negro in the Majors? Must be a gag.

The 1945 pennant races were almost over. It looked to be the Detroit Tigers in the American League and the Chicago Cubs in the National. Their lineups were so inferior to prewar standards that Chicago sportswriter Warren Brown wrote, *I don't think either team can win.*

World Series tickets, lower grandstand, were going to be priced at six bucks per game. Gasoline to drive to the game was fifteen cents a gallon. The average salary of the players was $4,500 for the season. Bonuses for World Series winners would be $3,500.

And the most important topic: When were we going to be rotated home? There was a point system based on time served and participation in combat engagements. Meanwhile, there was plenty of free time and good food. We watched movies almost every night. Among the memorable ones were *Anchors Aweigh* with Frank Sinatra and Gene Kelly, *The Picture of Dorian Gray*, *Mildred Pierce*, *The Bells of St. Mary's*, *State Fair*, *The Lost Weekend*, and *Spellbound*. There were also war movies. The Hollywood make-believe war movies were objects of ridicule to us. They were hooted off the screen. We had had enough of the War.

USO entertainment troupes visited us regularly and were greeted with huge enthusiasm. We loved them, especially the Hollywood starlets who were a must in every troupe.

Of course, the men also paid lots of attention to the 120 Army nurses on the island. There was plenty of ogling and flirting going on, much of it unwelcomed by the nurses. My men suffered an inordinate number of scratches, bruises, and sprains, with sick call bringing a long line to the infirmary every day.

A number of the nurses were very good-looking—girls who would have been attractive and desirable anywhere. Here on Okinawa, in this setting, with their fresh young faces, in their starched and neatly ironed uniforms, their beauty was magnified. Even ordinary-looking girls looked real pretty. *Okinawa lovelies*, we called them, as if Okinawa had thrown a spell over them. We were pretty sure they would all turn homely as soon as they left the island.

The Okinawa routine was easy and relaxed. Urges awoke in me that had been suppressed for three years or more. Nurse Sally Carol—a girl with two first names—wasn't one of the real good-lookers, yet I found her attractive.

8

Sally Carol

S HE WAS A REGISTERED nurse. She enlisted in the Navy a week after Pearl Harbor with an ensign's commission. When I met her, she'd risen to the rank of lieutenant commander. That's the equivalent of a major in the Army or Marines.

Sally reported to me at company headquarters every day with a list of the men seen, treated, and discharged and the men held for further examination or treatment, and the nature of their illness or injury. Although she outranked me, she stood in front of my desk, almost at attention, while she delivered her report. After two weeks, I managed to get her to sit opposite me, and sometimes she would even accept a Coke or an iced tea.

I guessed her to be about thirty. She was more pleasant-looking than pretty. Like most women, she got better-looking when she smiled, which she did rarely. She was serious about her duties and responsibilities as head nurse and commander of the infirmary and the sick bay. She had a great figure. The starched uniform couldn't conceal that. I liked her but had no romantic designs—not for a woman ten years older than me.

***

The night of August 25 was warm with a full moon in a cloudless sky illuminated by a million stars. The air was soft and fragrant. I strolled through the one-acre park we built after V-J Day, when we dressed up the barracks and company headquarters. I relaxed on a bench, smoking a cigarette, filled with thoughts of home. Mostly I was thinking of my girl, Alice, yearning for her and my family and friends. Now that going home was no longer a wish and a dream, I had little patience for the waiting.

In the distance, I heard the sounds of the big swing bands. A party going on somewhere. It was near midnight when I returned to my quarters and climbed into bed.

I was awakened by a knock on my door. It was Sally, in full dress uniform: navy military jacket with lieutenant commander's gold stripes at the bottom of her sleeves, navy skirt, white dress shirt, navy necktie, and that pert, handsome navy and white cap. That uniform enhanced the looks of every woman who put it on. I suspected, no doubt unfairly, that some WAVE enlistees were motivated more by the chance to wear it than the desire to serve.

"Sally," I said. "What is it? It's almost midnight."

"Can I come in?"

9

Knowing Sally

Y OU'LL HAVE TO excuse me, Jack," she said as she entered. "I'm coming from a party over at the nurses' dayroom, and I maybe had a drink too many."

"Wait a second while I put on some clothes," I said. I was wearing only a pair of boxer shorts.

"Not necessary, Jack," she said, moving toward me. "I'm not gonna wait. I'm tired of beating around the bush—I need a man tonight. It's not that anyone will do. You. You're what I need. I been thinking about you and this for weeks. You up for it?"

Wow! What to say? What to do? She looked so sexy in that uniform, in the dim light. Her eyes were wide and shining, searching my face for an answer as a bashful smile played on her lips. It had been so long. I swept her into my bed. "Sally," I grunted. "I don't understand . . . I never let myself think about you this way."

She pulled my head to hers and kissed me . . . deeply, hungrily, arousing me. "No more talk, Jack," she said. "I'm not here for conversation."

I swelled. I got huge. It felt as though it would burst as she took it in her hand.

"Oh, yes," she said, addressing it. "I knew you would be a big boy."

A condom appeared in her hand. She slipped it on me in one quick, smooth motion. Smooth and practiced.

"Now," she said, panting. "Give it to me."

Afterward, I lay on my back and smoked a cigarette. Blue smoke rose up in a cloud, drawn to the revolving fan blades. Sally sat up to take a cigarette from the pack on my night table and lit it. There is something erotic about watching a girl light up. Something about how she holds the flame while she takes the first drag and then exhales the smoke in a narrow stream, through pursed lips.

I leaned on my side to face her. She was beautiful. Her hair spread out on the pillow, framing her face. She smiled, serene. Her eyes were moist. She turned to me.

"Tell me, Sally," I said. "Tell me everything. Who are you? Where do you come from?"

She took another drag and exhaled before she answered. "I was married, Jack. I was working at the Baptist Highlands Hospital in Louisville. One of a couple hundred nurses. My husband was the chief of maintenance in the hospital. We had a good life. The Depression didn't affect us. Our jobs were secure. Not a lot of money but a lot of security. No kids. We tried, but it didn't work.

"He got drafted in June '41. The Navy. I joined up right after Pearl Harbor. I never saw him again. He was on a destroyer that went down in the Coral Sea. I'm glad I joined up. My work is important. And it's not bad being a commanding officer. I'd like to stay in, but that's not gonna happen. They're already downsizing. I'll go back to Louisville. It will be a comedown from lieutenant commander to just plain nurse Miss Carol. I'll have to get used to someone calling for me, *Nurse, Nurse, Miss Carol!* I'll go back to being just another gal from the nursing pool. Here I'm Commander Carol, in charge of a hundred and nineteen nurses and a hundred orderlies. I can have my pick of fifty officers in this regiment from captain up to full colonel. That's the letdown that's gonna be. I have to confess, this war has been good to me. These three years were everything, and not dangerous, really. I've never been in a dangerous area . . . always in safe, rear areas. The camaraderie is great. Here, I'm a desirable woman. I'm important. I'm respected by the doctors and the brass. Back home, my life will be dull. I'll live in a dark apartment. I'll wear dark clothing and work a dark job. Everything will be dark. I'm sorry the war is over."

"That's an adjustment we'll all have to make, Sally," I said, wanting to change the subject. "But why me tonight, when you could have any man on the island?"

"I like you, Jack. I know all about you. You're something special, and you don't have a wife back home. You're good in bed, too, like I knew you would be." She paused to stroke my cheek. "But don't worry, Jack. We're ships passing in the night . . . no involvement or obligation. We'll never see each other again, and that's perfect."

I sat up sharply. "Whattaya mean? You're dumping me already?"

"I'm shipping out tomorrow, Jack. That party tonight was for me and eight other nurses. They're reducing the nursing staff. Everything is winding down. Twenty-five of us will be on a C-47 at eleven hundred." She looked at her wristwatch. "That's less than nine hours from now." She sat up and swung her legs onto the floor. "I gotta get going," she said, reaching for her clothes.

I sat dumbfounded while she dressed, shaking my head in disbelief as I smoked my cigarette.

She opened the door and stepped outside, looking back at me one more time before disappearing into the night. "I love you, Jack," she said. "Have a good life."

10

Introspection

THE SALLY CAROL episode left me in turmoil. What, exactly, were my feelings for her? That night, I loved her, for an hour, before she told me she was shipping out the next morning. When she told me that, I felt a void. Something good was taken away from me. Crazy. How could that be, after a one-hour romance that consisted of good sex and a half dozen sentences?

I moped about it for a few days, guilt feelings about Alice. I pictured Alice back home in Atlantic City, missing me, waiting for me, *saving* herself for me. I was a heel, or was it just a case of letting in feelings that I shut out while at war? I surrendered to the first temptation that came along. What did that say about my character?

I settled back into the routine of daily drills and administrative duties. I kept the men occupied by forming a company baseball team and establishing a league of teams from each company, and a tennis competition and a volleyball league. The days dragged by, monotonously, filled with boredom and longing for home.

It was a day late in September when the colonel's adjutant came for me in the colonel's jeep. The colonel, who was the brigade commander, wanted to see me. It was outside the chain of command for me to be summoned at brigade level, skipping over the battalion major. Very unusual. What could the colonel want with me?

"You can take ten to get into suntans and a cap," the adjutant said.

11

The Brigade Commander

I CLIMBED INTO THE jeep, and we headed for brigade headquarters. "What's up?" I asked the adjutant.

"Don't know," he shrugged. "All he said was to find you."

I wracked my brain. One of my corporals was in trouble over a nurse—maybe it was worse than I knew. Or could it be about me and Sally?

Brigade headquarters was at the top of a ridge overlooking our original landing beach and the ocean. The brigade offices, the barracks, the officers' quarters, and the colonel's house were all newly built—handsomely done, bright, orderly and fresh, surrounded by well-kept lawns edged with white-washed stones, planted with trees, shrubbery, and flowers. And, of course, the customary sixty-foot flagpole.

Down below, on the beach and offshore, salvage and wrecking crews were busily cutting up and clearing away the debris of war: hundreds of beached landing craft, half-submerged ships, damaged amphibian tanks, burned-out jeeps, trucks, and artillery pieces. The bodies were all gone. They'd been removed within a few days of securing the beach. Ships offshore were receiving salvaged steel, while others towed unsalvageable wrecks out to sea to be sunk in deep water.

Looking down on that scene offered a glimpse of the enormity of the waste in men and materiel from the Okinawa invasion. And this was four months after the conquest. During the action, you saw the waste and the killing all around you, but here atop the ridge, I saw its remnants, stretched out over five miles of beach, under a soft blue sky with cottony clouds and a brilliant sun, a white sand beach tracing the edge of a sun-splashed ocean. Waves formed, sparkling, swelling, rising, rolling onto the beach with serene regularity, sometimes shifting a hulk of a ship or tank that wasn't deeply embedded in the hard-packed sand. Here, high on the ridge, a light wind freshened the air. The Pacific water was tinted with a warm blue. It was a silver and blue ocean, unlike the silver and gray Atlantic back home. Off in the distance, three jeeps were parked on the beach where six nurses and six sergeants splashed in the surf. Their laughter carried on the breeze.

I entered the HQ building apprehensively. What was I about to be told?

"Come in, Captain." The colonel returned my salute, motioning me into his office. What a contrast this office was with the makeshift tents that served as headquarters at company, battalion, and even brigade levels during the fighting. Here was a Hollywood set, neat and polished, the brigade and United States flags flanking the colonel's desk. Floor-to-ceiling maps of Okinawa and the Pacific theater covered one wall above a two-foot-high stage. The screened windows were open and a light breeze lifted white sheer curtains. Two ceiling fans kept the air circulating comfortably. An Oriental rug decorated the floor. This was a far cry from the thrown-together combat conditions I was used to.

The colonel pointed to the chair on the other side of his desk. I took a seat and he sat down opposite me. He was a study in crispness, dressed in freshly pressed suntans, the military's lightweight pale khakis. He had short, steel-gray hair and steel reading glasses. He sat erect, the silver eagles on his collars gleaming in the sunlight. I sat at attention as he smoked a cigarette and leafed through a manila folder on his desk. He closed the file and looked up. He leaned forward, his eyes fixed on mine, and studied me, impassively, for several seconds. I kept firm eye contact. It was an effort, but I knew not to look away.

"Captain," he said, jabbing the folder with his forefinger, "this is your file. I'm going to have a very serious talk with you right now."

What the hell was I in for?

12

The Choice

R ELAX, CAPTAIN," THE colonel smiled. "You're in no trouble."
He switched on the intercom. "Bring us a couple of iced teas," he said into the box. He offered me a cigarette, which I declined. Another draw on his cigarette, a flick of the ash into the ashtray. He leaned back. His expression softened.

"Your file is impressive, Captain. I'm Naval Academy. You're OCS. We regular officers always talk about you fellows who came out of OCS. How you stack up against regular Navy. In your case, you're as good as any of us. That's why I brought you here."

He reached into his drawer and took out a pair of gold oak-leaf clusters— major's oak leaves. He held them toward me in his palm.

"These can be yours, Captain," he said, pausing for effect. "Surprised?"

I pushed back against the chair as if struck by his words. I sucked in my breath. "I sure am, Colonel," I said. "What's it all about?"

"Your battalion commander, Major Stiles, is getting early rotation. He'll shove off as soon as we settle on his replacement. I'm offering you the job. Sign up for another tour—four years. The battalion is yours; so are the oak leaves. *Major* Laurel. You'll be the youngest marine major I know."

He took a short puff on his cigarette and ground it out in the ashtray. "The battalion is going to draw occupation duty in Japan. It's good duty—*real* good duty for a battalion commander. Maybe you'll wind up a career marine. It's a good life, the peacetime Marines. In five years, you'll be a light colonel. You'll make full colonel by retirement. You'll be less than fifty years old—a young man with a retired colonel's pension and a future that's comfortable and secure." He leaned forward, fixing me with his stare. "The Corps needs men like you, Captain Laurel. How about it?"

"Wow," I said, trying to wrap my head around the offer. "Not bad for a high school graduate. Otherwise . . . When does my rotation come up? I know I have enough points to go home early."

"Yes, you do. In fact, Major Stiles put you in for the next open slot to fly you out of here. But you have a choice to make: battalion commander or home real soon. Think it over. Your record shows you're good at quick decisions."

"When do you need my answer?" I asked.

"Let's see," the colonel said, studying his watch. "It's fourteen twenty, and there's a C-47 leaving for Hawaii at seventeen hundred. There's a seat on it for you. Or you can be Major Laurel. Take your choice."

I had a little more than two hours to decide what direction my life would take.

I stood up and saluted. "May I be dismissed, sir? If your adjutant will drive me back to camp, I'll send him back with my answer."

"Okay. Dismissed, Captain. You're a good Marine. Good luck to you, whatever you decide."

13

Decision

I WAS SILENT ON the ride back to company, but my decision was already made. I was going home.

Back at camp, I called for my first lieutenant. While I stuffed my duffel, I told him I would be on the transport at 1700 hours and that I was recommending him for promotion to captain and to take over the company. I tossed my combat knife into the duffel along with my field binoculars. They were my only wartime souvenirs.

"I don't have a lot of time," I said. "I have to see Major Stiles to get my orders and surrender my sidearm. So I'll say goodbye now. I need my driver and jeep for the next couple of hours. Otherwise, the company is yours."

"Yessir, thank you, Jack," the lieutenant said. He shook my hand. "Good luck, Captain—in whatever you do."

At 1640 hours, I was at the airstrip where the C-47 was fully fueled, with its passenger complement of soldiers, officers, journalists, and visiting congressmen on board and ready for takeoff. A company was lined up, facing the plane, at parade rest. The company commander and his staff faced the back of the company. The battalion band was at hand.

Must be a senator on the C-47, I thought. *They love this kind of reception.*

As my jeep neared the company, my driver sounded the horn—three short blasts. The band struck up the "National Emblem March." The company commander came to attention and barked a command, *"Companeee!"* followed by the echoes of the four platoon lieutenants, *"Platooon! Ten-HUT!"* The company snapped to attention. *"Abouoot FACE!"* The company and the commander's staff came about, facing me. It was my company! The commander was my first lieutenant, already wearing his captain's bars. He saluted me. I climbed out of the jeep.

"The company is here to see you off, Captain," he said.

I returned the salute. The company was suited up for a parade in sharply pressed summer dress with service cap and necktie, shoes shined. I don't think I ever saw the company looking so sharp and military—this band of ragged, bearded, grimy warriors who stormed the beaches and fought with me on this and the other islands.

I choked up. "Don't you have anything better for this company to do, Captain?" I was afraid my voice would fail. I hesitated, only for a moment, recovering my composure. "Thank you, Captain," I said. "Thank you. You're the best. The finest group of men I could ever know."

The new captain stepped forward. He offered me something wrapped in a khaki T-shirt. "It's your sidearm and holster, Captain," he said. "I got it back from the quartermaster. Put it in your duffel. I gave him one of the souvenirs instead. We've got six more of these at HQ and who knows how many more the men have collected." He saluted again.

I accepted the package and nodded. "Thanks," I whispered. I was finding it hard to speak.

"Review the troops, sir?" he asked.

"Sure," I said. I patrolled the ranks like a visiting general, peering into the smooth young faces. Here were those few originals who survived all three of our landings. And here the replacements who made it through the next two, and those who survived the last one. I knew most of them by sight, not all by name. And here were the forty-two replacements who brought us up to full strength after we took Okinawa. They looked like kids. There would be no island-storming for them. The A-bombs had spared them.

At the waiting plane, I threw a final salute and climbed aboard. I leaned out the door and shouted, "*Companeeee . . . dis-MISSED!*"

14

Going Home

IT WAS TWO flights from Okinawa to San Diego, with five days in between in Honolulu, Hawaii. The Marines take care of their own, especially combat officers, and when I reached San Diego, I requested a seat on an eastbound military flight. They put me up at the Marine Corps Recruiting Center where I had a private room and meals at the officers' mess. On the third day, I gave up on the flight and started east by train.

It was eight days and five different trains from San Diego to Atlantic City. The trains were crowded with servicemen headed home. Sometimes the wait was a few hours between connecting rides, sometimes a day or more. The trains were noisy and jubilant and smoke-filled. There were few civilians on the trains, mostly servicemen full of excitement, laughing and swapping stories and smoking like chimneys and catching up on a few years of not enough sleep. At every stop, there were welcoming banners and USO booths offering us coffee, donuts, and sandwiches, and there was often a spirited high school band too. All was celebration. America was the greatest nation in history, rejoicing in its power and exalting its heroes.

On one leg of my trip, from Oklahoma City to Nashville, I sat next to a black Army sergeant who'd lost his right arm above the elbow. The right sleeve of his uniform was pinned up, neatly, in the manner seen too often in those days. He was in the window seat, his right side against the window. I was on the aisle. He stared out the window, expressionless, removed from the general excitement around him, withdrawn. It was easy to imagine his thoughts.

"How are you, Sergeant?" I asked. "Where you been? And where you headed?"

He told me he lost his arm in the Philippines invasion at Leyte Gulf. He was headed for Newark, New Jersey.

"What're your plans?" I asked.

"They gonna fix me up with an artificial arm," he said. "I'm goin' to Rutgers College on the G.I. Bill. Gonna teach shop. I can't do much without a right hand, but I can teach."

He was twenty-eight, seven years older than me, a union steel worker drafted two weeks after Pearl Harbor. He'd gotten married the week before he left and had a three-year-old daughter he'd never seen. His background in construction had landed him in a construction battalion, the CBs—or Seabees, as the men were called—but as a cook. The services weren't integrated during the War. Black enlistees served as cooks, kitchen helpers, stewards, and waiters in the officers' mess. But when a unit got into a combat situation, *everybody* went into action, blacks along with everyone else. I admired the Seabees. They built roads and airstrips and bridges, sometimes under battle conditions.

"You know something, Sarge," I said. "You Seabee guys probably saved my life. Once on Peleliu, my orders were for my company to take a position on top of a hill overlooking a river two hundred yards wide. I asked my major, 'How do we get across the river?' He said, *Three half-tracks will follow you with twenty-five inflatable boats. When you reach the river, inflate the boats and row across, eight men in a boat.*

"So we forced our way to the river. What do we find at the river? A CB unit under fire from the hill we're supposed to take. The Seabees just finished throwing a pontoon bridge across the river. We raced over the bridge and took the hill. I lost three men. There was a sign on the far end of the bridge: *This bridge comes with the compliments of the 134th Marine Construction Battalion.* Those Seabees lost half their company, but they saved half of mine."

He nodded. "That's what we did. It's what I did when they didn't have me cookin' and cleanin' in the officers' mess." He took a drag of his cigarette before asking, "How 'bout you, Captain? What're you comin' home to?"

It was what filled my thoughts every moment since V-J Day. I rested my head on the back of the seat and spoke to the ceiling. "I have a mom and dad. And a sister. And maybe a girlfriend. I haven't seen any of them since I enlisted in June '42. I never held a full-time job. I don't know what I'm gonna do. Hell, I don't know what I *want* to do. I guess I'll join the 52-20 Club.

"I never let myself think about after the war," I continued. "I focused on today. It was a superstition: *Don't think about the future. Just hope and pray I'll make it through this.* Now, these last weeks, the future is *all* I think about. But I can't get anything in focus. Maybe it'll come to me once I'm home and out of uniform."

The car was full of servicemen, mostly Army. The seats were filled. So was the aisle, crowded with servicemen, some standing, some sitting on their duffel bags, the air around us filled with smoke. A soldier at the far end of the car was playing dreamy tunes, softly, on a harmonica, the music mostly drowned out by the din of voices and laughter. Time passed. Miles passed to the hypnotic *clack-clack* of iron wheels on steel rails. Through the windows, the telephone wires dipped and rose, monotonously, repeating the same arc over and over, endlessly.

A few flasks started to be passed around. The cigarette smoke thickened. The voices got louder, accented with loud bursts of laughter. A soldier, perched on his duffel bag, hollered to the harmonica player to "Stop playing that creepy shit. Give us something lively!" The harmonica struck up "Bless Them All," but of course, it was the Army version: *"Fuck Them All, The Long and The Short and The Tall."* They sang it over and over again, each time louder and more raucous. Noise filled the car, an ocean of noise, sweeping back and forth.

A good-looking soldier, a corporal, leaned over me. He was drunk, but his uniform was immaculate, pressed to perfection, his regulation khaki necktie tied in a perfect Windsor knot. I wondered how he managed to be so well-groomed. Most of us were wrinkled and didn't smell so good, and most of us had one or more days' growth of beard. He swayed unsteadily, holding the hand-strap, and leaned over me, snorting in my left ear, "Hey, Captain," he slurred, "how come youah sittin' next to a niggah?" Then, he hollered across me, "Hey, niggah, whyncha get up and give youah seat to a white man?"

I looked up at the corporal. "Where you comin' from, Corporal?" I asked, raising my voice to be heard above the noise.

He replied that he'd been an aide to a supply major at the quartermaster center in Sydney, Australia.

"I guess you didn't get to see any action," I said.

"Nope," he replied, "but I sure wanted some."

"Lean down here, Corporal," I said, asking him to lean lower over me. "I'll tell you something."

"Okay, Captain," he slurred as he lowered his head toward me, "but what 'bout the niggah? Aincha gonna make him give me his seat?"

"Tell you what," I said as I grabbed his perfectly made necktie and yanked his face down, sharply, into the top of my head. "Get lost, Corporal." I shoved him away and he fell backward into a couple of soldiers who'd witnessed the scene.

His nose and upper lip were bleeding. He wiped his face with his hand then stared at his bloody palm in disbelief. He started to get up and I rose out of my seat to stand over him.

"I'll give you about two seconds to get out of my sight," I said. I turned to the soldiers he'd fallen into. "Get this piece of shit outta my sight."

"Yessir, Captain. Yessir." They led away the bleeding corporal.

"That's what we fought a war for?" I scoffed to my neighbor as I sat back down. "What a laugh."

15

Homecoming

I CALLED HOME FROM Philadelphia station on October 24. It had been three years since I'd gone overseas, and Mom cried into the phone when she heard my voice. I told her there was a two-hour wait for a train to carry me the last sixty miles to Atlantic City. She and Dad could expect me in four or five hours.

I used the men's room to wash up and shave. I'd been saving a fresh T-shirt and shorts and socks. I lifted my dress greens out of my duffel where I'd folded and wrapped them in two yards of tissue paper so they'd be presentable when I reached home. I shined my shoes with the T-shirt I'd been wearing for the last five days.

Combing my hair, I studied the Marine captain in the mirror. He looked back at me, a level gaze through dark blue eyes. He looked older than his twenty-one years. His face was leathery, with permanent squint lines at the eyes. His hair was growing in, darker and thicker, after having been shorn down to a quarter-inch for three years. The eighteen-year-old recruit's untamed straw-colored hair was long gone, cut and discarded on the floor of the Marine boot camp barbershop at Camp Pendleton in 1942.

I put on the beige-colored necktie with a neat four-in-hand knot and strapped on the Sam Browne belt and shoulder strap. I fished out my six ribbons and pinned them to the green jacket above the left breast pocket. I knew Mom and Dad would get a kick out of seeing me in uniform with the ribbons. Dad had two from World War I. That war ended only twenty-seven years ago.

Mom showed them to me once when I was about twelve, after I pestered Dad to tell me about his war experiences. "Your father was a good soldier," she said, holding out the two ribbons in her palm. "They gave him these. He doesn't like to talk about the war."

I put on my officer's cap and sized up the complete image in the mirror: a Marine officer, experienced in the art of war, in leading and commanding men, witness to thousands of killings; coming home. To what? I'd never thought about a career. I was a high school graduate and a Marine captain with nothing but a war in between.

****

My family lived in Atlantic City in a rented third-floor apartment above Michaelson's Bakery on the 3900 block of Ventnor Avenue, between Dover and Annapolis Avenues. My father was the manager of the Nu-Enamel Paint Store uptown on Atlantic Avenue, near Missouri Avenue. He worked all the hours that the store was open, from eight o'clock in the morning until nine at night. When Pearl Harbor was attacked, his salary had just been raised to forty-eight dollars a week. By mid-1942, when I joined the Marines, he was up to fifty-two dollars a week, which was a pretty good salary considering the average family was then living on less than two thousand a year.

Dad wore a three-piece suit to work every day, with a white shirt and a conservative necktie. He was a quiet man. In my teens, I'd learned his mild manner and even temper were deceptive. They belied a toughness and a strong sense of pride and protectiveness for his family. He never spoke of his combat service in World War I, except to say he prayed I would never have to go to war.

Mom was a perfect homemaker. Our household was always fresh and orderly. My sister and I wanted for nothing. There were no frills in our family's life, nor was there any sense of deprivation. Mom stuffed envelopes to earn extra money. There were always piles of envelopes and marketing pieces on our dining room table. If my girlfriend, Alice, came to visit and I wasn't home yet, she helped Mom with the envelope stuffing. Mom thought the world of Alice.

My sister, Evie, was a good kid; pretty, two years younger than me. I adored her. Defending her honor when I was fifteen got me into trouble, but it had to be done. I almost killed the man who molested her—beat him with a piece of iron pipe. I was lucky I didn't serve a long prison sentence, which was thanks to Bobo Truck and Alan Goren. I'd done some favors for Bobo back in 1939, when I was fifteen. He was Atlantic City's mob boss; he ran the Atlantic City rackets.

Alan Goren was a commodities trader, a mystic, my mentor, and my introduction to history, literature, economics, and philosophy. It was Goren who introduced me, Bobo, and Benny James to the mysterious world of commodities futures. He was the most important influence in my life from 1939 until I left for the Marines in mid-1942. We made a curious foursome in '39, Bobo and Goren and me, and Benny, a boardwalk pitchman with charisma to burn. We were thrown together in an unlikely partnership speculating in cocoa futures.

Eddie Dunauskas was my best friend. His father owned the Polish delicatessen next door to us, and his family lived above the store. Eddie and I were inseparable before we went off to war. He was a month older than me and two inches shorter. He was broad and muscular and dark and good-looking—not at all like me. I was tall and skinny and nondescript. I had unruly straw-colored hair and a fair complexion with a hint of freckles across my cheeks and nose.

We were closer than any brothers could be. Eddie was smart and strong. He was always serious. He spoke slowly, deliberately. He had to know how things worked. He was a tinkerer. He could fix just about anything. Like me, he enlisted the day after we graduated Atlantic City High School, except that I wanted the Marines. He joined the Navy.

Before we went into the service, my sister, Evie, managed to be home whenever Eddie was in our apartment. I knew she'd had a crush on him since she was twelve and he fourteen. He took notice of her, finally, a few months before he enlisted. About the only time he ever spoke to her before that was to say, *Hey, Evie, where's Jack?* For New Year's Eve, 1941, twenty-four days after Pearl Harbor, he asked her to a party being thrown by one of Alice's friends. I thought she would faint, between her excitement and worrying that she shouldn't screw up.

Eddie was his usual self that night, polite and good-natured with little to say. Evie talked enough for both of them. At the stroke of midnight, he kissed her, a big kiss that I think he copied from Clark Gable in *Gone with the Wind*—the last scene in part 1, right after Rhett and Scarlett drive the carriage through the burning streets of Atlanta. Evie all but swooned. Her slender, fifteen-year-old figure collapsed into his arms. Eddie was embarrassed. But after that he dated her every week, and it was Evie who did the farewell scene six months later at the bus station when Eddie swung onto the bus, destination Norfolk and the Navy.

I hadn't seen any of these people since 1942, when I boarded the bus on my first leg of the journey to Camp Pendleton.

16

Family and Friends

***

THEY WERE ASSEMBLED, waiting for me: Mom and Dad and Evie and Eddie, and my friend Harvey Geek—Blinky, we called him, because of the way he blinked when he got nervous or excited. Lots of hugging and kissing. Mom cried and hugged me with her face pressed sideways into my chest. She tried to speak, but the words wouldn't come. Dad embraced us both. "Welcome home, son." I felt his tears on my cheek.

Everything was the same as when I left. Or was it? The apartment felt smaller. The furnishings looked tired. Mom and Dad looked older than just the three years since I left. I tried to say I loved them and how wonderful it was to be home. My voice cracked. My eyes got moist. I embraced them and kissed them.

Evie bubbled with excitement. "Jack, you're so . . . so handsome! Oh, I love you." She hugged me and kissed my cheek. She was nineteen. She was a pretty girl when I left. Now she was a beautiful young woman. Eddie was wearing his Navy chief petty officer dress blues. He hugged me, too, a great, powerful bear hug. I pounded his back. A flood of emotion came over me. I really loved the guy. It felt like a miracle that we were here, together, safe, after three years of war.

I studied Eddie closely. He went away a boy, a strong, tough boy. Now, every trace of the boy was gone. He'd come back a man, stronger still. I saw he had the same permanent squint lines that I had and his face was leaner.

"I wanted you to see me in the monkey suit just once," he laughed. "It's goin' back in the closet now."

***

The Navy taught Eddie telecommunications. He was chief radio operator on a heavy cruiser, the *Wichita*. He left for the Navy two days before I left for the Marines. Until my homecoming, I hadn't seen him or heard from him. All I knew, from one of Alice's letters, was that he'd been wounded late in the war. It was a minor wound, as war wounds go: he lost a piece of meat out of his left calf. He spent a month on a Navy hospital ship then was discharged. He arrived home two months before me. The wound left him with a slight limp, almost unnoticeable. In the service we called this kind of injury *a million-dollar wound*. It sent you home, hardly impaired.

Eddie was in love with telecommunications. He knew Morse code. He was applying for a ham radio license. He was building a ham radio and erecting a twenty-five foot antenna on the roof of the Dunauskases' delicatessen. He was sure he would bring in Australia. He told me about the International Ham Radio Operators Society. "Telecommunications, that's the field for me. It's the wave of the future, just like cars and radios were the big thing in the '30s."

He had just taken a lease on a store uptown on Atlantic Avenue. He was going to sell and repair radios, television sets, telephones, electrical parts and supplies. He painted the sign himself on the storefront window, "Eddie's TV and Radio," and under it, "Sales and Repairs."

Mr. Dunauskas gave up on Eddie in the delicatessen. Anyone could see that his son was not for the white apron, waiting on women and slicing kielbasa. "And I won't work for anyone," Eddie said. "I been ordered around enough to last a lifetime. I'll be in business for myself. I'll do fine."

* * *

Blinky was wearing a brown leather flight jacket with the Eighth Air Force shoulder patch. He was a major; he'd been a navigator. He flew thirty missions over Europe in a B-17 bomber, five more than the requirement. I would never have recognized him. What happened to Harvey Geek, the short kid with no friends except me and Eddie? The kid who had a hopeless crush on my little sister before finally accepting she was Eddie's girl?

Blinky wanted to be a pilot. He enlisted in the Army Air Corps, and they sent him to flight school, but he washed out as a pilot and became a navigator instead. He must have been a good one. He ended the war as lead navigator of his bomber group, with the rank of major.

Eddie and I had matured. We changed physically during three years in the War. But we were still Jack and Eddie. Not Blinky—the War had completely transformed him. The nervous squinting was gone. He was taller, straighter. His voice and manner had the ring and bearing of command. The mustache topped it off. No one who saw that bashful little kid leave for the service would recognize the Air Force major who came back in his place. He was poised, his speech confident. There was a rich timbre in his voice. He went into the service a tenor and returned a bass-baritone.

"Blinky," I said, putting my arm around his shoulders and pulling him to me. "I hardly know you. You must've grown four inches. Goddamn, you're a good-looking dude, *Major Geek*, and the mustache. You look like Errol Flynn. No—Errol Flynn *wishes!*"

He laughed. "Yeah, Jack, we've all grown up. Those of us who made it, anyway… and, oh yeah, I'm not Blinky anymore. I'm not even Harvey Geek. I changed my name last week. I'm Howard Gordon. I aim to make a lot of money in the insurance business. Not like my old man. He's still working a debit. How's it sound to you? *Howard Gordon?* Would anybody buy a twenty-five-thousand-dollar life insurance policy from *Harvey Geek*? Nope, I'm Major Howard Gordon, Eighth Air Force. I'll sell a million!"

I laughed and slapped his back. "I bet you will, Blinky!"

"*Howard* is the name, Jack. *Howard.* Can you say it?"

"Sure, Blink—I mean, *Howard.* I'll get used to it."

I turned to Mom, "Hey, Mom," I asked. "Where's Alice?" Alice, my girl. Was she still my girl?

Mom answered. Her voice revealed nothing. "She asked me to phone her when you arrived. I'll call her."

"No, Mom, I'll call."

Alice sobbed into the phone. "Jack! Oh, Jack . . . I'll be right there. Meet me outside. I have to see you alone."

"Alice? Why? What's wrong?"

She had already hung up.

17

Alice

ALICE KEEVER WAS my girl since 1939, when I was fifteen and she fourteen. Mom adored Alice, and she was like a big sister to Evie, who was one year her junior. Before I left for the Marines, Alice was at our apartment almost every day. High-spirited and outgoing, she was slender with long, lovely legs, big brown eyes, and a generous smile. She could carry on a conversation alone. I wasn't much of a talker when I met her, but a comment here and there was enough to keep her going. In fact, an occasional grunt would do.

Alice aimed to be a naturalist. She read voraciously and showed a keen interest in virtually every aspect of life and culture. I was always surprised how much she knew, and on so many subjects: history, literature, astronomy, biology, archeology. When did she have time to learn all that stuff?

During the three years we were together before I went to war, our sexual relationship had never gone beyond heavy petting. That's where she drew the line, as she was determined to be a virgin when she married. That's difficult to imagine today, but before the War, it was not unusual. Those days, the good girl's mantra was *Save yourself*—give up your virginity to a husband. Sacred matrimony was an American ideal, along with lifelong dedication to one's partner.

The War changed everything. Young men going off to war put a strain on the idea of feminine purity. Girls, swept up in patriotism and the anguish of partings, maybe forever, compromised the ideal of virginal marriages.

* * *

Alice and I talked about it a few days before I left for the Marines. We had never *done it*, though I was not a virgin. My own initiation had come at fifteen with a high-priced hooker—a gift from Bobo Truck. Repayment, I guess, for an errand I did for him.

Alice interrupted one of our heavy petting sessions to ask, "Should we do it before you go, Jack?" She looked into my eyes, from one eye to the other, her expression absolutely serious, not even a hint of her smile. "I love you, Jack. I want to do it for you. Who knows how long before we'll be together again," and the unspoken *Who knows if you'll come back . . . or if you'll come back whole.*

There were a hundred times when I would have seized the invitation, but with only a few days remaining before I left, I discovered a surprising reluctance. Integrity? I wasn't sure.

"Alice," I said, "I love you more than I can say. I want us to be together . . . always. But I'll be gone in a few days. Who knows what'll happen. Who knows if I'll even come back. I'm saying *no* for my sake as well as yours. I hear about guys getting married because they're leaving and girls wanting to get pregnant. That's nuts. It's tough enough to go. A guy doesn't need to be worrying about a responsibility he left behind.

"And listen, if you fall for someone while I'm away, I'll understand. It will hurt and maybe I'll get angry, but I won't blame you. I could be gone for years. I might not come back at all. Or if I do, maybe not in one piece. I don't want you feeling obligated to me. No, I'm not gonna take it from you," I said. "Not until it's right—the way you always wanted it."

It was the most I'd ever said to her by far, and my words made her cry. She cried that night and every day until we said goodbye a few days later. The parting was painful. We both cried.

In spite of leaving Alice behind, I was full of patriotism, and the thought of being a Marine was exhilarating to me. I was going to be tough and smart—a man's man. I couldn't wait to go, and I think I cried only because I felt Alice's pain. Later, I thought about her every day. She was my emotional anchor, my link to the real world. I wanted to come back to her. I wanted her to be there when I got back, thinking of me, loving me, missing me, saving herself for me. Soldiers get all filled up with sentiment about the girl back home. Memory makes her better looking, sweeter, and brighter. I could close my eyes and see Alice smiling, laughing, so honest, so loving, so happy, so sad. And I remembered, dreamily, how it felt to hold her and touch her.

In the beginning, I wrote her two or three times a week. When we shipped out for Australia, I wrote less frequently. I was superstitious. I imagined her getting a letter from me after I'd bought it. You heard such stories. Guys sending letters that start out, *If you receive this letter, you'll know I'm dead,* and just ordinary letters saying, *I'm doing fine,* arriving weeks after the War Department has sent the condolences telegram. I was afraid to write, afraid to tell her I was okay. Superstition.

She, on the other hand, wrote me every week. Sometimes two or three or even four times a week. Her letters caught up to me in batches during the short breathing spaces between the fighting and the shipping out to the next amphibious operation. I loved to get her letters, but seldom did I respond. Superstition.

Superstition. A letter could take a month or two to reach her. What was the point? She would know I was okay, let's say, on November 8, but the letter arrives on January 26. What does she think? Is he all right today? Who cares that he was all right seven weeks ago? What about today?

* * *

So now it had been three years since the tearful farewell, and I was about to see her. Was she as pretty as I remembered her? I carried a snapshot when I left, a great photo. It caught her at her best, leaning against a boardwalk railing in a light cotton dress. Big smile, soft hair, dress and hair lifted by a summer breeze, smooth round arms and perfect shoulders. And those great legs.

I carried the picture with me throughout my service. It was on every one of those hellish islands with me. I studied it every day. But was she really that good-looking? Had the years coarsened her? Was she still in love with me? Was she angry that I'd sent so few letters?

Had she met someone else?

18

The Beach

I WAITED OUTSIDE IN the dark, near the corner. The streetlamp gave me a thirty-foot shadow, across the avenue and twenty feet high up the side of a building. I smoked a cigarette.

"Where is she?" I stared at my watch. "I'll give her five more minutes, then I'm going to her." In the darkness, I heard the clicking of her heels before I saw her, across the street, half a block away.

I couldn't make out her features. The streetlight behind her turned her into a black silhouette striding toward me. She broke into a run for the last twenty yards, her arms reaching out to me. She fell into my arms, her arms around my back.

"Jack, Jack, Jack!" she sobbed, her cheek pressed against my shoulder. She looked up at me. Now I could make out her features. I felt her tears. Her face shone in the lamplight. Her eyes glistened through her tears. She was smiling. That great smile. How many times had I dreamed of this moment. I pulled her close. I wrapped her in my arms.

"Alice . . . darling." I tilted up her chin and kissed her. Salty tears blended with the sweetness of the kiss.

She burrowed into my chest. I hugged her to me. We stood that way for a few minutes, silently. I was filled with emotion. I could not speak. Words would not come.

When she broke away, she examined my face, there in the dim light, restless eyes scanning every feature.

"You're so . . . grown up," she said, "and so . . . handsome." She looked into my eyes. "Is my Jack in there? Inside that uniform?"

"It's me, all right," I said. "Nothing different—just a little older."

The evening was warm. The sun was down but its light lingered, giving the darkening sky a last trace of color before night fell.

"Let's not go in," she said, her head resting against my shoulder. "I want to be alone with you."

"Sure," I said. "Let's walk. I want to see the ocean."

What did I expect to find? The boardwalk was unchanged. The steel railings, the cone-shaped circle of light around every light pole, the deserted benches, the distant lights of the grand hotels. All as if I'd just left it yesterday. We walked to the ocean, across the boardwalk and down to the beach. A silver half-moon rose in the east. Scattered clouds lit up like lanterns, dramatically, as the moon slipped behind them.

The beach was wide. The tide was out, leaving behind a wide swath of tightly packed sand. The ocean was black, almost flat. A silver beam of moonlight lay across the water. Low swells rolled in toward the shore, forming, rising up, leaning forward, displaying a glistening underbelly for a few moments before tumbling into white foam, turning into a transparent sheet of white lace, gliding onto the beach across the outgoing remnant of the previous wave then slipping back to the sea under the new lace of its successor. In the distance, a luminous splash marked the arc of a dolphin.

"Nothing has changed," I said, staring out to sea. "It's the same as three years ago."

Alice pressed to me and leaned her head on my shoulder. "It's the same as three *million* years ago."

"I'll take fifty or sixty years of it, for us, together," I said.

"I came here all the time," Alice said. "I used to look out to sea, thinking about you. And I prayed for you. Every day. Every night. Especially here, by the ocean."

"I was afraid to think this day would ever come," I said. "I don't have words."

It was a warm night. We kissed. I filled with desire. She pulled me to her hungrily.

"Let's swim," I said.

We shed our clothes. I lifted her; carried her to the water, into the surf. She was a black silhouette of polished marble. Her body glistened in the moonlight. She was delicious. I was filled with love for her.

"Do you remember that night, all those years ago, when we swam out here?" I asked. "The back-to-school party?"

"I'll never forget it," she said.

"I was fifteen and you were fourteen. That was only six years ago. It feels like a century."

We swam out fifty yards, beyond the breakers. Her wet hair hung across her forehead and down across her shoulders like an Egyptian headdress, just as I remembered it. We embraced and kissed and laughed. We groped for each other. We floated over the forming waves. The water was still warm after baking for months in the summer sun. We talked of old times before the War. I was bursting with the joy of being alive, safe, back at home, and with Alice.

We emerged from the ocean, laughing, trotting through the surf and onto the warm sand. I cradled her onto the beach. Our wet naked bodies touched. She stopped laughing. I kissed her face, her shoulders, her breasts. I swelled with passion. I caressed her breasts and the smoothness of her body. I stroked her leg and the velvet creaminess of her inner thigh. "Oh my god," I breathed heavily. I wanted to shout, to laugh, to cry with joy.

She moaned softly. "I'm still a virgin, Jack," she whispered, arching up to me, smiling, her eyes shining. "Nobody has touched me ... I'm a little scared."

"It's okay," I panted. "Don't be scared. Relax. People been doin' this a long time."

She opened to me, moist and hot. Her breathing became rapid and heavy. She pulled my face down, smothering me with great, wet, open-mouthed kisses. "Do it!" she whispered in a small hoarse voice. "Do it, do it."

I pushed at her. She was tight; I pushed again. I entered, just a little.

She stiffened. A low groan escaped her.

"Does it hurt?" I asked.

She arched to me. "More," she breathed.

I entered, slowly, and stopped. She was warm, wet, delicious. I was hot with desire.

"Ooh," she moaned. "Ooh, Jack." I went deeper. She thrust at me. "Ooh ... Jack ... you're so ... *inside* me!"

"I love you, Alice," I breathed into her ear.

"I love you, Jack," she panted, breathlessly pushing at me. Pushing. Pushing. Tears filled her eyes.

"Alice, am I hurting you?"

"Don't stop," she moaned. She pulled my head down again and raised her chin to kiss me, hot, feverish kisses on my lips, on my eyes, all over my face. She stiffened and arched her body. "Oh my god, oh my god, oh my god, oh . . . oh . . . ooh . . . OOH . . . OOOH!"

Afterward, I took a cigarette out of my uniform pocket and lit it. Our heavy breathing slowed. We relaxed. We lay side by side, looking up at the sky, the end of my cigarette a small red light glowing in the darkness.

"This isn't how I thought it would be my first time," she laughed. "But it sure wasn't bad."

I didn't know what to say. I just looked at her, loving what I saw.

"Look, Jack," she said, pointing at the sky. "There's Orion, right where we left him three years ago."

I drew on my cigarette, the red glow brightened. The smoke drifted skyward. "Now," I said, turning toward her, "I guess you'll just have to marry me."

"You betcha!" she laughed as she rolled on top of me and kissed me a dozen times.

* * *

I think about that evening often. Can you know what it was like for me? Words can't capture the feeling. I wanted to stand up, up on my toes, throw my arms in the air, and call out to the sky: "It's me, Jack Laurel! I'm home! I'm back! I survived!"

If I were alone, I might have done it.

19

Bobo Truck

THE NEXT MORNING, I slept in until ten. When I arose, I saw Mom had washed all my cotton clothes, including my khaki chino uniforms. They were all hanging on the looped clothesline that stretched to the Dunauskas house next door. There was a pulley on either end so the clothes could be sent out to hang above the alleyway between the buildings and drawn back in when dry.

When I finished showering and shaving, I pulled on shorts and a T-shirt and found Mom ironing my dress greens.

Without interrupting the strokes of her iron, she leaned away from the ironing board to kiss me. "Good morning, son," she smiled. Then, looking at me carefully, "My, what a physique you've developed. You must have put on thirty or forty pounds, and it looks like all of it is muscle." She turned back to her ironing.

"These should go to the cleaner," she said, running the hot iron over the tunic. "I brushed them off as well as I could. I turned out the pockets and brushed them out. There was sand in the pockets and in the pleats."

"I have to get some new clothes, I guess. I don't think I can get into my old stuff, and I don't want to wear any of the Marine issue."

"Jack, you are so handsome and soldierly in this uniform. Why don't you wear it for a day or two so everybody can see what you look like as a captain before you put it away. Your father's old uniform is still hanging in the storage closet. Yours will go next to it."

"Okay, Mom," I said. I hugged her and kissed her cheek. For her, I'd let everybody see me once in uniform. Then, goodbye Marines. I'd buy some clothes that fit.

So, when I took the jitney uptown to visit Bobo Truck, I was in full dress greens with a Sam Browne leather belt and leather shoulder strap and service cap and the double rows of ribbons above the left breast pocket. I smiled, thinking I would have been on my bicycle but it would be unseemly for a Marine captain in full dress greens to be pedaling along Atlantic Avenue.

* * *

His name was Benno Trucci, born in 1896 to poor Italian immigrants who arrived in Philadelphia three years earlier. He was drafted into the Army during the First World War. Soon after his discharge, he discovered Atlantic City. He adopted a different name. He became *Bobo Truck*. He was big, powerful, smart, and ruthless. In a few years, he built the organization that ran Atlantic City.

I met Bobo accidentally in 1939 when I was fifteen. He liked me. He tried to draw me into his organization, but I remained wary and never got too close. I ran errands for him until I left for the Marines at age eighteen. He saved me from a criminal prosecution after I beat two bullies with an iron pipe for molesting my sister, Evie, when she was thirteen. I almost killed one of them. I never dared to ask for Bobo's help. He knew my problem. He helped, unasked. I would have done anything for him.

Bobo had a fatherly attachment to me. He had no children. He once said if he ever had a son, he would want him to be like me—the best flattery I ever received.

Knowing Bobo was like having a pet leopard. He was dangerous. He could be ruthless. Sometimes people who crossed him disappeared. But, like many powerful and dangerous men, he could be a charmer. I always felt his affection for me was genuine. I liked him. I feared him. I admired him. I counted him as a sincere friend.

Bobo was the boss of Atlantic City. He controlled every form of gambling: the numbers, bookmaking on horses, football, baseball, basketball, on boxing. He liked to brag that there were no drugs in his town and prostitution was confined to the big hotels. He operated like one of today's franchisors. He had the city divided into territories geographically. In addition to the geographic territories, each big hotel was a territory unto itself. Some of the big hotels had gaming rooms, complete with crap tables, blackjack, roulette, and baccarat. While the small hotels didn't have such facilities, every small hotel had someone who would cover your number or a bet on a ball game, but no girls. They were confined to the big hotels only. And no drugs, absolutely none anywhere.

Every territory had a franchisee. Bobo didn't call them *franchisees*. That word wasn't around in 1939. He called them his *piedi*, his *mani*, his *diti*, the Italian words for feet, hands, fingers. He gave out rights in a territory like one of today's franchisors. Every territory had a *piede* who had the rights to write numbers in that territory. Every territory had a *mano* who had the rights to bookmaking in that territory. Every big hotel had a piede with rights to write numbers, a mano with rights to bookmaking and gaming, and a *dite* with rights to prostitution.

Sometimes one *uomo* (man) had more than one set of rights. Sometimes one *uomo* had rights in two territories. Many of the *uomi* held down regular jobs besides being a piede or a mano or a dite—regular jobs such as barbers, bartenders, desk clerks. Some were small businessmen, shopkeepers, barbers, tailors, shoemakers, owners of small restaurants, grocery stores, delicatessens. Bobo's network was big; some four hundred men were in his organization.

Bobo's bookie joint behind Royce's Shooting Gallery was the one hands-on operation he ran. He didn't want any more than that.

Every piede, mano, and dite paid Bobo a weekly royalty. Bobo called it "the dues," from as little as ten dollars a week to as much as two hundred. It depended on Bobo's evaluation of how profitable the territory was.

In Bobo's office on the second floor, above Trucci's, which I visited many times, there was an eight-by-four-foot map of Atlantic City mounted on the wall. The territories were outlined and numbered and marked with the name of the man who operated each territory.

Altogether, there were sixty territories including the hotels. The territories were grouped into five districts. Each district had a district boss. These were Bobo's *capi*, which is the Italian word for *heads*. The capi were on Bobo's payroll. Bobo also had twenty soldiers to help him keep the peace. Bobo protected his people by taking care of the police, the district attorney, the county prosecutor, and a few judges; he was always trying but couldn't get them all. The chief of police was on his payroll. So were a half dozen police lieutenants and a dozen policemen.

If somebody tried to muscle in on one of Bobo's people, Bobo's man had only to report it to his *capo*. Usually the capo sent an invitation to the intruder for a meeting. That one meeting was usually enough to convince the intruder to seek another means of livelihood. The intruder would receive a warning, nothing physical. If an intruder failed to heed a warning, something bad happened to him, such as a broken arm or a few loose teeth. That was the second warning. If the second warning did not convince the intruder to keep out, the problem was erased. There was hardly ever a need to go beyond a second warning.

Bobo's soldiers were his police force. They were his *soldati*. Georgie and Frankie were his two trusted generals and bodyguards. They ran the army. They ran the capi. They noticed everything. When they were with Bobo, their eyes were in constant motion, scanning the room or the street, watchful for any stranger or any suspicious motion. They knew everything that happened in Atlantic City. They guarded Bobo the way the Secret Service guards the president.

* * *

I entered Trucci's, Bobo's restaurant and club on Arctic Avenue. Trucci's vied with the 500 Club as Atlantic City's most upscale restaurant. Its small stage always featured a piano player and a singer. Well-known performers and their bands could often be heard there, the likes of Frank Sinatra, Louis Armstrong, and Billie Holiday.

It was early afternoon. The club was only partly lighted. The outdoor lights and the glittering interior were resting, waiting for evening. Bobo's office was upstairs. The maître d' approached, wearing his best welcoming smile, eyebrows raised. "May I help you, sir? We're not open yet."

"Nick, it's me, Jack," I said, clapping him on his upper arms. He stopped, studied me sharply. "My God! It *is* you, Jack! I can't believe it. Look at you. I can't believe it. Wait till Bobo sees you. Go on up. Surprise him. Boy, will he be surprised!"

I ran up the carpeted stairway and knocked. An old pattern from years earlier: *Tap-tap, tap-tap, tap-tap.*

The peephole opened. "Yeah, who is it?" It was Georgie's voice. Georgie, Bobo's chief lieutenant.

"Open up, Georgie," I commanded. "The Marines are here."

The door flew open. Georgie stood in the doorway, arms spread to embrace me. He was even wider than I remembered. He pulled me into a bear hug.

"Oh my god! Oh my god! Jack! It's Jack, Bobo," he called out over his shoulder. "Look at him. He looks like a fuckin' general!"

Bobo was up, approaching. He waved Georgie aside. He gripped me by my upper arms, held me at arm's length, studying me for a few moments before pulling me to him in a powerful embrace. I could feel the steel in his arms through the sleeves of the dark blue suit. Still the powerful Bobo. He must have been almost fifty. Still the boss. He looked the same except for a touch of gray that had invaded his thick black hair at the temples. He wore his hair the same way, brushed straight back from his broad forehead. He still looked sleek, massive, powerful, important.

He cupped my right jaw and chin in his palm. "Jack, it's good to have you back. Here, sit down over here. Hey, Georgie, get us some sandwiches over here, and some sodas. Or do you want a beer, Jack?"

"A Coke will be fine, Bobo," I said, sinking into a sofa.

He wanted me to tell him everything about the War. He'd been in the American Expeditionary Force in France in 1918 and had fought at Chateau-Thierry on the Marne, at the Battle of Saint-Mihiel. He called it *Saint Millie Sally.* He'd never talked much about it except to say that General John Pershing was a fucking butcher. But here, now, he wanted me to tell him about every battle and *every one a them fuckin' islands.*

"I can sum it all up this way, Bobo: It was one hellhole after another—three of them that I was in. Lots of good boys getting killed. And lots of good boys gettin' worse than killed. I never got a scratch. Just luck. You know how it is. Why that guy and why not me? Who knows? You start to pray. And when you get through one engagement, you think it was the praying so you pray even harder the next time. Meanwhile, the guy next to you takes one in the middle of praying. Were my prayers better than his?"

I bit into my sandwich and studied the room. Everything was as I remembered it. Bobo's office was furnished like a gentlemen's club. He had a huge desk built of polished cherry wood. His chair was a soft red leather judge's chair, high-backed, a swivel chair. There were thick carpets, and thick drapes pulled aside to let the breeze in through the open windows. Two ceiling fans kept the air moving. He had a big red leather sofa and four red leather chairs and a huge radio set, about five feet tall and nearly three feet wide. Off to one side was an oval-shaped cherry wood conference table and eight high-backed wooden chairs, also cherry. A full-size Wurlitzer jukebox played popular ballads and quiet Italian melodies from a corner of the room.

The walls were of satiny walnut paneling, so highly polished that you could almost see yourself reflected in them. Set into the paneling were prominent raised millwork squares framed in two-inch molding. A wide, millworked chair rail encircled the room. A life-size painting of Pope Pius XII in a heavy gilt museum frame hung on one wall, facing a large crucifix on the opposite wall.

I leaned back into the sofa and realized this was the first time I'd ever relaxed in this room. Always, before I left for the Marines, I was apprehensive in Bobo's presence. He had an aura of great strength, always calm, confident in his power, a coiled spring that might lash out at any moment. But today, I was beyond such apprehension.

"So tell me, Bobo, how're things with you? Is the bookie joint still there behind the shooting gallery? How is Frankie?"

"Hey," Bobo exclaimed. "Where *is* Frankie? Georgie, get ahold of Frankie over here. Get him up here. Tell him we got a surprise for him." Georgie left and Bobo turned back to me. "Frankie'll get a kick outta seein' you, Jack.

"Things been pretty good for us," he continued. "The War brought lotsa money over here to Atlantic City. The Army took over the Chalfonte and Haddon Hall and the Marlboro-Blenheim and the Shelburne. Made 'em into hospitals and recuperation centers. The town was full of servicemen, all lookin' for fun. It was great. My club did fantastic. So did my numbers guys. And the bookmakers, they did real good too. But the guys who ran the whores, they really cleaned up. They had to bring in girls from Philly and New York. Our hometown girls couldn't handle the demand." He laughed. "They was wearin' themselves out. Remember little Patti, the blonde?"

I sure did. I lost my virginity to Patti in a night of ecstasy at fifteen. She was a gift from Bobo for an assignment I carried out for him. I nodded.

"She just now quit the game," Bobo said. "She told me she sometimes pulled in a grand a night. Can you imagine that? That's more than I clear! She told me she's got over a hunnert thou saved up. She took it and headed for California to start a new life. She offered me a goodbye fuck, but I'm exclusive with Loretta. You remember Loretta. I don't whore around anymore."

Bobo moved to his desk and half sat on the front of it, his weight on his right leg, his left knee up on the desk. He lit a cigarette.

"Yeah, Jack," he said, waving the match to extinguish it and exhaling a cloud of smoke, "the War was good for business. Everybody did good. Except the boys who got killed or hurt. Too bad. Too bad it took a war to get the country back on its feet over here. You'd think those smartasses in Washington could figure out how to have good times without shipping a few million boys overseas and gettin' a half million of 'em killed. You'd think."

"You lose anybody close?" I asked.

"Yeah," he shook his head through another cloud of smoke. "A cousin in Cleveland lost a son. Nice kid. Georgie lost two nephews. Loretta, she lost her younger brother. A couple of my boys bought it. One in France. One in the Pacific. But the worst, I think, is Nick Pezzi, one of my *capos*. He lost an eye and an arm. He's collecting a hunnert and ten bucks a month disability pension. He can't work. I let him keep his territory. He can't work it, so I got him a gopher. I cut down his dues from sixty bucks a week to ten. At least he's okay for money.

"So, Jack, what's your plans? Remember what I told you. You can come in with us. I told you that when you were a snot-nosed kid. Look at you now over here. A fuckin' captain. You filled out. You went away a boy and come back a man. You look pretty tough. And smart—I know that from those days. Whattaya say? Join my organization. You'll be like Georgie and Frankie. My right arms. Georgie and Frankie could use some help. They know you. You know them. It will be good. Whattaya say?"

When Bobo put on the charm, he was hard to resist.

"Thanks, Bobo," I said. "That's a great offer. Can I think about it?" I rose out of the sofa and paced as I spoke. "I'm going to get married, Bobo. To Alice. Remember her? Maybe I'll go to college. The government will pay for it and give me twenty bucks a week besides. I ain't made up my mind what to do. Only been thinking about it a few weeks—before I came back, I was afraid to think about *anything* except the next couple hours. Superstition, you know. How could I know I'd be coming home tomorrow or next week or next month, or ever? My company shipped out in October 1942 with 186 men. Only 85 of us originals made it back. Meanwhile, there were another 150 replacements that joined the company, some after each engagement. Only 101 of them made it to the end.

"So I don't really have any firm plans yet. The only thing I'm sure about is that I won't go to work in a retail store or manage one. My dad's a great guy, but I'm not gonna live that life."

"Come in with us," Bobo repeated.

"Thanks again for the offer, Bobo. I'm gonna think about it, seriously." I got up to leave. "I gotta get going. I'm gonna see Alan Goren. You remember Alan."

"You bet I do," Bobo laughed. "The toughest little guy I ever knew. Hey, give him my regards. I always liked that guy. And you give my proposition a good think."

I was about to leave when Georgie returned with Frankie. He was built like Georgie and Bobo but a couple inches shorter and forty pounds lighter.

They were all about the same age, but the years had brushed Frankie only lightly. He looked tough as always. He gave me the big hug and slapped my back.

"It's great to see you, kid," he said. He actually choked up; there was a quiver in his voice.

Frankie? Of all people, Frankie was the least likely to get choked up over anything. He must have liked me more than I knew. I always liked him, but I felt closer to Georgie. Frankie was not a talker. He never wasted words. He was sort of background to Georgie and Bobo. I looked at the three of them, big men, sleek, tough. When I left them behind in 1942, I was a boy and they were men. Now I was a man, and tough and powerful as they were, and age was beginning to do its relentless work on them. I felt their envy at my youth.

"So, Jack," Bobo said in a quiet moment. "What was the biggest thing that you'll remember always from all those landings and all the killings? For me, it was those days at Chateau-Thierry in 1918. I expected to get it every minute for four days. I'll never forget it. It's with me alla the time." He leaned back, blew smoke in the air, relaxed. "What about you? Alla them landings and battles. Ya got one big memory, bigger than the rest? The one that sticks out the biggest? The one you'll always remember?"

I thought for a moment then pursed my lips and leaned forward. "Yeah," I murmured, "there was one thing . . ." I straightened up, and they gathered closer. "I got laid on Okinawa—a Navy nurse, a month after the Japs surrendered."

A moment's silence. They looked at each other. Bobo tried to suppress a laugh. It came out as a big snort. Then an explosion of laughter. Heads thrown back. All of us. The kind of laughing where you cannot catch your breath and you start to cry from the exertion. *Haaaah!* Roaring, raucus laughter, near hysteria. Our roaring filled the room—loud, rollicking, shrill. *Haaah!* Bobo leaped from his chair onto the sofa. He wrapped me in his arms. Tight. I couldn't catch my breath. Torrents of laughter, grunts, even farts filled the room. *Haaaaah!* . . . me gasping for air.

"Hey," I tried to say, "it ain't all *that* funny," but I dissolved into laughter before I could finish. Bobo kissed my cheek as the laughter brought me to tears. They streamed down my face. Georgie and Frankie convulsed. Then came another wave: *Ha Ha Ha Ha!* This went on for what seemed like ten minutes. We were unable to control it or stop it. Finally, the chaos subsided but only for a moment before returning in an even greater wave.

"So that was the big thing of your war—you fucked a Navy nurse!" Bobo gasped and choked as he hugged me. "You son of a bitch!" he laughed. "I love you." He punched my shoulder then sat up and stopped to catch his breath. "You are somethin'," he whispered, breathing heavily.

Finally we quieted down, exhausted. We sat, silenced, for a minute. Then the tumult returned, deep, deafening, uncontrollable. *HAHA! . . . OH MY GOD!* Eyes shut, full-mouthed roars. All of us weak from more waves of the chaos. Georgie and Frankie were sprawled out on the sofa, trying to catch their breath.

It was another ten minutes before I was composed enough to stand and straighten my uniform.

Bear hugs all around.

"Don't forget, Jack," Bobo said. "You belong with us over here."

It's a good deal, I thought. *I could do real well with Bobo. And I wouldn't need any special training.*

"I'll remember that," I said.

As I descended the stairs, I heard the laughter burst out again, and I laughed as well. I was still laughing when I reached the street.

20

The Boardwalk

F ROM BOBO'S, I walked to the Atlantic City Boardwalk. It was three years since I had last seen it. How had it changed? During the War, the Army took over forty hotels as hospitals. Collectively, they were called the Thomas M. England General Hospital. After V-J Day, the Army gave up all but three of the largest: the Chalfont, Haddon Hall, and the Traymore were still being operated as rehabilitation centers. Their broad decks overlooking the board-walk were crowded with injured servicemen, some in uniform but most in pajamas and robes.

It was two hours before noon, and the boardwalk was bathed in sunlight. The sun was still low enough in the eastern sky to throw long morning shadows onto the boards. The big hotels in the heart of the city were clean and fresh, glistening in the sunlight: the Traymore, Shelburne, Marlboro-Blenheim, gold and ivory arabesque palaces; and the big, solid-looking Dennis and Claridge and Mayflower.

I paused before Krilow's Kitchen Gadget stand. A pitchman was giving his spiel and demonstrating the gadgets. I studied him with the eye of a connoisseur. He was pretty good but no Benny James. Benny was my role model in the summer of 1939 when I worked at this very stand. He was the best of the pitchmen, handsome, smart, ten years my senior. A quick thinker with a quicksilver personality. It was Benny's remarkable gift with numbers and arithmetic that led to the most improbable partnering you can imagine. There were four of us: me, a fifteen-year-old boy, and three men: Benny, Bobo, and Alan Goren. A high-stakes game of commodities trading served as my introduction to Bobo and Goren.

On the boardwalk opposite the kitchen gadget stand was Steel Pier, alive with a thousand flashing lights. A queue inched forward to buy tickets. Three movies were being shown: *Anchors Aweigh, Abbott and Costello in Hollywood,*

Adventures of Rusty. The headliners were comedian Eddie Cantor and a big band, the Casa Loma Orchestra with Glen Gray. Nothing had changed except the names of the movies and the headliners.

The day was one of Atlantic City's mid-October beauties. A few wisps of vapor hung low over the horizon. The sun was a shining silver disk, climbing to its noonday peak, slowly tracing an autumn arc across a cloudless sky.

The tide was receding, leaving behind a slick, wide swath of hard-packed sand at the water's edge. The ocean sparkled. Swells rolled toward the shore, rising into waves that spilled on the beach. Seagulls wheeled overhead, their cries a lively concert. Flocks of sandpipers ran and turned and circled at the water's edge like a drill team, in perfect unison. It always amazed me, and still does, how they behave as if they are a single organism, with a shared consciousness. All was as it had been.

The boardwalk was crowded with visitors drawn to the town by the perfect weather. I couldn't quite put my finger on it, but there was something about these visitors that was different from their 1942 predecessors. These 1945 strollers were well-dressed, as their earlier counterparts had been. The men wore English blazers and English tweeds and soft, creamy flannel trousers, with women on their arms dressed in smart suits and pretty dresses, the latter a bit longer than in 1942. The men wore hats—felt fedoras, same as in 1942—but the women's hats had changed. They were simpler. Their brims were wider, influenced by a moist-eyed Ingrid Bergman, looking out at Humphrey Bogart and Paul Henreid from under a wide brim in the final scene of 1942's *Casablanca.*

There was something else, though . . . or was it my imagination? These modern strollers seemed more erect, with a jauntiness in their step. You could see they were the victors. They had just won the War. They were confident in themselves and their country. These were the invincibles, the greatest generation, for whom all things were possible. I was one of them.

My uniform attracted the admiring looks of women and the respectful notice of men. Suddenly, I felt uncomfortable wearing it. I was an impostor. I was no longer a captain of Marines; I was a twenty-one-year-old boy with no career and no job. I took off the uniform for good after that day.

21

America

MERICA WAS SUPREME. Never in history and never again would a country be so powerful, so rich, so dominant. The War's cost in lives was staggering. America mourned its 416,000 dead servicemen, but no civilians died. But the others: Germany with 5.5 million military deaths and 2 million civilians; the Soviet Union with 9 million military deaths and 3 million civilians; Japan with 2.1 million military deaths and 1.7 million civilians. Those countries lost a whole generation of young men, and then there were the 6 million Jews killed in Hitler's *final solution* concentration camps. Britain suffered 382,000 military deaths, fewer than we did, but Britain had several hundred thousand civilian deaths.

Of all the combatants, only our country was unscathed. No bombs fell here. No invaders came to our shores. In Britain, Germany, France, Italy, China, Japan, and throughout the Soviet Union west of the Ural Mountains, industrialized cities were in ruin. Here in America, the war effort produced a giant new state-of-the-art industrial base. American economists worried about the big letdown when war production stopped. No need to worry. For almost four years, all of American industry was given over to the war effort. At war's end, there was a bottled-up demand for everything: cars, building materials, bridges and roads, housing, major appliances, schools, furniture, buses and trains.

Returning servicemen formed new families and made babies in record numbers. Industry shifted quickly to civilian products. Civilian demand filled the factories. The country burst with prosperity and confidence while other countries struggled to rebound. We leaped forward. We were the envy of the world. Providence and history had blessed us. Ours was a country and we were a people who could do anything. Jobs were abundant. Wages rose. New towns were formed. The future beckoned. It was good to be an American.

That was the America that awaited me when I came home.

* * *

It was three years since I allowed myself to think or plan about anything except the combat I was in or the next one coming.

Between island invasions, the time was never empty. On the contrary, the time was full of activity. There was preparedness work to do: integrate the replacements, put the entire company through training exercises, resupply the company, learn about our new weapons, check all our weapons and supplies, exchange ideas and survival tips with my lieutenants and with other company commanders, study the maps and pictures of our next target—all done with the deadly seriousness of the fear of overlooking anything that could keep us alive through the next invasion.

So what now? All that effort and fear and frenzy was over, forever. What value did it have for getting on with life? Probably none.

The moment I took off my uniform, I would be a high school graduate with no training for anything. What a letdown. From Marine captain to unemployed kid with no skill except to lead an infantry company into combat. Wasn't it strange that a twenty-one-year-old should have a three-year blank space in his history called the War?

22

Alan Goren and Zena

I VISITED GOREN AND Zena that afternoon. They were living in the same apartment, just as I left them three years earlier. The living room windows were open. The sheer white curtains lifted in the light breeze. Goren was reading the paper, wearing his khaki pants and a gray cardigan sweater over a white shirt; same gray ragg socks and loafers, surrounded by newspapers, as always, and a fragrant pipe. Books were everywhere. He rose from the sofa to answer my ring. When he saw it was me, he stood motionless for a moment then embraced me wordlessly.

"Zena, come here, Zena," he called out over his shoulder, his voice choking. "It's Jack."

She ran from the kitchen, wiping her hands on her apron. She squeezed between us and hugged me and kissed my cheek four or five times. Then she wept. Goren was also a little misty-eyed.

They wanted to hear everything, especially Zena. She wanted to hear about every day of the three years I'd been away.

Goren was one of the commodities trading foursome, together with Bobo, Benny James, and me. He'd somehow stumbled into Zena's fortune-telling parlor on the boardwalk and fell under her spell. He firmly believed Zena could see into the future, in spite of her occasional protests to the contrary.

Goren was in the First World War. He came out an infantry captain, decorated for valor. There was no need to describe the War to Goren. He studied my face carefully. "Are you all right, Jack?" he asked. "In every way?"

I understood him. "I'm fine, Alan," I said. "But please—I want to hear what you've been up to since I last saw you."

Goren said he traded crude oil futures during the War and made a lot of money. It was an obvious call to go long and stay long, as he put it.

From the beginning of the War until Pearl Harbor, crude prices inched up steadily. "It was easy money," he said. "The war in Europe made me rich until we got in it. But then, in early 1942, a few months after Pearl Harbor, Roosevelt created the OPA, the Office of Price Administration; the idea was to control wages and prices and keep inflation under control. Otherwise, we would have had runaway inflation. Price fluctuations in the commodities markets became very narrow. I managed to make some money, not much; my big score came before the OPA."

Zena was still *the* boardwalk fortune teller. During the War, most of her customers were soldiers. They stood in line outside her little parlor, anxious to know. Now things were back to normal. She welcomed the end of the soldier customers. Too often, she said, she had a hard time murmuring soothing ambiguities to an anxious young face.

"Now, here's something for you to ponder," Goren said to me but looked at Zena. "About three months ago, July 16 to be exact, the War was over in Europe but not in the Pacific. It looked like it would go on and on—maybe for years. I'll never forget that day. I was in Zena's parlor. I brought a couple of sandwiches. She hung out the *CLOSED* sign and made tea. It was a daily ritual. Very nice. We ate at Zena's table. That day, she must have touched the light switch on her globe accidentally. It lit up. I'm sure you remember when something like that happened back in 1939 when you and me and Benny were there. She got that in-a-trance look, staring into the globe. I didn't see anything in the globe—just that milky cloud around the perimeter and a dark spot in the center. I said, *Zena, what is it? What's in there?* She stared into the globe for almost a minute, then she blinked a few times and straightened up. I asked her what happened."

Zena broke in. "It was terrible, Jack. I saw something horrible and dark, enormous, and deadly. It wasn't clear. I told Alan something terrible was happening, or about to happen, but I couldn't see what it was except that it was destruction and death. Bigger than anything. And I couldn't see where it was happening."

Alan interrupted, "It was an omen, something big. Maybe a volcano. Maybe a tornado or a hurricane, or maybe a new weapon. What can it mean? If it's happening here or to Americans, it might prolong the War. But if it's happening to the Japs, it could shorten the War. A prolonged war would mean a little strengthening in crude oil prices—not much. Victory over Japan was certain. It was only a question of how long and how many more deaths. But if it meant a quicker end to the War, then crude prices will drop. I was long over a hundred contracts. I got up from the table and went to my broker and closed out my positions.

"Then nothing happened, just the daily war news, air raids on Japan, preparations to invade Japan. Nothing new or startling. I started thinking about going back long into crude futures. Everything pointed to a long, long war. Then August 6 and the bomb fell on Hiroshima. That meant the end of the War, which was the big headline, but a detail that came out was that the bomb had been tested in Alamogordo, New Mexico, several weeks earlier. Can you guess the date of the test, Jack? It was July 16—the very day Zena saw her globe go dark. She really has the gift!"

"I don't know what I have," Zena said. "I am not a clairvoyant. Sometimes I see things, but I never know what they mean. Alan does the interpreting. I keep telling him to stop. I shouldn't tell him anything. One day, he'll get hurt bad from thinking I know things."

"I'm still trading," Alan continued, "but it's hard work. And I'm not always right. I'm thinking of quitting. I have enough money. I think I'm going back to real estate. That's going to be big; so many new households are going to form, and there's been no new housing built for three years."

He wanted to know my plans. I said I didn't have any yet but I was thinking about it every day. "Do you have any suggestions?" I asked.

"I can think of lots of things for you," he answered, "but you'll decide on your own. Take your time. You'll succeed at anything you try. Make sure you don't get into a dead-end. Make sure you do something where there's opportunity and you're part of the big economy and you understand everything that's happening in the world. It's not about just making a living; it's about really living and learning about everything.

"Jack," he continued, "this is a unique moment in history. When, ever, did a country have a monopoly on the most powerful weapon ever imagined.

There has never been a country like ours, in all of history, so superior in everything. Ours is the greatest economy, the most powerful military, the strongest industrial base, the richest. Ours is the land of opportunity, more so than any time in our history. People and nations all over the world look to us for help and guidance. The world is in awe of America. Americans abroad are seen as supermen, whether it's MacArthur in Japan, or Stilwell in China, or Eisenhower and Marshall in Europe, or just an American businessman. We are respected everywhere, sometimes with admiration, sometimes with envy, sometimes with hostility, but always respected, and maybe a little bit feared.

"We have such enormous power, the A-bomb. There's never been anything to equal this in all of history. Even the Romans don't compare. Their reach was small compared to ours. America can project its power to any spot on earth. We won't have a monopoly on the bomb for long—maybe a couple of years, maybe five. We'll have problems with the Russians, but until they have the bomb, they'll be easy to manage. Once they have it, there will be a power struggle with them. They shouldn't be underestimated. They have a big new industrial base east of the Urals, all new, built during the War, and they're smart. But we have at least five years to work things out with them before they have the bomb."

He put into words the vague ideas I had about being part of an exciting new post-war economy. New things were happening. Wars always accelerated new things. I knew the post-War economy was going to be big and crowded with new things.

"Tell me about Harry Truman," I said. "What about him?"

"I've studied him," Goren said. He paused to draw on his pipe. A fragrant cloud of smoke rose, was drawn to the open windows, and floated out. "Truman has a tough deal. Roosevelt was a giant. Nobody can stand up to that comparison. But I think Truman will be okay. He gets very high marks for how he ran the Truman Committee as a senator. That committee did a great job of stopping defense contractors from gouging the government during the War. Before Roosevelt picked him for vice president last year, people who know Washington used to say he was the best informed man in the Senate.

"He's tough, and smart, and he's his own man. He's not afraid to make hard decisions—like dropping the Bomb. And he's smarter than Roosevelt when it comes to understanding Stalin and the Russians. I think he'll be as good as we could get to contain the Russians with no misunderstood signals. I'm for him, Jack. He's got a tough act to follow, but he'll do it and do it well."

"I don't know anything about him," I said, "except every man in my company says he saved our lives by dropping those bombs. We'd probably be fighting in Japan by now, or maybe we'd all be killed by now."

Goren said, "You get an idea about him from his response to MacArthur and Chester Nimitz on the eve of the Japanese surrender ceremony on the battleship *Missouri*. Their press attachés received instructions from Washington to be *politically correct* concerning remarks about the Japanese. It was a new term. MacArthur and Nimitz sent a joint telegram to Truman asking what it meant—*politically correct*. Truman answered, 'It's a new term coined by members of the media who think you can pick up a piece of shit by the clean end.'"

* * *

Roosevelt was president so long that it was hard to imagine any other man in the role. Roosevelt was a patrician. He was not readily accessible. He came to be invested with godlike qualities—all-knowing, decisive. He made all the politicians look like pygmies. Truman was the polar opposite. He was a man of the people. He came from humble beginnings. He was a decorated artillery captain in World War I, and after that, a failed haberdasher. His entry into politics was as a flunky in the powerful Tom Pendergast political machine. They put him in office and expected him to do as he was told. The machine got him into the Senate. There—unlike most politicians, whose integrity is at its peak before being elected and downward thereafter—Truman's integrity, questionable at the outset of his senatorial election, developed once elected.

* * *

I asked about Benny James. Had Goren heard from him?

"Yes, he's an intelligence officer stationed in Washington, and—oh my," he interrupted himself. "That reminds me. Remember Benny gave me four thousand dollars to invest for him in 1939 when he went to England? He thought I should go long on crude oil futures, and I had the same idea. We sure were right. And you. Remember you gave me two hundred dollars? Well, Benny's four thousand dollars is worth more than forty-five thousand, and your two hundred dollars is about three thousand. I closed both your accounts when I unloaded. I'll get you a check for your balance. Benny wants to partner with me, trading commodities, but I don't want the responsibility. I may never go back to it. I made enough."

Zena served tea. It was old times again.

23

Going to Work

ISPENT A MONTH doing not much of anything. It was time to go to work, but I had no plans.

Bobo's offer didn't need any particular skills. That was a big plus. The training would be on the job. And the money would be good. A tempting thought, but I set it aside. Bobo was, after all, illegal. Worse, he was dangerous. He was a charmer when in a good mood, but I'd seen his dark side. I wouldn't want to be there. And I'd had enough of soldiering. I didn't want to be a soldier in Bobo's army.

Eddie opened Eddie's TV and Radio with his saved-up service pay and a $3,000 gift from his dad to help him get started. His was the first store in Atlantic City to carry television sets. He carried RCA and Philco as a retailer, and he was trying for a South Jersey distributorship for Motorola.

I visited him every day. Business was slow. Mostly he was doing repair work. When he sold a TV, he usually sold a rooftop antenna and got the installation job. Reception was poor in Atlantic City. Rabbit ears didn't pull in a signal. A rooftop antenna was almost a necessity. Programming was meager. Television in Atlantic City got off to a slow start.

Eddie was optimistic, but it was obvious that he was disappointed at his rate of progress. One day he had a lead for a local grocery distributor for an intercom system. He asked me to come along. He thought Eddie's TV and Radio would inspire more confidence if represented by a systems designer *and* an installer.

"Who's the designer?" I asked.

"You are, Jack," he said.

"Are you kidding?" I said.

"You don't have to say much," he said. "Take this clipboard. Just ask where they want the boxes. We'll walk through the place. Every box is both

"

a sender and a receiver. Write down the locations. Tell them we'll draw a sketch and be back tomorrow with a quote. If you're stumped, I'll chime in. Don't worry."

We got the job. Eddie was elated. I even returned with him to "oversee" his installation. It was a hoot.

* * *

I knew a guy at Atlantic Phone Company, though nobody called it that. APC was the name everybody used. His name was Fred Walsh, a thirty-one-year-old master sergeant in my second platoon. I knew him real well. He was a replacement after Cape Gloucester. He survived the last two of our invasions, but on Okinawa on the last day of fighting, he received a million-dollar wound. It got him home; a piece of Japanese shrapnel tore through his left side without touching any organs. The surgeons at the mobile surgical hospital sterilized the wound and sewed him up. He was shipped out for home in July. The rest of us in the company envied him. We were preparing for the invasion of Japan. Who knew how long the War would go on and how many of us would survive it?

I drove Fred to the airstrip when he got booked out on a C-47 flight to Honolulu. That was when he told me he had a wife and a good job waiting back home in Trenton, working for APC. He wished me and the company good luck. He was going home. We were getting ready to invade Japan.

Fred knew I was from Atlantic City. He gave me his address and phone number. "Look me up, Captain," he offered. "You never know . . ."

Could that have been only five months ago? It was worlds away, an era ago. I called him in early December. He seemed excited.

"Captain!" he bellowed into the phone. "Great to hear your voice. Hey, c'mon up to see me—tomorrow. Oh boy, it will be great to see you."

I borrowed clothes from my dad: a white shirt, tie, and navy blue suit. The shirt sleeves were an inch short. So were the suit sleeves and trousers. The shirt collar was too small. I left it unbuttoned and pulled up the necktie to cover the gap. And the jacket buttoned too tight. I would have to keep it unbuttoned. Dad had a gray herringbone overcoat that looked presentable because it was too big for him. I also wore Dad's gray felt hat and scarf. Every man wore a hat those days. Sizing myself up in the mirror, I looked presentable, marginally. I thought I'd pass muster as long as I stayed seated.

To get to the APC office in Trenton involved two trains and a trolley and then a seven-block walk in a light snowfall. When I arrived, I may have looked better than I felt, which was damp, deflated, and wrinkled.

The receptionist was a pretty girl. She raised her eyebrows and smiled. "Yes, may I help you?" When I gave her my name, she broke into a big smile, jumped up from behind the reception desk, and came around to shake my hand. That was unusual back then in 1945, for a girl to shake hands, especially with such enthusiasm.

"Captain Laurel! Mr. Walsh told us all about you. It's so good to meet you. Wait here. I'll get him."

She ran across the open office area, picking her way between rows of desks, then disappeared behind a door with a dimpled glass panel on which the painted lettering read:

FREDERICK WALSH

Regional Operations Manager

After a moment, the door flew open and Fred Walsh burst out. He bore down on me, arms outstretched. "Captain!" he bellowed. "Look, everybody. This here is my captain, my commander. Captain Jack Laurel . . . who I told you about . . . the best officer in the whole brigade! Probably in the whole goddamn First Marine Division!"

Everyone smiled and nodded. Several of the employees stood up and actually clapped.

"Captain!" He ignored the handshake I offered. Instead, he threw his arms around me and pulled me tight, slapping my back. "God a'mighty, it's good to see you," he said as he stepped back.

"And it's great to see you, Sarge," I said, as pleased as I was surprised by the big welcome.

"C'mon in, come into my office. Hey, Betty," he called out, "how 'bout getting us a couple coffees?" He took my arm and pulled me into his office.

I studied Fred across his desk. He was a big man, same height as me but broader. I was uncomfortable—me, an unemployed twenty-one-year-old ex-captain, and he, my ex-subordinate, a thirty-one-year-old man with a solid position in America's most prestigious company, in a navy blue pinstriped suit and snowy white shirt and highly polished black shoes.

"Congratulations, Sarge," I said. "Looks like you're really well settled in. And how about let's drop the *Captain Laurel*. I'm Jack. You're Fred."

"Okay, Captain . . . I mean, Jack. Gee, that sounds strange. But you're right. All that is old news. Yes, I'm doing great. Did you know I'm a married man? I had a wife when I joined up. She was in a family way. I didn't even know it. Now I've got a three-year-old son and another one on the way and I have this great job. It doesn't hurt that my uncle is the US congressman representing this district."

We talked a bit about old times. Then I told him I was ready to go to work. Maybe there was something for me at APC. He didn't have to think about it. "You bet there is," he said. I need a guy just like you in sales in South Jersey. I just canned a guy down there, a lazy son of a bitch. He hardly ever worked, just collected commissions on the orders that came in from his territory by themselves. The job is yours. You'll be reporting to the district manager for that location. Look here . . ."

He picked up a twenty-four-inch stick leaning in the corner. I saw that it was the end of a tree branch, reasonably straight, that had been shaved clean and smooth, although some of the knobs hadn't been shaved down completely. "See this stick, Jack?" he said. "I cut it off a tree my last day in Okinawa. It's my only war souvenir."

He pointed the stick at a three-by-five-foot map of New Jersey pinned to a wall. A heavy east-west red line ran across it, following county roads from Lambertville on the Delaware River, twelve miles north of Trenton, passing above Princeton and South Brunswick, and reaching the Atlantic Coast at Sea Bright. The area below the red line was subdivided with blue lines into three areas. For a moment, it felt like I was in a situation meeting back there on one of the islands. "This is my region," Walsh said. "Everything south of this red line. All of South Jersey."

He tapped the map with the stick. "These are the three districts in my region. This one—District NJ2—covers Atlantic City to Camden and everything south of that. You'll work in this district."

What a surprise! I wasn't expecting a job offer. I thought he might say he'd keep his eye out for me—you know: *I'll let you know if anything comes along.*

"Wow, hey, thanks, Sarge," I said. "I mean, Fred. I didn't expect this. It's a big break for me. But how can I handle the job? I have no experience."

"Never mind," he said. "I'm gonna go to bat for you. You're perfect for APC. A military man. A captain. Decorated. We'll train you. You're the right image for APC. And anyway, Captain—I mean, Jack—anybody can sell APC. We're the only game in town for anybody or any company that wants phone service."

He told me about the work, the territory, the money I'd be making, the training they'd give me. I was elated. "I sure didn't expect anything like this when I came here," I said. "Sarge, I don't know how to thank you. But you can be sure I won't let you down."

I was eager to get on my way. The job sounded fine, but I was uncomfortable with our role reversal and was feeling seedy in my damp, secondhand clothes.

When I stood to leave, Fred asked, "Did you have any trouble finding the place?"

"Not at all," I answered.

"How did you get here?" he asked.

"By train," I said. "I haven't gotten around to buying a car yet."

"Well, c'mon," he said. "I'll drive you to the station."

Fred had a 1942 Pontiac, one of the last cars built before the car companies switched over from civilian to war production. The first of the post-War cars hadn't yet arrived in showrooms.

"Nice car," I said.

"Beats bumping around in a jeep," he grinned.

When we got to the train station, I shook his hand and thanked him again for the job. "I'll do a good job for you," I said.

"I know you will," he answered. Then he smiled and said, "Jack, get some new clothes. And you'll need a car."

My boss, the sergeant. I flushed with embarrassment.

* * *

I liked the idea of working for the phone company. I wanted to sell communication systems. The War had accelerated the development of electronics and telecommunications, and I believed that to be competitive, companies were going to want newer and better. It was exciting, and I wanted to be part of it.

Alice greeted my news with a smile, a hug, and a kiss. "But what do you know about telephones?" she asked.

"Never mind," I said, holding her in a strong embrace. "Never mind that I have no training and I sure know nothing about telephones or electronics. APC wants me because they're looking for young veterans. I'm a Marine captain. They have a training program, and they'll back me up technically when I need help."

"Let's celebrate," she said with that great smile.

"What did you have in mind?" I asked.

"Come with me," she said, taking my hand and drawing me into her bedroom. "No one's home but me."

A week before Christmas 1945, I became an APC salesman. I bought two new suits, a gray flannel and a navy blue; four white button-down shirts; four silk ties, two striped and two with patterns; a gray felt hat and a brown cocoa straw hat for spring and summer; a gray gabardine topcoat by Alligator; brown wing-tip shoes, and a pair of black round-tip bluchers.

That was a uniform of the sort that APC salesmen wore. IBM salesmen wore the same uniform, as did salesmen for US Steel, General Electric, Pfizer, and most of the other leading American corporations.

I bought a used 1939 Plymouth for $300, maroon. Alice and I cleaned and polished every inch of it. It was quite presentable for a young APC salesman.

I sold communications systems. The company gave me a three-week training course and half of South Jersey as my territory. I enrolled in the night school program at Atlantic Cape Community College in a two-year course that led to a certificate in clectrical-electronic engineering. They were difficult courses but not as difficult as Officers' Candidate School.

The selling was easy. My APC business card got me in everywhere. Almost every company I visited wanted something new. I designed telephone systems and sold them and conducted training sessions on how to use them. My military service made it easy to get personal with potential customers. "What did you do in the War?" It was the icebreaker, whether the question was asked of me or I asked it. I capitalized shamelessly on my military service. By April, I was earning more than sixty dollars a week, pretty good money in the spring of 1946.

24

Eddie and Evie

EDDIE'S BUSINESS WAS doing okay. He worked long hours and almost every day. He spent as much time as he could experimenting with inventive ideas for improving the technology of radios and telephones.

Since his return from the War, he and my sister Evie were inseparable. Within a few weeks, she was wearing his engagement ring. She had a job as receptionist in a medical practice, although she had no particular training. She was smart, pretty, and a quick learner who handled the job well. Patients liked her. The doctors liked her. Even the nurses liked her.

Because Eddie worked such long hours, he and Evie had little time together, but their bond was strong. When they talked of a wedding date, Eddie said he wanted his business to get stronger. He wanted to be a good provider. His traditional ideas told him he wasn't ready to marry and start a family.

"We're hardly ever together," Evie complained to me. "I love him. I want him, but I need him to be with me. He works all the time. When I get to see him, he's tired. He never wants to go out, not to a restaurant or a movie. I make dinner. We spend an hour or so having a late meal and listening to the radio. Then he goes home. I want to get married. We'll be all right. I'm working, and he's doing pretty well. I don't think he has to work as hard as he does."

"Give him some time," I said. "He's really caught up in his business. He thinks of nothing else. It's only a few months old and everything he has is in it. He's not like me. I'm doing fine without anything invested. I have nothing at risk. When I quit for the day, I'm done. I don't carry any problems home. Once I open up an account, it's like an annuity. The orders come in by themselves, for upgrades, additional equipment, installations. And my commissions just roll in.

"Eddie works hard. You know what he says: *When I stop rowing, the boat stops.* Nothing just rolls in for him like for me. He needs your support. Don't complain. Encourage him. Always be there for him. He loves you, Evie. Everything will be okay—you'll see."

She sighed. "I know all that, Jack, but it's hard. I can tell you these things, but I never say anything to him. I'm patient; I love him so. He's worth everything. And I'm really proud of him. He's not even twenty-two, and he has his own business. And anyway, we're young. What's the hurry?"

With a wink and a sigh, she added, "But it would be nice to go out once in a while."

25

The Good Life

ALICE GRADUATED FROM Atlantic City High School in June 1943 and enrolled at Princeton University. As part of the war effort, Princeton was on a three-semester year. An eight-semester undergraduate program could be completed in less than three years. The school offered the courses she wanted: archeology, anthropology, and evolutionary biology. The weekday commute was two hours each way—a tiring schedule but well worth it, she said. Those courses were not available at any college closer to home.

When I returned from the War, Alice was in her eighth and final semester. Her evolutionary biology professor had gotten her a part-time job with the Department of the Interior, cataloging the animal and plant life of southern New Jersey. Her area was everything south of and including the Lebanon State Forest. On weekends and on days off from school, she traveled to the parks and wildlife reserves within her territory with a camera, binoculars, and a notebook. She filled journals by the dozen with descriptions and photos of birds, mammals, insects, trees, shrubs, grasses, and flowers. After graduating in January 1946 with multiple degrees, her job became full-time. She was earning forty dollars a week.

I was very pleased with my growing career at APC. By May 1946, my commission income was closing in on $400 a month.

"So, Alice," I said, "it's time for a wedding. What do you think?"

"I was ready the day you came home," she smiled.

So we did it. It was a June wedding.

Not to be outdone, Evie persuaded Eddie to follow suit two months later.

* * *

We lived with Alice's parents for six months while we saved up for a house. We found a 1928 three-bedroom, Spanish-style house in Marven Gardens in Margate. We bought it for $8,000 with a twenty-year, $7,500 GI mortgage at 3 percent interest. Our monthly payment was $41.60. Eddie and Evie bought a house nearby.

By the time we moved in, my monthly earnings were over $400 and Alice was good for another $160. That was a solid income in 1946, in the upper range of middle-class America.

My father, still manager of the Nu-Enamel Paint Store and enjoying post-War prosperity and rising wages, was earning $285 and was very proud of his success. But even as he told me how proud he was that my success had eclipsed his, I sensed a melancholy that his achievement was so modest after decades of toil.

* * *

Atlantic City witnesses a disgraceful phenomenon every year on Labor Day. It is *summer dog abandonment day.* Some families who move into summer rental houses at the shore buy a dog, or pick one up at an animal shelter, as a child's pet for the summer with no intention of keeping the animal when they give up the rented house and go home at summer's end. On the way out of Atlantic City, on the Black Horse Pike and the White Horse Pike, summer dogs are let out of the car, abandoned on the highway. You saw a number of such dogs on the highway every Labor Day, following the mass exodus from the shore.

I found Max a day after Labor Day, wandering along the Black Horse Pike. He was a mixture of German shepherd and Labrador retriever. He was big-boned, handsome, and smart. He trained so easily that it never felt like training. Within weeks, Alice or I could take him anywhere without a leash. He walked alongside my left ankle, stopped when I stopped, started up when I did. He obeyed hand signals; *stop, sit, lie down, up, go there, come.* I don't even remember teaching him. He just seemed to know what I wanted.

He was protective of us. He made our house feel secure. Alice took him with her when she drove into the forests and national parks. It was reassuring to know Max was always with her in her station wagon and at her side. His pleasant demeanor and wagging tail stopped when he went into guardian mode, confronting a stranger. Unleashed, his head thrust forward, eyes leveled at the stranger, tail stiff and held straight behind him, a low growl barely audible.

"It's okay, Max." Those were the words to set him at ease. Nobody was gonna mess with Alice with Max at her side.

Foolish people, they who abandoned him, I thought.

* * *

In February 1947, Alice asked me would I like to become a father.

"Sure," I said. "Shall we give it a try?"

"I guess we already did," she laughed. "I'm two months pregnant."

26

Walkie-Talkies

IN APRIL 1947, I'D been with APC for fifteen months. On Monday, during our regular sales staff meeting, a man from our Bell Laboratories Division in Camden came to give a talk on new products under development. He brought with him twenty pages of government surplus inventory and carried a tape recorder, a device none of us had seen before.

The state of the art, we thought, was the wire recorder, which had been in use for two years but was not, in fact, an efficient device. Its fidelity was poor. Its spool tangled easily or broke, and it held only twenty minutes of recording. The Bell Labs man's tape recorder was in a handsome, polished wooden case with a hinged lid that opened to reveal dual tape reels, microphone, and controls. All of us were intrigued by his demonstration. We took turns speaking into the mic and listening to our own voices. It was interesting to hear your own voice. I'd never heard mine recorded, and it didn't sound at all as I imagined.

"Where did this come from?" I asked. "It doesn't look like an experimental model. It's so well-finished. I've never seen anything like it."

"It's from Germany," the Bell Labs man said. "The Germans have had similar recorders since 1940. Just about every serious military office had one—and not just in Germany but in France, and Holland, and all the other countries the Germans occupied. Our army commandeered them, probably a few thousand. They sold them here as government surplus. Bell Labs bought ten at sixty-five bucks apiece. They have to be worth a couple hundred or more. Anybody want one?"

I spoke up first, and he said I could have the one he'd brought. So I bought it. *What a great piece of equipment,* I thought. *Alice will love it, and Eddie will go bananas.*

Then I studied the electronics section of the inventory pages. There was one item in particular that caught my attention: 1,487 Handie-Talkies, new and unused in their original packaging, for sale at $2.15 each, originally purchased by the Army in 1944 for $62.00 apiece. They were twenty-four inches long, single crystal, with a twenty-four-inch whip antenna.

These were second-generation walkie-talkies of the type used in the War since 1942. The original model had a heavy battery pack and was carried in a sack with a forty-eight-inch antenna. I had one in the War. In the field, I always had an aide with me with a backpack that held the battery and the antenna. He carried the walkie-talkie, as well, so I could be hands-free until I needed it. By the time we went to Okinawa, we had the next generation, the Handie-Talkie. It was self-contained and much easier to use, but we still called it a walkie-talkie. Like the original, it had only a line-of-sight range and its reception was pretty spotty. I'd have to talk to Eddie about this equipment.

Eddie and Evie came for dinner that evening. Eddie showed up in a suit and tie while Evie wore a white blouse, flowered skirt, and high heels. The cut of her skirt was called *A-line*. It was an attractive style those days for young women, especially pretty ones with slim figures. That's the way we dressed back then, not only when going out to visit but even at home alone.

When I arrived from work, I always found Alice looking fresh and dressed attractively. I wore a suit and tie every day to work. I washed my hands and face when I got home, but the suit and tie remained on through dinner and the rest of the evening. Eddie observed the custom of dressing to go out, even to a casual dinner at someone's home. I knew it was an inconvenience for him to leave work early, come home, climb out of his work clothes, shower, and dress for dinner. For Evie, an evening out of the house with Eddie was a treat, and she'd obviously been looking forward to this evening.

Alice made a big antipasto and cooked up spaghetti and sausage with her own tomato sauce and fresh-grated Reggiano cheese. Eddie brought the Chianti.

Before we sat down for dinner I showed off my new toy, the tape recorder. It was fun talking and singing into it and listening to the playback. It was technology on the march. That it had been in use in Germany for six years was puzzling. Didn't we have a corner on all things new? I guessed not. Here it was, almost two years after the War, and there was no American-made tape recorder on the market.

After dinner, while Evie and Alice cleaned up the kitchen, I told Eddie about the walkie-talkies. He said he knew them real well. They worked best in open areas. In congested areas, they didn't perform well at all.

"When I was on the *Wichita*," he said, "we put in at Pearl Harbor in February 1945 for supplies and an engine room check before heading to Okinawa. The skipper picked up four of them. He gave me one, he gave one to the chief engineer, he kept one, and he gave one to the exec. He thought they could be a backup for our intercom system. But it was no good because they're all on one frequency. When anybody used his, he came across on all the others. So the skipper took away the engineer's and the exec's. Just him and me had them. But they were still no good because there was so much steel everywhere and you never knew when a signal would carry. If the skipper was on the bridge, we could reach each other most of the time, but when he moved around the ship, sometimes we connected but most times we lost communication."

"Do you want them?" I asked. "They're going for two dollars and fifteen cents. The Army paid about sixty dollars apiece."

"I'd like to have them," Eddie said. "They have valuable components, and I could probably sell a few. The cases alone are worth a few bucks if I can find a use for them—so are the vacuum tubes. But I have to tell you, Jack, I can't spare the money. My business is okay. I'm making a living, but it's tough, and every extra buck goes into more inventory. I'll have to pass."

"Tell you what," I said. "I'll buy five hundred. It's not a gift and it's not a handout. We're going to make some money out of this. As an APC man, I can't sell them myself, but I can give you leads. I'm with people all day long who might want a couple."

"Okay, Jack," Eddie said. "If you buy them, I'll sell them. I'm sure we can make a few bucks that way, and I'd like to see if I can increase their output. This could be interesting."

27

The Antenna Job

June 1947

IF WE KNEW what we were in for that day, maybe Eddie would have turned down the job.

He'd asked me to come with him on Saturday to do an antenna installation for a nineteen-inch RCA TV. The customer took the set to his office, but the rabbit ears were not pulling in a signal.

I was glad to go along. It gave us some time together, which was rare because Eddie was always working. He had little time or patience for socializing.

"Where we goin'?" I asked, climbing into his station wagon.

"It's out on Route 206," he answered. "It's about thirty-five miles from here, halfway to Philadelphia, in the Pine Barrens. The guy has a building supply company out there. No wonder he can't get reception—it's in the boonies, the middle of nowhere."

I settled down for an hour-long drive. "So how's everything?" I asked. "Seems you're always working. Is the business doing well?"

"Business is okay," he said, "but it ain't easy, Jack. I'm a one-man show. I do the selling. I do the repairs. I do the installations. I pay the bills. And meanwhile, I've been playing around with our walkie-talkies. I have an idea to make them one-on-one instead of a call going out to everyone in range. They're like radios and receivers. I'm trying to make them like telephones. You know, one-on-one.

"Also, they're too big. I can use a different, better battery, smaller, rechargeable, less than half the size. I can cut off about six inches from the lower half and put the bottom back on. And I know how to increase their range using a repeater and a relay station.

"They're full of vacuum tubes that take up a lot of space. Someday, somebody will invent something to replace those tubes. It will be small, maybe the size of a cigarette. These tubes not only take up too much room, but they blow out, like light bulbs. Any day, I expect something to replace them. There was an article in *Scientific American* about some guys at Bell Labs working on a solid-state device. They call it a transistor. I know I'm onto something; the trouble is finding enough time to work my ideas through."

"Well," I said. "I hope you're making decent money for all that work. Look at how I landed: I'm making good money and the work is nothing. It's all conversation and a little bit of sketching. No nights, evenings, or weekends, and when I quit for the day, it's over until the next day. But you—your work-day has no end. You're at it *all the time* . . . when you're not at your store or out on a job, you're home thinking and planning. And worrying, too, I bet."

"Listen, Jack," Eddie said earnestly. "I'm real glad you're doing so well, and yes, sometimes when I'm working late, I envy your schedule. My business is tough, and like you say, it's with me all the time. I know that when I'm not working, nothing happens. It's hard on Evie. She understands, and I tell her it won't always be like this. Maybe in a year, I'll be able to afford an assistant. But I'll tell you this: I couldn't work for anyone. I'm my own man. As good as it is for you, you're still an employee. One of these days I'm gonna make you quit and partner up with me. You'll see."

"So just how well are you doin'?" I asked. "I'm good for better than four fifty a month. How about you?"

"When my accountant was in last week, he said I'm clearing better than a hundred a week."

"Wow," I said, "I'm impressed. I didn't know you were doin' that good."

"Well," Eddie said, "I had to correct my accountant. I told him I'm not really making money; I'm making parts and inventory. You gotta plow any profit right back in if you want to grow. But Evie and I are okay. She's making thirty-five dollars a week, and I draw sixty dollars every Saturday. The money's okay; the stress is the problem."

The road turned into a two-lane county road, walled in by mile after mile of pines and dense shrubbery. "Are you sure you got the directions right?" I asked.

"Positive. I'm watching the speedometer. There should be a sign on the right exactly eight point six miles from that last railway crossing. Keep your eye out."

The sign was nearly hidden by foliage. "Spencer Building Supply Co.," it said, with an arrow pointing to a break in the trees. We turned onto an access road and drove another two hundred yards, ending at a cyclone fence with a closed gate and a security station. A guard asked us who we were then spoke into an intercom box to announce us.

"Two guys from Eddie's TV and Radio." Receiving an okay, he opened the gate and waved us through.

"What kinda place is this," I asked, "out here in the middle of nothing, fenced off, with security?"

"I got no idea," Eddie said, "but we'll know soon enough."

28

The Spencer Building Supply Company

WE ENTERED A LARGE rectangular clearing cut out of the forest of pine and brush, about nine hundred feet across and twelve hundred feet deep. A one-thousand-foot-long, one-story building stood off to the left, a short distance from the gate. At the far end of the clearing was what must have once been a rocky cliff that had been quarried until little of it remained. A line of railroad track ran across the far end of the clearing, close to the remnants of the cliff.

Stacks of various kinds of brick, building blocks, stone, and slate stood in neatly arranged rows between aisles wide enough for pickup trucks and forklifts to navigate. An American flag floated lazily at the top of a sixty-foot flagpole near the entrance to the building. A grassy lawn, well-tended with flowering shrubs, was bisected by a walkway to the front door. The lawn and the path were outlined with painted white stones, just like an Army headquarters building. The company's name was mounted above the entrance: "Spencer Building Supply Co." Alongside the door was a painted military emblem and the words "United States Army, 108th Ordinance." The door itself carried a lieutenant colonel's insignia above the word "Headquarters."

Several company trucks were parked close to the building in striped parking spaces, with customer pickups scattered throughout the grid of aisles that separated the stacks of building materials. I counted four forklifts transferring materials from the piles to the waiting pickups. There was activity everywhere: building supplies being transported, men walking briskly up and down the aisles, trucks and other vehicles on the move.

We entered the building into a reception area. To our left behind a low railing, a half dozen women worked at their desks. To our right was a room marked "Office." Beyond it, stretching off to the right, the rest of the long building was a warehouse heavily stocked with lumber, hardware, and building materials. Mr. Spencer was waiting for us in the reception area.

"Dave Spencer," he said, introducing himself as he offered us his hand. He appeared to be in his late forties.

I introduced myself, and before Spencer could respond, I asked, "Dave, what kind of place is this? It looks like an Army base."

Spencer answered, "Used to be a limestone quarry. Got played out a long time ago. During the War, the Army took it over for a staging center—trucks, jeeps, field pieces, half-tracks. I was the CO here. I used to be a traffic manager at the Baltimore and Ohio Railroad. The site is twenty-four acres. The rest of this building used to be a barracks. Back there"—he motioned toward the far end of the clearing—"is the rail line from Baltimore to the New York docks. You can't see it, but we have a siding back there in the trees. During the War, when the New York docks were overloaded, cargo was stored here until they could accept it.

"The Army gave up this place at the beginning of 1945 when it looked like the war in Europe was just about over. When I got discharged, I leased the site from the state, and now it's my store and warehouse. I sell building materials. I have forty thousand feet of warehouse space, and it's filled. You name it, I have it—every kind of stone, a dozen kinds of brick and block, lumber, hardware, steel cable, structural steel rebar, cement, electrical equipment, roofing, doors and windows. If you wanna build a house or a ten-story building, everything you need is right here. If I don't have what you want, I'll get it for you. I have catalogs for everything." With that, he waved us into the private office.

"Sit, fellas," he said, nodding to the two pull-up chairs at his desk. "There it is," he said, pointing to a nineteen-inch RCA television set with a pair of twenty-four-inch rabbit ear antennas, sitting on a row of two-drawer file cabinets.

Eddie turned on the set, and the screen filled with a fuzzy test pattern, hardly discernible behind the curtain of snow. Other channels were the same: faint images and undecipherable audio obscured by static and snow. Nothing you could hope to watch or understand.

"Whattaya think, fellas?" Spencer asked. "This set cost me four hundred and ninety dollars, and that's what I get. Nothing."

Eddie said he could help then explained, "The stations send out a shaped signal—not a circular one like you might think. The station draws the shape of the area they want to cover with the power they have. The transmission towers are arranged in that shape. Amplifiers, relays, and repeaters help send out the signal in that shape. The station wants to send the signal as far as it can to pick up cities and places with high population density. No sense wasting signal in remote areas, from their perspective. The signal must be very weak here, though it's strong in Atlantic City, only about forty miles away. Those rabbit ears aren't doing anything."

He showed Spencer the flat three-foot-long corrugated carton he brought with us, eighteen inches wide and four inches deep. "This is RCA's Hi-Lo Stacked Array Antenna, Model SK203. When I put the pieces together, it will look like an 'H.' Here's a picture of it on the carton. The sides will be four feet long. The cross piece is two feet. It comes with two one-foot vertical antennas. They stand up straight from the sides of the H. It's made of one-inch tubular steel with irridite zinc plating."

"Looks impressive," Spencer said, studying the picture. "You think it'll pull in a signal out here in the woods?"

"Up on the roof, it's going to pull in something. Maybe not great." Eddie paused then stood up and walked over to the window. "But that flagpole . . ." he mused. "Maybe." He turned back to the proprietor. "Dave, do you have a pair of binoculars? I'd like to take a good look at the top of your flagpole— that could be the ideal place for your antenna."

"Up there?" Spencer said. "That's crazy. Put it on the roof like we discussed."

"Dave, if I can get the antenna up there, you'll have ten times the reception you'll get from the roof," Eddie said. "Let me study the flagpole."

"Sounds nuts, but go ahead, have a look. I'll do better than binoculars. I have a telescope."

"The top is flat, which is good," Eddie said a few minutes later, looking through the telescope from a distance of some thirty yards. "But there's a ball on top—a ball on a ten-inch stem that's about an inch around. Looks like chrome-plated steel or maybe anodized aluminum. It will work, and a hacksaw will take it off.

"The pieces slip into these female flanges." He pointed to the parts of the antenna as he spoke. "The only piece I have to set into the pole is the anchor plate with the female receptacle standing up. Every stem part locks into place without any screws or metal straps. It's a really good piece of engineering. If I can't reach up there because I can't get up high enough to where I'll be able to drill into the top of the pole, I'll curve the anchor plate a little and set it into the side, close to the top. There's an elbow in the carton for that kind of installation. In that case, I won't need to cut off the ball and stem."

"Are you serious?" Spencer asked.

"I sure am," Eddie answered. "Dave, do you have any three-eighths-inch Romex cable?"

"Sure, we carry it. How much you need?"

"About a hundred and fifty feet."

"You really mean to put the thing up there, don't you?"

"Oh, yeah," Eddie answered. "I was gonna mount the antenna on your roof, but on that flagpole, if there's any signal at all, no matter how weak, this antenna will gather it in and send it down the Romex, into the building, and into your set. You'll pull in New York, Philadelphia, Baltimore...maybe even Washington."

"How're you gonna get it up there?" Spencer asked. "That pole is actually sixty-six feet. You'll need a motorized hoist and bucket, and I don't have one. You gotta rent them for a whole day, with an operator. That's about two hundred bucks, and it might take a few days to get one. What's this gonna cost me?"

"I don't need a hoist," Eddie said. "I'll go up the pole on the halyard."

"Come on, Eddie," I interjected. "You're not really goin' up that pole."

"Not to worry," he answered. "When I was on the *Wichita*, the skipper used to send me up the masts all the time, and they're a hundred and twenty feet above the waterline. Whenever our reception got bad or spotty, he used to send me up to check out all the antennas. This'll be easy. I won't have a pitching ship under me—or rolling. Rolling was the worst. And there's no wind today. Piece of cake."

"Eddie," I tried to reason with him, "that halyard ain't gonna hold you. What're you, about a hundred'n ninety pounds?"

"Jack," Eddie said, "you been taking that engineering course for a couple months. How much stress you think that halyard and pulley can take? Can you figure it?"

"I don't have a clue," I answered.

"Look at it like this," Eddie said. "That flag is about six feet by nine feet. How many pounds of pressure you think it puts on the halyard and the pulley in, say, a forty-mile wind?"

"I have no idea," I said.

"Me neither," Spencer added.

"Well," Eddie said, "I don't know for sure, but it's gotta be a helluva lot more than I weigh. Maybe four hundred pounds or more, don't you think?"

"Anyway," I said, "forget it. I'm not gonna carry you home in pieces. Evie will kill me. Let's put the damn thing on the roof."

"I agree," Spencer said. "Put it on the roof. I don't want you getting killed in my yard."

"Stop worrying," Eddie said. "This'll be neat. Nothin's gonna happen. You think I wanna get hurt? I know what I'm doin'." He turned to Spencer. "Can you spare a couple strong men to help me?" It was clear that Eddie meant to do it.

"Okay." Spencer shrugged. "I'll give you two big guys and the Romex. But wait a minute. How long will this take? And what's it gonna cost me?"

Eddie pursed his lips and held his chin between his thumb and forefinger. He thought for a half minute. "It'll take about two hours tops. You supply the Romex and two guys. I have everything else I need. I'll charge you a hundred and eighty-five, complete, antenna and installation."

"Okay." Spencer agreed. "I gotta see this."

"Okay," Eddie repeated. "Let's do it. First thing I gotta do is build a bosun's chair. I need two pieces of wood, eighteen inches long, two by twos. And some half-inch line."

He drilled holes in the wooden pieces and laced the half-inch rope into an eighteen-inch-wide seat. He tied a five-foot line to each of the four corners of the seat and joined them. Then he fashioned a back support to the seat by tying five horizontal lines to two of the five-foot vertical lines. Now he had a wooden seat with a rope back and the four lines tied together. When they were raised, they formed into a hollow pyramid shape.

He lowered the flag and fastened the top of the bosun's chair to the upper flag hook on the halyard. Next he drilled a one-inch hole at the base of the flagpole. "This is for the Romex," he explained. "The pole is hollow. It's made out of aluminum tubes, about seven of them. They're about twelve feet long. They're nested, making a real strong pole. I'll drop a light line down inside the pole. You'll fish it out and tie on the Romex. I'll pull the Romex up the inside of the pole and connect it to the antenna."

A half-dozen customers, attracted by our activity, gathered near the flagpole to watch us.

Eddie filled a canvas sack with tools: the electric drill with 150 feet of electric cord, stainless steel screws, pliers, screwdrivers, a rubber mallet, a hammer, a wire stripper, and a jar of exterior patching compound. He coiled an eighty-foot line and put it across his right shoulder and under his left arm like a bandolier. He climbed into the bosun's chair and tied himself to the rear vertical lines. "Don't wanna slip out," he explained.

He grabbed the down side of the halyard and hoisted himself a few feet. He looped a line around the pole loosely and tied it to his belt. "This is so I don't swing away from the pole," he explained. "All right, guys. Start lifting me. Only four feet at a time. Cleat the halyard every four feet. That way, if you let the halyard slip, the most I'll fall is four feet.

"When I get up there, I'll drop the line. You fellows tie on the canvas sack but leave the cord from the drill hang out and plug it in when I get it up there. When I'm ready for the antenna, I'll send down the line again for the antenna pieces. They're marked. Send up a piece at a time. I'll tell you which."

Spencer's two men and I put on cotton work gloves and did the hoisting. "Okay, heave," I called out. We hoisted four feet at a time, slowly, then cleated, then again at my command, *Heave*, and another four feet. Eddie helped by pulling on the downside of the halyard. He wrapped his legs around the pole as he went up and helped the lifting by sort of climbing the pole with his legs. It seemed to be going well, and safely. He was at the top in a few minutes. We made fast the halyard to the cleat.

He tied the half-inch line to the bosun's chair and dropped the line to us. We tied on the sack. He pulled it up. We drew the cord into the building and plugged it in to a receptacle. Eddie began to drill into the pole. I couldn't see exactly what he was doing, but he seemed satisfied that all was going well.

After a while, he sent down for an antenna piece. Then another. And another.

Suddenly I heard a creaking sound, and fear gripped me as I realized the cleat was starting to pull out from the pole.

"Grab the halyard," I shouted to the two helpers. "Dave, get over here. Grab hold. Pull. Hold him up there!"

The four of us strained to keep Eddie up there. Without him pulling himself up and wrapping his legs around the pole, he was now dead weight.

"You two," I ordered, nodding to the two biggest bystanders. "C'mon over here. Grab the halyard. We need more strength. Dave, get a car and bring it here. We'll use it as an anchor.

"Hold on with your legs," I hollered up to Eddie. "The cleat is coming loose. We'll bring you down."

"Don't bring me down," he called down to me. "I only need fifteen minutes. You guys can hold me up."

"Bullshit, Eddie," I hollered. "I'm bringing you down."

"No, you don't. I'm gonna finish." He never stopped working.

Spencer had already started running for his car. He drove it right up to the flagpole, the front bumper almost touching the pole. We tied on the halyard. You couldn't do that with one of today's cars. But in 1946, the front bumper was a separate component. It stood away from the front of the car about four or five inches, anchored onto the car by two steel extensions of the frame of the car's chassis. It was a safe arrangement. Eddie didn't even slow down to watch us.

More people gathered to see what was happening. The crowd grew to about fifteen people.

Eddie hollered down, "I'm ready for the Romex. I'm dropping the line inside the pole."

We fished out the line through the one-inch hole that Eddie had drilled open at the base of the pole and tied on the Romex. Eddie pulled up the Romex through the pole. In a few minutes, he connected the Romex to the antenna and sealed the hole with the exterior patching compound.

"Okay, guys," he hollered. "You can bring me down."

We lowered him to the cheers and applause of the onlookers. Everyone wanted to shake Eddie's hand or pound him on the back. "What a job!" "Great work!" "Never saw anything like it!" "You're really somethin'." *All right!*"

We dug the trench for the Romex from the base of the pole to the wall outside of Spencer's office then through the wall and to the TV set. The reception was good. Spencer was ecstatic.

"Eddie," he said, "you're some guy. Wait a minute while I get you a check. It's gonna be two fifty. One eighty five isn't enough for what you did. Hell, I'd a paid a hundred bucks just to watch you."

"No, thanks," Eddie said. "I'm a one-price shop. One eighty five it is."

"But I have a question for you, Dave," I said. "This is a big place. I see you have men and machines all over the place and inside the warehouse. How do you communicate with your people? Do you have an intercom system in the warehouse? How about when you want to talk to somebody all the way over there?" I pointed to the far end of the clearing where a man on a forklift was transferring pallets of cinder block from a stacked pile onto a customer's flatbed truck.

"If I need him, I send somebody to bring him into the warehouse. There's an extension phone in the middle of the warehouse, at the service desk."

"Maybe I can improve on that for you," I said. "Can I work up a proposal?"

"Sure thing. You guys are good. By the way, Jack, what did *you* do in the War?"

"I was in the Marines," I answered. "I was a captain. Infantry."

"It shows," Spencer said.

* * *

Back in Eddie's station wagon, we drove in silence out of the compound and back onto the highway. After a few minutes, Eddie asked what kind of proposal I had in mind for Spencer.

"I'm not sure," I said. "I have sort of an idea. Let me think about it." I had a sense of having witnessed something important, but it was elusive.

"It's the flagpole, isn't it?" Eddie asked. "I thought about it while I was up there. If I could send a signal from a walkie-talkie up to the top of the pole and then—"

"Hey, look," I interrupted, pointing ahead of us through the windshield. "Is that a scene from *Tom Sawyer* or what?"

29

Wilkens Lake

W E WERE OVERTAKING two boys in overalls, shirtless, walking along the road with fishing poles over their shoulders. They carried straw baskets. They weren't barefoot. Their feet were partially covered with the torn remnants of black Keds sneakers tied together with pieces of torn shoelaces. They wore battered, wide-brimmed straw hats. It was an image straight out of *Life on the Mississippi*. The poles were six-foot-long tree cuttings, knobby, and not exactly straight but reasonably so.

As Eddie pulled up alongside, I leaned out the window. "Hi, fellas," I called out. "Where you headed?"

They stopped. The taller of the two came closer to the station wagon. I pegged him as twelve or thirteen, at most. "Hello, mister," he said with a grin. "We goin' fishin'."

"Where's fishing around here?" I asked. There was nothing but forest on both sides of the road, and we hadn't seen a house, a sign, or any other evidence of habitation for miles, not since we left Spencer's.

The shorter boy came over. "We goin' to Wilkens Lake."

The taller one added, "It's up ahead another few miles."

"We didn't see a lake on the way here," I said. "Which side of the road is it on?"

"It ain't on the road," said the little one. "It's off in the woods. Good fishin' there."

"No kidding," I said. "I didn't know there was anything like that around here."

Eddie leaned toward them, "C'mon, fellas. Hop in. We'll drive you."

"Gee, thanks, mister." They climbed into the back seat, their poles set into the rear of the station wagon and resting on top of the seat.

"You'll have to direct me," Eddie said as he started up again. "I didn't see any roads leading off of this one on the way here."

"Sure, mister. It's up ahead on the right. I'll show you."

"What's your names, fellas? Where do you live?" I asked.

"I'm Jimmy," said the taller one, "and this here's my brother, Timmy. We live over in Irontown 'bout six, seven miles back that way."

"I don't know the town," I said. "How big is it? I mean, what's its population?"

"What's *population*?" Jimmy said.

"I mean, how many people live in your town?"

Jimmy asked Timmy, "How many folks you think, Timmy? My guess is about fifty."

Timmy nodded in agreement.

"And what kind of work do your folks do?" I asked.

"They's a cranberry bog. Mom and Dad work there. And we grow some corn and tomatoes. And we pick blueberries. We got a rooster and some hens and a cow."

"How about school? Do you fellas go to school?"

"Sure, but not in summer." He grinned at me and rolled his eyes as if to say, *Don't you know there's no school in summer?* "They's a schoolhouse in the next town; that's Brewster. That's only a couple miles away. Teacher comes on Monday, Wednesday, and Friday. But not in summer," he repeated. "They's no school in summer."

I looked in the straw baskets. There were scraps of towel, twine, knives, pieces of fried chicken, bottles of water, a box of bait. I studied the fishing poles. The fishing line was brown sisal twine, wrapped around and along the pole, tied through a hole that had been drilled near the end of the pole. The business end of the line was hand-tied to a homemade wooden float then, eighteen inches later, to a sinker, which was a metal washer. The hook was tied to the metal washer with a twelve-inch line. Not exactly state of the art.

"Do you catch anything with these poles?" I asked.

"Betcha, yes," Jimmy answered. "Slow down. We gonna turn off right around here."

There was a narrow opening to a dirt road in the otherwise solid line of forest. The road was only about ten feet wide; it turned to the right after only thirty feet, so that from the road we were on, it was hidden. The entry to the dirt road appeared to be only a small barren spot at the side of the road. The road had a set of wheel ruts dug into it. After driving slowly for about a half mile, Eddie asked, "How far do we go on this road?" He sounded a bit anxious, and I understood why. There was no possibility to turn around. The dirt road was closed in by solid forest on both sides; walls of pine and cedar rising above thick shrubbery.

It was a primeval forest, ripe with nature's splendor, untouched by humans. The sky was visible wherever the canopy of trees did not close fully. Birds soared above the trees, their cries breaking an otherwise silent world.

"How far?" Eddie asked again.

"Couple miles," said Jimmy.

"Is there a clearing up ahead?" I asked.

"Yeah," answered Jimmy. "They's a sandy beach up ahead at the lake."

We drove on, not much faster than we could have walked, the station wagon bumping and rolling from side to side. We finally reached the lake, pulling onto a thirty-foot-wide sand and gravel beach. The boys hopped out. I got out to take a closer look while Eddie backed up and turned and backed and turned again and again until he had the station wagon pointed back to where we came from.

"C'mon out, Eddie," I said. "Have a look at this place. It's a ghost town."

A narrow stream fed into the lake fifty yards off to our left. Where the stream entered the lake were the remnants of a small village: a cluster of a half dozen abandoned frame houses, their roofs gone or collapsed, front porches falling away. Off to the side was a long, low, partially collapsed building that must have been an industrial building or warehouse, and behind it was a massive wooden structure about forty feet long with a faded painted sign: "Furnace."

"What is this place?" I asked Jimmy.

He shrugged and said, "My dad said it used to be a place where they made iron. He didn't tell me a name."

"I heard about places like this," Eddie said. "We're in the Pine Barrens. These towns died out around the time of the Civil War. Some people still live here. They're called *Pineys,* like these boys. They're still living in the last century."

We had stepped back in history, on a clear sunny day. That had something to do with the beauty of the lake. The lake stretched off in the distance and disappeared around a bend. Thick pitch pine forest came down to the water's edge except in a few places, like where we were, where patches of sugar sand beach interrupted the solid line of forest. The water was clear but stained with a brown, almost reddish tinge. There was a good breeze, and the surface rippled and sparkled. The tiniest of waves, not even an inch high, lapped at the sandy beach.

"What do you catch here?" I asked.

"Some bass, but mostly pick'rel," Jimmy said, making a face. "They's boney." The two kicked off their sneaks, rolled up their overalls, and waded into the water.

"Betcha we take home eight, ten fish today. It'll be good eatin', spiten the bones."

The boys quickly unrolled the lines from their poles and baited their hooks with a couple of plump earthworms. They gathered up their floats, sinkers, and bait into bundles that they pitched out into the lake. Timmy made a good cast of about thirty feet, with Jimmy's bait hitting the water just a few feet further.

"Well, good fishing, fellas," I said as Eddie and I climbed into the station wagon.

The boys waved as we started up. "Thanks, misters. Thanks for the lift. Just follow the dirt road like we drove in and it'll take you back to the main road."

"Boy, this sure is desolate," Eddie said as we started off.

"It would be a rotten place to get stuck."

Worse than getting stuck was waiting for us.

* * *

The dirt road from the lake back to the main road was about three miles long. We'd bumped along about halfway when a man stepped out of the woods into the center of the dirt road and motioned for us to stop.

30

Confrontation

HE WAS WEARING SOILED Army fatigues and dirty boots. I guessed him to be about thirty, but a scruffy beard and long hair that hung down below a wrinkled Army fatigue cap made it hard to tell. A canvas bag hung from a strap across his chest. What made him dangerous-looking was the rifle in the crook of his left elbow. If Eddie could have driven by him, I suppose he would have, but there was no way to drive out of the ruts, and even so, we were completely hemmed in by forest on both sides. So we stopped, and the man approached.

His rifle was an Army Garand. The semiautomatic MI infantryman's rifle. I'd seen plenty of them. It was a heavy piece, not what you'd want as a hunting rifle. It hung from his left elbow, half pointed at the ground.

Eddie leaned out the window. "How 'bout moving aside so we can pass?" he said.

"Get out of the car," was the reply. The man's face twitched nervously.

"Whattaya think, Eddie?" I said quietly. "Keep moving; he'll get outta the way."

Eddie inched the wagon forward.

The man didn't move. "Get out of the car," he repeated, beginning to raise the rifle.

"I don't want to run him down," Eddie said to me, stopping the wagon. He shifted into neutral and let the car idle as he opened his door and stepped out. So did I.

"What's the problem?" I asked.

"Come 'round front," he said, "and keep your hands where I can see 'em." He wet his lips. He transferred the rifle to an *at ready* position: right hand on the stock, over the trigger; left hand under the barrel end of the stock. This was getting serious.

I repeated, "What's the trouble, fella?"

"Get away from the car," he answered.

"Go to the left," I said to Eddie as I moved to the right. Better we shouldn't be close to each other. Better he would have to swing the rifle to take a shot.

He took a step toward us. "I want your money," he said hoarsely. His eyes shifted back and forth from Eddie to me. "Quick. Let's have it."

"Is that all?" I said. I watched his eyes following my right hand as I reached into my rear pockets where I had my money folded in half. "Here," I said, handing it forward. Then I barked out the command *Ten-hut, soldier!* and tossed the bills to him.

A moment of confusion—the combination of my command, the Army version of *Atten-shun*, plus the money fluttering to the ground. He glanced down at the falling bills. In that instant, I dove at him. I caught the rifle barrel in my left hand and pushed it aside as I crashed my right shoulder into his chest. He went down, me on top of him. I wrenched the rifle out of his grasp and jumped to my feet.

"Get up, soldier," I commanded.

He climbed to his feet awkwardly, rubbing his chest where my shoulder hit him. He raised his arms.

"I didn't mean no harm," he said, his eyes focused on the ground. "Just need a few bucks."

"Get movin'," I said, pointing the rifle at him.

He turned and started away along the road.

"No, not that way," I said. "Into the trees. Get goin' until I can't see you."

"How 'bout my rifle?" he said.

"Get goin'," I answered.

"Didn't mean no harm," he mumbled as he pushed into the woods, brushing aside branches and shrubs. He turned around once to look back at me, saw me with the rifle still pointed at him. He turned and continued into the depths of the forest.

When he was out of sight, I turned to Eddie. "C'mon, let's get movin'," I said, gathering up my money. "This rifle is coming with us."

We climbed into the station wagon.

"Chrissake, Jack," Eddie said as he slipped into gear. "You're really somethin'. I didn't know what to do. How did you figure it out? He might've killed you."

"I learned a lesson from you, Eddie, six years ago. Act. Don't talk a lot. Act . . . *hit!* Do what you have to and do it quick. You taught me that. Do you remember? It was my mantra in the War. Act! Shoot! Run! Don't spend a lot of time thinking about it. I guessed the guy had been a soldier—the fatigues, boots, cap, and the Garand. My command stopped him for a second. That and the money in the air. I figured he wouldn't react fast enough to get off a shot. It's hard to shoot an M1 from the hip. You gotta get it into your right shoulder to get off a good shot. Besides, I think he aimed to take our money and the car. And maybe work himself up to shoot us as well. If he dragged us off the road, nobody would find us in these woods. We'd just go missing. So the way I figured, I didn't have much to lose. The real danger would've been to obey him, one piece at a time, while he worked up the courage to shoot us.

"Let's not tell the girls about this. No sense upsetting them. I'm gonna keep the rifle. This Garand is a great weapon—the Army's best piece of equipment, according to Patton."

31

Pine Barrens

AT BREAKFAST THE following morning, I was absorbed in a newspaper article about the Marshall Plan, Secretary of State George Marshall's plan for economic aid to rebuild Europe. There was also editorial comment about the Truman Doctrine, announced two months earlier: $400 million of military and economic aid to Greece and Turkey. A staggering sum at the time.

The remnants of the wartime alliance with the Soviet Union were fast dissolving. The Berlin blockade was only a year in the future. The US was strengthening Western Europe to confront the Soviets and stop their expansion into the Eastern Mediterranean. I wondered whether the news was significant to me.

Next, I turned to a story about how Jackie Robinson was doing with the Brooklyn Dodgers and his stoicism in the face of racial insults.

I set the paper aside and asked Alice about the Pine Barrens. She was standing at the stove, cleaning up. "Alice," I asked, "where do you go to catalog your plants? Are you in the Pine Barrens?"

She turned to face me. "I go to various sites, Jack, in and out of the Pine Barrens, but mostly in. Some are just a few miles from here, like the Absecon wetlands near Brigantine, or I'll drive over to Wharton State Forest, about twenty miles. And there are places without a name right along the White Horse Pike, and others along the Black Horse.

"The Pine Barrens are a mysterious place, Jack, covering more than a million acres. Almost a quarter of New Jersey is Pine Barrens. You only need to go a few miles outside of Camden or Trenton or Princeton or Vineland to find them.

"Throughout the southern part of the state, especially, when you're on a road with forest alongside, you're probably in the Pine Barrens. Stop your car and walk in a few hundred yards without a compass, and it's easy to become disoriented. You may not find your way back to the road."

"I've heard the Pine Barrens mentioned over the years," I said, "but never paid much attention. I thought it was one particular place, a big marshy wilderness that never got developed because it was too wet and densely wooded."

"Not at all," she said. "The Barrens are widespread, and every year more of the forest is cleared and developed for farming, business, and new homes. But it's a diverse environment—not just woods but lakes, streams, marshes, and rivers. The densest woods are in South Jersey."

"I hear there are villages down there," I said. "The people are called 'Pineys' and they live without electricity or running water, cut off from the civilized world."

"I'll tell you about the Pine Barrens, Jack," she said with attitude, hands on hips, "but eat your eggs before they get cold." I bit in, and she pulled up a chair next to me.

"The Pine Barrens have a unique soil. It's mostly sand, which limits the types of trees and vegetation that grow there. There are beautiful lakes and rivers in these forests. I'm not sure that every part of the woods have been explored. For the most part, it's a pine and cedar wilderness, full of deer, wild turkey, small mammals, birds, turtles, and snakes. The timber rattlesnake is the only poisonous native snake, but it's pretty rare.

"The forests are prone to fire; every ten or fifteen years, a big fire burns up hundreds or even thousands of acres. The fire clears the ground vegetation and burns the pine trees, which helps to release seeds from the pinecones. The burnt stuff falls and covers the ground. The pines and shrubs reestablish and come back quickly.

"And yes, there are people living in the Pine Barrens. There have been since early colonial times. In fact, it was once a prosperous region because of the combination of bog ore that can be made into iron and a plentiful supply of wood for charcoal."

"What's with the iron?" I asked.

"I believe there's only one other place in the world that produces bog iron," she said. "Somewhere in Eastern Europe, I think. It happens like this: the soil is rich in iron, and certain minerals in the groundwater in the bogs and swamps act on the iron particles to form lumps of ore. Early settlers realized you could put the stuff in a furnace and refine it into useful iron. There's plenty of wood that can be burnt into charcoal to fuel a furnace, so villages developed in places where the bog ore was. It's a renewable resource that's easily dredged from along the banks of the bogs, rivers, and streams where it forms.

"So people built big brick furnaces to . . ." She looked down at her hands. "I guess you'd call it *smelt* the ore into iron, and they cast the iron into all kinds of things—pots and pans, horseshoes, lampposts, axles, gun barrels, cannons, and cannonballs."

She looked up to be sure I was listening then continued. "During prerevolutionary times, the English forbade the colonies to make iron. Without iron, the colonists couldn't make cannons or cannonballs or temper iron into steel for swords and bayonets. It was a way to protect the English iron industry and keep the colonies from becoming heavily armed. Whatever iron or steel the colonists needed was supposed to be bought and shipped from English iron and steel mills, but they made iron in the Pine Barrens anyway. It was an underground industry—like the hidden-away whiskey stills during Prohibition.

"During the Revolution, all the iron products needed for war were produced in about twenty different towns in the Pine Barrens. They were prosperous towns in their day. For some time after the war, they continued to make most of the iron in the United States, and they manufactured glass—lots of glass, and paper too. Sand, or silica, went into the glass, and there was no shortage of fine 'sugar sand' there for the taking. The main ingredient in the paper was marsh grass, also in almost endless supply in the region.

"Initially, there wasn't a huge farming industry there because of the sandy soil, but with fertilizers, certain crops like corn, tomatoes, and soybeans did fine. Later on, the locals developed cranberry bogs and cultivated blueberries. Wild blackberries are everywhere in the Pine Barrens. Some years the fruit is so plentiful, you can just rake it off the ground into bushel baskets."

"What happened to the iron industry?" I asked.

"In the 1850s, a better grade of ore was discovered in Pennsylvania, and they figured out how to make the iron using a blast furnace. It was a more efficient method and produced superior iron. By the time the Civil War began, commercial iron production had ended in the Pine Barrens, and the paper industry died off not long after. They couldn't compete with the way paper is made in the big paper mills, mainly from hardwood pulp.

"Glassmaking also had a lot of competition, and eventually people began leaving for better opportunities. The company towns died out, and the families that remained had to live off the land. Progress passed them by— in some areas, it's like living in the mid-nineteenth century. No electricity, no municipal water or gas or sewage systems. They're like the Okies, in some cases maybe even more primitive. Pineys slaughter a few hogs each year for their own consumption and sell a little to meat lockers. I see them sometimes in old trucks when they come to the farmer's markets to sell blueberries, corn, and various handcrafts, like baskets. Most of the women and kids are barefoot. The few dollars they earn from what they sell lets them buy things they can't make on their own—cotton dresses, coats, overalls, shoes. I understand there are a handful of small schoolhouses where teachers come a few times a month, but there's a lot of illiteracy."

She paused, fixing me with an intense gaze. "And then there's the legend of the Jersey Devil."

"A myth," I said. "Like Bigfoot. An old wives' tale."

"People swear they've seen it," she said, "carrying off sheep, even children. I suppose it's just fanciful imaginings." She gave me a curious look. "Why the sudden interest in the Pine Barrens, Jack?"

"Me and Eddie were in the woods yesterday." I told her about Eddie installing the antenna and our visit to Wilkens Lake. I didn't mention our encounter on the way back from the lake.

"Alice," I said. "I don't want you going into the Pine Barrens alone. It's too wild, and I don't think the Pineys are noble savages. I got a feeling it's a dangerous place, especially for an unescorted woman."

"Don't worry about me," she answered. "I know where it's safe and where not to go. I only go into places that are closed off and have security stations. And I always have Max with me. He's a pretty good bodyguard, don't you think? Plus, I have one of Eddie's walkie-talkies."

"A walkie-talkie won't do you any good if there isn't somebody nearby with another set, and its range is going to be very limited out there."

"Please don't worry, Jack. I'm not brave. I don't go anywhere where I could run into trouble. Now, finish your breakfast."

"Okay," I said, "but tell you what. Next Sunday, if the weather's good, take me to all of the places you go to. I want to see them. And we'll visit a village. I want to see for myself."

"Sure, Jack," she grinned. "but not too early. I have important plans for Sunday morning."

32

An Hour with Blinky

August 8, 1947

IT WAS FIVE FORTY-FIVE on a Wednesday afternoon, and I was headed home after a day of appointments in the Camden area. I stopped at Gene's Diner, twenty miles before Atlantic City.

It had been a good day. I closed a $2,000 deal for phones for a new lab and model shop for RCA and was invited to submit proposals for a metal stamping shop in Cinnaminson and a new Pontiac dealer on the Black Horse Pike. I wanted to use the men's room and then relax with a cup of coffee at Gene's while I wrote some notes for the proposals. I took a window booth.

I saw him pull off the road onto the gravel parking lot. I was headed east, toward home. He was headed west. It was Blinky, stepping out of a new forest green Buick Roadmaster, the General Motors model that proclaimed its owner could afford a Cadillac but was restrained by modesty. I hadn't seen him in months. He spotted me through the diner window, waved, and gave a broad smile. I stood as he approached my booth. We embraced.

"Blinky! I mean, Howard. Where you headed?" I asked.

He slid into the booth. "I have an appointment in Camden, a prospect for a policy. My best appointments are in the evening. I like to meet the prospect with his wife, after dinner. I'll have dinner here and get there at seven thirty."

I studied him. He was a work of art. He glowed, a smooth tan. Faint squint lines along his eyes added a touch of rugged outdoors. His hair had a soft sheen, pencil mustache, a flash of perfect teeth when he smiled, a Douglas Fairbanks Jr. smile—devilish yet warm, friendly, trustworthy. His clothes were perfect, a white dress shirt with a subtle herringbone pattern, a gold and red repp tie tied in a perfect Windsor knot, and a matching silk handkerchief in the breast pocket. The suit, in double-breasted navy blue with faint, almost invisible maroon squares, was perfectly pressed. He took off the jacket and hung it up. He hiked up his trousers before he sat down, a middle-class habit that parents taught their young sons in order to maintain a fresh crease. I'm told men from a more affluent background don't do it, I suppose because their trousers were regularly cleaned and pressed; I haven't really studied the matter.

I was glad to see Blinky. The image in my mind of him and Bernie backing off on an April day in 1939 while the Mackey brothers gave Eddie and me a beating had begun to fade. That was a long time ago, and he was a different man now from the timid fifteen-year-old Blinky, the appeaser who urged me to humble myself to a bully rather than confront him.

"Jack," he said abruptly, squinting at me as if looking into the sun. "Do you think about the War?"

"Yeah, sure I do," I answered, "but I try not to. How about you?"

"You know what I think about? What it felt like up there, in the sky, in the clouds, alone in the world, the drone of the engines, my feelings for the crew. The fear on the way to the mission. The magic of it on the return. It was a kind of love to be up there. I flew twenty-five missions. Then I volunteered for five more—thirty missions without a scratch. I'm blessed, like you. We have to live up to the gift we got."

"You're right, Blink . . . Howard. Every day is a gift. I never forget that."

"Jack," he said. "I'll tell you how I improved my chances up there."

"Improved your chances?" I asked. "With prayers? A lucky shirt? A Saint Christopher medal?"

"No," he said. A serious, faraway look took hold of his eyes, and his lips curled into a grim half-smile. "After the first raid, I figured it out. The safest plane is the lead bomber. The German antiaircraft guns start calculating the range and altitude as soon as they see the formation coming. By the time they have it all figured out, the formation is on top of them, so they are shooting into the heart of the formation. The guys in the middle got plastered. The guys in the rear got it the worst. Same thing goes for the German fighter planes. By the time they reach the formation, the lead planes are over or past the targets. The fighters go after the middle planes and the ones at the back—the planes that didn't drop their loads yet.

"So I figured it out my best chance was to be the lead navigator, the best navigator. That's who's in the lead plane. I studied all the time, all those altitude calculations and the celestial stuff and the charts. By my fourth raid, they had me in the lead plane. And they made me a major. I was the best. Out in front. A hundred planes following me, sometimes five hundred—a few times, a thousand. That's how I improved my chances. What about you?"

"I didn't do anything smart like you did," I said. "I don't know how I made it through. Just lucky, I guess."

"I salute luck," he said, saluting the air. "Luck beats smart any day."

He lit a cigarette and waved out the match. "How's your work, Jack? How's Alice? Tell me."

I brought him up to date. Then I asked him the same. His answer surprised me.

33

The Insurance Game

BLINKY SAID THE image had never left him: him and Bernie standing back that day in April, all those years ago, while me and Eddie were being beat up by the Mackeys. He said the two of them used to talk ashamedly about their cowardice that day and that he'd dedicated his life to atonement. He said the extra five missions over Germany seemed to bring catharsis.

Sad about Bernie. Eddie and Blinky and I survived the War, but in early December 1944, Bernie was one of the thousands of hastily trained draftees shipped over to fill in the spaces in Omar Bradley's First Army. He arrived just in time for the Battle of the Bulge and was killed in St. Vick, Belgium, on December 19, 1944.

Now here was Blinky, no more the awkward little boy whose friendship with me and Eddie was all but crushed in one fateful moment but a war hero with a flashing smile and the voice and stature of a paladin. I told him to stop apologizing. The incident was behind us, he'd more than atoned, and I would always count him as a friend.

"Jack," Blinky said. "Let me tell you about the life insurance game. It's a pushover for guys like me and you. All these ex-servicemen are getting married. They're gonna start making babies. They need life insurance. It's an easy sell, not even a sell—all you gotta do is feed 'em the pitch. I get my leads from the American Legion posts and the Veterans of Foreign Wars, the VFW. I give the post commanders a few bucks and I get every post member's name, address, marital status, number of dependents, war record, and discharge rank. And you know what? It's for real. It's not a scam. These guys *should* have it. Here, listen—here's the pitch:

Now, look here, Sarge, you're a married man. You have a family, or if you're not a father yet, you will be soon. You've got responsibilities. You're just starting out. God forbid if something happens to you and you never had enough time to build up a nest egg. What will happen to your family? You gotta protect them. At least for the next ten years or so until you can accumulate enough savings. How much will they need? A year's income? Maybe two, or three, or maybe five? It's a question you have to ask yourself and factor in how much you can afford in premiums. You can't take the chance of leaving them broke. The first job of a man is to protect his family. Did you buy the VA insurance? If you did, that's great. And it's cheap. But it's only ten thousand dollars. That ain't enough. And my product is from Metropolitan Life Insurance Company, the biggest, strongest insurer in the world.

"The average guy I'll be selling is twenty-five to thirty. A basic, no frills, five-thousand-dollar, ten-year term policy costs about sixty to eighty dollars a year. I try to pitch a renewable term policy, or a whole life policy."

Here you go, soldier, the Cadillac of policies: whole life. It builds cash value. In ten years, the cash value is as much as all the premiums you paid. It's only a few bucks a year more than the basic ten-year term, but it's permanent. You'll keep it all your life, and someday, when you're well-fixed financially, you can cash it in and get back every cent you invested in it.

"How's that, Jack? It's a cinch. And me a major. Major Howard Gordon, Eighth Air Force. I score about seven out of every ten leads. I like to see them at home, in the evening, at the kitchen table, with the wife. How can they resist?" He flashed the Douglas Fairbanks Jr. smile.

I had to admit it. He was good. "How much do you make at this, Blink… I mean, Howard?" I asked.

"It's great, Jack," he answered with enthusiasm. "I get anywhere from sixty-five to ninety percent of the first-year premium. Depends on whether the policy is a stripped-down basic term policy or one of the better ones. Say it's a ten-thousand-dollar whole life policy with an annual premium of two hundred dollars. I'll get ninety percent of the first-year premium on that one. Even if the premium is paid on a quarterly mode, fifty dollars every three months. I get one hundred eighty dollars up front. I give the post commander five dollars for each lead and five dollars more for every one I close. But that's just between you and me, Jack. I could get fired for that. I don't give it to him exactly. I make a monthly contribution to the post. What he does with it is his business.

"And I get an ongoing commission, two percent every year thereafter; they're called *trails*. In time, the trails will amount to a lot of money every year. I figure in ten years, I'll have fifteen thousand dollars a year coming just in trails, and that will increase about fifteen hundred dollars every year that I keep selling. Right now, I'm good for about twelve hundred dollars a month in commissions. And every once in a while, I get a lead out at the country club. Those guys are usually businessmen or guys with some sophistication about money. They're a harder sell. And the pitch has to be slow and subtle, and in installments. I can't come at 'em all at once. But they're bigger policies when I close 'em. I closed a thirty-thousand-dollar whole life about a month ago. The guy was forty-one years old. The premium was one thousand twenty dollars. My commission was nine hundred eighteen dollars!"

"Howard," I said, "I gotta say I'm impressed. I didn't think selling insurance was such a moneymaker. But I'm sticking with APC. I'm not even making half of what you're making, but my commissions are getting bigger and it's a growing company, lots of opportunities. I won't be a salesman for long. I expect to work myself up the ladder. My district manager is up in years—he's past sixty. I aim to have his job in a few years. I hope in time I'll be doing as good as you are."

"Sure, Jack," he answered, "but when you get to where I am now, I'll be up to twenty-five hundred dollars a month."

I thought he was probably right. But what he was doing didn't appeal to me. Telecommunications was exciting, with new developments happening all the time.

"Something else, Jack," he said. "What I do is not a job. I'm my own man. Those policies I sell—they're mine. If I leave Metropolitan, I still get the trails. They're mine for as long as the policy is in force. And as for new business, I can sell Prudential or New York Life just as easy. Metropolitan will never fire me. I might fire them. I could probably get a signing bonus to sign on with another company. I'm a big producer, and I'll keep getting better. I don't consider myself an employee. I learned a lesson from watching my old man work like a horse on that *debit*. He was lucky to pull in sixty dollars a week, and if he got canned, he was just plain out of a job. He couldn't take the *debit* with him.

"About you, Jack, ask yourself, what is your job security? You could be canned any time, and you take away nothing."

I didn't respond. I knew he was right that I had no job protection. I thought about that sometimes, but I had a vague idea I'd be moving on one day to a business of my own; probably Eddie and I would join up to do something together, something big and exciting.

"For now, I don't see APC letting me go," I said. "I'm a solid producer with a sponsor at the regional level."

Even as I said it, I knew I was vulnerable. I remembered how quick they canned the guy I replaced when he lost his protection. But I wouldn't dwell on it.

34

Good Advice

Blinky CONTINUED. "There's this guy in the office. He wasn't in the service. He's thirty-five. He did back-office work in a small over-the-counter shop for a few years before he started selling life insurance. He's not a great salesman. He doesn't make what I do, but he knows the brokerage business inside and out. His name is Mike Randolph. He wants to start a brokerage company with me. We'll be Randolph and Gordon Securities, or Gordon and Randolph. We'll toss a coin. Meanwhile, Mike's taught me a lot. He has me in the market, and I'm doin' real good. Do you own any stocks, Jack?"

"I'm not in the market at all these days."

"Well, Jack, old friend, we'll have to get you investing some of your money. You know we're at the beginning of the biggest economic boom that any country ever had in all of history. The stock market will follow suit. The Dow-Jones is at one eighty-five, and the New York Stock Exchange trades three hundred thousand shares a day. Mike says the day will come when the Dow-Jones hits one thousand and there will be a million shares trading a day. *A million shares a day.* You gotta get in it!"

"Are you kidding?" I said, raising my eyebrows almost derisively. "Why not a two-thousand-dollar Dow? Why not *two million* shares a day?"

He was right, of course. Imagine: a thousand-dollar Dow and a million shares traded a day. But as right as he was, he never guessed that the Dow would stand at 1,003 on November 15, 1972, that million-share days would begin in 1953, and that by 2017, we'd see the Dow at 20,000. And not one or even two million shares trading a day, but *two billion or more* traded daily since the beginning of 2001.

35

The Crank Note

IN 1947, FEW people locked the doors to their houses and hardly anyone ever locked car doors, especially in a solid, respectable middle-class neighborhood like Marven Gardens, New Jersey.

When I left home for work that morning and climbed into my car, I found a plain white envelope on the passenger seat. It was not addressed. It had no return address. It was not sealed. Before I opened it, I turned it over and again, looking for a clue to its origin. There was none. There was a crude note inside fashioned by pasting letters from a newspaper or a magazine, like the ransom notes you see in the movies:

YUR

NO

HERO

TO ME

WACH

OUT

I got out of the car and looked up and down the street and the sidewalks and the houses, looking for someone who didn't belong. It was early, not yet seven o'clock. The street and sidewalks were empty.

I studied the note front and back. There was nothing but the pasted letters. I held it up to the light, not knowing what I was looking for. The paper was a ruled sheet from a tablet or a notepad. There was nothing to betray its origin. I got back into the car and drove to the Margate Police Station.

* * *

The desk sergeant told me to lay the note on the desk. He put on gloves before lifting it to study it front and back. "I guess it's got your prints all over it," he said.

"Yes," I said, "I didn't think of that at first. When I did, I'd already handled it."

"We might still find the guy's prints, but there's no detectives here right now. Leave it with me. Somebody will call you."

"I don't want my wife or anyone else to know about this. Don't call me at home or at my office number. I'll call you."

It was three days before I reached the detective who had the case. He asked me to come in early the next day.

***

"I'm Detective Al Burns," he said, offering me his handshake. "I'll tell you what we know and what we don't know. These letters, here, here, here"—he pointed to them—"came from a newspaper. These letters, here, here," he pointed to the colored ones, "come from an advertising supplement. The paste is an ordinary school paste. The paper is from a pack of ruled paper that you can buy in any five-and-dime store. We couldn't find any prints except yours. The guy must've worn real thin gloves. He couldn't handle these little letters with regular gloves. The newspaper could be any one in thousands—most likely it's from Atlantic City or nearby, but it could come from anywhere. It would take thousands of hours to pin down the exact paper and the exact date. And what would that tell us? Nothing.

"You got an enemy out there, Jack. You think who it could be. We'll interview whoever you think."

"I can only think of the Mackey brothers. I had trouble with the two of them back in 1939. They molested my sister, Evie. She was only thirteen. I beat them with an iron pipe and got arrested."

The detective stroked his chin, thoughtfully. "Ya know, I remember that," he said. "It was an Atlantic City case. I was rootin' for you. I was glad you got off. They deserved what you gave 'em."

He took down the names of the Mackeys and their addresses and said he would visit them.

"Anybody else, Jack?" he asked. "Maybe somebody from your old Marine outfit?"

"I can't think of anybody from my old company. If there was somebody with a hard-on for me, I would have known it. The only person I can think of besides the Mackeys is a guy whose job I got a couple of weeks after he was fired. But I had nothing to do with that. I never met him and I don't think he even knows my name."

Detective Burns took down his name. "We'll talk to him," he said.

"So what can I do?" I asked. "What should I do?"

"Just be careful, Jack. It could be anybody. But I don't think you're in danger. If this guy wanted to hurt you, he could have done that. Why send a note?"

"I'm not worried about me," I said. "I'm worried about my wife."

"Try to live your life. I agree you shouldn't tell your wife. There's nothing you can do. If there's a crazy guy after you, nothing can protect you. If you and the missus had twenty-four-hour bodyguards, they couldn't protect you unless you want to live your life locked up in your house. And even then . . ."

We arranged that when he called me, he would be Al Green from the Atlantic City Bell Telephone office. I didn't want Alice or anyone at work to wonder why a detective was calling.

Ten days later, he reported he'd met with the Mackeys. "They seemed to fear you," he said. "They acted like it would be stupid to hurt you in any way because of retaliation—maybe not from you but from somebody they wouldn't want to mess with. I don't suspect them.

"The guy who lost his job didn't even know your name—or at least, that's what he said. He's working for a lawyer in Toms River. Says it's a better job than what he had at APC—no travel. So we're at a dead end. If I hear anything, I'll let you know."

I felt that cloud over me all the time, for days, for weeks. I studied every man I saw. I told Alice to be careful all the time. "There's crazies out there." I didn't drum in the message. She would have suspected something.

Gradually, the concern faded—never completely, but I had to dismiss it or else I couldn't function.

36

Vision of a Wireless Future

Sunday, September 7, 1947

EDDIE WANTED TO meet Sunday morning. He had something to show me. We met on the pavilion near Albany Avenue. It was a perfect day. The air was crisp and clear under a cloudless sky. An easterly breeze carried the ocean's salty tang ashore. We sat on a bench at the end of the pavilion, facing out to a silver sea, squinting in the sharp sunlight reflected from the water.

Eddie spoke. "Y'know, Jack, sometimes I miss the Navy. Do you know what it's like out there on a day like today when the ship is cruising to somewhere, or on a patrol with no combat mission? Like being on an ocean cruise, slipping through the water, cutting through a swell. I sure don't miss the War, but I miss that."

"I don't miss one day of it," I said, "except the day on Okinawa when it was over. So, Eddie, whattaya have to show me?"

"First, let me tell you I been thinking about our walkie-talkies," he said, "ever since you bought them. They represent the future. Know why? Because they're wireless. Like radio is wireless. Like shortwave is wireless. Like TV is wireless. Telephone is today's state of the art, just like telegraph was state of the art for sixty years. But telegraph will be a relic in a few more years, and one day, wired telephones will be too."

I nodded as he continued.

"At one time, the steam engine was the new big thing, then it was electricity coming into our homes—refrigerators, light bulbs, radios. Now, it's like these things have always been with us and we're in the early days of the next big thing in communications. That will be the wireless telephone. The big breakthrough will come when we can get enough range."

He looked out at the horizon, squinting in the sunlight for a moment before turning back to me. "The line of sight for a walkie-talkie is only about three miles when it's held by a guy five-foot-nine, a little more if the guy is six-two. Or more if the guy is standing on a platform two feet high. Every foot higher extends the line of sight to the horizon by about a quarter mile. So, if the walkie-talkie is ten feet high, its range is almost five miles. There's a formula for it, but I don't remember it. That's because the earth is round and that's the distance to the horizon. So the walkie-talkies don't have the range to be practical.

"Besides that, here's what's wrong with them. One, they're too big and too heavy. When you were in the service, somebody carried it for you. Two, they broadcast like a radio.

"I sold five of our walkie-talkies last week to the Absecon Country Club. That's the right kind of user—a golf course, not too big, because remember the range is only about three miles. The groundskeepers carry them in their carts, along with their tools. If they had to carry them all day, or even with a shoulder strap, they wouldn't use them. Did I tell you about that sale? I got ten dollars apiece. Our profit is seven eighty-five each. You have thirty dollars and thirty-seven cents coming. Six dollars and seven cents apiece— your cost plus half the profit."

"Well, Eddie," I said, "together with the four I sold a month ago, that makes nine we've sold. At that rate, we'll be all out of them in about fifty years. It wasn't a great investment."

"That's not the point, Jack. They turned me on to something. Something big for you and me." He stood up from the bench and leaned against the railing. "I want to make them work one-on-one like a telephone. Not so easy, but I have an idea about that."

"How come radio and TV have such range?" I asked, "And shortwave? How come we can get radio from thousands of miles away?"

Eddie explained, "Regular radio is transmitted from transmission towers that are at least a couple hundred feet high. They're still line of sight, but where our walkie-talkies' line of sight is only three miles or so to the horizon, the line of sight from a two-hundred-foot tower is about twenty miles, with the signal transmitted to another tower that's maybe only fifteen miles away.

That tower has a repeater that picks up the signal and reflects it, and the next tower picks it up and reflects it, and so on. It was the Spencer antenna job up on that flagpole that got me thinking about how we can increase the range of our walkie-talkies."

He continued, "Shortwave radio travels so far because it bounces off the ionosphere. With good atmospheric conditions, a shortwave radio can reach a few thousand miles, and in time, as the senders are improved, I'll bet that shortwave can reach anywhere in the world."

"Well, Eddie," I said, "if communications is the next big thing, let's you and me do it and get in early. Let's think it through and make a plan."

"I'm already on it," he said.

37

The Printed Circuit

EDDIE BECAME ANIMATED. He paced. His words tumbled out, tripping over each other.

"You know the wrist radio that Dick Tracy wears, Jack? Someday, it will happen, but not like the comic stuff. There will be a handheld radio. It will send a signal to one particular radio. It will be just like a telephone. You'll punch in a number and connect to another telephone. Except it'll be wireless. It's gonna happen. Our walkie-talkies are the first generation."

"Why isn't it happening now?" I asked.

He sat. His words slowed and became measured.

"A bunch of problems to be solved," he said. "The main one is miniaturization. To get the kind of power you need, you'd have an instrument as big as a refrigerator, with a hundred vacuum tubes and miles of wiring and a battery as big as a breadbox."

"What's gonna change that?" I asked.

"Things will be invented that don't exist today. One by one, they'll come into use. Things that are small but more powerful than the big things they'll replace. There's stuff being developed right now—like the transistor I told you about, to take the place of a vacuum tube. It's made out of gold, plated onto something called germanium. It has three leads coming out of it to connect to wiring, the way a vacuum tube plugs into a socket. It isn't fragile like a vacuum tube. It's unbreakable—*solid-state*. Imagine, getting rid of the vacuum tube! There's six of them in every one of our walkie-talkies. Replace them with these little transistors, and that alone reduces the size of the walkie-talkie by three-quarters. I could make our walkie-talkies act like phones instead of radios if I had the transistors, but there's no chance of that. It takes a big corporation like Bell Labs or General Electric or RCA to manufacture transistors.

"However . . ." He stood up again, suddenly more animated. "There's another option: a circuit board that's small and solid-state to take the place of all the wiring and replace the steel chassis. The Army developed the technology during the War, and they've made it available to anybody who wants to use it—for *free*. They call it a printed circuit and, Jack, I've made one!

"Instead of wires from socket to socket in a steel frame chassis, the circuit board has copper lines etched onto the board that take the place of wires. The board uses less space than a steel chassis, and it is solid-state, nothing to come apart or break, so it's more reliable. No more wires corroding and coming loose.

"There's three ways to make them. I made my prototype the cheapest way, without expensive equipment. The beauty of it is, it's made-to-order for an assembly line. We can mass-produce with very little extra investment in equipment." He reached into a paper bag he'd been carrying. "Here's the prototype, Jack."

The board was a finished piece of work, smooth and polished. The copper lines etched onto the board were perfectly uniform. I counted sixteen lines connecting the holes for the tubes. The copper shone in the bright sunlight.

"Eddie," I said, "this looks like it came off an assembly line. How did you do it?"

"Like I said, Jack, the Army developed three ways to make the printed circuit, two of which require serious machinery. The method I used needs only a punch press and a die designed to stamp out channels for the copper."

He continued. "I don't have a punch press or a thousand bucks lying around to have a tool and die maker build a die for me. I made mine out of a five-by-ten-foot sheet of cardboard that I coated with liquid wax to make it an insulator. Then I made a cardboard mask. I punched out the receptacle holes for up to twenty-eight vacuum tubes. I drew the channels on the mask. Then I cut out the channels with a box cutter. It took a long time—I had to be real careful so the copper lines would be uniform and perfect.

"There's a guy with an induction furnace over in Pleasantville. I melted the copper there and quick-brushed it over the mask. When I took away the mask, I had a printed circuit board. I won't need these socket holes where the vacuum tubes go. The next generation boards won't have vacuum tubes. Instead, there will be small transistors, as soon as I figure out how to get hold of them.

"The whole board with the transistors will be smaller than this one—only about three inches by five inches and less than a half-inch thick, and it'll weigh less than six ounces. That replaces the chassis that's in the walkie-talkies that weighs almost two pounds and is three inches by seven inches by two inches and needs three more inches of space around it for the vacuum tubes to stand up on the chassis.

"This is just a prototype, but it works. I used tubes in the holes, and I built a radio *without wires*! This printed circuit board can be used *today* as a chassis for a radio or TV, using tubes. When transistors are available, the design of the board will have to modify, but essentially this board will serve as the chassis for a transistor radio and a TV. The boards have to be made with the right equipment. I figure there should be about five models to start with. I need a punch press, dies to stamp out each size board, dies to stamp out each circuit design, and an induction furnace to melt the copper. The process will use manual labor, but it will be done with a slow-moving belt running along a long table. I'm putting together a budget for the equipment and rent for a shop and payroll for a couple of men and three girls. I think I can build about a thousand pieces in an eight-hour shift with five people, maybe six. You have to help me with the numbers. I have an idea I can build the boards for less than a dollar each and sell them to companies like RCA, Motorola, and GE for about two dollars and fifty cents. There's a real business here, Jack. I figure the market for these among all the radio and TV manufacturers must be at least five thousand a day."

"But, Eddie, you told me that all the manufacturers are using steel chassis with vacuum tubes and wiring. When will they switch over to transistors? And when they do, won't they make their own printed circuits, by the tens of thousands, with high-speed equipment?"

"That's what's so great," he answered. "Sure, mine may be made in a primitive way, but they will look and work like they're made in a million-dollar factory. And at the outset, I'll be cheaper than a company that designs expensive high-speed equipment to build the boards. That takes time and investment. RCA won't look for the cheapest way to make printed circuits. They'll design an expensive high-speed system and, meanwhile, I'll be making them almost as cheap as they will and I'll be in the market first. By the time RCA makes their first printed circuit, I'll be making second-generation boards.

"It won't be a pushover to sell the first ones. There's a lot of inertia to overcome with the radio and TV makers. But this is a better mousetrap, built at a fraction of the cost of hand wiring. I'll be embedded in the industry before the big guys even get started.

"Jack," he said, "come in with me. I'll build 'em; you'll sell 'em. I even have a name for us, *Dunlaur Electronics—Dun* for Dunauskas, *Laur* for Laurel. So whattaya say?"

I studied his face, smiling, eager.

"Eddie," I grinned, "I say you don't need a salesman."

38

Decision-Making

MONDAY WAS THE weekly sales force meeting day at the APC district office in Camden. Driving there in the early morning, my thoughts were filled with Eddie and the printed circuit board. It was an exciting idea, could be a big business, could be an opening to the expanding world of telecommunications, and opportunity for big success—but dangerous. I made a *for* and *against* argument list as I drove.

For joining up with Eddie:
1. I had confidence in Eddie. The guy could build anything.
2. I did some calculations in my head that told me how profitable the printed circuits could be—potential annual profit in the hundreds of thousands.
3. The printed circuit was only a first step. Off in the future was a wireless phone, small enough to carry, linking the world in communication without wires. What an idea! I wanted to be part of that.
4. Being a business owner was a seductive thought. I missed being Captain Laurel, with a company of men to command. My job at APC provided a good living with no stress, but I was an employee. My predecessor was fired without warning, and I knew it could happen to me. It didn't matter that I did a good job. There was no congressman or commissioner protecting me. And anyone could write orders for APC—there was no competition.

Against:
1. I was making good money at APC. With Eddie, the financial situation would be tight. I knew that between us, we didn't have enough cash

resources to tackle the printed circuit. My rough guess was we'd need $20,000. Where would it come from?

2. Going into debt was scary. What if we were a failure?

3. We would have to be in the market very soon with a worthwhile product at the right price. Dozens if not hundreds of guys like Eddie had to be experimenting with printed circuits, and no doubt some of the big companies as well. We could be edged out of the market before we even got in.

4. What about security for my family? The baby was due in a few weeks. Could I risk everything going after a big win?

What a dilemma. I almost wished Eddie hadn't shown me the printed circuit board. I turned it over in my mind, over and over, without reaching a decision.

It was difficult to concentrate during the sales meeting. Eddie and the printed circuit were like a film covering my thoughts, and I wasn't focused on my work. I hoped it wasn't obvious. When the meeting ended at three thirty, the sales manager took me aside. He wanted to see me privately.

What's this about? I wondered.

39

APC Comments on My Performance

J ACK," MY BOSS said, "I'm putting you in for a performance bonus. Your productivity this quarter is outstanding. There's three weeks left, and if you don't bring in another sale between now and September thirtieth, you'll still have set a record for a quarter. Congratulations!"

"Thanks," I said. "That's great. I just keep beating the bushes. I had no idea I might be setting a record. What is the bonus?"

"An all-expenses-paid one-week vacation in Miami Beach or seven hundred dollars. Your choice."

Seven hundred dollars was more than a month's pay. "I'll take the seven hundred," I said without hesitation. "Alice and I are expecting our baby this month. The money will come in handy—thank you!"

"You're welcome," he said, shaking my hand. "You earned it. But, Jack, are you all right? You seemed distracted in there today."

"I'm fine," I said, feeling my face flush. "Maybe a little anxious about the baby."

* * *

Arthur Koestler, in his book *The Act of Creation*, says that life is temporarily suspended during the decision-making process, when confronting the choices drives away all other thoughts. It's true, in my experience. When I started the return trip from Camden, I could think of nothing else but Eddie and the printed circuits. The APC bonus added another weight to staying with my job.

I needed to air my thoughts, and I wasn't ready to discuss the idea with Alice. Alan Goren was the man. I called him from a pay phone and asked whether I could see him that evening.

"Sure, Jack," he said. "C'mon over."

40

Goren, the Analyst

THE GOREN APARTMENT was delicious with the fragrance of dinner in the oven.

Alan and Zena greeted me warmly at the door. "You'll stay for dinner," she said. She waved away my apologies for not visiting more often and for barging in this way on such short notice.

During dinner, I told them about Eddie and the printed circuits. I recited my reasons for and against. I told Goren I needed him to help me reach a decision.

"I understand, Jack," he said. "Let's finish dinner, and then we'll talk."

After dinner, Zena cleared the table and served tea. We sat in silence for some moments. Surprisingly, Goren had no questions. He drew on his pipe thoughtfully. He looked down at his teacup, in deep thought. Then he straightened up and studied me.

"Jack," he said, soberly, "this is a big decision for you. It's a fork in the road. Here is comfort... and safety... I suppose, unless you get let go from APC. Even so, you're a good salesman. You'll always make a decent living. It's a lifestyle that doesn't stretch you. It's a lifestyle that settles for what is in easy reach. No one could fault you if you turn down Eddie, but that's not my choice for you. If you succeed with Eddie, you'll be in the heart of the biggest scientific and economic boom in history. You and Eddie will be part of that. And you're liable to become very rich along the way. That's my choice for you. Zena, what do you see for this young man?"

"Don't ask me that, Alan," she said. "I don't know of such things. What I saw for Jack back in 1939 was a good, successful life."

She turned to me. "Jack, that's what I saw for you then, and that's what I see for you now. You'll succeed. Success is what I see, but I don't see the form it will take."

"There you are, Jack," Goren said. "Go with Eddie. It's exciting—and don't be put off because it might fail. It could. But so what? You're young. You'd succeed at something else. I know it's scary, but if you don't do this, you'll wonder all your life if you should have been part of the glory days that are coming for this country.

"One word of caution. Don't try to do it on a shoestring. I don't know the numbers. Make sure you are properly capitalized. Figure out your needs. Don't cheat yourselves. Allow for everything. When you know how much you need, come to me. I have a lot of money, Jack. You and I have a good track record—the cocoa beans in 1939, and crude oil during the War."

"Alan," I said, "I didn't come here to wheedle money from you. I just wanted your advice. Forget about money."

He turned to Zena. "What say, Zena? The money is not mine, it's ours."

She nodded her head in my direction. "I'll invest in anything he does."

41

Leaving It to Alice

IT WAS ABOUT NINE o'clock when I got home. Alice was waiting in the living room, listening to the radio. The *George Burns and Gracie Allen Show* was ending. She rose to open the door when she heard my car.

"Jack, are you all right?" she asked, studying my face. My anxiety must have shown.

I embraced her with a big hug and kissed her. After two years of being together, her kiss was still erotic, and the feel of her body was sensuous in my arms. The big hug was not so easy this late in her pregnancy, but I loved the feel of her swollen belly against me. The baby was due almost any day.

"Come, let's sit here," I said, leading her to the sofa. "We have a big decision to make."

I told her everything, just as I had explained it to Goren, but I didn't tell her I'd been to see Goren or about Goren's reaction.

She frowned in deep thought. "This is so difficult," she said. "We are doing so well; we're comfortable, and what with the baby coming . . . I see Eddie working so hard, all the time, and Evie getting frustrated. Leaving a good job to start a business is risky, but I know that if it weren't for me and the baby, you'd join up with Eddie tomorrow morning."

She paused and leaned into my shoulder. "And that's what I want you to do," she said, her voice quivering.

I lifted her chin to study her expression. Her eyes were moist.

"I love you so," she whispered, "and I know you will succeed at anything. Yes, I am frightened, a little, but that's all right. You'll do well and I'll be fine. And if you didn't do this, it would hang in the air always, that we didn't have the courage to reach for the brass ring. Not the money—that's only a small piece of it. It's you, Jack. The APC job is fine, but it will make you smaller. This thing with Eddie will expand you. You two will be important players in what's coming. It does not occur to me for one second that it might fail. You'll never fail at anything."

What a woman!

42

Decision Time

I TOLD EDDIE THAT Alice was behind me either way, joining up with Eddie or staying with APC. "How about Evie?" I asked him.

Eddie said Evie was thrilled with the plan. She saw it as Eddie having more free time and easing the ever-present worry about being a one-man business. She paid little attention to the numbers, such as the immediate effect on our take-home drawings and how much additional expense we were undertaking. For Evie, all was positive. She was ready to launch right away.

"But I'm not ready," I said. "It's a big risk. Alan warned me not to start out without enough money to see us through. We could go broke before we catch on if we don't have staying power. He said he'll lend us as much as we need, but I don't want to borrow money from friends. I did some rough figuring. I think we need twenty thousand dollars. I have about five thousand. You're stretched thin as it is. I gotta think this through carefully. I'm going to talk to the Boardwalk National Bank to give me some time."

"Okay, Jack," Eddie said soberly, "but you gotta make up your mind soon. Getting in the game first, or very early, at least—that's what it's all about."

"Sure, Eddie. I won't procrastinate."

43

Lunch with My Dad

IARRANGED MY AFTERNOON appointments to be near Atlantic City and made plans to have lunch with my dad.

Over lunch, I told him about Eddie and the printed circuits and quitting APC. He listened carefully. I expected him to urge me to stay at APC, as it represents security, or to decline an opinion out of concern for having me follow a recommendation that didn't turn out well. So I was surprised when he cut me short and said I should go with Eddie. His words were such a surprise; they made me sit up erect and even tilt backward a little.

"Son," he said with a proud smile, "go for it. You don't have to go into such detail with me. I know you, better maybe than you know yourself." He paused as his eyes swept my face. "And I know Eddie. You two can't fail. Don't aim for a life of security and dullness. Look at me. I have a solid job, but that's all it is, a job. It's dull, boring, dead-end, nothing ever new. Jack, I have a great wife, two marvelous children, a little money in the bank, but—and you must never, never, ever repeat a word of this—my life is a giant bore. I feel like I'm sleepwalking through it."

I rose. I lifted him up from his chair and hugged him. All I could say was, "Dad, I love you."

Yet my mind was still not made up. I guess I wasn't as confident in myself as he was, as Goren and Alice were. I told myself I was unafraid for my sake, but there was Alice and the baby to consider.

44

Adam

September 15, 1947

A DAM WAS BORN at one in the morning on September 15, 1947—the third anniversary of our attack on Peleliu. He was big and healthy, the most perfect baby ever. My love for him and Alice was overwhelming. Only a father knows that feeling of a father's love for a first-born son. I could not have imagined it, and the welling up of love for the wife and mother, until it happened. She looked so precious on that pillow—tired, her hair fanned out around her pale face. Her eyes sparkled with happiness. She gave me a great, wide, joyous smile that lit up her face with an inner light as she moved aside the soft blue blanket to show me our boy.

She observed that September 15 was only a week away from the autumn equinox—the second time each year when there were the same number of daylight and nighttime hours. "That means a well-balanced personality," she said, "and the ability to see both sides of serious matters."

She was right all around. She always was.

We did have it all.

45

Announcing Adam

I LEFT THE HOSPITAL at four o'clock in the morning, caught three hours of sleep, then woke, showered, and dressed for work. It was Monday—sales staff meeting. I didn't want to miss it, even though I would be late.

On the way, I stopped at a tobacco shop on Atlantic Avenue to buy a box of cigars. It was the custom for a new father to pass out cigars.

On the ride to Camden, my thoughts were everywhere: dreams for our son, plans for Alice. She'll need help. Will she want to work or give up her job? And the big thing that Adam had crowded out: going into business with Eddie.

I decided to set aside the Eddie question for a few weeks. There was too much to do. Alice and Adam would be coming home in a couple of days. We hadn't bought any baby stuff yet, out of superstition. I had to do it now, and I had a list: crib, bassinet, two dozen diapers, baby oil, baby powder, pajamas, blanket, sheets, bottles, nipples, and a mobile to suspend above the crib. Evie said she would help me with the shopping.

I threw open the door to the office. "It's a boy!" I cried out. The staff rose to greet me, but I continued on to throw open the door to the meeting room. Everyone turned around.

"It's a boy!" I cried. "Eight pounds, four ounces. He's big and handsome. His name is Adam!"

Everyone jumped to their feet and crowded around. They shook my hand. They pounded my back. They offered good wishes and congratulations. I handed out the cigars—good ones, Partigas, genuine Cuban, thirty cents apiece.

After twenty minutes of celebration, the staff returned to their desks and the sales meeting resumed. The wall charts were in place; the sales manager resumed his report. When the meeting ended, the sales manager asked me to come into his private office.

"What's up?" I asked, still glowing from my new fatherhood and the warm reception from all my colleagues.

"Have a seat, Jack," he said. He frowned. "I have bad news for you. I'm sorry. Especially on a day like this, such a great day for you."

"What is it?" I couldn't imagine. I must have lost a big account or that big installation at RCA.

"We're letting you go, Jack."

I couldn't speak. I couldn't mouth the words to ask why. I was stunned, a body blow to my stomach. I groped for a chair and fell into it.

He continued. "It's not me, Jack. You know how I feel about you. It's an order from Regional. They're replacing you with a young man with some kind of relationship with the state attorney general. They told me to drop our biggest earner. That's you by a longshot. That's bad, 'cause you're the best. This kid is going to be straight salary. He'll be making half of what you're making. Regional says anybody can sell our stuff—that we're the only game in town. I'm sorry, Jack. No decent job around here is safe unless somebody protects you. Give me all your leads and clean out your desk. You'll get two weeks termination pay."

I recovered my speech. "Will it do me any good to talk to Fred Walsh at Regional? He's the one who hired me. He was my staff sergeant in the War."

"Sorry to have to say this, Jack, but it was Walsh who gave the order."

46

Alice Gets the News

I DROVE TO THE hospital. Alice was propped up in her bed with Adam at her breast. She was startled to see me. It was only eleven o'clock.

"Jack! What's wrong? Why are you here? Are you okay?"

I told her.

"Bend down here," she said.

She hugged me with her free arm. "Is that all? You frightened me. I was afraid you were hurt . . . or sick. What happened?"

I gave her the details.

"So," she said, "it wasn't Dunlaur. You were already fired before you decided. Sit down. I'll get a nurse to bring you coffee and a sandwich. You have to relax. You look so tense."

"Alice, aren't you worried about this? Just a few days ago, we were talking about how good we have it. And I know you were at least a little bit nervous about me giving up the APC job, what with Adam about to arrive. You didn't fool me. I knew you were worried even though you did a good job of hiding it."

"I'll admit, I had a nervous moment. But only a moment. I knew we'd be all right. Now this news doesn't bother me at all. Nothing is gonna stop you and Eddie. It's best to be your own boss. No matter how attractive a job is, you're always just an employee. That's not for you. Or Eddie. Not you two. Me, worried? Not for a minute. Here, sit. Relax."

I threw my arms around her and held her close. She looked up at me with that always smile and shiny eyes.

"Not to worry," she whispered.

Now to see Eddie. He won't be so upbeat.

47

Bringing the News to Eddie

EDDIE WAS IN his store, explaining the features of a Philco TV to a couple. He was wearing his blue denim pants and shirt with *Eddie's* embroidered above the left breast pocket.

I studied the store carefully, as if seeing it for the first time: a retail store in front and a rear counter behind which was Eddie's cramped workspace. The retail area was only a twelve-by-twelve-foot space, and I thought it resembled a workshop more than a store, with its white walls and shelving unadorned except for a few marketing posters from Philco and RCA. The floor was a bare yellow and brown geometric-patterned linoleum. Cabinets lined both sides of the store, with long countertops. A few TVs stood on the counters, together with several small radios, record players, telephones, antennas, an intercom box, and several catalogs. The shelves held electrical parts: cords, plugs, headsets, lightbulbs, electric sockets, switches, and the like.

While I waited, another customer entered carrying a small radio. "Can you fix this?" he asked Eddie, holding it up.

"Be with you in a few minutes," Eddie answered.

"Take care of your customer," said the man who was looking at the Philco TV. "We'll think it over and let you know."

"Sure," said Eddie, with a smile. "Think it over. It's a good set and a good price." He turned to the new customer. "What seems to be the problem?" While he examined the radio, another customer arrived.

I stood by for an hour and a half while Eddie waited on six customers before I had a chance to talk to him. I asked him to hang the *Out to Lunch* sign on the door so we could have a serious talk. Then I told him.

He stepped back as if the news slapped him. He groped for a response.

I spoke up. "So what's it gonna be, Eddie? If we go ahead with the plan, I start out as deadweight. If you want to call it off, it's okay."

"Deadweight?" he snorted with excitement. "What a break for us!" He grinned and gathered me up in a bear hug. "This is great news, Jack. My God, if you don't sell one phone installation a week, I'll be shocked. At least four installations a month—average profit anywhere from three hundred to twelve hundred dollars. APC can take their five hundred a month and stick it!"

That's how I became Eddie's partner. Not my proudest moment. The decision was made for me. I'll never know whether I had the balls to quit APC.

"Okay, Jack," Eddie said, offering his hand. "Shake on it. We're in business as of right now. But before we do anything else, I want us to drive up to the University of Pennsylvania, right now. I want to show you the future."

"What's there?" I asked.

"ENIAC," he said.

"What is it?"

"You'll see."

48

ENIAC

O N THE DRIVE TO Philadelphia and on the return trip, we worked out a business plan. Eddie said Evie would be elated to hear I was partnering with him. We decided she was going to be part of Dunlaur Electronics. She would quit her job and take over the store.

ENIAC—it stood for "Electronic Numerical Integrator and Computer"—was the world's first electronic computer. It was built for the Army during the War but wasn't finished until 1946. It was shut down in November for improvements to its functionary reliability. It was reactivated in July 1947, about two months before our visit.

It wasn't just a big piece of machinery. It was twenty-four thousand square feet of wired panels with a total weight of thirty tons, covering three walls of its own room with a control tower in the center. A sign for visitors listed some details. The monster device had 17,468 vacuum tubes, 7,200 crystal diodes, 1,500 relays, 70,000 resistors, 10,000 capacitors, and 5,000,000 hand-soldered joints. It could perform 100,000 calculations per second and store half as many results.

The ENIAC cost $500,000 to build. That's more than $10 million at today's prices.

"The day will come when all this"—Eddie indicated the entire room with a sweep of his arm—"will be housed in something no bigger than a TV set." He was wrong, of course. Today's desktop computers and even our handheld devices outperform the ENIAC by a factor of twenty thousand using a microchip smaller than a fingernail.

Eddie continued, "But this is the future. Miniaturization and transistors—they're the key, and we're right here with our printed circuits, right at the beginning."

** * **

Here is the business plan we developed:

1. Keep the existing business of installations and sales of radios and TVs.
2. Hire a man who can take over Eddie's role in installations, sales, and repairs.
3. Rent space in an industrial building for developing the printed circuits. That will be our model shop and production facility and is where Eddie will work.
4. Turn over Eddie's store to Evie. Wall off an area in the rear for supplies and the repair shop.
5. Redecorate the store. Put down carpeting and dress up the store. Make it look upscale, with soft lighting, carpeted walls, and counters. At least twenty TVs on display, all turned on.
6. Change the name. The store will be Dunlaur Electronics, Retail Division, Store #1.

My job would be to sell phone installations and prepare customers for our printed circuits, with delivery starting in forty-five days.

49

Selling

MY FIRST SALES CALL was to Dave Spencer. He gave me a big hello and pumped my hand vigorously.

"Hey you, Jack," he grinned at me. "It's great to see you. How's your pal? I tell everybody about Eddie up on the flagpole that day."

"How's the TV working?" I asked.

"Just great," he said. "I pull in New York, Philly, Baltimore—sometimes even Washington on cold, clear days. Here, c'mon in my office. Marylou, get Jack a drink. How 'bout a coffee, Jack? Or would you like tea?" We sat. "So what brings you out this way, Jack?"

"I'm not with APC anymore, Dave. I'm partners with Eddie. Here's my card—we're Dunlaur Electronics. I want to show you a couple of things I think you should have. First, you need another telephone at the far end of this building, beyond the warehouse on an outside wall. When you want to talk to one of your people in the yard, you'll be able to call him to that place—he won't have to come all the way into the building. I'll wire the line through the warehouse and tie it in to the outside phone. It's an easy installation."

"But how will we call the guy to the phone?"

"Take your pick: I can install a public address speaker on the roof, strong enough to carry all over the yard, or I can sell you some of these." I opened my case and took out one of our walkie-talkies.

"You've seen these, Dave," I said, handing it to him. "Two-way radios, US Army surplus. Brand new. The Army paid sixty-two dollars apiece for them. I can sell you a few for twelve dollars each. I had the original version on New Guinea. I got this model, the improved version, when I got to Peleliu, and I carried it on Okinawa."

As Dave turned the device over in his hand, I continued. "Your men ride around the yard in those covered golf carts. They won't have to carry the radio. It can sit in the cart. You call out, *John, please go to the outside phone,* or you communicate with him through the radio. Its range is about three miles—way more than you need. And your yard is open. No obstructions. Reception will be good. I have another one in my car. C'mon, I'll show you. I'll drive to the far end of the yard and call you." I drove to the far end of the yard and called.

Spencer received my call and responded. "Sounds good, Jack," Spencer said, "but how can you install another phone. Doesn't APC have that locked up?"

"They have the monopoly on the telephone lines. But once it's inside a building, anybody can distribute the signal. The telephones are available from Western Electric. They have to sell them to anybody, at the same price APC pays. You have one incoming line into the receptionist's phone. Your other eight phones get their signal from her phone. They can communicate with her or with each other, using her phone as a switchboard. I'll add another line and another phone, or APC will do it for you.

"They own your phones," I reminded him. "You're paying a dollar fifty per month to rent each phone and a service for running each line from the receptionist's phone station. The phone I sell you for twenty-four fifty will be yours, no rental. You just pay me for the phone and to run the line. I'll service it as good as APC, and you'll be striking a blow for small business.

"So, Dave," I finished my pitch, "how 'bout I work up a proposal in a few minutes while I'm here. I'll figure in a public address unit as well."

I made the sale. But more important, I secured a good reference for my next prospect.

On the way home, I detoured to the Buena Vista Country Club. I got a *Maybe, we'll think about it,* regarding my proposal for a telephone line into the men's locker room but came away with an order for four walkie-talkies.

50

Grinding It Out

BUSINESS IS NOT easy.

I called on prospects every day. As many as I could. I made Saturday and evening appointments when I could. The more appointments, the more sales possibilities. The biggest obstacle was being a nobody company. APC could do everything we could do, and maybe better, even though Eddie said our installations were just as good. We were using components made by Western Electric, Westinghouse, and General Electric. Our customers who wanted to give a break to a small company were never disappointed, and our prices were usually 40 percent less than APC. I calculated that, on average, one sales call in four resulted in an opportunity to bid on an installation, adding phones, installing a public address system, upgrading phones to eliminate an operator-operated switchboard. Typically I landed one out of three bids. That meant that when a receptionist said *Mr. So-and-So will see you now,* I had a one in twelve likelihood of a sale. I got my share. I was averaging about three deals a week.

We hired a guy to do TV and radio repair in the store and assist Eddie on installations. When a job was completed, there was no automatic reorder. I called on completed-job customers regularly to see if they needed anything new. Since I was out there all the time, we took on a line of electrical components: wire, small transformers, motors, industrial strength batteries. I sold a few walkie-talkies every week. I carried catalogs of the TV, radio, and radio phonograph brands we carried in the store and sold a little of everything.

I stayed with the night school program at Atlantic City Community College. I completed the course in February 1948 with a certificate in electrical-electronic engineering. The course helped me technically and gave me good credentials on a sales call.

Evie gave up her receptionist job at the medical practice to take over the store. We paid her the same thirty-five dollars per week that she'd been earning. She was a natural retailer. The first thing she did was to update the store. She scraped *Eddie's TV and Radio* from the window and designed a professional-looking sign:

DUNLAUR ELECTRONICS
RETAIL DIVISION

She redid the interior. She closed off the workshop area. She covered the floor, the cabinet fronts, and countertops with medium-gray Berber carpeting. She took down all the shelves and put all the parts and miscellaneous products out of sight in the cabinets. She brought in more TV sets. She added DuMont to our line. She brought in radio phonographs. She lined up all the TVs on one carpeted countertop and all the radios and radio phonographs on another. She kept the TVs on all the time, all on the same channel. She dimmed the lighting in the store so the TVs provided most of the light.

Evie was good at selling. She learned everything she could about radios and television sets and the relative merits of the different brands. Almost every sale resulted in a rooftop antenna sale as well. Our retail sales improved. Why not? A good-looking girl with a welcoming smile and a lively personality. Plus, she knew her stuff, and her prices were competitive.

We traded in Eddie's station wagon for a white panel truck on which we had the company name and phone number professionally inscribed.

We ate into our cash account despite the new business I was bringing in and the improved retail business. The repairman's and Evie's salaries; money spent to update the store; the new truck; my car expenses; buying more TVs, radios, and radio phonographs for a better display; and our weekly draws—it burned through our cash at an alarming rate. And there was Eddie's printed circuit development. We put off starting up a separate shop, but to build the prototypes, we had expenses for materials, outside vendors for die-cutting, laminating, induction copper melting, applying the molten copper through the die-cut mask, and punch press work.

At one point, Eddie said to me, "Maybe we should stop the printed circuit project and let go the repairman."

"Nothing doing," I said. "The printed circuit is the key to our company becoming serious. The rest of what we're doing is a holding operation so we can do the printed circuits. I'll borrow a thousand from my dad. Do you think your father will spring for another thou?"

Two months later we went back for another $2,000. The borrowing got us over the crisis until job completions and collections caught up with the sales I was generating. But I could see more crises coming. Poring over the books and bills was a depressing job, spreading insufficient over all the bills and expenses. I got Evie to take over the job. She was better at it.

51

The Home Front

W HEN ADAM WAS born, Alice had to take a leave of absence from her job. That took away her forty-dollar weekly contribution to running our household. Eddie and I cut our weekly draws to fifty dollars each. Eddie and Evie were getting along all right with Eddie's fifty dollars and Evie's thirty-five, but I was struggling. It was tough times, even though Alice was great at stretching the money. She persuaded her boss to let her do some work at home, a few hours per week. That brought in ten dollars a week. We sure needed it.

We couldn't afford anything but basic necessities. Entertainment was evening TV and radio. I listened to Edward R. Murrow's nightly seven forty-five news program when I was at home . . . *and listen to Murrow tomorrow.* There were enjoyable weekly half-hours with Eddie Cantor, George Burns and Gracie Allen, *Big Town* with Edward G. Robinson, Jack Benny, Red Skelton, *Superman,* Bob Hope, *Sherlock Holmes,* Jimmy Durante, Fred Allen, Abbott and Costello, and lots more. There were few good TV shows, but there was extensive coverage of a UFO that supposedly crashed in Roswell, New Mexico. Immediately, there were hundreds of alien sightings and reports by people who were abducted onto spacecrafts.

Until February, I was committed to three evenings per week for my night school course. That didn't leave much time for evening relaxation, and all too often, our evenings consisted of Eddie, Evie, and me going over accounts and plans while Alice served up tea, cake, and encouragement. She never had a moment of doubt.

Even relatively small unexpected expenses put us in a financial tailspin, like a fifteen-dollar heater repair or a new twelve-dollar tire for Alice's station wagon. Yet we were far from being impoverished. Average annual family income was $3,000, which is where we were. All our basic daily needs were covered. The house was always clean and neat. I policed the outside and kept the grass and bushes cut. I went to work well-dressed. We ate well. Alice sent me off with a sandwich and piece of fruit in a brown bag. I always ate near a water fountain, water being my beverage of choice.

Max the Wonder Dog was an exceptional animal. I walked the beach with him every morning and evening. Alice and I loved him. But our budget was so tight that for a fleeting, shameful moment, I considered giving him away. I think that was my low point. I never mentioned it to Alice.

* * *

In December, Bell Laboratories announced the invention of the transistor to replace glass vacuum tubes. Eddie showed me the story in the *New York Times*.

"This means we're running out of time with the printed circuit board. Transistors will be on the market in six months, maybe sooner. We have to be showing prototypes by May. We gotta be in the game early, or we'll be shut out."

I knew he was right.

52

A Summons from Bobo

January 1948

WHEN I GOT home from work, there was a message from Georgie. He was going to come for me at eight o'clock that night. Bobo wanted to see me. I'd planned to write up two follow-up proposals for sales calls I made that day. But you didn't say no to Bobo.

Georgie was driving a new Cadillac.

"Nice car," I said as I climbed in. "What's up, Georgie?"

"Bobo wants to see you," was his answer.

"What about?" I pressed him.

"He'll tell you."

Georgie drove to Trucci's. It was a step back in time.

Atlantic City's two most popular restaurant clubs were the 500 Club and Trucci's. They were both on Arctic Avenue, within a block of each other. The clubs were the hangouts for celebrities, prominent local citizens, and tourists who came to see the celebrities.

The clubs featured live entertainment seven nights a week. Well-known performers, including Louis Armstrong, Frank Sinatra, Billie Holiday, Dizzy Gillespie, Cab Calloway, and Carmen Cavallaro appeared from time to time. Most nights, however, dinner patrons were entertained by a duo of pianist and singer who would never made it big but could be counted on for a good show.

Trucci's was bright enough to be seen from six blocks away. Moving lights circled its marquee, formed out of light bulbs that blinked on and off every half-second. Searchlights threw moving crisscrosses of light beams across the sky. A row of bright goosenecked lights mounted on the roof parapet shone down on the pavement below. A tall black uniformed doorman stood outside, dressed in an ornate, full-length military coat with broad lapels, lots of gold buttons, heavy gold-braided trim, and handsome epaulets. He looked like a Russian Cossack general. A steady stream of expensive cars pulled up to the curb, discharging well-dressed men and attractive women. Valet parking attendants whisked away the cars.

Only known patrons could enter Trucci's. The doorman asked my name. It meant nothing to him, but before he stepped inside the vestibule to ask someone about me, he saw Georgie, who waved him aside.

The entrance to the dining room was through the bar, all polished cherry wood with paneled walls. Behind the bar was a wall of smoked glass, reflecting the good-looking women sitting on the high barstools in their little black dresses, with lovely arms and legs, and the self-assured men who stood at their elbows. The bar was dark. It opened into a brightly lit dining room. We followed Georgie to a table set for seven in the center of the dining room.

This night, Trucci's featured a young pianist, who performed mostly soft dinner music and an occasional jazz piece or ragtime, played quietly. The singer was a good-looking girl with a pleasant but unexciting voice. The dining room was packed. The men wore suits or expensive sport coats and dress shirts and neckties. Some wore dinner jackets. The women wore evening dresses. Jewelry glittered.

The circling lights were silver and crystal globes fashioned from hundreds of small facets. Light danced and sparkled from them, making the entire dining room seem in motion. The table linen was pure white; a live floral arrangement was centered on each table. Laughter filled the air, along with the babble of a hundred conversations and lots of smoke from cigarettes and cigars. Most adults smoked in 1948, when a pack of cigarettes would set you back about twenty-one cents.

Georgie and I entered the dining room, and I spotted Bobo immediately. He was at his favorite table with Loretta and Frankie and two other men. Loretta Mauriello was a black-haired beauty in her midthirties. She wore a low-cut white silk sleeveless blouse that revealed perfect shoulders and arms and a tantalizing look at the inner curve of her breasts. Her necklace was made of flat silver bars suspended Egyptian-style from a silver circle, studded with diamonds and emeralds. She wore a heavy silver bracelet covered in diamonds. A broad smile displayed perfect white teeth framed in bright red lips.

One of the other men at the table had that big, sleek, rosy look that seemed characteristic of important racketeers. As I approached the table, they all rose to greet me, with the exception of the man I didn't know, who remained seated and unintroduced. Bobo and Frankie gave me the big hug. Loretta's eyes lit up when she saw me but only for a moment; she knew better than to rest admiring eyes on any man except Bobo. Her hand touched my arm briefly as she reached up to kiss my cheek. Her touching me at all was unsettling. I guessed Bobo would remember the gesture, fleeting and innocent as it may have been.

Loretta hadn't seen me since I returned from the service. Her comments were the usual: "You've grown, Jack … You went away a boy and came back a man … I know about your combat record," and so on.

Bobo motioned for Georgie and me to sit. He looked around for his waiter and waved for him to come. "Whattaya drinkin', Jack?"

I ordered a bourbon and water, no ice.

"Bring that for Jack and bring Georgie his usual. Now then, Jack." Bobo leaned forward. "Drink up. Then let's go up to the office. We got things to talk about over here. Georgie, you come on up with me and Jack. Frankie and Loretta, entertain our guests."

53

A Favor for Bobo

U PSTAIRS, I SETTLED into an easy chair. Bobo did that half sit at the front of his desk, one foot on the floor. He lit a cigar, his motion slow and deliberate. His bottom lip jutted out to release smoke gently up at the ceiling, softly, pensively.

"What's up, Bobo?" I asked.

"What's up?" he asked. "First, I gotta tell you I heard about you and your friend Eddie goin' into business. Electronics, ain't it? Radios and telephones and all that? I was hoping you'd come in with me. I still ain't givin' up on the idea. And I heard you was turned down for a ten-thousand-dollar loan from the Boardwalk National Bank, right?"

I rose out of my chair, and I must have looked agitated. "How do you know about that?" I demanded.

"Relax," he said. "I know everything what goes on in this town over here. That's my business. Don't let it bother you."

I felt my face flush as I sat back in the easy chair. *So much for bank confidentiality*, I thought.

Bobo took another draw on the cigar and released the smoke in a narrow stream through pursed lips. "But Jack," he said, hands out, palms up, and eyebrows raised, "why didn't you come to me if you needed money? You know I'll help you over here. Anyway, let it go. We'll talk about that another time."

Another stream of smoke. He rose and went around the desk to sit in the tall judge's chair.

"Anyway, you wanna know what's up? A lot is up over here, Jack. I'll tell you what's up. Things is changin' over here. It ain't like it used to be. We had it real good for a long time. No interference from New York. No interference from Philly. Pretty much we did what we want. No interference from nobody.

157

Not from City Hall. Not from the politicians. Not from the newspapers. And the police, they're under control." He stopped to relight the cigar. He sipped at a Coke.

"What's happening, Bobo?" I asked.

"It was real good here during the War," he continued. "Now things is changin'. I see it comin'. I got some hints what's comin' our way. Philly wants in. So does New York. But it's gonna be Philly. They're closer, and they already got some guys in place over here. It's a matter of time. Maybe a year. The guy you saw downstairs—he's sort of a scout for the Philly organization—come down to see me for a chat, friendly-like, to let me know they're around. They're not ready. They'll come to see me not so friendly when they're ready.

"Right now, I got to know what's coming down, and when . . . and who. You and your friend Eddie can help me. I need a favor. I need you guys to bug the police chief's office and put a tap on his phone. You guys must know how to do that. That's the favor I need. Nobody's comin' here to murder me without he's got the chief. Do this for me, will ya?"

I didn't answer right away. I thought hard about what he was asking.

I stood. "Bobo, I can't turn you down, but I have to talk to Eddie. He's the brains when it comes to that kinda stuff. If we can do it, you'll have to get us in, and there's things we'll need." I looked at my watch: nine forty-five. "C'mon, Georgie, take me home. I'll get with Eddie on it first thing tomorrow."

Bobo walked over to me. He took my hand and looked into my eyes, with a slight squint. I remembered that look from years earlier. It was an effort for me not to look away. "Okay, Jack," he said. "I know you can help me. Don't worry about getting in. I got two detectives and five cops in that building on my payroll. Tell me what you need. You'll have it."

"You need a phone away from here," I said. "We'll bring the tap in on a phone line. If it gets discovered, you don't want it to be coming in here to you."

Bobo gave me a telephone number. Georgie had taken care of that already. The phone was in a boarded-up derelict house above Arctic Avenue, known as "the colored part of town." The last deed to the house was in 1911,

Bobo explained. The real estate taxes went delinquent in 1930. In 1936, the deed was transferred and recorded to Julius Brown, and the taxes were paid with a mailed-in money order. The phone bill got paid with mailed-in money orders.

"Who's Julius Brown?" I asked him.

"I'm surprised at you, Jack," he said. "There ain't no Julius Brown!"

54

The Tap

BOBO'S JOB NEEDED two visits to police headquarters. Georgie fixed us up with coveralls that read *South Jersey Electric.* He gave us name badges, one for *Wilmer, T.*, the other, *Borden, E.* He brought us a South Jersey Electric panel truck. I wore heavy-rimmed eyeglasses and a South Jersey Electric cap over a shaggy blond wig. Eddie wore a paste-on mustache. His South Jersey Electric cap covered a dark brown wig with the hair pulled straight back into a ponytail. We both wore thin cotton gloves.

At noon, we drove to the headquarters building and parked the truck out front. Before we entered the building, we took the ladder off the truck and set it against the rear wall of the building where the electric service entered. Eddie climbed up and switched off the power. He waited two minutes then restored power. He waited five minutes and cut off the power again. After four repetitions of power off, power restored, we walked to the front of the building and entered the precinct door, wheeling in a box with three dials and three control knobs and a handheld dial that was attached to the box by an eight-foot electric cord. It was a phony piece of equipment, assembled for the occasion. A uniformed police sergeant was waiting for us. I gathered he was one of Bobo's cops.

"You the guys from the electric company?" the cop asked in a voice loud enough for all in earshot to hear.

"That's right," I said. "We'll have to test all the outlets on the third floor. That's where the trouble is." I knew the chief's office was room 305.

"Okay," I said, after going through half of the offices on the third floor until we reached room 305. "Here it is." I unscrewed an outlet switch plate, fiddled with the switch, then replaced the plate. "That does it," I said "Problem solved."

We took off. That's how we got to size up the chief's office to know where and how Eddie would install and hide the listening device. Today, a listening device would be the size of a dime, and it would be wireless. The microphone we were going to use was the size of a salad dish, and it needed 75 watts of electric power.

* * *

At one o'clock that morning, we returned to police headquarters, which was open twenty-four hours a day. Georgie gave us a driver dressed just as we were, in South Jersey Electric coveralls.

"Why is he coming with us?" I asked.

"You might need him," Georgie answered.

"Okay," I shrugged. "Let's get started. Get your gloves on." The three of us walked in carrying the ladder. "We're back," I announced. "More trouble."

The desk sergeant waved us through to the elevators.

Another Bobo man, I thought. Uh-oh. The door to the chief's office was locked. I tried it a few times. "Problem. How we gonna get in?"

"That's what I'm here for," said the driver. With that, he kneeled before the locked door with a ring of skeleton keys and had the door open in twenty seconds.

Eddie placed the tap into the phone, which took nearly no time at all. The listening device went into the base of the overhead light and fan. He spent fifteen minutes up on the ladder, cutting, adding, and splicing wires, then another fifteen snaking the added electric cord inside the ceiling and wall down to the phone jack, where he tied it into the phone service. With everything put back in order, we left, locking the door behind us.

55

Reporting to Bobo

HE NEXT MORNING, Eddie and I brought the tape recorder to Bobo's office.

"Here's how it works," Eddie said. "The mic in the fan will turn itself on whenever there's a sound in the room. It will hear and record everything that goes on in the room, except when the telephone is in use. When the telephone is in use, the mic will cut out and the telephone will record. When the telephone hangs up, that will reactivate the mic. I wired a dedicated line into the phone number you gave us. The police department's phone bill will go up by five dollars a month, but they have so many lines into that building, they'll never know about this one.

"Get me into the house so I can hook up the tape recorder. It will record up to two hours, and I've included two extra reels of tape. You can erase and reuse them as often as you like. We'll get you another machine so you can listen to the tapes here or wherever you want to."

"Well, thank you, guys," Bobo said. "I knew you could do it. Whatta I owe you for this? Don't be bashful over here. This is worth a lot to me. How 'bout a couple thou'?"

"You owe us nothing, Bobo," I said without hesitation. "This is for old times' sake."

The job had cost Eddie and me five hundred dollar in materials, but though we really couldn't afford it, we'd decided that, this time at least, we preferred Bobo's gratitude to his money.

56

Conundrum

OUR INSTALLATION BUSINESS and retail store had to generate enough income to nourish our printed circuit ambitions. The printed circuit effort was a demanding master. It had to be launched in a hurry. We had to be in the market soon with our first-generation boards designed for use with vacuum tubes.

Transistors were less than a year away, maybe only six months. Once they were available, the entire radio-TV industry would change overnight from vacuum tubes to solid-state. We had to have a customer base for our printed circuit board designed for vacuum tubes so we could immediately replace them with boards designed for transistors. If not, we would be shut out of the market with no chance of getting back in. We were in a race against the calendar.

The only reason we had a chance was that the big companies were not interested in an in-between step of printed circuits designed for vacuum tubes. They were waiting on solid-state boards and planning to switch over to transistors as soon as they were available—no more vacuum tubes.

I dedicated almost half of my time to prospecting for printed circuit customers, though I had no base of contacts for potential users. This cut in on my time selling installations.

Meantime, Eddie had to do some of the installations and troubleshoot problems, leaving little time to develop a high-output shop to make printed circuit boards. If I broke through with a sample order, we would have to be ready for a volume order soon after. A production shop would have to be ready and waiting.

Eddie was also working on a redesign of our walkie-talkies, but that took a back seat to the printed circuits.

Our work days lengthened. Eddie was in his shop every evening and on weekends. Evie and I did paperwork at nights, paid bills, mailed out statements, typed up proposals, and struggled with a voracious checkbook. Eddie's shop ate up all the income that we generated from sales and installations. I tried to schedule sales calls on Saturdays. Saturday was a normal workday in 1948, although there was a growing movement to make it a half-day.

Our initial cash contributions were exhausted quickly, and so did another $4,000 borrowed from our fathers. Our cash went to the store makeover, the new van, additional payroll, and the basic start-up expenses of Eddie's printed circuit shop: rent, worktables, the induction oven, a secondhand punch press, a guillotine cutter, telephone service, and all the miscellaneous hand tools and supplies that are part of a shop that makes things.

So, even as we were moving ahead and making money with our installation business and retail store, we were eating through money too fast.

I didn't see much of Alice and Adam. I was always tired. I tried to stay energetic and positive. It was hard to do. All that work, and the whole thing could collapse at any time. My unspoken thought was, *Should we give up on the printed circuit? It could break us financially. We could make a decent living without it.*

We could settle for a moderately successful business consisting of installations, service, and the retail store. We would be like hundreds or even thousands of small installers and small TV-radio stores.

But that's not what we were after. Dunlaur Electronics was to be an early entrant in the new world of electronics and communications.

57

The Berlin Blockade

June 24, 1948

THE VICTORIOUS ALLIES divided post-war Germany into four occupation zones: US, British, French, and Soviet East Germany. The Soviet zone was quickly converted by Stalin into a Soviet satellite with a puppet government under his control.

East Berlin, deep inside the Soviet zone, was itself divided into four zones, while the US, British, and French zones collectively formed West Berlin. The Soviets created checkpoints on all the roads, railways, and canals leading from West Germany through East Germany to East Berlin. Periodically, the Soviets put pressure on the Americans. It was a way to demonstrate Soviet dominance over East Germany and to wring various concessions from the Americans by delaying or stopping truck convoys bringing supplies into West Berlin, or by stopping trains and subjecting the passengers to questioning and passport inspections.

By June 1948, such incidents had become frequent. The concessions were usually minor, with the Americans agreeing and the incident quickly over and forgotten.

American hard-liners advocated military confrontation to teach the Russians a lesson. It was unrealistic thinking it was the US that won the War in Europe and that the US could defeat the Soviets militarily. The reality was that at War's end, the Soviet army was the biggest and most powerful in the world, and, by 1948, the US Army had demobilized to 1938 levels. A military confrontation with the Soviets was unthinkable. True, only the US had the atomic bomb, but it was not going to be used. The entire world, including the US, recoiled from the horrors of Hiroshima and Nagasaki.

On June 24, 1948, the Soviets blockaded Berlin. They offered to lift the blockade if the Americans would agree not to introduce the new German deutschmark into Berlin.

The Americans would not agree. Instead, President Truman responded by feeding and supplying the entire population of West Berlin with the Berlin Airlift, a constant stream of cargo planes flying into Tempelhof Airport at the rate of one landing every four minutes, around the clock; fifteen hundred flights daily, delivering five thousand tons of cargo to feed and supply the city. As winter approached, the need for coal to heat West Berlin increased the daily cargo requirement to over nine thousand tons of cargo daily.

It was an unprecedented and masterful demonstration of American know-how and military skill. Each plane landed, taxied out of the way of the next plane, discharged its cargo, refueled and turned around for the return flight in less than thirty minutes. If a plane missed its landing slot, it turned around and flew back to its original take-off location. The stream of planes was not to be interrupted; the Soviets did not attempt to stop it for fear of bringing on a real war. The airlift lasted 322 days until the Russians lifted the blockade on May 2, 1949.

The Berlin Airlift demonstrated how Cold War provocations by the Soviets could be handled through skillful, patient responses by the Americans. Truman resisted pressure from American war hawks who argued for military responses. His policy of resolving Cold War provocations without direct confrontation held through seven subsequent American administrations until the Soviet Union's collapse in 1991.

58

Don't Stop for Corn

SUMMER CAME. I rose every morning, had breakfast with Alice, and spent some precious time with Adam before climbing into my car and riding out to do battle. I saw so little of him, even on weekends. If I was not seeing prospects, likely I was in the store with Evie, poring over accounts and relieving her for a couple of hours so she could be with Eddie.

The daily routine was joyless. I put on a brave front, cloaked myself with a smiling air of confidence and success, all the time trying to quiet the insistent voice that said Dunlaur was not going to make it *regardless* of how much we made on installations and retail sales. Eddie's shop burned through it all and then some.

Meanwhile, I hustled to sell installations and beat the bushes for a break-through with our printed circuit. On this day, I was returning home from Allentown, Pennsylvania, where I'd signed up a new installation but struck out trying for a sample order of circuits. It was a long drive—sixty miles from Allentown to Philly and then sixty-five more to Atlantic City.

My radio was tuned to Philadelphia station WCAU and a program featuring the leading singers of the day: Peggy Lee, Perry Como, Vaughn Monroe, and, of course, Sinatra. I wasn't listening. My mind was searching for a solution to Dunlaur's race against time and the financial crisis that was overtaking us.

Between Camden and Atlantic City, I pulled off the road at Rose's farm market, opposite Gene's Diner. I picked up a dozen ears of corn and two quarts of Jersey tomatoes—fifteen cents for the corn and ten more for the tomatoes.

A rusty old Ford pickup truck, vintage 1932 or thereabouts, was parked at Rose's. A rough-looking man, apparently the driver, was talking with Rose. He wore dirty overalls over a bare chest, old Army boots, and a dirty, torn straw hat. He had a scruffy beard. I thought he must be about thirty. He had a girl with him, barefoot, in a thin, dirty cotton dress. Her hair hung loose, covering her face. She was young—I figured sixteen at most. Her arms and legs were browned by the sun, covered with scratches and bruises. She had just finished taking pails of berries out of the truck and lining them up on an empty table.

"I count twenty quarts of blueberries," Rose said, "and seven of blackberries. Give you eight cents a quart for the blueberries and a dime for the blackberries."

"C'mon, Rose," the man said. "You kin do better'n'at. How 'bout ten cents fer the blueberries and fifteen fer the blackberries. I know you'll sell the blueberries fer fifteen cents a pint and twenty for the blackberries."

"That's what I'm payin', mister. What I told ya. You want it or no?"

"All right," he grimaced. Then he said to the girl, "Pour out the blueberries into that big washbasin over there, and pour out th blackberries into that one next t' it."

Rose counted out the money, "A dollar sixty for the blueberries, seventy cents for the blackberries; here's two thirty. And here"—she handed a tomato to the girl—"this is for you."

"Thanks, Rose," the girl said. "Look Earl, see 'em sandals? They's only thirty cents a pair. Kin I have a pair?"

"Nah, you don't need no sandals." He pushed her away. "Get busy emptyin' the pails. I'm goin' up the road," he said, climbing into the truck. "Gonna buy some rope and have a beer."

I put my corn and tomatoes into the trunk and walked across the road to the diner. I hadn't had lunch, so I ordered a sandwich and coffee and read the diner's copy of the *Camden Courier*. Someone put a nickel in the nickelodeon, and Perry Como's "Temptation" filled the diner. The music was infectious. It drove the printed circuit problem out of my mind for a few minutes. The waitress half skipped to the tune while one of the men seated at the counter sang along enthusiastically but terribly off-key. The music and singing competed with the diner's radio, which was describing the first DCTs in the Berlin Airlift landing at Tempelhof Airport.

I paid the bill, crossed over the road, got into my car, and started off. It was one of those perfect days, the sky wearing its summer blue, the air fragrant with wildflowers. As I cruised along, my thoughts returned to the problem of getting a sample order for the circuits.

I'd driven about ten miles when I heard a rustling in the back seat. I pulled off the road onto the shoulder and turned around. At first, the back seat seemed empty, but then I saw her, on the floor, squeezed between the seats.

"Hey," I said. "What's the idea? What are you doing in my car?"

59

The Stowaway

170

S HE PULLED HERSELF off the floor onto the seat.

"Please, mister," she pleaded. "Take me with you. Anywhere. You kin let me out in the next town. I gotta get away from 'im. Please, please, mister. Just get me away as far as you kin."

She burst into tears.

60

Violet

ALL RIGHT, ALL right, stop crying," I said. "What's your name?"
"Violet," she sobbed.

"C'mon outta there, Violet."

She climbed out of the car. I got out as well.

"Tell me about it," I said. The tears ran down her cheeks, turning her face into an abstract picture of dark tan, dirt, and pale tears. I saw that her teeth were yellow and she was missing one near the front. Her stunning feature was her eyes. They were violet, truly violet, a deep violet. The look was startling, those violet eyes peering out of that dirty face, behind the tangled mop of dirty hair.

"I gotta git away," she repeated. "I cain't live like that no more. I'll die, or I'll kill m'self. Look at me. Ain't I a picture? That's how he keeps me lookin', so's nobody will be inter'std."

"Who is he to you?" I asked.

"He's a cousin. But just 'bout ever'body is a cousin. He works me. I pick the berries. I takes care of the chickens. I makes his meals. He takes me whenever he wants. He even lends me out, for a quarter or for a couple fish hooks or a piece o' rope or a beer. I have to stuff m'self with towels so's I don't get preggers. I wanna die. I bin lookin' fer a way out. Today, I seen you and yer car at Rose's. You look like a good man. So I hid in yer car whiles you was in the diner."

"All right," I sighed. "Get in the car. Here, up front. No need to hide in the back. I'll take you somewhere."

She smelled bad. Everything about her was covered with dirt. I would have to clean the car and spray it with air freshener once I got home.

But what to do with the girl?

61

Life in the Pine Barrens

I COULDN'T JUST DROP her off somewhere or leave her along the highway, so I decided to take her home. Alice would know what to do. This was women's business.

While we drove, the girl told me more about her life in the Pine Barrens. It was all bleak. Nothing good ever happened in Arnold's Crossing, the place where she was born. She never knew a father. Her village had thirty old frame houses, of which just three were occupied. The rest were derelicts, with missing doors and windows, caved-in roofs, and collapsed floors. She had two girlfriends when she was younger, but when her mother died, Cousin Earl took her to his house. He lived in a falling-down old house that somebody abandoned many years ago. One room had heat in the winter, from a cast-iron wood-burning stove, but there was no plumbing. Water was pumped from an old well half a mile away. There was a fenced yard with some chickens and a rooster and a cow. Violet looked after the animals, collected the eggs, milked the cow, tried to keep the house orderly, fetched the water every day, carried it home in two three-gallon wooden buckets. Earl didn't do much of anything. He fished a little. He had an old rifle and a rusted shotgun; sometimes he hunted rabbit or deer.

There was a one-room schoolhouse in the next village. A teacher came twice a month, together with a doctor. Nobody learned much. The doctor could take care of small problems, but if a person was really sick, he said he'd send an ambulance to take the person to a hospital, but usually the ambulance never came.

62

What to Do with Violet

A s her story developed, I decided it wouldn't be fair to Alice to bring Violet home. Alice was too occupied with Adam and trying to do part-time work from home. And we were struggling to manage with little money. She shouldn't be burdened with this problem. On the other hand, knowing Alice, she'd take her in. But I shouldn't do that to her.

I took the girl to my mother instead. I didn't know what else to do with her. Mom would know what to do. My dad wasn't home from work yet.

"Who is this?" my mother asked, motioning at her with an outstretched hand.

The girl stammered, "I'm . . . I . . . I . . ."

I put my hand on the girl's back and urged her forward. "Mom," I said, "this is Violet. She's in some trouble and needs a place to stay . . . for a few days, until I can figure out what to do with her. Maybe she can have Evie's old room—just for a day or so?"

Mom studied her curiously while I explained. "All right, son." She smiled. "Let's clean her up."

"Oh, thanks, missus," Violet said. She smiled, not a pretty smile with that missing front tooth.

"Come, dear," Mom said. "Let's get you into a nice warm bath."

"Thanks, Mom." I gave her a hug and headed to the door. "I'll bring Alice back," I said. "We'll figure out what to do with her."

* * *

When Alice and I returned, my dad was home. "Most kids bring home stray dogs," he said with an amused smile. "C'mon in."

Mom had set out a pot of tea and a plate of cookies. She said Violet was asleep in Evie's bed.

"I never imagined anyone could be so dirty," Mom said. "And so bruised and scratched. And her hair. It was a rat's nest. I brushed it as best I could, but I couldn't get out all the knots. I had to cut off a lot. She wanted to hug me and kiss me. Poor child. She told me everything. Jack, you don't know the half of it. Can you believe how those people live, only thirty miles from here? She didn't remember ever bathing in a tub with warm water and soap. She didn't want to get out. I gave her one of Evie's old nightgowns. When she saw Evie's bed, with the clean sheets and pillows, she began to cry."

She poured tea and offered us the cookie plate. "Now, then, what are we to do with her?"

"There's a child welfare agency," Dad said. "They'll take her."

"How old is she?" Alice asked.

"Seventeen, as best as she can figure," Mom said. "She said she picked Easter Sunday to be her birthday so she wouldn't have trouble remembering the date. The trouble with that is, the date changes every year!"

"Can she read and write?" Dad asked.

"Not much," Mom said. "A teacher used to come twice a month to her village, together with a doctor, but that stopped when the War started."

"Well," said Dad, "I can call the welfare agency tomorrow."

"How about we wait a few days?" I said. "I wouldn't want to think they'll take her back to Cousin Earl. Maybe we can get her a job as a live-in maid or babysitter."

Alice looked at me. That big smile. "Jack, shouldn't we—"

"No, dear," I said. "You have enough on your plate, and with the baby and all. But no need to worry; we'll make sure she's okay."

I turned to Mom, who said, "Let's leave it alone for the time being. She can stay here until we decide what's best. The house is very quiet with you and Evie gone. See, she's already our responsibility."

And that's how we left it. Violet was still asleep when Alice and I left.

"Jack," Alice said in the car. "Violet is a big, big responsibility. She should be in school. But I'll take her in if we don't find a good solution."

I stopped the car and embraced her.

I hadn't thought about Eddie and the printed circuits since finding Violet, but now, on the drive home, the challenges we were facing slid back into my thoughts.

63

The End of Dunlaur Electronics

Labor Day, 1948

EVIE CALLED AN emergency meeting—all of us, including Alice. Evie wasted no time. She spoke soberly. She had financial notes in hand but did not have to consult them.

"We're finished," she said. "We can hold out two or maybe three months."

"What are you saying?" Alice asked. "Do you mean we have to drop the printed circuits?"

"It's too late for that." Evie shook her head. "Our vendors will cut us off in two months. I've been shorting our bills for months, making on-account payments. The delinquent balances are way too big. I've heard from just about every vendor that they are stopping selling us. No more radios, no more TVs, antennas or wire or junction boxes. Western Electric will stop delivering phones in ten days. I've been running an account with Benzinger's gas station. He says no more credit. He won't sell us gas unless we pay cash and add twenty percent to each fill-up to be applied to our account. Rent for the store is two months back. Rent for Eddie's shop is two months back. The phone company will turn us off next month."

"What about our accounts receivable?" I asked. "Can't we borrow against them?"

"I did that with the bank last month," she said grimly. "That money's gone."

"How much do we need to keep going?" I asked.

"Eight thousand dollars to get through this crunch," she said, "but we'll continue to fall behind twenty-five hundred dollars every month. If we find the eight thousand, in three months we'll be back where we are now. If we go down, everything goes down—the installation business and the retail business. And that's the end of the printed circuit."

64

Searching for Money

W E HAVE TO FIND money. Where to find the money? I'd been to the Boardwalk National Bank three months earlier, looking for a $10,000 loan. They turned me down. They offered to finance the accounts receivable, but I said that was no good. It would damage our reputation with our customers that we were not adequately capitalized. Now I heard that Evie had already exhausted that temporary fix.

"I know only two places," I said. "Bobo or Alan Goren. I'm not going to Bobo. Better to close up than to owe him money. And I don't want to go to Alan. I would have to tell him the loan is too risky. It's not like start-up money. It's a temporary bailout. In a few months, we'll be right back here again. My dad is tapped out. I think yours is, too, Eddie. I could go to every vendor and tell them we're shutting down the printed circuits. That will have us generating a profit. In time, we can get current."

Evie sighed as she answered me. "I've been there, Jack. Nobody will go along. Looks like it's Goren or Bobo, or we're done."

65

The Traymore

THE FOLLOWING MORNING, I called Alan Goren and made an appointment to visit him the next day.

"Anything special, Jack?" he asked. "Is this a social visit? Or is it business?"

"Can't fool you, Alan," I answered. "Dunlaur Electronics is in trouble. I need your advice. Can I see you tomorrow?"

"Sure, Jack," he said. "And if it's money you need, I've got it."

That evening, there was an article in the *Atlantic City Press* about how the Traymore Hotel was going to install a new phone system that would allow guests to dial calls directly from their rooms without going through a central switchboard. The article said calls would be billed to the guest's room and added to his bill at checkout. It would displace twelve telephone operators and a bookkeeper.

I was at the Traymore Hotel at eight o'clock the next morning. I sat in the manager's reception room until eleven thirty. I might be sitting there still but for a local businessman, a Marine veteran, who recognized me as he walked through the reception room and stopped to chat. I told him why I was there. Ten minutes later, I was seated in front of the manager, another Marine veteran. I asked for an opportunity to bid on the telephone job.

"You'll be bidding against the phone company," he said. "What are your credentials for the job?"

"I worked for APC before my partner and I started Dunlaur Electronics. Your telephone job is easy. Big, but easy. Just a lot of labor. All the equipment comes from Western Electric. I know we can underbid APC by twenty-five percent. But I have a better idea using new technology. I'll try my idea in the first ten rooms. If it works to your satisfaction, I'll revise my bid, using the new technology. In that case, I'll probably be fifty percent below APC. Can I have the specs so I can figure out the pricing?"

He stroked his chin. "There aren't any specs," he said, stroking his chin. "APC knows what we need—they designed the system. But let me think about it and maybe talk with the hotel's ownership. I don't want to give you false hope. It won't be easy to stray from APC, because they service our entire switchboard system. But give me your card, Jack, and I'll get back to you."

"Thanks for even considering it," I said, rising. "Can I get a look into one of the back panels in the switchboard? If our new printed circuits are appropriate for the job, you'll have a system that's better than what you're aiming for, at half the price."

"Sure," he said. "C'mon, I'll take you to the telephone room."

66

The Traymore Job

I DIDN'T GO TO Alan Goren. I called to postpone my visit and headed instead for Bobo's office. He was glad to see me. He pointed to the tape recorder. "This is the best thing I ever owned," he said. "I listen to the police chief—every phone call, every visitor. I never heard so much bullshit over here. He's on the take all day long. He must have big money salted away. And I was right about Philly wanting to move in. But the chief ain't ready. He's afraid of me. Remember the thing back in 1939 with his daughter? Even though it was my guys who found the guy what raped her, he thinks maybe I arranged it."

"Bobo," I said. "I won't beat around the bush. I need a favor, if you can do it."

I told him about the Traymore job.

"Can you get us into the bidding, Bobo? We can do the job better and cheaper, but we're up against APC. I figure, real rough, the job is anywhere from a hundred to a hundred twenty thousand dollars if we do it the APC way. If we can do it with our new printed circuit boards, I can cut the price down to maybe seventy-five to a hundred thousand. APC will want at least a hundred and fifty thousand, more likely two hundred. If we had a sales rep, we'd be paying a seven-and-a-half percent commission—if you can help me, you can have the commission."

"Calm down, Jack," he said with that squinty look. "You're all agitated over here. This must be real big for you. I never seen you looking so nervous. Relax. I'll make a couple calls. If you get the job, my commission is ten percent." Grinning, he added, "But 'cause it's you, I'll take five."

"If I get the job, I'll have to borrow twenty-five thousand dollars from you to get started," I said.

He laughed. "Hey, Georgie," he said, "didja hear that? I love this kid. What balls!" He slapped me on the back, almost knocked me down. "Sure, kid. You're on."

67

Success!

THE TRAYMORE JOB launched our company. It was more than the windfall profit that saved us; it was a breakthrough that established Dunlaur Electronics as a serious player in the telecommunications world. To do the job, we had to hire five more installers. Suddenly, we were a ten-person company with a successful major hotel phone system upgrade in our credits.

All the big hotels in Atlantic City wanted the same upgrade. We took on four more jobs: the President, the Breakers, the Chalfont, the Chelsea. A detailed brochure I wrote, emphasizing the benefits and cost savings of our printed circuits, was being well-received by potential customers. I traveled to major cities, searching out electronic components distributors. I offered protected territory distributorships for our printed circuits. Within six months, we were producing and selling one thousand printed circuits a week and working on four hotel jobs. The successful use of our printed circuits in hotel jobs brought, at last, a test order with Motorola for use in their radios. That test order expanded into a production order.

By the time transistors were available, we were the leaders in printed circuits. As transistors replaced vacuum tubes, we were the country's largest manufacturer of printed circuits. By the spring of 1949, Dunlaur Electronics was successful beyond our dreams.

My income soared. I hired a three-day-a-week housekeeper for Alice. She resumed her old job out in the field, cataloging the wildlife of the Pine Barrens and the state parks in southern New Jersey. I bought her a new Ford station wagon, with the wooden rear and side panels. She drove everywhere in it, with Max as her constant companion. She took Adam along, too, on the days when Mrs. Wilson, a widow who had become our part-time housekeeper and babysitter, was not scheduled.

Our house was clean and inviting and filled with love and laughter. Life was good. It was better than good.

68

The Best of Times

DUNLAUR ELECTRONICS FLOURISHED, and going to work was a joy for me. Evie's retail store was successful. In April 1949, she opened a second one on Market Street in Philly. The new store was different: much bigger, for one thing, and offering more than TVs, radios, record players, and accessories. Evie had a more expansive vision. She brought in major appliances like refrigerators, clothes washers, and ovens, along with smaller items like toasters and coffeemakers.

At the center of the store was a rectangular customer service center, fifteen by twelve feet. It was made up of customer counters on three sides with high swivel stools for customers' comfort. The sales and clerical staff had desks with areas inside the rectangle. Philadelphia was a huge market relative to Atlantic City, and the store outperformed our expectations immediately.

In July 1949, a third Dunlaur Electronics store opened in Trenton—another strong market. Evie was a smart and tireless businesswoman. She kept the stores up to date in every way. Each had the same look of quiet technical proficiency: the same gray Berber carpeted floor, walls, and countertops; all the TVs playing, tuned to the same channel; dim store lighting, most of the lighting coming from rows of TV sets; and rows of bright white home appliances.

The employees were all thirty-somethings, attractive, polite, and well-spoken. Evie hired each employee personally. She took full-page ads in the Sunday editions of the *Philadelphia Inquirer*, the *Atlantic City Press*, and the *Trentonian*. After opening the Philadelphia store, it had occurred to Evie that the Dunlaur stores should be on the highways, out of the traditional center city market sites, wherever possible. The Trenton location was a freestanding store on the Olden Avenue Bypass with off-street parking. She began planning store number 4 in Allentown. The store, to be located on the Seventh Street Highway, would be similar to the one in Trenton, freestanding with off-street parking.

Eddie thought it was time to have a child. Evie said no, not yet. She was too busy at the moment—maybe in another year or two.

The *Atlantic City Press* wanted to run a story about Dunlaur Electronics. The reporter who contacted us suggested a headline: "LOCALS MAKE GOOD. DECORATED MARINE, WOUNDED NAVY VET, AND BEAUTIFUL WIFE RUNNING RETAIL DIVISION OF BOOMING ELECTRONICS BUSINESS."

I would have welcomed the publicity and imagined using the article in our marketing materials, but Eddie nixed the idea. "We're doing fine without everybody knowing everything about us," he said. "We're just small potatoes, but our customers think we're a big company. Why tell the world our plant is only fifteen thousand square feet and the whole company is only fifty people? Motorola and RCA and Westinghouse probably think we're many times that size. That's why when we get visits from their people, I keep 'em in the office and the conference room and the model shop. I never let 'em see the plant. That's why I have the partitions all the way back there. If somebody gets a peek, he'll think he's seeing only one section of the plant."

While we saw his point, Evie and I were disappointed.

Meantime, we were still trying to decide what to do with Violet. Mom and Dad took her to a dentist, who gave her teeth their first good cleaning and fitted her gap with a false tooth. Mom had her hair washed and brushed and cut. It was a rich dark brown color, almost black. When brushed thoroughly, it took on a satin sheen, pulled straight back into a ponytail. She was a pretty girl with beautiful eyes and a great figure, but more than that, she was smart, funny, and big-hearted.

* * *

Bobo's lawyer was Lawrence Durells, managing partner of Durells, Clarke, McCauley and Levy, Atlantic City's most prestigious law firm. He was close to the judges and the politicians and the district attorney's office. It was Larry Durells who had successfully represented me in 1939, when I was fifteen, for beating the Mackey brothers with an iron pipe after they molested thirteen-year-old Evie. The attorney did it as a favor to Bobo—I could never have gotten him to take my case otherwise—and never charged me a fee. Now, he was Dunlaur's lawyer and general counsel.

Durells arranged a birth certificate for Violet and a new name. And a birthday that didn't change every year like Easter. She became Eddie's cousin, from Coshocton, Ohio. Her birth was recorded in the Coshocton County records: Violet Dunauskas, born April 20, 1931, daughter of Herbert and Shifra Dunauskas.

As that was underway, Durells got Violet into the eleventh grade at Atlantic City High School. She was far behind her classmates in every subject, but she was a remarkably quick learner. The boys crowded around her, but she had no interest at all—not in any of them. The football captain expressed bewilderment that she wouldn't give him a tumble; she had little interest in socializing with the girls in her class either. She studied tirelessly. She had so much ground to make up.

She spent every spare moment reading. She soaked up history and music. Her speech improved. The makeover was remarkable. It was the *Pygmalion* story. No more talk of sending her away. She was mom's new daughter and Evie's kid sister.

* * *

Eddie couldn't seem to stop working sixty-hour weeks. He built a state-of-the-art facility for manufacturing the printed circuits. I established a network of dealers. New generic designs were developed regularly, but our strength was in our model shop where Eddie and his engineers designed dedicated boards for a customer's specific manufactured product. Orders were pouring in. I hired a sales manager. We had fifty employees in the factory and seventy in our three retail stores.

Eddie started on the wireless phone. He had already reduced the size of our walkie-talkies by two-thirds. He built a fifty-foot tower atop our factory building and put a relay and a repeater on it, tuned to a frequency we used only for the walkie-talkies. We could communicate directly with twelve units within a radius of eighteen miles. He hadn't yet solved the problem of making a walkie-talkie work more like a telephone than a radio, but I knew it was only a matter of time.

Our lives seemed perfect. That's dangerous. You should not tempt the gods with human perfection.

69

The Soviet A-Bomb

August 29, 1949

IN A STUNNING turn of events, President Truman announced that the Soviets had tested an atomic bomb, catching the United States intelligence services by surprise. They'd assessed the Soviets as at least five but more likely ten years away from developing such a weapon—adequate time, it was hoped, for US-Soviet relations to shift from adversarial to cooperative.

For the most part, America shrugged off the news, but the backyard bomb shelter industry appeared seemingly overnight, and school children were trained to duck under their desks when the siren sounded.

70

Such an Ordinary Morning

IT WAS THE WEEK of the Miss America Beauty Pageant in Atlantic City. The *Atlantic City Press* dedicated four pages to stories about the pageant and photos of the contestants in the surf, on the boardwalk, leaning against the railings, and riding in rolling chairs. The favorite was Jacque Mercer, a dark-haired beauty from Litchfield, Arizona.

The day started like every other. At breakfast, I asked Alice her plans for the day. She said she was going to visit a nearby wildlife area. A rare bird, a black skimmer, had been spotted there, and she hoped to photograph it. I suppose she told me the name of the place she intended to visit, but it didn't register. I was absorbed in a story in the *Press* about a sheet metal workers' strike at the RCA plant in Camden. Eddie and I had been wondering if and when an organizational attempt was going to be made at Dunlaur Electronics. We talked about it often, speculating on the cost of having a union in our shop.

"Are you taking Adam with you?" I asked her, barely looking up from the paper as I worked on my eggs and bacon.

"No, Mrs. Wilson is coming today," she said, leaning over the range. "He'll be okay with her. And I'll be home before she's ready to leave."

She was preparing breakfast for Adam. Her hair fell forward over her forehead. She was wearing a white, masculine-looking shirt. Its sleeves were rolled up revealing her forearms, slim, round, tanned; capable hands and rosy arms, slicing, mixing, stirring. A drop of perspiration dropped into Adam's cereal. She dipped her forefinger in the cereal then sucked on it.

"Needs a pinch of cinnamon," she murmured to herself. As she turned to face me with her finger still in her mouth, her eyes crinkled with suppressed laughter.

She'd aroused me. I set down the paper and went to her. I held her close.

"Wait a moment, Jack," she said, backing off. "I just remembered . . . I have something for you upstairs. Finish your eggs and come on up."

She was in our bedroom, smiling that great smile. It lit up her face. Dancing eyes—they shone.

"Whatcha got for me?" I asked.

"Me," she laughed, throwing herself on the bed, arms spread wide, reaching up to me. "Now take off those silly pants."

I had no problem being late for work that day.

* * *

I adjusted my necktie before the mirror in our hall entryway as Alice stood at my side, brushing imaginary lint from my shoulder. We smiled at each other in the mirror. She handed me my hat and briefcase and held Adam up to me. He put an arm around my neck and kissed me on my cheek. "Bye, Daddy. I love you."

"Bye, Adam," I replied. "I love you too. And you, too, Alice. I love you too." I smiled as I kissed her. "Thanks for a wonderful morning. I hope you find your bird."

She and Adam stood in the open doorway as I left. "Goodbye, darling," she waved.

"Goodbye, Daddy." Adam copied the wave.

Such an ordinary morning.

* * *

Mrs. Wilson called me that afternoon.

"Mr. Laurel, it's almost five o'clock, and Mrs. Laurel isn't home yet. I usually leave at four."

71

Disappearance

I QUESTIONED MRS. WILSON. "Did she telephone you?"

"No, Mr. Laurel. Not a word. And I can't leave Adam alone."

"I'll start for home. Wait for me, please."

Alice kept one of our walkie-talkies in her car, and I carried one in my briefcase, but away from our tower in Atlantic City, their range was just a mile or two. If she was not near a telephone, there was no way for her to communicate.

"Mr. Laurel, that woman Zena called for Mrs. Laurel, but she'd already gone. That was 'bout eleven-thirty."

I asked Eddie to make some calls, to my mom, to Alice's mother, to Evie. I said I'd call him when I got to the house.

On the drive home, I worried about the possibilities. Had her car broken down in some remote place? I knew some of the wildlife preserves were large and desolate.

Had she been in an accident? Or maybe she went deep into the woods and misjudged the time. What was the name of the place? I was sure she'd told me, but I hadn't registered it. I was angry with myself about that.

Other bad images. Alice in a hospital following an accident. The station wagon stuck in a rut, or sinking in a swamp, or it won't start. Alice sitting on the running board, trying to figure out how to get help, broadcasting on her walkie-talkie, hoping for a response from someone, anyone.

What was most likely? She'd misjudged or lost track of the time. She will be home when I arrive. The thought buoyed me. By the time I neared our street, I was sure her station wagon would be in the drive.

It wasn't.

***

"Mrs. Wilson, has Alice called?"

"No, sir, not a word. Only Mr. Dunauskas. He said he called around but nobody knows anything."

"Can you stay late and give Adam dinner? I have to find Alice."

"I'll stay as long as you need me."

I called Mom. She said she'd come with Violet and stay as well. I said I would call in every half hour. Before I left, I wrote down as much as I knew and everything Mrs. Wilson knew. I knew what Alice was wearing, which camera she took. The binoculars, the earrings, her diamond ring. Was she wearing a necklace or a pin? Which one? Mrs. Wilson didn't know where Alice was headed. "To see birds" was all she knew.

I called Alan Goren's apartment. I wanted to talk to Zena.

"Zena, Alice hasn't come home yet. Mrs. Wilson said you called soon after she left this morning. Why did you call for her?"

"I'm sure it's nothing, Jack," she said. "I had a thought about her and was checking to see that everything was all right."

"What kind of thought?" I pressed.

"I'm sure it's nothing," she repeated. "I had a thought that she should stay home today, but by the time I called, she'd already gone out."

I rushed out and started the car. Wait. Where was I going? Where to start? The police. Of course. That's where I'll get help.

72

Margate Police

Cops were in line, waiting to book three arrests with the desk sergeant: a shoplifter, a drunk and disorderly, a mugger. All were in good humor—the cops, the prisoners, the desk sergeant. It was almost an hour before the sergeant waved me over to his desk.

"What's your story?" he asked.

I told him then asked to see Detective Al Burns. Burns knew about the threatening note back in 1947. After taking a brief statement, the sergeant called Burns. Burns came in a few minutes later and led me to a small room with a table and a few chairs.

"Have a seat, Jack," he said as he scanned my statement. "Tell me all about it."

I gave him as much detail as I could. A description of Alice. A description of her station wagon; a description of our dog, Max. I included Mrs. Wilson's description of how Alice was dressed: her half-carat diamond engagement ring in the gold setting and her plain gold wedding band, the mosaic broach, the binoculars and the camera.

"This is very early, Jack," he said. "She's probably stuck with a broken down car. If she doesn't show up by morning, I'll send a car tomorrow to the Brigantine Wildlife Preserve. Does that sound familiar? That's the closest one. Or maybe Makepeace Lake? That's less than forty miles from here. There's also Goose Pond Preserve. Jack, there's a lot of places she could have gone."

"I'm sorry. The name of the place didn't register when she said it. But the bird she was looking for is a something-or-other *skimmer*. It made me think of a straw hat."

He wrote it down. "Okay, Jack. You go home. Hopefully she'll show up tonight."

He wrote his telephone number on a memo pad. He said I should call him in the morning after ten o'clock. I called the house before I left the station. Eddie and Evie and Mom and Violet were there, but they had no news. I headed home, despondent. What had I expected the police to do? Start a search tonight? To search where?

On the way home, it occurred to me that Alice may have been kidnapped. It was a chilling thought.

73

Burns on the Job

I CALLED BURNS AT ten the next morning.

"It's Jack Laurel. Any news about my wife?"

"No, Jack. I'm sorry. I was hoping you'd have heard from her by now."

"Not a word."

"I know the name of the bird she was looking for," he said. "It's a black skimmer. It's uncommon in the area but has been spotted at the Brigantine Preserve. I'm sending a car over there."

"I'll go with," I said. "Maybe I'll see something they won't recognize."

"Okay," he said. "C'mon down. Now. I'll go with you."

74

The Brigantine Wildlife Preserve

THE BRIGANTINE WILDLIFE Preserve covered fifty-six hundred acres. An eight-mile dirt road circled through the preserve. Most of the preserve was salt marsh, with a built-up road cutting through it to give clear sighting opportunities for great distances.

About eight hundred acres of the preserve was an impenetrable, jungle-like swamp of wild shrubbery, pine trees, thick weeds, and grasses. In that area, nothing was visible from the dirt road except the immediate growth at the edge of the road. Even on a bright day, the interior was black. The swamp growth was too dense for sunlight to penetrate.

We cruised the road at less than a walking pace. Nothing. The dirt surface was packed hard. There were faint traces of many sets of tire treads. When we came to the swamp, we stopped the car and walked along both edges of the road. Visibility into the swamp was not even six feet. We walked along the entire perimeter, searching for any clue—something on the road or some sign of disturbance in the swamp. Nothing.

Burns said the Trenton Police had a helicopter. They would lend it for a flyover of the swamp. Maybe from the air we'd see something.

The ranger on duty couldn't recall a Ford station wagon entering or leaving the preserve the day before but said that didn't mean one didn't. The gate to the perimeter road had been open for months, and the administration building was set fifty yards off the road. Cars entered and left regularly with no one paying attention. The ranger suggested we talk to the maintenance man. He cruised the road regularly. Maybe he saw something.

We waited a half hour until the maintenance truck arrived. Burns called the driver over. Did he see a Ford station wagon yesterday?

"Well, I saw a station wagon. Didn't notice if it was a Ford."

"When did you see it?"

"Yesterday morning. Drove in around ten, left around noon."

It was a dead end, as Mrs. Wilson said Alice didn't leave the house until eleven. We drove back to the police station, dispirited.

75

Nothing

A L," I ASKED. "Could this be a kidnapping?"

"Doesn't feel like it. You'd have heard something by now."

"What do I do?" I asked.

"There's nothing you can do," he answered. I'll write up a missing persons report with the information we have. You'll need to provide a photo. The report will go out to every state and local police station in South Jersey up to and including Trenton. There's a good chance the station wagon will get spotted."

"I have to do more than that," I said. "I'll get a story into the *Press* with a picture. I'll make up reward posters and circulars with her picture. I'll get them posted and distributed everywhere within fifty miles of here."

"That could help," Burns said. "But you'll have trouble getting more than a little piece into the *Press*, and I doubt they'll run a picture. But go ahead, give it a try. Meanwhile, we'll be working our end."

* * *

For the next few days, I clung to the hope that I would get a ransom call or letter. Nothing. Violet moved in. Someone had to be home with Adam. I was busy calling reporters, putting up posters, and very little else.

I brought a Dunlaur secretary to the house to answer calls in response to the posters. There were dozens of them. She typed up the information from every call, and I delivered her reports to Burns daily. I thought he was starting to get annoyed with me. One day, he suggested I hire a private investigator to run down all the leads. He said he didn't have the manpower.

I went to see Attorney Durells. He gave me the name and number of his private investigator, whom I hired immediately. His fee was forty dollars per day plus expenses. He said he took only one assignment at a time and he'd be working my case seven days a week, including nights if something came up that needed immediate action.

What else could I do? Burns said our chances of finding Alice were diminishing. "Sorry, Jack, but that's the reality. These cases get cold and the more time that passes, the colder it gets."

* * *

Violet was a take-charge kind of a girl. She began supervising Mrs. Wilson, who had been kind enough to increase her hours and take over the cooking duties. Both of them looked after Adam, who continually asked, *Where is Mommy?* We told him she was visiting an old friend. *When will Mommy come home?* Just as soon as she can. He pouted and cried. His bewilderment and sense of loss tore at my heart.

Eddie and Evie came every night. Weeks passed. Nothing.

Violet prepared dinner every night. One night at dinner, a few weeks after the disappearance, Eddie pulled me aside, nervously, to say, "Jack, I'm sorry to ask, but I have to. Can you start coming in to work, for at least a couple of hours a day? I'm trying to handle everything, but it's getting out of hand. I moved another desk and an expeditor into your office. He's a help, but we can't keep up. Your sales reps are on the phone all day long. We deal with them the best we can, but they need you. I don't want to lay this on you, Jack, but I have to. And actually, I think it might be good for you. There's only so much you can do at home. Whattaya think?"

"You're right, Eddie," I said. "I've started to think the same thing. I'll start tomorrow. Nothing happens in the early morning. I'll come in at seven for a couple hours. Then I'll come back at six in the afternoon for a couple of hours."

Eddie was visibly relieved.

Poor guy. He must have struggled with that speech for a week.

76

Back to Work . . . Sort Of

I WENT TO WORK the next day. I had been away for almost a month, and the backup was overwhelming. Everyone was very deferential. They spoke to me in somber, hushed voices, as if plain straightforward talk would wound me in some way. I picked at the work, made phone calls, did my best, but I knew I was not functioning well. I couldn't summon the energy to sound positive and vigorous on the phone. I would have to try harder.

It was a life in limbo, a fall from a cliff. Hope for a good ending faded with a growing certainty. I dreaded the terrible news that would come one day.

Ironically it was during this time that Dunlaur got its biggest contract for printed circuits. Our North Central rep closed a deal with the Westinghouse factory in Minneapolis. A week later, Eddie showed me through our new printed circuit facility that did away with almost all handwork and quadrupled our capacity.

"We're now the state-of-the-art plant," he said, sweeping his outstretched arm across the motorized conveyor belt that carried the finished product to the packing area. "Nobody's gonna edge us out by making a better product or making it cheaper. But we gotta keep improving and lowering costs. We're number one in this business, and we gotta hold our position."

* * *

Two days later, I got a call from Georgie.

"Bobo wants to see you," he said. "I'll pick you up in an hour."

"What's it about, Georgie?" A summons from Bobo was not to be ignored.

"Bobo wants to see you," he repeated.

He came for me in the new Cadillac. Frankie was with him.

I climbed into the back. "What's up, guys?"

"Relax, Jack, nothing bad. Bobo wants to see you."

Bobo was waiting for me in his office over Trucci's. He was not alone. Two men sat in semidarkness in a corner. They wore hats with brims pulled low. I could not make out their faces.

"Jack, c'mon in over here," he said, greeting me with a strong hand-shake. "I just heard about your Alice. You shoulda come to me right away. I had to read about it in the *Press*? Ya shoulda come to me right away," he repeated.

"Who are these guys?" I asked, indicating the two men in the corner.

"Never mind them, Jack," Bobo answered. "They're a coupla my boys. You don't have to know them. Now, tell me everything."

I told him everything. Why? Did he know something? Did he have a lead?

"I got nothin' over here, Jack," he said, somberly, "but I'm gonna get on it. Get me some a'them posters with her picture." He turned to the men in the corner. "Write down everything," he said, "*everything*, especially what she was driving and what she was wearing. And any jewelry and anything else valuable. The camera. Binoculars. Anything and everything."

One of the strangers spoke. "What kinda camera?"

"It's a Leica," I said.

"What's it worth?" he asked.

"Kind of expensive," I said. "Maybe three hundred fifty."

"See if you can find the bill," the man said. "I want the model and serial number. Same for the binoculars."

"Okay, Jack," Bobo said. "That's it. Georgie, take him home. I'm sure he has stuff to do."

"You don't know how much I appreciate this, Bobo," I said. "The police have nothing. My private investigator has nothing. Even if you find nothing, you have my thanks."

"It's okay, Jack. For old time's sake. Go home. We'll do what we can over here." He turned away. I was dismissed. As I left, he turned back for a moment. "And fire the PI," he said. "We don't need him."

77

Coping

IRETURNED TO WORK. There was relief in working, in focusing on something other than Alice's disappearance and Adam's unhappiness. I slipped back into a full-time routine, more than full time. I made it a point to go home every day from noon until one and again from five to six so I could be with Adam. He greeted me always with the same question, "Is Mommy coming home today?"

After dinner, I went back to work for several hours more. I wanted to be tired when I came home. It helped to sleep.

Violet moved in, now a senior at Atlantic City High. I hired Mrs. Wilson for extra hours so Violet could finish her school day and spend an hour or so on after-school activities before coming home and taking charge. She ran the household. She was like a big sister to Adam, a mother figure at times.

More than one friend told me it didn't look good for Violet to have the role of homemaker, mother, and . . . what else? They said, "You know, Jack, she's a beautiful young woman, and you're only twenty-five." I made it a point to avoid those friends thereafter when I could.

In truth, Violet had blossomed. More than her good looks, it was her manner that made her so attractive. She was always smiling, soft-spoken, an eager listener—possessed of many of the qualities I adored in Alice. But there was no romance in the relationship. I felt like a brother to her.

It was four months after the disappearance that I got another call from Georgie.

"Bobo wants to see you," he said. "I'll be right over to pick you up."

78

Danny Merino

B OBO WAS IN HIS office. Frankie was with him. Also another man, someone I didn't know. He looked to be about sixty, slightly stooped, a full head of bristly white hair, thick eyeglasses. He seemed comfortable and relaxed. He was drinking a cup of coffee.

"Jack," Bobo said. "This over here is Danny Merino. He is a pawn broker, has a shop in Trenton. Listen to his story."

He turned to the man and said, "Go 'head, Danny. Tell Jack over here what you told us a couple months ago."

This was Danny Merino's story:

"I own and manage the Old Gold Pawn Shop, on Olden Avenue in Trenton. That's near your Dunlaur Electronics store, been in business there twenty-five years. I know everybody in Trenton—all the cops, judges, politicians, most of the crooks. Me and Bobo go way back. I used to be a *nomo* for Bobo. I had a territory up around Maryland Avenue. I had the bookmaking and the numbers. I owe Bobo big time for what he did for me once back then. I always stayed in touch.

"I run a legit business," he added. "Ain't been in trouble in twenty-five years."

"Get to the point, Danny," Bobo said.

"Sure, Bobo," Merino said, "but I want Jack to know something about me so he'll understand what I'm gonna tell him." He took a sip of his coffee before continuing. "One day, this guy comes in with some stuff to pawn. He has a half-carat diamond ring, no inscription on the band, good quality, maybe a VVS1. He has a one-inch mosaic broach—a country landscape, gold back and rim."

My eyes widened. Was he describing Alice's stuff?

"The guy has a pair of Bausch & Lomb binoculars, eight by twenty-five millimeters with a three-quarter-inch brown leather strap and a light brown leather case. An expensive pair of binoculars."

I jumped up. "It's Alice's stuff! What else? What else?"

"The guy has a Leica camera, a 1946 Model III C."

"It's her stuff!" I cried out. "What happened?" I wanted to grab him, get the story out faster. "Tell me, tell me."

Bobo stood and wrapped an arm around my shoulder. "Take it easy, Jack," he said. "You'll hear it all. Sit down."

Merino continued, "The guy didn't look kosher. He was obviously nervous. I figured it was stolen goods. He kept looking at the door. I opened the camera. There was no film in it. A serial number was on the insert side of the film box.

"I told him I was only guessing at the value of the diamond ring. I told him I could go a hundred and a half for the four items, but, if he could wait a day, I'd get the ring appraised and might do better. He says no, he'll take the stuff someplace else.

"I said, tell you what, I run a legitimate shop. I'll let you have two hundred now. You come back tomorrow and maybe I'll be able to give you more, if you give me a chance to appraise the ring. I don't want to cheat you. The stuff may be worth more—maybe two fifty or three hundred for the lot. He says, *Gimme the two hunnert*. He'll call me tomorrow to see if he can get more.

"I filled out a pawn ticket. He said his name is Tom Barnes. He gives me the address of a cheap hotel in Trenton, the Jefferson on Sixth. I figured I'd never hear from him and the name and address was phony. When he left, I stuck my head out the door. He had a car parked a couple stores away, a dark blue Chevy sedan, maybe just a couple years old. I caught the license number when the car passed by, Pennsylvania tags."

I was on my feet. "You let him get away!"

"Stop it, Jack," Bobo said. "You owe my friend over here. Shut up and let him finish."

Merino was unruffled by my outbursts. "The Leica is an expensive camera. I thought I could trace the owner through the serial number. It took me a few days, but I got the name on the warranty. Alice Laurel."

I broke down. I was choking.

Bobo sat me back down and sat beside me. He rubbed my back. "Take it easy, son. Take it easy."

Merino went on. "I recognized the name, Alice Laurel, from a police flyer. She's an Atlantic City girl, so I called Bobo to ask him what to do. Bobo asked me to describe the guy and every detail about him. I said I'll do that and even better. I have a camera up on a shelf behind my counter. I got it rigged so I can take a picture of whoever is at the counter, just by pressing a plate on the wall behind me. I press it with my ass—doesn't alarm nobody. I cough to hide the sound of the shutter. I held the ring up like to get a good look under the lamp. The guy looks up too. I bump my ass. I get his picture."

I stood again, but before I could find any words, Bobo handed me a photograph. "Here's the guy," he said.

I felt faint, and Georgie saw me stumble. He put an arm around me and helped me back into the chair. I recognized the man in the photo. It was that guy, the bum with the rifle who stopped Eddie and me in the Pine Barrens. That day back in June 1947, when we were driving away from Wilkens Lake—that day when we did the aerial installation at Spencer's and gave two kids a lift to the lake to go fishing.

"Where is he?" I said hoarsely. "Did the cops find him?"

"I'll tell you the rest," Bobo said. "Then you'll tell me. I got connections in Trenton. I sent those two guys you met over here. The car was stolen in Jersey. The license plate was stolen off a different car, a Pennsylvania car. That made it harder to trace, but my guys are good. Took them two months, but they found him in Newark."

"You found him? Where is he?"

"Easy, Jack. There's more to tell you. We got the whole story from him. I got it on a tape offa that tape recorder you and your partner gave me. We had to rough him up, but we got the whole story. We made him take us to where it happened. That's an ugly story. His real name is Norris, Charles

Norris. You'll have to think about what you want to do about this. I got the guy himself tied up and gagged in the cellar of a boarded-up farmhouse out past Absecon. There's two guys with him all the time. He's yours, Jack. Do what you want with him, or you can give him to us. Your choice.

"And here, Jack," Bobo said, lifting a paper bag from the floor under his desk. "Here's Alice's stuff."

Spilling the bag's contents onto the desk, I sobbed uncontrollably before uttering through clenched teeth, "I want . . . to see him."

"I knew you would," Bobo said. "We'll go, but first, listen to the tape." He opened the lid to the tape recorder and placed a forefinger on the play button.

79

What Happened to Alice

I T'S AN UGLY story you're gonna hear," Bobo said.

"How did you get him to talk?" I asked.

"We know how over here," Bobo said. "We prepare the guy with a work-out. Then we strap him to a chair. He's hurtin', and gettin' real scared what's comin' next. Then I get real close to his face. I tell him like this:

"Look here, you piece of shit. I know what's true when I hear it. And I know bullshit. And we gonna hurt you ... bad, when you tell me bullshit. When I'm satisfied you told me everything, the truth, I'll make you tell me again. And again. Maybe three more times, maybe five, maybe ten. When you tell me the truth, you'll repeat it, always the same. If you lie to me, we'll hurt you, bad ... real bad. In the end, you gonna tell me everything, just as it happened. You gonna be glad to tell me the truth because you don't wanna get hurt no more. I been gettin' the real story outta shits like you for twenty-five years. Save your-self. Tell me everything ... the truth. The truth ain't gonna hurt you as much as tellin' me bullshit.

"Jack," Bobo continued. "I got his whole story on this tape machine. It's the truth. I know the truth when a guy finally spills."

This was Norris's story, told haltingly, with long pauses:

"I'm Charles Norris. I killed Alice Laurel. I was out to punish her husband, Jack Laurel. He and his friend beat me up in the Pine Barrens back in 1947, near Wilkens Lake. They were drivin' a station wagon. I got the license number. It took me a long time to trace it to the owner. More'n a year. That was Edward Dunauskas ... but it was the other guy who beat me up. I found where Dunauskas lived. I watched him for a long time, every day, until one day I spotted the other guy with him. I found out the other guy's name: Jack Laurel. He's an Atlantic City war hero. But he ain't no hero to me. I was in the War, same as him. I was in combat, same as him. Bet I saw more combat than him. I found out where he lived. I watched his house. I put a note in his car. That scared him. He went to the cops. I saw his wife. I watched her drive away in that Ford station wagon, almost every day. I got even with Jack Laurel."

Norris stopped. The tape ran on silently for ten seconds. There was a sharp slapping sound. Norris stifled a scream, then continued.

"I used to hang out where Wellington Avenue runs into the Black Horse Pike, 'cause Alice Laurel usta go that way most mornings around ten or eleven. That day, I stood by the road on the Pike, and when I spotted her coming in the station wagon, I thumbed for a ride. I was shaved. I was clean, wearing a new pair of chinos and a clean white shirt. I needed to look clean and respectable so's she'd stop and pick me up. I had a canvas bag with me. That's where I had my stuff, a knife and some rope, rags, a roll of tape. I asked her where she's headed. She said she's going to Makepeace Lake. I said great, I know where that is. You can drop me off on the Pike near the entrance. She had this big black dog in the back of the wagon. I knew she would have the dog with her, so I had a half a hotdog for him with a pill in it. When we were about ten miles from the lake, I turned around and scratched his head and said he's a good dog. I gave him the hotdog. He was asleep a coupla minutes before we got to the entrance.

"She told me she was going to look for a certain kind of bird, a black skimmer. I asked could I come and watch. She said okay, I could help her maybe by taking pictures if she spotted the bird in her binoculars.

"When she stopped the wagon and we got out is when I grabbed her and stuck my knife against her belly. I only wanted to keep her from screaming but she tried to punch me and kick me. I punched her in the stomach. I punched her hard on the side of her head. She fell down. I hit her again, a coupla times until she passed out. Her skirt went up above her knees. I saw way up her legs. It turned me on . . ."

The tape went silent again. Then a thud, like a fist going into Norris's face. A groan, a whimper. He resumed.

"I pulled off all her clothes. I spread her legs. I stuck it to her . . . then she started to come to. I was still in her. She was gonna scream . . . I pressed a bundle of her clothes against her face. She kicked and tried to push me away. She twisted her head from side to side but I pressed down. I smothered her. She stopped moving. It was an accident. I didn't mean it. I only wanted to keep her quiet. I ain't no killer, I just wanted to punish Jack Laurel for what he did to me.

"After, I cleaned up. I dragged the dog out and killed it. I dragged her and the dog about twenty-five feet into the swamp. Once you're in there, you might as well be a mile into it. Nobody's gonna find you. But I didn't mean to kill her."

"That's the end, Jack," Bobo said, turning off the tape recorder. "What do you want us to do with him? We can finish him off, easy or hard. We can tape up his mouth and leave him there in the dark to die. That will take a few days. Or you can finish him off yourself. You killed a few Japs. You can kill this piece of shit. What's your pleasure?"

"Take me to him," I said.

<h1 style="text-align:center">80</h1>

<h1 style="text-align:center">Face-to-Face</h1>

I CLIMBED INTO BOBO'S Cadillac with Georgie and Frankie. It was a forty-five-minute drive. We pulled up behind a decrepit old farmhouse, far back from the road, boarded up—no other houses or buildings as far as I could see, just hundreds of acres of untended weeds and scrub and tangled vines.

The house had a below-grade windowless root cellar. There, under the dim light of a single bare bulb, was Norris, naked, strapped into a wooden kitchen chair with duct tape. A strip of tape was across his mouth. The chair had a mesh seat that had been torn out so that Norris's testicles and penis dangled over a bedpan on the floor. The bedpan needed dumping.

His face was bruised. His arms, chest, and legs were covered with deep welts, as if he'd been struck repeatedly with a thin strap or a whip. A line of dried blood ran down his chin from the corner of his mouth and dropped down onto his shoulder and continued onto his chest.

I tilted up his chin and looked into his eyes. "Remember me, Charlie?"

He closed his eyes and nodded slightly.

I resisted the impulse to beat him. Or maybe to kill him.

"I want him to take me there," I choked. "I got to see her."

Bobo put his hand on my shoulder. "No good, Jack," he said quietly. "We was there. It's been eight months. Animals got to her and the dog. You don't want to see it."

I broke down completely. I sank to the floor.

Bobo and Georgie lifted me to my feet. "C'mon, Jack," Bobo said. "We'll take you somewhere where you can be alone. Charlie over here ain't goin' nowhere. Whattaya want us to do with him? You got some thinkin' to do."

81

What to Do with Charlie Norris?

I FELT WEAK. BLOOD pounded in my temples. I had to sit. I had to rest. I had to think. I had to be alone. I asked Bobo to take me back to the Dunlaur plant.

When we neared Atlantic City, I made two calls from a pay phone. I told Eddie I wouldn't be returning to work that day, I had something pressing to take care of. I told Mrs. Wilson that Violet should have dinner with Adam and not to wait up for me. I wouldn't be home tonight.

Georgie drove me to the Dunlaur plant. I did not enter the building. I went to my car and drove away.

The very northern end of Brigantine Island is empty for a half mile before the Brigantine Wildlife Preserve begins. I sat on the beach, resting against a piece of the broken sea wall. I had to think.

82

Alone

SPRING IS A TIME of great beauty at the Jersey shore. It was May, and the days were lengthening. It was late afternoon, but the sun was hanging halfway above the horizon, reluctant to set, growing larger as it descended. It wouldn't slip below the horizon until eight forty-five.

The sun is a giant red ball when it rises, then shrinks as it arcs across the sky until it is only a small silver disk at noon, then it grows big and swollen again as it finishes its arc and sinks to its sunset. I didn't learn the answer to that spectacle until twenty years later.

I stared at a serene world. Blue sky, bluer sea, bright with silver flashes. The breeze was fresh, delicious with the salty tang of the ocean. Seabirds wheeled overhead, their cries filled the air. My thoughts slipped back to that sunrise on December 26, 1943, the day of our assault on Cape Gloucester. The scene was the same. I was back there, on the troop ship, scanning the horizon through my field glasses before the action began. The same song sprang into my head, *I'll be seeing you . . . in all the old familiar places . . .* I could not turn it off. I choked back tears. I was alone.

Until today, Alice's disappearance was a crushing mystery, with me all the time. I had been unable to accept that she was gone forever. Had I held out hope? For a while, yes, but now there were no more illusions. All hope was gone. The image of Alice's horror flooded my mind like a one-second snippet of a movie. I saw her, swinging her arms like pistons, trying to hit him, flailing, kicking at him, those lovely legs that opened for me that very morning while we laughed and loved only four hours earlier.

That scene would flash into my head, uninvited, over and over again for years. I didn't want to see it, but I could not stop it. Even now, all these many years later, it still comes to me, uninvited and unannounced. Not too often, thankfully, or I would be unable to function in any way. To myself, I call it *the scene*.

Her murderer was mine. What would I do with him?

The air was turning cold. A wind sprang up. I climbed in my car and drove to a nearby motel. I had to be alone.

* * *

The next morning, I washed up and drove to Bobo's office above Trucci's. I knew what I wanted done with Charles Norris.

83

Bobo: The Way It Is

GEORGIE ANSWERED my knock.

"It's Jack," he said opening the door.

Bobo came to me and put his arm around my shoulder. "Sit over here, Jack," he said. "You don't look so good. Had any breakfast?"

"If I could have a coffee . . ."

I sipped at the coffee. My hand trembled. I tried to compose myself. "Bobo," I said. "You said he's mine. I done a lot of killing in the War, but I'm not a killer. I want to turn him over to the police."

Bobo and Georgie looked at each other then back at me. Neither spoke for a few seconds. Then Bobo: "No good, Jack. You ain't thought it through over here. How ya gonna do it? You gonna walk him in to a police station? Or maybe leave him tied up on the pavement in front of a precinct building . . . with his confession taped onto him?

"No, Jack, it won't work. All you'll do is get me and my boys in trouble. Big trouble. And you know what'll happen to Charlie? Nothing! He'll tell 'em we beat the confession outta him. He'll deny everything. And he'll finger me and some of my guys and Danny Merino, the pawnbroker. Alice's stuff? He stole a car and found Alice's stuff in it. The only real evidence will be one of the boys what saw Alice's remains and the dog's because Charlie took him there. But you think I'll let my boys testify? C'mon, Jack, get real. *We'll* be in trouble. Charlie will walk.

"Jack, he's yours to do what you want, but not that. You're one of us. Jack, you're like a son to me. You're my family. Do you think I'da done this for anybody? When that bastard lowlife hurt you, he hurt me. We protect each other. Killin' is what he needs. And that's too good for him."

I let his words sink in. He was right, of course.

"I can't be his executioner," I said.

214

Bobo stood over me. That look. Hard. Brow knitted. He studied me, motionless, silently, with unblinking eyes. Nobody spoke for quite a while. Then he spoke over his shoulder. "Georgie, get Durells over here."

84

Waiting for Durells

WE SAT IN SILENCE, waiting for the attorney.

Bobo sat at the desk, smoking cigarettes and studying handwritten reports on ruled yellow pages. Georgie read the *Atlantic City Press*. I closed my eyes and tried to shut out everything.

Durells arrived. He entered with a broad smile and a cheery hello. He saw me. "Hey, Jack," he approached with a firm handshake. "What's up? Nothing serious, I hope." He turned to Bobo. He started to say something but sensed the grim atmosphere. He sat, and his demeanor changed. "What's wrong, fellows?" he asked, soberly.

Bobo turned to me. "Jack, whyncha go downstairs. You ain't had breakfast. I'll get Nick to fix you some ham and eggs. Take your time. Me and Larry got a lotta thinkin' to do over here. I'll call down when you should come back up."

I picked at the breakfast. My heart was still racing. The pounding in my head subsided, leaving behind a dull headache. I called Eddie.

He wanted to know what's wrong. He was worried. "Where are you, Jack? What's goin' on?"

"I'm taking off a coupla days. It's a personal thing. Don't worry. I'll explain when I see you."

I called Violet with the same message. She was not as easily put off as Eddie. "Jack, I know something is wrong. Tell me. Can I help?"

"It's okay," I said. "Just look after Adam, please. I'll be okay." I hung up before she could ask another question. I tried to relax, to make my mind a blank.

It was an hour before Nick told me Bobo wanted me to come back up to his office.

85

Durells for the Defense

I SLUMPED INTO AN easy chair. "What's to do?" I asked.

Durells answered. "Bobo told me the whole thing. Jack, Bobo is correct. We can't turn Charlie over to the police. If I were his lawyer, he would never even get indicted. Take away the confession, which won't be allowed because it was coerced, and there's nothing except a stolen car. Not a piece of hard evidence except he took two of the boys to the crime scene. Even that might not get in because he was coerced, but anyway, we can't let the boys become witnesses. God only knows what I would get out of them if I were the defense lawyer doing the cross-examination. Yes, I'm good, but so are most of the public defenders—good enough for that—good enough that the whole organization is jeopardized if any one of the boys ever is examined in a courtroom."

He paused. "No, Jack. Bobo's right—there's no turning him in. He'll get off and we'll be in trouble."

"What then?" I asked. "I'm no killer, and I don't want anybody doing any killing for me."

Durells studied me through half-closed eyes. He leaned toward me. "I have a solution," he said.

86

The Durells Solution

JACK," DURELLS SAID, "I'm talking to you as though you are part of Bobo's organization. Not even as though. You are. The organization lives by this rule: Protect one another. Without that, the organization would collapse.

"What Bobo did for you is what he would do for anyone in the organization. And everyone knows that every other one has his back. Maybe Charlie should have been dealt with in the normal way. But Bobo has such regard for you that he wanted to give Charlie to you to do what you want with him—anything . . . anything, that is, other than leaving him to the judicial system. Charlie doesn't deserve that. Killing is what he deserves. That's what justice demands. Even if the system got a conviction, most likely, he'll get life. New Jersey doesn't like the death penalty. Up here in a New Jersey prison, he will spend the rest of his life being fed and clothed and getting medical attention without having to work. He'll get magazines and watch movies. Probably a better life than the one he's used to.

"You don't want to mete out real justice on your own, so we have a quandary. But there is a solution. This is it: I know a man who runs a small southern county. I won't tell you the county's name or the state it's in. My man is the boss of everything, including the judge, the DA's office, the police, and the prison. They call it a prison farm—sounds benign, but it isn't. It's a hellhole for the prisoners. They are all lifers. They are put in ankle chains the day they arrive, and the chains stay on permanently until they die. No prisoner ever leaves alive.

"Every county has unsolved crimes—killings, rapes, multiple robberies. My man will get Charlie railroaded, convicted of a crime in that county and sentenced to life. Charlie will never make a phone call or send a letter. No one will ever know what happened to him. He'll disappear. He'll never have a good minute. His life will be work, work, every day, hard work, bad food,

"

not enough of it, not enough sleep, a life not worth living, until he gets sick and dies or just dies from being played out. That's the solution, Jack, and it's worse than being killed."

Durells paused to study my reaction. I was having trouble absorbing what he'd said.

"There's something else, Jack. Alice's disappearance will always be a mystery. You understand that, don't you? You can never tell anybody anything. No one. Not your partner, Dunauskas, not your family, not even your own son when he grows up. Do you understand that?

"And one more thing," he said. "Money. You're doing well in your business, so you should be able to handle this. There's twenty-five hundred dollars for my southern friend, a grand for Danny Merino, the pawn broker, and eight grand for Bobo and his boys. Okay?"

"Do it," I said, "but there's something I want. Gather up the remains, Alice and the dog. Have them cremated and bring me the ashes."

87

What Now?

So, I thought, NOW I belong to Bobo. If he calls on me, I will have to respond. And Larry Durells knows it too. How will that cloud Dunlaur's client-attorney relationship with Durells?

The worst of it is that I can never reveal what happened to Alice, not to anyone. Not to Eddie, or Evie, or Alice's parents. I will grieve alone and carry the secret to my grave.

Instead of hope being my constant companion, I had a new dark companion. It would be with me always, the knowing and being unable to share it and unable to shed it. The secret was only two days old. I knew its enormity had not even begun to touch me.

I had to go away, to be alone. I needed to grieve, alone. I had to adjust to my new reality.

I left Bobo's office and went home. Mrs. Wilson was there, having temporarily moved in to help with Adam. Violet was still in school.

I put on a cheery face. "Hi, Mrs. Wilson, I'm home. Gotta pack a few things for an extended trip to visit some of our distributors."

I showered, shaved, and put on clean clothes. I went to Adam.

He missed me. "Daddy, I miss you," he hugged me. "Is Mommy coming home today?"

I held back tears. I lifted my boy onto my knee and kissed him. "No, Adam, not today. I'm sorry."

88

Getting Away

I TRIED TO COMPOSE myself as I drove to the Dunlaur plant to see Eddie. He was at his desk, studying a drawing so intently he didn't hear me come in. He was wearing the special glasses he'd built for himself. Their one-inch long cylinders with magnified lenses acted as a microscope, allowing him to study intricate drawings while keeping his hands free.

"Eddie . . ." I said, and he leaped out of his seat.

He swept off the glasses and came to me. He grasped me by my upper arms and peered into my eyes. "Jack, what's going on?" he asked. "You look so tired. Where've you been? We've all been worried."

"Nothing much," I lied. "Sometimes I get overwhelmed about Alice. I had to be alone for a while. But I'm okay. Really. And you know what? I'm gonna go on a goodwill trip. I'm gonna make a short swing around our east central territory. I'll visit our eight distributors in the territory. I'll show them our latest stuff and fill them in on what's coming, and I'll find out what other electronics companies are offering them. It will be a great customer relations move, and it will be good for me. I'm trying to build my life around the idea that Alice is never coming back, and I need some time alone to sort things out."

Eddie relaxed. He motioned me to sit and spoke into his intercom. "Kathy, will you bring me and Jack a couple coffees, please?" He studied me carefully, his eyes scanning my face. After a moment, he looked away. "Okay, Jack," he said. "Sure. Great idea. But it will feel strange. Do you realize we've been together every single day since we formed Dunlaur? It was a weird feeling that you weren't around for two days and I didn't know where you were. When do you intend to make this trip?"

"I'll start off tomorrow. I'll be gone—"

"You can't go tomorrow, Jack," he broke in. "Violet is graduating on Friday. You know that. You gotta be here."

I sucked in a breath. I'd forgotten about Violet's graduation. "Sure, Eddie," I said. "I clean forgot. I'll wait until Monday."

89

Graduation Day

I HADN'T VISITED ATLANTIC City High since I graduated in June 1942. Could it be only eight years? It felt like a lifetime since that bittersweet day marking the beginning of my journey into manhood. Every boy in my class had been in the service within a few months of graduation. Too many never came back.

Images from that day flooded my mind. My folks smiling through tears. Alice clinging to me, looking up at me with the shadow of fear and sadness showing through her brave smile and moist eyes. Evie hanging on to Eddie, trying to be brave but failing at it, as Blinky looked on. Blinky was a little guy in 1942, with that habit of blinking hard and fast when he was excited, or embarrassed, or worried, or for no reason at all. He'd had a thing for Evie since 1939, and it showed on that June day, although she belonged to Eddie now. No one would guess that little Blinky would return as the imposing and handsome Major Howard Gordon three years later.

As those 1942 graduation festivities had drawn to a close, Eddie punched me on the arm. "That's it, Jack," he said. "End of boyhood. You go to the Marines. I go to the Navy..." He turned to Blinky. "How 'bout you, Blinky?"

"And me to the Air Force," he said, blinking furiously.

* * *

On this 1950 graduation day, I felt so alone. Violet, in her cap and gown, was a woman. In the company of her classmates, she was an adult among children.

Maybe she guessed wrong about her age, I thought. *Maybe by a couple of years. She doesn't look like an eighteen-year-old.*

Out on the front lawn after the ceremony, a half dozen of the school's football heroes gathered around her. She had ignored them for two and a half years, to their puzzled bewilderment. They were the school's most desirable. What was her problem? This was their last chance to get near her. They were such little boys next to her. She smiled graciously, had a kind word for everyone, but remained unapproachable.

I tried to participate in the good feelings of the graduation. I managed a wooden smile and tried to join in conversation but had trouble speaking coherently. My mind and thoughts were a tangle of grief and depression. I could not focus. All my friends were sensitive to how I was coping with Alice's unresolved disappearance, unaware that my remoteness was the result of what I knew and could never reveal.

"Jack," Eddie said, taking me aside. "We need to talk about Violet. She's in your house every afternoon and at night, but I don't think you have a clue about her. Do you even know she's enrolled at Penn for September? She'd rather come to work at Dunlaur. When can we talk about it?"

90

What about Violet?

EDDIE'S COMMENTS SURPRISED me. I looked at Violet, smiling, laughing, in animated conversation at the center of a ring of people she loved and who loved her: my mom and dad, Goren and Zena, and Blinky. Blinky? What's he doing here? I didn't know he even knew Violet.

Eddie was right. I barely knew her. I studied her as if for the first time. She was a miracle, a lovely transformation from the dirty little creature who had hidden in my car and begged me to drive her out of the Pine Barrens.

"This is serious stuff," I said to Eddie. "Can we leave it till I come back? I'm starting out tomorrow. Be back in ten, twelve days."

"Sure," Eddie said. A frown slipped across his face. It was plain that he couldn't make me out anymore.

91

On the Road

THE ROAD TRIP was therapeutic. The first stop was Philadelphia, just sixty miles away—hardly a trip. But after that, each trip was hundreds of miles. The 1950s highway system was primitive compared to what we have today. The great expansion of our highways was an Eisenhower initiative. On average, I covered less than thirty miles per hour, a leisurely pace through small towns and open farmlands. I made frequent stops. I tried to blank out all thoughts of Alice and of the terrible secret I carried. That did not happen, but I was learning to function regardless so that I could carry on. I stayed in close contact with the office and with Mrs. Wilson and Violet. I spoke to Adam. My voice was reassuring to him. After a few days, he believed me that I was not far away and would be home soon.

The distributors welcomed me. It was a tonic. Dunlaur Electronics was an important vendor to them. They gave me worthwhile suggestions. I learned what their customers wanted. I gathered ideas for new products. And, of course, there were complaints, though not many. I felt I was performing well. But the nights spent in small hotel rooms were hard. My mind filled with replays of all that had happened and the terrible, unintended consequence of Bobo's great favor.

92

Sally?

L EAVING CHICAGO ON the evening of the seventh day, I studied my map for the route to St. Louis. My eye caught on Louisville, southeast of Chicago, as I recalled that Sally Carol lived there. Louisville is the same distance from Chicago as St. Louis is to the southwest. I calculated that going to Louisville for a day and then driving to St. Louis would add three days to my trip.

Was it worth that kind of time for me to try and find Sally in Louisville? What was the name of the hospital she'd mentioned? The APC information operator read off the names of the Louisville hospitals. "Louisville Baptist Highlands Hospital"—that was the one.

The thought of Sally would not leave. I lay in bed, waiting for sleep to come, but instead came the vision of Sally that night in Okinawa, so poised and desirable in her WAVE uniform. And the firmness of her body, giving herself to me. The thought was erotic, and the first such feeling I'd had in the months since Alice's disappearance. In a perverse way, the terribleness of knowing the full truth had hollowed me out. I was empty. Erotic feelings came uninvited.

93

Nurse Carol

THE NEXT DAY was Saturday, June 24, 1950. As I climbed into my car that morning, I reflected that it was the fifth anniversary of the final conquest of Okinawa. Would I ever experience that kind of jubilation again?

I phoned Sally's hospital. "Yes, we have a Sally Carol. She's here now. I can page her for you."

"Please do," I said.

I arrived in Louisville that afternoon, arriving in the main lobby of the hospital at five thirty. At six ten, she emerged from the elevator. I might not have recognized her if I were not expecting her.

She came toward me with a big smile, almost running. "Oh, Jack," she sang out. "It's so good to see you . . . so good!"

I embraced her in a big hug and kissed her cheek. "So," I said, "there really is a Sally Carol. Sometimes I thought I imagined you. Let's look at you." I held her at arm's length and studied her. "Yep, it's you—Lieutenant Commander Carol. C'mon. Take me to a restaurant. We've got five years to catch up on."

"Jack," she smiled. "It was such a surprise when they paged me this morning. I haven't gotten over the shock. You're all I thought about all day. I had trouble focusing on my job. I'm not taking you to a restaurant. I'm taking you home. I'll feed you. I want you all to myself."

94

Sally Revisited

S URE," I SAID. "My car is right outside."

Sally lived in a one-bedroom walk-up on the third floor of a converted house only a few blocks from the hospital. Her apartment was tired-looking, almost shabby. It was not neat. She shooed away a cat that greeted us. Her kitchen table held the morning's newspaper, a cereal box, and a rumpled blouse and slip. Plates, cups, and silverware were piled up on the sink counter. A raincoat was draped over the sofa. Two pairs of shoes were on the floor. The cat's litter box was in the center of the living room.

"Excuse how the place looks," she said. "I wasn't expecting company this evening. Come," she said, taking my hand and leading me into the bedroom. "You know I don't beat around the bush. Take me to bed."

I did the job, but it was not a good performance. Though it was tempting to blame the effect of time and gravity on Sally's appearance, I knew my lackluster performance was more to do with me than her. Good lovemaking needs a kind of mental clarity. My thoughts and emotions were a string of guilt, loneliness, grief, and a bleak outlook.

"Thanks, Jack," she said afterward. "I needed that. Haven't had any since you five years ago. I'm quite a comedown from those days, I know it. I told you back then what I was facing as just another gal in the nurses' pool. Dullness. Nurse Carol. *Nurse Carol to the fourth floor nurses' station.* My life is dull as dirt. I have trouble with men. I don't get asked out often. Once in a while, somebody fixes me up. It's always the same. A cheap dinner and I'm expected to put out afterward. I don't, so that's the end. Another creep down.

"Oh, Jack," she sighed. "I dream of those days in the South Pacific. I was *somebody,* Lieutenant Commander Carol. I felt young and strong. I looked good. I know I did. All the officers were after me. I was a queen, a couple hundred men and women under my command. Remember what I told you that night? The War was a good time for me. I knew what I was coming back to—to this." She took in the little apartment with a sweep of her arm.

Sally lit a cigarette. "I'm not going to ask about your life," she said. "You know mine. I told you what my life would be. It's exactly that. You can see it, can't you?

"But you, you were a blank canvas. Your life hadn't begun. What were you, twenty-one? You could have gone in any direction. You look good, Jack. You have that look of success . . . well-groomed, nice clothes, good car, traveling on business. But something is wrong."

I broke in. "What makes you say that?"

She drew on her cigarette then exhaled the smoke, staring up toward the ceiling. She looked into my eyes. "I know this," she said. "I know enough about you that you wouldn't travel this far out of your way to get laid unless you're not getting any. So you're not single, or you'd be getting plenty. A guy like you, good-looking, great lover, okay for money. So you must be married, but something is wrong there. You're not the kind of guy who cheats on a wife—something else . . . I don't know."

Her words struck like a whip. I sucked in my breath and said, "Wait a minute, Sally, what—"

She stopped me, putting her finger to my lips. "Let's forget it, Jack," she said. "We're ships that pass in the night. Let's just enjoy each other for these few hours."

Just as well, I thought. *Leave it alone.*

She gave me a sad, wistful smile. "I hope you'll spend the night," she said softly.

The next day was a shocker. Everyone remembers how and where he heard the news.

95

June 25, 1950—War!

"WAKE UP, JACK!" Sally was shaking me.

"What is it, Sally?" I asked, not fully awake, looking at my watch on the night table.

"War, that's what it is!" she cried. "I just heard it on the news while I was fixing breakfast."

I sat up suddenly, fully awake. "What? What war?"

"Korea," she said solemnly. "The North Koreans have invaded South Korea." Her voice rose. "Truman says we'll defend South Korea! We're mobilizing! The Armed Forces have to be brought back to full strength. All officers, soldiers, and noncoms who are still eligible to serve are being called back."

I was too stunned to speak, trying to absorb it. What did it mean for me, for Dunlaur? Could they call me back?

Sally roamed around the little apartment, quietly, smoking heavily, absorbed in her thoughts. Then she sat at the kitchen table. She stared down at her coffee cup.

"Jack, do you know what this means? They'll call me up." She brightened. She looked up from the table. She looked at me, directly, with a wry smile. "I'll get my grade back. I'll be Lieutenant Commander Carol again."

"Sally," I said, "war means killing. Didn't we have enough the last time? My God, it's only been five years. You almost make it sound like good news."

Throwing her arms in the air, she laughed. "It is for me, Jack!"

96

Heading Home

I SHOWERED AND DRESSED quickly. "Sally, I've got to get going," I said. "I've got to get home."

"Sure," she said. "But here, I fixed breakfast for us. Sit and eat before you take off."

We ate in silence, our thoughts filled with the news of war.

For Sally, the future was clear. She would be Lieutenant Commander Carol, back in uniform, back in command and running a military hospital somewhere in the Pacific, maybe on board a Navy hospital ship. She was invigorated and eager to begin.

For me, all was confusion: this war, Dunlaur, Adam, acceptance of a new life alone. I was impatient to be home. Would I be called up?

We parted with a kiss and a long hug. She looked up at me. "Goodbye, Jack," she smiled. "Have a good life."

They were the same parting words from 1945 Okinawa. For a moment, I loved her again. Then I was gone.

97

A New Life

MY LIFE BACK HOME was filled with the new war. Activity at Dunlaur was frenzied. Every military agency came to see us with urgent needs. They needed everything. Korea had caught the country unprepared. After 1945, the military had slipped back to a fraction of its size, almost to 1939 levels. War industries had faded away or found other purposes. The factories that had built our tanks and bombers were back to making cars.

A new war was impossible, we thought at the time. Who would be the enemy? Our only dangerous adversary was the Soviet Union, and it seemed inconceivable that Stalin would engage in a shooting war with us. Korea came as a complete surprise. The Soviets and the Chinese were the real enemy, using the North Koreans to fight for them while the US sent its own boys into war.

I learned quickly that as a father, I would not be called up. That role, and being essential for war production, exempted me. I was relieved. My sense of duty to the Marines was outweighed by my responsibility to care for Adam.

Eddie was off the hook because of his war wounds and work at Dunlaur, but Blinky was called up. He was single. He did not want to go. He was angry. His business career was going so well. He applied for a deferment.

* * *

I thought a lot about Alice's remains. Bobo had said his people would return to the scene and gather up what was left of her and the dog. I couldn't call him about it though; I'd learned that lesson once, a long time ago. You did not talk serious stuff on the phone with Bobo. I had to go see him. But I was busy fielding the demands of military procurement officers. They wanted everything, more than we could deliver.

"Expand," they told us. "Add equipment, put in assembly lines."

I was overwhelmed with work and meetings, pushing to do more and do it faster. The busyness was a blessing. It kept my mind full. It shut out everything except work.

After two weeks, I found time to slip away for an hour when an Air Force procurement colonel canceled an appointment. I jumped into my car and headed for Bobo's place.

98

Alice's Remains

S IT DOWN, JACK," Bobo said, drawing on his cigarette. "Georgie, bring Jack a Coke and a sandwich over here." Bobo was seated behind his big desk.

I remained standing. "Thanks, Bobo, but I got to get back to the plant as quick as I can. It's a madhouse. We already started up a second shift. We can't keep up, and they want more of what we make and they want new stuff. Stuff we never made before. Tell me about Alice."

Bobo stabbed out his cigarette, stood, and approached me. "Let's sit here for a moment," he said, drawing me to the sofa. "We got a mystery over here."

"Mystery?" I repeated. "What kind of mystery?"

He hesitated then said quietly, "The remains is gone, Jack. They ain't there anymore. That's the mystery."

I jumped out of the sofa. "Whattaya mean? That can't be! They must've forgotten the exact place."

"No, they didn't forget," Bobo said, thoughtfully. "My guys are too good. They don't forget. They don't get lost. They marked the spot. They cut a slash in a tree right across the road. They don't make mistakes over here, and they're thorough. They took pictures."

He opened the desk drawer and took out an envelope. "Look here, Jack. My guys took these pictures when Charlie took them to the spot." He removed a handful of photos. "See here. This is Charlie. Recognize him? And look here. Here's the slash mark in the tree." He put the next four pictures into his drawer. "I'm not gonna show you the remains. They're right in here." He poked a finger into a spot in the photo of the hidden entrance into the brush. "About ten yards into here. They know the spot all right. The remains is gone. And no sign of nothin'. It's a goddamn mystery."

"But Bobo, how can that be?" I felt a great pressure rising up in me. I wanted to shout. My head got dizzy. I could not stand. I collapsed into the sofa. I could hardly speak.

"Get him that Coke," Bobo repeated to Georgie. He lit another cigarette and took that half-sitting position on the front of the desk, left foot on the floor, right leg swinging lazily. "I don't know what to tell you, Jack. I wish I understood it."

After a moment the dizziness went away. I stood up. "I want to go there," I said. "Get your guys to take me there."

"Sure, Jack. When you wanna go?"

"Right now," I said.

They took me. I saw the slash mark. I saw the spot Charlie had pointed out. I went in. There was nothing to see. The forest and swamp and choking grasses and shrubs spread in all directions, dark and moist, with the buzzing sound of a million flies and mosquitoes and an occasional birdcall.

How could the remains have disappeared? It was madness.

* * *

I did not return to the plant that afternoon. I went home.

Adam climbed all over me. "Daddy, Daddy," he cried. I held him close. I rocked back and forth. I rubbed my cheek against his and soaked him with my tears.

Violet arrived home a little after five o'clock. Eddie and Evie were with her. I did not want company but tried to compose myself and act normal.

99

Violet Again

EDDIE CAME CLOSE and studied me.
"What's wrong, Jack?" he asked. His face showed his concern. "What happened to you? You left at eleven. You didn't tell anyone where you were going. And you didn't come back. I'm worried, Jack. What's wrong? Something's happened. You seemed okay the last coupla weeks. Now this. When you came back from the trip, I thought you were over whatever it was."

"I'm okay, Eddie." I tried to manage a smile. "I may have a cold coming on, but it's nothing to worry about. A good night's sleep and I'll be back to my old self by morning."

I turned my attention to Evie. "It's good to see you, sis. It's been too long. Eddie keeps me up to date on you and the retail division. You're doing a great job."

"Thanks, Jack," Evie said. "Things are going well. I'm working hard, and so is Violet. She's been helping me every day since graduation—I can't say enough about her."

She turned to Violet. "Violet, want to tell Jack what you think about Dunlaur Retail?"

Violet became animated. She talked about Dunlaur almost with reverence. She admired it as a company and as our creation.

As I listened, the conversation grew muffled, as if the room was stuffed with cotton. I couldn't focus on what anyone was saying. Dimly, I understood that Violet wanted to be part of Dunlaur Retail. Evie asked my opinion. I couldn't offer an intelligible response. They all eyed me curiously.

"What's wrong, Jack?" Eddie said, moving closer with that worried frown that came over him lately whenever we were together. "Are you feeling all right? You seem so . . . remote."

Evie sat beside me on the sofa. She put an arm around me and rubbed my shoulder. She started to say something but I interrupted.

"I'm sorry," I said. "I don't feel well. You'll have to excuse me. I need to get into bed."

Everyone wanted to help. Maybe a glass of warm milk. Should we call a doctor? Violet felt my forehead. She said it was cool.

With difficulty, I persuaded them that all I needed was sleep. That I'd be fine in the morning.

Evie and Eddie left. I said goodnight to Violet and dragged myself to bed.

* * *

Sometimes revelation comes in sleep.

100

Mystery Solved?

I TRIED TO SLEEP, but sleep would not come. *The scene* pushed into my head, over and over again. The mystery. How could the remains have vanished? If I didn't have confidence in Bobo's two guys, I would think it was all a hideous prank. But the photos, and the ones Bobo didn't want me to see, were real . . . and the bodies were gone. *The scene* wouldn't leave me.

Toward early morning, a sort of half-sleep came. I pleaded for sleep, but all I got was that same feeling of being in a room stuffed with cotton, dulling my senses, and so I half-dozed and *the scene* revisited me over and over.

Suddenly, I was wide awake. I sat up abruptly. I knew the answer.

101

Solving the Mystery

THE NEXT MORNING, I was outside Bobo's office at six thirty. The door was locked. I waited in the hall for an hour until Georgie arrived and let me in.

"What's up, Jack?" he asked.

"I gotta see Bobo," I blurted. "I know what happened."

"Take it easy, Jack," Georgie said. "Bobo won't be here till eight. What happened to *what*? Wanna tell me?"

I sat on the sofa and leaned back and stared at the ceiling. "I'll wait, Georgie," I said after a minute. "No sense going over it twice."

When Bobo showed up, I leaped off the sofa. "Bobo," I blurted almost hysterically, "I know what happened to the remains!"

"Calm down, Jack," he said, taking me by the arm. "Sit down over here. Tell me what you know."

"It's Charlie," I cried out. "He escaped and came back to remove the evidence. There's no other explanation. It has to be that."

Bobo rose from the sofa. He stood over me, saying nothing. His eyes squinted, piercing me. He stood that way motionless and silent for what seemed an eternity. Finally, he turned away and sat behind his desk. "Georgie," he said. "Tell Nick to bring us some coffee over here and some ham and eggs for Jack. He looks like he ain't eaten for a while."

He turned to me. "Jack," he said quietly, almost in a kindly manner. "I want you to sit there and try to relax. I gotta think this through. You try to relax. You'll eat breakfast while I think about this. Don't be anxious to do something over here. Nobody's going anywhere."

He sat still in his big judge's chair. He lit a cigarette and tilted back. He jutted out his chin and exhaled a stream of smoke at the ceiling. From time to time, he stroked his chin between his thumb and forefinger.

What was he thinking?

When Nick brought up the breakfast, I ate it. I was hungry. Appetite overcame my weariness and chaotic agitation. I ate slowly, sipping at the coffee. When I had eaten, I closed my eyes. I was so tired, so tired. I murmured to myself, "So tired." I dozed off, and we must have sat that way for almost an hour.

Then Bobo straightened in his chair. He swiveled toward me and leaned forward, his head thrust forward, lips pursed for a moment. He spoke in a quiet monotone. "Jack, this here is still a mystery. I can't figure it out, but it ain't Charlie. That's for sure."

"How can you be so sure?" I asked.

"Jack," he said soberly, quietly. "Did you really believe that bullshit story that Charlie is in a southern prison?"

I was startled. "What do you mean, Bobo? I don't understand."

He paused before he answered. "It's like when the father has to put the old dog down and he tells his little boy that old Pal is goin' away to live on a farm. You believed that bullshit story about Charlie in the prison down south because you wanted to believe it. You didn't want his blood on your conscience, and I didn't want it there either."

Bobo leaned back in his chair. He let his words sink in. Then he resumed. "About the money. You'll get around to thinkin' about that. That was to make it real. The money went like Durells said—a thou for Merino, eight thou for my guys what tracked him down and caught him, and a little for me. The twenty-five hundred for the southern big shot, that was for Durells."

102

A Cask of Amontillado

BOBO WAS WEARING that dangerous face now—cold, dark, piercing eyes looking out from under hooded lids, his mouth a thin slash across a thickening, jutting jaw. How I used to cringe from that face. For how many men, I wondered, was that the last face they ever saw?

"That's right, Jack. Charlie ain't the answer. Charlie is dead."

I struggled to catch my breath. "I don't get it," I croaked. "Tell me."

The dangerous face left him, replaced with one of friendship and concern for me.

"It ain't hard to understand," he said. "The son of a bitch needed killin' and you wasn't gonna have any part of it, so I done what hadda be done. Me and Durells, we made up the bullshit story for your benefit."

"Where is he?" I asked. "What did you do with him?"

Bobo answered evenly, as if he were telling me something of no particular importance. "He's at the bottom of the Atlantic, Jack, in concrete leggings out past the continental shelf, about seventy miles out, at the bottom of five thousand feet of ocean. That's where Charlie is." He snorted. "Where he belongs."

He stood up and approached me. He took me by the shoulders, his eyes boring into me. "Don't get bent outta shape, Jack, and don't let this be on your conscience. Charlie was a bad guy what needed killin'—and by the way, you shouldn't be fooled by the hillbilly act. He was a two-bit thug from Philly who fled into the woods to beat some serious mob heat. I'd never heard of him—he was low level, a nobody—but I got the story from a reliable source, and I can tell ya, Jack, Charlie was messing with the wrong guys. So did I do it for you, because of Alice? Maybe, but it had to be taken care of anyway. That fuckin' animal wouldn't have stopped with Alice."

Bobo took a deep breath, his eyes piercing mine, before continuing. "Now listen closely, Jack, and I'll tell you how it was done. You prob'ly don't think about me as somebody what reads. I mean books and lit'recher, do you? Well, truth is, I *ain't* much of a reader, but I read a short story once in high school. Did you ever think of me as a schoolboy over here? Well, I was. Not much of a student, but I got by.

"My family came here from Italy when I was nine. We lived in a poor neighborhood full of Italian immigrants. There was this little Italian theater the old folks had for entertainment. They did plays, and some movies, and sometimes they read from a book. Everything was in Italian. So one night when I was fourteen, my Uncle Pietro comes by and says he's takin' me to the theatre. We're gonna see something called *Il Barile d'Amontillado*. They translated it into Italian from a short story by a guy named Poe. Edgar Allen Poe. Ever hear of him? I liked that story so much, I bought a book of his short stories, but I ain't a reader. I never read any of his others. I could barely make it through *The Cask of Amontillado*. That's the English name. It's about revenge, a good revenge. Know what's a good revenge? I'll tell you.

"First, the guy you're gonna kill, he has to *know* he's gonna be killed. Next, he has to know *who* is gonna kill him—*you*. Third thing he has to know is *why*. And he has to watch it happen and know he can't stop it.

"Charlie hollered, *Please don't do this . . . give me a break . . . give me to the cops. I didn't mean it. It was an accident.*

"The fucker wanted a break, Jack! Like he gave Alice a break!

"My guys are humane. Before they tossed him in the water, they smothered him—like he done to Alice. Then, just to make sure he'll never be identified if the body gets pulled up twenty-thirty years from now, they pulled out his teeth and cut off his fingertips. And that's what we did to Charlie Norris."

"So, Bobo," I said, "what happened to Alice's remains?"

"It's a fuckin' mystery, Jack."

103

Therapy with Bobo

BOBO SAT ALONGSIDE me on the sofa and looked at me with a kind of tough sympathy.

"Son," he said softly, "I'm gonna tell you something over here what might help you."

His use of the word "son" startled me, in a good way; he had my full attention.

"Alice was a great gal," he began, "but she's gone, and you gotta get on with livin'. Chrissakes, look at you. You're young, you're smart, and you ain't bad looking. You're doin' good in business. You got a little boy, and he needs you to be there for him. Someday, you'll have all this behind you and you'll be functioning again. Right now, you ain't even functioning ten percent. So look here—since you're gonna get this behind you someday anyway, why wait? Do it now."

He stood up, towering over me. "Get over it now. Don't nurse it along."

With that, he turned and went back to his desk. After taking his seat, he leaned forward and continued. "I lost a lot of people myself, Jack. Most in not nice ways. People who meant a lot to me. Family, friends, guys what worked for me. Guys in the Army back in '18. I learned something from losin' people. Know what I learned? You get over it. Then you get smart. You get over it fast. Better this way. Slow is no good. You had a big loss, sure. But gettin' over it slow will cost you more losses. Go home, Jack, and start livin' again."

I let his words sink in for almost a minute before responding. "You know somethin', Bobo?" I said finally. "You're a real friend. Next to Eddie, I guess the best friend I've got. And I appreciate everything you've just said.

"But," I continued, "there's a piece missing. Nobody knows she's dead except me and you and your guys. People used to say, *Jack, they'll find her.*

Maybe she's okay. Nobody says that anymore. After the first few weeks, people don't know what to say. My own mom and dad and Alice's parents, and everybody we know—they don't know what to say, so they don't say anything. They just look at me with pity.

"The problem is, I can't grieve openly. I carry the secret like I'm carrying an elephant on my back. I can't figure how to grieve and get it over with."

"I understand, Jack," Bobo said. "You'll just have to bear it. You're right about your friends. They don't know how to deal with you. If you was a widower, they know what to do—fix you up with their nieces. But this way makes it tougher for you. But what I said still goes. You gotta get on with it. I'll help you any way you want. Don't know how, but whatever you need."

After a moment's pause, he added, "Getting laid might help."

104

Getting It Together

I WAS BACK AT work the next morning. As touched as I was by Bobo's empathy, it wasn't his words that made me go. People were counting on me.

Dunlaur had become almost 100 percent a defense manufacturer. What it didn't make for the military, it made for other defense manufacturers. Korea had forced us to produce, more and more, and to expand. We'd added a full second shift, and after realizing that Monday start-up slowed down full production, we were in the process of adding a limited weekend shift to keep things moving at all times.

President Truman rushed American troops and matériel to South Korea. The war went badly for us. The North rolled through the South with ease. The South Korean army was a mere twenty thousand men. The North Koreans made quick work of them, and it looked like our forces were going to be overrun as well.

The American military knows how to rise in a crisis. Reinforcements poured in from Americans stationed in Japan and Hawaii and airlifts from the States. One hundred thousand American reinforcements stopped the North Koreans at the southeastern tip of the South Korean Peninsula around the city of Pusan. "The Pusan Perimeter," it was called. It held long enough for more American troops to reinforce, assemble, and finally to break out and begin the long and costly maximum effort to drive back the North Koreans. Before the war ended, three hundred fifty thousand Americans served in Korea.

My work at Dunlaur was endless—not enough hours in the day. My thoughts were dedicated solely to the company. Eddie, our key personnel, and I met every evening to hone our effort and seek ways to improve production. I was rarely home at a reasonable evening hour.

Violet kept the household in order. She rearranged Adam's sleeping pattern so that when I showed up at ten o'clock, hungry and exhausted, she had a hot meal ready and Adam was awake to spend a half hour or so with me.

My conversations with Violet were brief and predictable. She was always polite, soft-spoken, and reserved. And solicitous. Was there anything I needed? Anything she could do for me?

"No thanks, Violet. Is everything okay? Adam okay? Any problems?"

One evening, on a Sunday when I returned home earlier than usual, I asked her about herself. "Violet," I began, "I noticed my friend Blinky—Howard Gordon, that is—was at your graduation. I didn't know you knew him."

She blushed and turned slightly to avoid direct eye contact. "Howard came to the retail office one day to see Evie about life insurance. He asked about me, and Evie told him I'm Eddie's cousin and that I'm working at Dunlaur for the summer. He asked me to dinner, but I said I can't manage it. He took me to lunch instead."

"Really?" I was surprised that Blinky would react to Violet as a woman rather than as a child. Although taking a good look at her, objectively, I could understand. Alice was only twenty when I came back from the War. Violet did not seem any less mature. "Tell me about . . . Howard," I pressed her. "How is he with you?"

She spoke to the tabletop. "He's nice. He's handsome and personable. But you know that. He's the same age as you. He was called up for the war. He's a bomber navigator. They need men like him. But he got a deferment to settle up his business affairs. After we had lunch, he wanted to take me out again—for dinner and a show, he said."

She paused for a long second before continuing. "I haven't had anything to do with men since you took me away from Earl, and Howard's attention makes me a little uncomfortable. I told him it's best we don't date."

What was that I felt—a twinge of jealousy? No, more like a sense of ownership . . . or of ownership being threatened.

"Violet," I said, "tell me about your work with Evie at Dunlaur Retail."

She brightened and straightened up. The reticence left her. She looked at me straight on, smiling. The words came tumbling out, full of energy and enthusiasm.

"I love it there!" she said. "And I so admire Evie. What a woman! She seems to know everything, and everybody respects her. The sales reps come to see her. They don't want to talk business on the phone or by mail—they want to see Evie. She knows every employee. She's planning store number five, and she has a retail scout looking to locate number six.

"I want to be part of Dunlaur. I want to be like Evie, and like you and Eddie. You didn't need college, and neither do I. There's more education in a month at Dunlaur than in four years at Penn." She turned away as her shyness returned. "I'm sorry if I got excited."

I studied her for a moment before I spoke. "Violet, it occurs to me that when we talk, you never address me by name. What do you call me when you are talking about me? Jack? Mr. Laurel? Adam's father? Eddie's partner? *Him*?"

She hung her head a little. "I'm sorry," she whispered. "What do you want me to call you?"

"How about Jack?" I suggested. "It's my name, after all."

The smile returned. "Okay, Jack," she said and rushed out of the room.

* * *

On a Thursday night late in July, when I got home, Violet handed me a telephone message from Detective Burns. The message was brief: "Ask him to call me. Al Burns."

105

News from Al Burns

I CALLED DETECTIVE BURNS early the next morning.

"Al," I said. "It's Jack Laurel. Do you have news for me?" I tried to sound as if I knew nothing.

"Yes, I do, Jack," he replied. "Can you come to the station?"

I wanted to sound excited. "What is it?"

"I'd rather you come to the station," he said. "This is not for the telephone."

* * *

"What's the news, Al?" I asked, walking into Burns's office. I struggled to adopt the right demeanor. The detective was a perceptive man; he mustn't think I knew anything.

"I'm afraid it's not good news."

"What is it, Al?" I looked at him intently. Did I look worried and anxious?

He rose from his chair and came around. He rested his hand on my shoulder. "Alice is dead, Jack."

"Dead?" I repeated. I tried to choke on the word as I stepped back, play-acting, as if his words had struck me in the chest. "I guess I knew," I said. I eased myself into a chair.

"We're not sure what happened to her yet, Jack, but here's what we do know. A man—a bird-watcher—was in the Makepeace Lake Wildlife Management Area about three weeks ago. The entrance is off the White Horse Pike some thirty miles from here."

I knew the entrance was actually off the Black Horse Pike but stifled the impulse to correct him as he continued.

"This guy has a dog, a pointer, and they were on one of the dirt paths. He's watching for birds through his binoculars when the dog runs into the bush and starts barking. The guy goes in to follow the dog. It's like a jungle swamp in there. He pushes in about twenty yards. The dog is barking at two bodies—one human, one canine, badly decomposed."

He paused. His eyes scanned my face. "Jack." He paused again. "I waited to call you because I wanted to be sure it was Alice. Yesterday, the lab confirmed it."

I held my head in my hands and stammered, "What happened to them, Al?" I needed to show more shock, more grief, but wasn't sure how.

"There's not much left of them after nine months. Animals got at them. The local cops collected the remains and put out an all-stations bulletin for a hundred-mile radius, though I can't say they were very efficient about it. The bulletin finally reached my desk a couple of days ago while I was in the field on another investigation. Yesterday, I went to the morgue. There was nothing to see from the remains, mostly just clothing shreds and a dog collar. A tag on the collar identified the dog as Max."

I almost fell over, and now I wasn't acting. Burns drove me to the morgue. When I saw what remained of my wife, I broke down, sobbing uncontrollably as I collapsed into the detective's arms.

106

Pretending

Burns drove us back to Margate. I was silent, but he wanted to talk. "It appears the dog was killed with a knife, Jack . . . we don't know about Alice. Did it happen where we found them, or were they moved there later? We have nothing to go on at this point. I'm so sorry."

"Do something for me, Al," I said. "Get something in the newspaper so people will know. I can't be calling people. Except my folks and hers and Eddie and my sister."

* * *

So the secret was out that Alice was dead. Not the whole secret. The real facts and details were still mine to take to the grave. I asked Burns for her remains. I wanted a regular funeral and burial as soon as possible. He said he'd contact an undertaker to arrange it with the Vineland Police.

Perversely, now it was in the open that Alice had been murdered, my secret felt smaller. I realized a part of me would be able to function better because everyone knew of her death, if not the details. I was officially widowed. What had happened would never be known except to me and Bobo's guys and Lawrence Durells. In time, I believed everyone else would close the book on it.

* * *

I used Al Burns's office phone to call my dad, Eddie, Alice's mom, and Goren. I would see Bobo the next morning. I knew that within a day, everyone who knew me would have heard the news.

My first face-to-face was with Violet. She rushed home early. Telephoning the others was easy compared to that conversation.

107

Goodbye, Alice

VIOLET RUSHED INTO the house. She found me on the sofa with Adam. She picked him up and sat next to me.

"Tell me what I can do for you," she said.

"There's nothing to do," I said. "Alice is gone. Life goes on. I have Adam. He needs me more than ever. I'll pull myself together. I'll manage. I have to."

"I'm here for you," she said. She handed Adam back to me and went upstairs. She was crying.

Adam leaned against me. "Is Mommy coming home today?" he asked.

"No, son," I said. "Mommy is not coming home. She went away to a faraway place. She is all right. She sent a message to tell you she loves you. She will always love you. She is happy. She wants you to be happy, to be a good boy, and always listen to Daddy. Can you do that, Adam?" I hugged him close.

He was bewildered. "Why?" he asked.

"It's a big story, Adam," I said. "You will not understand it now. Later on, you will, but right now, we can't wait for Mommy. She isn't coming home."

He cried himself asleep. Then I cried.

108

Closure

November 5, 1950

I KNEW FROM CHARLIE'S confession that Max never had a chance to defend Alice. He was cremated and his ashes went into a small urn, which I placed in Alice's coffin. They died together, and I wanted them buried together.

It was a graveside ceremony on a gray, overcast day, in keeping with the occasion.

Alice's mother and father stood together with my own parents, close together, as if drawing warmth and strength from each other, their faces filled with terrible sadness. Violet and Blinky were together. His arm was around her shoulder, drawing her close. They cried.

Eddie and Evie huddled together, he stoic, broad, powerful, capable. She sobbed and clutched his arm, leaning against him as though needing him to keep her upright. I studied Eddie as though I hadn't seen him for a long while. He wore a black suit with a white shirt and black necktie. The collar was tight; he stretched his neck and inserted a finger inside to try and loosen it. It occurred to me that I hadn't seen him in a suit and tie since his wedding day. He was always in work clothes in his office, which was really a workshop, or in the model shop or on the factory floor; absorbed in our product line, always tinkering, always improving, always trying something new. Dunlaur's success had not changed him. A wave of love for him came over me.

The funeral was cathartic. Well over one hundred people attended. In addition to family members, dozens of Alice's friends and colleagues from the Department of the Interior and the New Jersey Wildlife Service came. Over and over, I heard how her passion for her work as a naturalist had inspired everyone around her, and I wanted to cry every time I heard it. I'm not sure how I managed to hold back the tears. A number of Dunlaur employees attended, along with well-wishers from the newspaper and radio stations. Al Burns and a dozen detectives from Vineland, Margate, and Atlantic City were on hand to show their support. There was no sign of Bobo or any of his men, which was no surprise, as Bobo always protected me from being linked to him. Larry Durells was there, however—he was Dunlaur's lawyer, so it was only right and proper that he would be there—and when I saw him, it struck me that of those assembled, only he and I knew the circumstances of Alice's death. I did my best to put it out of my mind.

A light, cold rain began to fall as the ceremony began. A sea of black umbrellas opened over the crowd, adding more darkness to the day.

Zena stepped forward. "I want to recite something," she said quietly. She paused, wiped away a tear. "This is by Christina Georgina Rossetti."

> *Remember me when I am gone away,*
> *Gone far away into the silent land;*
> *When you can no more hold me by the hand,*
> *Nor I half turn to go yet turning stay.*
> *Remember me when no more day by day*
> *You tell me of our future that you planned:*
> *Only remember me; you understand*
> *It will be late to counsel then or pray.*
> *Yet if you should forget me for a while*
> *And afterwards remember, do not grieve:*
> *For if the darkness and corruption leave*
> *A vestige of the thoughts that once I had,*
> *Better by far you should forget and smile*
> *Than that you should remember and be sad.*

Many of those in attendance wept as she read the poem. Adam clutched my hand and turned his face into my sleeve.

* * *

The ritual of funeral and burial is a good thing. It is a punctuation mark, a period, the end. It is society's permission for those left behind to resume their lives. "You may mourn," society says, "but go on living."

I returned to work two days later.

109

Back to Work

THE WAR IN KOREA had expanded our product list, and Dunlaur was now receiving major defense contracts. Army procurement officers continued to show up with orders for items we did not make, pressuring us to take on the work. We began to make a variety of electrical and electronics equipment, all new to us, from microwave-activated switches, transmitters, and receivers to relays, boosters, and relay-boosters. Every order came with full specifications and drawings. We created a team of electronics engineers and draftsmen. Sometimes an order came with a working prototype. Under Eddie's relentless management, each new item was fully understood and in production in a matter of days. We added factory space.

The military demanded every imaginable kind of electronics and communication equipment. All our effort was focused on production. The Dunlaur sales force did no selling. They became wartime order takers. Receive the orders, write them up, prepare delivery schedules, follow the orders through the manufacturing process, try to expedite production, respond to short-tempered customers who, too often, seemed to read from the same script: *"Where the hell is my order? It was due three days ago and I'm gonna be late with my shipment because you screwed up. There's a late penalty for every day since last Thursday, you know!"*

It wasn't only Dunlaur that couldn't keep up. Just about every company we did business with had the same problem. It was the debilitating pressure of too much business. Jobs were forced on us even when we protested that we were already beyond capacity. Those discussions with Army procurement officers always ended with me, or Eddie, or our production manager saying, wearily, "All right, we'll take the order. But I'm telling you now, we'll never be able to meet that delivery date."

The response was always the same: "Do your best. We'll help you if you run into delays."

"How will you help?"

"Not sure, but we'll figure it out. We need this stuff!"

Eddie and I wondered what it must have been like after Pearl Harbor. Korea was a small war, compared to the Big One.

Our product catalog grew into an eighty-page book. We now had more than one hundred different printed circuit board designs. We made items that went from idea to prototype in a few weeks and from prototype to production in a few days. Eddie's new smaller, stronger walkie-talkies, with improved range, became the state of the art for field communication. We also made the khaki-colored steel container for the walkie-talkie's battery pack and antenna.

Dunlaur was a prosperous company when the Korean War started. When the war ended, the Dunlaur factory had more than three hundred employees in a factory that had grown to one hundred thousand square feet. Our profits were enormous, to the level of embarrassment.

For companies such as ours, and for families with men serving in Korea, the Korean War was all-absorbing, as was WWII. But for the population at large, this war was remote and life went on normally. War news was a regular backdrop to life, but it seemed to touch few lives and interfered hardly at all in American life at home. It was, truly, the Forgotten War.

110

Eddie's Wartime Inventions

E{DDIE WAS CONTINUALLY} experimenting with our walkie-talkies, finding new ways to reduce their size and increase their range while trying to solve the problem of making them work more like telephones, with one-to-one communication. He installed an antenna atop the spire of the Claridge Hotel, which at four hundred feet was the tallest structure in Atlantic City. He installed a relay on the antenna to collect and resend voice communications from the walkie-talkies, extending our range from three to about twelve miles.

* * *

Eddie's latest idea was to install a relay on a battlefield blimp that could hover in a small circle at about five hundred feet above a military area, extending a walkie-talkie's range to twenty miles. When the concept was tested on a Navy blimp over Fort Dix, it worked, but as blimps were highly vulnerable to enemy attack, the Navy ended the experimentation.

* * *

One of Eddie's inventions that survived the Korean War is the portable biomass generator. The device is powered by anything that releases methane as it decomposes, including leaves, weeds, grasses, tree branches, garbage, animal carcasses, and manure. The biomass is fed into a cylindrical tank where its natural decomposition is accelerated by an internal press. The generator can be set either to release combustible gas or to fuel an internal electric-producing turbine.

Once mounted on a wheeled four-by-eight-foot flatbed, the generator could be towed almost anywhere, and it could supply enough gas or electricity to power a small remote village, farm, or field battalion.

* * *

There was nothing new about the way Eddie's portable water purifier worked: a combination of filters, membranes, and chlorine converted water from polluted ponds and streams into potable water. What *was* new was its small size and portability. As with the biomass generator, the unit could be mounted on a wheeled four-by-eight-foot flatbed in order to bring clean water to a village or town whose wells had become tainted from polluted groundwater, a common occurrence in war zones.

Bringing a biomass generator and a portable water purifier to a remote village drastically improved the quality of life there. Thousands of villages were able to flourish and grow as a result of one or more sets of the equipment pioneered by my friend.

111

A Distant Cloud

March 1951

BUSINESS GROWTH BROUGHT change and kept me very busy. In the spring of 1951, we opened Dunlaur's fourth outlet in Allentown and moved our retail division offices into the Philadelphia store. The latter space, which had originally housed a bank, occupied almost the entire first two floors of a Chestnut Street high-rise. A thirty-foot-high vaulted ceiling rose above the sales floor and a half floor of offices located on a balcony level. A restricted elevator operated between the sales floor and balcony. Traffic in and out of the store and all activity on the sales floor could be observed from the balcony level.

Evie's office at the center of the balcony had a commanding view of the first floor, including the entry foyer. Other balcony offices housed purchasing, bookkeeping and accounting, quality control and testing, and marketing, along with a large conference room where vendors' sales reps pitched new products and company meetings were held around a large conference table.

I wanted to discuss a marketing idea with Evie, which was to promote Dunlaur Retail as a division of Dunlaur Electronics, emphasizing that the stores carried state-of-the-art Dunlaur Electronics components. I wanted to display big posters on the store walls—professional photos, greatly enlarged, of the Dunlaur factory, both exterior and interior shots. My thinking was that advertising Dunlaur Electronics products in this manner would demonstrate to our retail clients that the stores were just one aspect of a significant company—that Dunlaur Electronics was building parts for the military in addition to the TVs, radios, phones, and other electronic components featured in the stores. The image I hoped to present was of up-to-the-minute retail stores, everything state of the art, as part of a flourishing electronics manufacturer on the cutting edge of American ingenuity.

I hoped to see Violet during my visit. She was now a full-time Dunlaur Retail employee, serving as Evie's assistant and second in command. They were closer than sisters, Evie and Violet Dunauskas. "The Dunlaur girls," as an increasing number of customers had begun to call them.

* * *

It was midafternoon on Friday when I arrived at the retail offices. As I stepped out of the elevator, Evie emerged from her office, together with Blinky. I was never able to think of him as Howard or Major Gordon. Blinky? What the hell was he doing here?

"Hi, Evie, Blinky—um, Howard," I called out. After exchanging greetings, I asked Howard what had brought him to Philadelphia.

Howard flashed the big smile. "Actually, it's business, Jack. I've been trying to sell Eddie on a life insurance policy, and he said to take it up with Evie. I thought that while I was at it, I'd pitch her on some partnership life insurance for all the senior people here and maybe a retirement policy for your employees. How about you, Jack? Maybe I can help you with some coverage too—you know, to be sure Adam is protected. Can we get together to talk about it?"

"Sure, Blinky," I said. "Call my secretary to set it up."

"Yes, sir!" he said, throwing a salute as he left.

As I turned to Evie, something in her expression told me something wasn't right, but I couldn't put a finger on it. I let it go for the moment. "Where's Violet?" I asked. "I'd like to say hello."

"She's in Allentown today," Evie said. "She'll be home tonight."

We sat in her office and talked about my marketing idea, which Evie liked. She said she'd get on it right away, beginning by producing photographic images for the walls of the retail floor and planning a display of our products in the conference room.

"What's this about life insurance, Evie?" I asked as I rose to leave.

"Oh, that . . ." Her eyes looked away for a moment. "It's not a bad idea."

"What is he recommending? How much premium for how much coverage?"

"He rattled off some numbers," she said distractedly, shuffling a pile of papers on her desk. "He said he'd mail me a proposal."

"Okay, Sis." I kissed her cheek and left.

Something was definitely not right, but whatever it was, it faded away quickly in the general busyness of my daily routine.

* * *

The following morning, the *something not right* thing returned when Eddie said, "Jack, last night, Evie said she wants to talk to Blinky about life insurance for me. I said, 'Sure, why not? A partnership policy for you and me.'"

"Good idea," I said. *But that's wrong,* I thought. *Blinky said he and Eddie had already talked about it.* I had a troubling thought, low level, like the first dull-ache warning of something you know will only get worse.

A few days later, a courier delivered a fat proposal from Blinky. It was for individual life insurance for Eddie, Evie, and me, and a partnership policy, and a comprehensive benefits package for employees. It was more than two hundred pages, full of graphs and tables. It was completely unintelligible to me.

Eddie felt the same. He set his copy aside, saying it was too complicated for the average person to understand. It was a big package, with a lot of premium, and I knew Blinky would follow up for an appointment to go over it with us.

When a week went by and he hadn't called, I didn't get it. What's going on? Blinky should be all over us for a piece of business this size. Then I remembered that uncomfortable feeling from the day I bumped into Blinky coming out of Evie's office.

Something was not right.

112

Wrestling with Success

DUNLAUR WAS DOING well before Korea, but the conflict fueled our growth. I wrestled with the uncomfortable recognition that war had brought wealth to me and Eddie. He and I talked about it, sharing our guilty feelings that Korea was good for us at the cost of so many lives. We raised salaries across the board at the plant and retail stores. We contributed generously to a dozen war-related charities, especially those that provided prosthetics and rehabilitation for wounded servicemen. We knew it was only an accident of fate that kept us home, safe and prosperous, while men we had served with in the Big One were fighting and dying.

Financial success barely changed our lifestyles. I brought Mrs. Wilson to live with us officially as full-time nanny, cook, and housekeeper. That freed Violet and me to work longer hours; I didn't care much for socializing, and Violet seemed to have no interest in men. Blinky's romantic overture ended when she rebuffed him, though an easygoing friendship took its place. Evie introduced a number of eligible young men to Violet, all of whom were enamored, but she never gave any of them a chance.

One evening, I asked her about it. "Violet," I said, "you're a lovely young woman with so much going for you, but I worry that you don't have a social life. You haven't any friends I know of, other than my sister, and I can't recall even one date. When Evie introduces you to a young man, it's always lunch near the office and then a brush-off. Don't you ever think of marrying and starting a family?"

She took a moment to gather her thoughts. "Maybe . . . someday. I can't say for sure. You know what my life was like before you got me away from Earl. He sold me for a quarter, a shotgun shell, or a couple of potatoes, and used me himself anytime he felt like it. After that, is it surprising I have so little interest in men?"

113

Evie and Blinky

May 11, 1951

THE DUNLAUR ELECTRONICS Philadelphia representative set up a lunch meeting between me and a small manufacturer of electrified board games. The customer was using Dunlaur printed circuits and switches.

We met for lunch at Old Bookbinders Restaurant, just two blocks from our Philadelphia store. He unfolded a drawing of a wiring diagram for a new board game that was essentially a mounted map of the United States. Players had to match up the names of 150 state capitals and other points of interest with their corresponding states. A correct matchup consisted of one plug in the hole that located the subject place on the map, a second plug in the hole alongside the name of the place within a list, and a third plug into the hole alongside the name of the state in another list. A correct matchup of the three plugs caused a small, recessed circular glass panel to light up.

I was commenting on the educational merits of the game when I spotted Evie and Blinky seated across the room. Their table had been cleared except for a couple of coffee cups and the check. They lingered, engrossed in conversation. She leaned forward, looking into his eyes intently, smiling. He leaned in toward her and flashed his best Douglas Fairbanks Jr. smile before leaning back again in his chair.

I excused myself and rose to greet them, but I stopped, halfway out of my seat as Blinky reached across the table and took her hand and murmured something. I sat and shifted my chair so as not to face them, but although they didn't acknowledge me, I knew they'd seen me. They stood and left the restaurant abruptly.

It was as I'd thought. Something was not right. Indeed, something was very wrong.

114

Evie

I CONFRONTED EVIE IN her office at five o'clock that afternoon. She could not look at me.

"Tell me," I said. "Tell me everything."

She dabbed at her eyes with a tissue, sobbing. I waited for her to compose herself.

"Nothing happened, Jack," she said finally. "Please believe me. You know he always had a thing for me, though I never paid him any attention—even since he came back from the War, all handsome and charming."

More tears. I waited for her to continue.

"Please, Jack," she sobbed. "Help me. I love Eddie. He's one in a million. We've made a big success together, but he takes me for granted. We never go out. We never entertain. We have no real friends, just business associates. He works late, so I work late, and we're like ships that pass in the night."

I winced at the expression. Sally Carol had used it.

She continued. "Howard is so different. He's Mr. Personality, very success-ful, and he hardly works anymore. At most, he might see ten prospects a week. He has time, and he's relaxed about things. He's not *always* thinking about business, like me and Eddie . . . and you.

"I was flattered by his attention," she went on. "I asked him why he hasn't gotten serious with a woman. Know what he says? He says there's no one like me. He sees women, but none that can hold his attention. There's only me."

She was calmer now. She spoke evenly, almost as if we were discussing a business matter.

"Do you know how flattering and romantic that is, Jack? To be pursued by a man like that when you're feeling lonely? But believe me, nothing happened. I've been afraid to let myself go. I haven't even let him kiss me."

"Evie," I said, looking at her with my eyelids lowered, "don't give me any bullshit. It doesn't make any difference to me if you kissed him, fucked him, or just held hands. You're a cheat! Am I going to tell Eddie? No. But I'll tell you, it's *over* between you and Blinky. And if I find out it isn't . . . well, I don't know, really, but I better not."

With that, I got up and walked to the door. She called out to me, but I kept going.

From there I got in my car and drove to Blinky's office. I thought he might be expecting to see me.

He was.

115

Blinky

I PAUSED OUTSIDE THE paneled door of Blinky's office on Central Pier. The bronze plaque read:

Major Howard Gordon, Retired
United States Eighth Air Force

Smaller painted lettering lower on the door read:

Life Insurance, Annuity Programs, Financial Consultant

I pushed the door open, hard. It slammed against the wall. He was in an inner office, in a dark brown, high-backed judge's chair behind a great polished desk. He was smoking a cigarette.

"Have a seat, Jack," he said, snuffing out the cigarette. "I've been expecting you."

"I'll bet you have," I answered. I was hot with anger. I felt my temples throb. I approached the desk and leaned on it, bending toward him. "Blinky, I guess you remember what I did to the Mackeys back in '39, right?"

He remained silent, but I could see his right hand shaking. He began to blink, furiously, just like the old Blinky.

"Let me tell you something," I continued. "You're a decorated war veteran. So am I. But you never got close to any fighting. You dropped bombs and flew away. You never saw the enemy close up. But I killed men, Blinky. Plenty of them. I could beat you to death and it wouldn't bother me." I paused, fixing him with a hard stare. "I think you're a coward under your new good looks and persona, Blinky . . . the same coward that stood by while Eddie and I got beat up by the Mackeys. Ain't that right, *Major Gordon?*"

I let out a harsh breath then stared him down, waiting for his response.

After a few seconds, he spoke, hoarsely, lips quivering. "You don't need to worry about me, Jack," he said nervously. "I won't be around after Monday.

I got the call-up letter yesterday. I'm reporting to McGuire in six days for a flight to Travis Air Force Base in California. They're going to give me update training on the B-29. That's the bomber I'll be in—you know, the Superfortress. We used it in the Pacific in '44 and '45. It's the plane that dropped the bombs on Hiroshima and Nagasaki.

"So I asked Evie out for lunch. I didn't even tell her I've been called up. I just wanted to see her one more time before I take off. I'll be on a B-29 over Korea in three weeks. If I make it back, I swear I'll never come near her."

I gave him the silent treatment; he kept talking.

"Look, Jack, we've been friends a long time. Give me a break," he implored. "Nothing happened."

Give me a break, hah! The same thing Charlie Norris said to Bobo's guys. It's what they always say when they get caught. I shook my head.

Still, the hot anger had begun to dissipate. I looked away from him and studied his office for the first time. It was elegant. The walls were panels of polished cherry wood with four-inch moldings and chair rails. There was a cherrywood conference table with eight red leather chairs plus a red leather sofa and a red leather lounge chair. The floor was covered with an expensive-looking oriental rug. I was struck by how much the whole setup resembled Bobo's.

A model B-17 flying fortress hung from the ceiling, large, with a three-foot wingspan—the bomber he'd flown in the War. A framed photograph on the walls showed him in his heavy leather airman's jacket with the crew of his B-17. Another featured a squadron of B-17s flying in formation, and there was a picture of him being awarded the Distinguished Flying Cross by Major General Carl Spaetz, commander of the Eighth Air Force. There was a photo of him shaking hands with Eisenhower. A framed black velvet plaque displayed his military decorations: the Distinguished Flying Cross, the Air Medal, the European Campaign Medal, the World War II Victory Medal. It was an impressive presentation, one I couldn't help but admire.

I turned back to look at him again, directly, for a few seconds. When I spoke, my voice was calm and controlled. "Well, then," I said, "the best of luck to you. They're not taking me because I'm a father, and they're not taking

Eddie because of his injury. Makes me feel guilty. I see the First Marines are there, including my own company—I checked on its personnel and I know a lot of those guys. My first lieutenant moved up to captain and became company commander when I got discharged. He's back. They made him a major and moved him up to battalion commander."

"You don't have anything to feel guilty about," Blinky said. "You did your part, more than your share."

I turned and left, thinking about the situation. Would I have hurt him if he wasn't on his way back to the service? I don't really know. Maybe. But he *was* going away. Maybe forever. The B-29s were not doing well in Korea. Russians were flying MIG jets against them. The casualty rate for B-29 crews was high. Much too high. Blinky had the cards stacked against him.

Removing the Tap

October 1951

GEORGIE CAME FOR me.

"What's up, Georgie?" I asked as I climbed into his car.

"He wants to see you," came the standard reply.

* * *

"What's up, Bobo?" I asked as Frankie swung the door open.

"Good to see you, Jack," Bobo replied, greeting me with a bear hug. "Want somethin'? Coffee, soda, coupla eggs?"

"I could use a coffee," I said, settling into the sofa.

Bobo sat in the easy chair next to the sofa. I couldn't help but notice the tape recorder sitting on the coffee table.

"I got a story to tell you over here," he said, leaning forward, his voice and face expressionless, "and then I need you to do something for me." He leaned back, lit a cigarette, and exhaled a cloud of smoke.

"You know how I feel about you, Jack. You're like a son to me. We done a lotta stuff together. And I always hoped you'd come in with us. But that's okay. You're one of us, anyway. Remember what I told you a few years back? That the Philly organization was gonna muscle in on us? You and Eddie fixed me up with that recording machine over here. It was a big thing you did for me. After I tell you what's happenin', I'm gonna ask you for another favor.

"First, I gotta tell you I got a kid into the Philly organization. He's twenty-one, been in their organization about three years, a good smart Italian kid from South Philly—reminds me of you in some ways, but he ain't gonna be a big industrialist like you. They didn't take him for Korea because he has a mother and three sisters to support. He wanted to go, but I wouldn't let him. He also wants to leave the Philly organization and come to us, but I won't let him, not yet. I need him where he is, keeping me informed. You have to know about him to understand what I'm gonna tell you over here. I'm listenin' to the recording machine one day and I hear this. I'll play it for you."

He pressed a button on the recorder and the machine spoke.

"Chief, it's time for us to move in."

"How come now? Anything special happen?"

"Korea's got everybody distracted. Everybody what counts is busy makin' money. Even you, I bet. I bet you're coinin' it, and so are half your cops. The big businesses pay anything for your guys and the government to leave them alone. It's time."

"Whatcha gonna do?"

"Not really sure, but I'm sending some muscle. Gotta get on site before New York."

"How you gonna do it? When?"

"Some guys. They'll be there soon."

"When? Where they stayin'? How many guys?"

"You'll know when they contact you. No need for you to know."

"Whatsamatta? Don't you trust me?"

"No, Chief. I don't trust nobody 'cept my own."

Bobo stopped the recorder.

"So I knew they're comin'," he said. "That's why I told you about the kid. He hears stuff. I knew when and where."

"Why are you telling me this?" I asked. "This doesn't concern me—does it?"

"I'll tell you why, Jack," he said, "because it already happened, and pretty soon the chief will wonder if he's been bugged over here. He ain't too smart, but he's smart enough, maybe. You and Eddie gotta get that stuff outta his office."

I sat in silence for a moment, considering what I'd just been told. "Whattaya mean, it already happened?" I said. "*What* already happened?"

"You're one of us, Jack. I can tell you."

He paused, took a drag on the cigarette. "The kid calls me one day. *Uncle Bobo*, he says—that's what he calls me—*three guys gonna show up in your town, and I know when and how. They're startin' out tomorrow. Two of them gonna drive in a brown Roadmaster on the Black Horse Pike. The third guy's gonna join them at Gene's Diner 'bout three o'clock. They're real tough guys, Uncle Bobo. That's all I know."*

"So what happened?" I asked.

"My guys intercepted them. They're gone."

"Whattaya mean, gone?"

"Gone, disappeared. Nobody will ever hear from them. That's what I mean. Gone."

"Well, but where are they? What happened to them?" I asked, thinking about Charlie Norris.

"Jack . . ." Bobo said pensively, drawing on his cigarette. "Jack, you don't have to know."

"Isn't the Philly organization doing anything about it?"

"Like what? They don't know what to think. Here. Listen."

He raced the tape forward and started it up again.

"Chief, what happened to my guys?"

"Whattaya mean, Carmine?"

"I told ya never to use my name!"

"Sorry, sorry . . . but whattaya mean? I don't know anything about your guys. Are they supposed to be here? In Atlantic City? I didn't hear from them."

"That's it. Nobody heard from them. They disappeared! And you're the only one knew they was comin'."

"Wait a second," the chief sounded very nervous. "Ya don't think I did anything to them . . . ? You wouldn't even tell me how many and when."

"Maybe, but you're the only one knew they was comin'. How d'ya account for that?"

"Now look, Carm—I mean, now look here—"

At that point, Bobo stopped the machine.

"Get it, Jack?" Bobo said. "These three guys are gone. And the brown

Buick, that'll be discovered in the Miami City Airport lot in about three weeks. The car will be cleaned out. Nothin' but fingerprints of the three guys on the wheel and stuff, and then a little piece of an airline ticket stub, too little to tell you anything. So maybe they went to Italy?"

I didn't think so.

He continued. "Carmine will wonder about this. He'll be sure the chief over here had something to do with it, but he can't figure it out. I'll get a breather. At least a year, I figure. Maybe more. Anyway, I need you and your partner to get all that stuff outta the chief's office. You understand, don't you?"

"Sure, Bobo. We'll do it for you, for old times' sake."

"Attaboy," he said. "I knew you'd do it for me."

* * *

When we put in the tap in January 1948, we were just kids, trying to start up a business. Now, three years later, we were successful businessmen—the owners and operators of a respected company with over three hundred employees—and Bobo had been instrumental in our success. He'd nailed down the Traymore job for us back at the end of '48, which saved Dunlaur from going broke and turned the corner for us. This was 1951, and we were no longer brash twenty-four-year-olds with nothing to lose, yet we couldn't refuse Bobo. With strong feelings of trepidation, Eddie and I went back to the routine we'd used to wire the chief's phone in the first place.

117

Korea

HISTORIANS CALL IT "the Forgotten War." It was a grim, desolate conflict that went on for three years. The draft brought the US Armed Forces up to 5.7 million servicemen and women, three hundred fifty thousand of whom served in Korea. The UN declared war on North Korea. Small contingent forces came from Britain, France, Canada, Australia, Turkey, and fifteen other countries. They were largely symbolic. It was an American effort.

Korea was not a "good war" like WWII. First of all, our safety and survival as a nation were not threatened. American forces were often bloodied, badly, but Korea did not arouse and unify the country. Thirty-nine thousand American servicemen were killed there, with another one hundred three thousand wounded, but here at home, the war went largely ignored and unnoticed, despite the magnitude of the effort.

By 1950, the post-WWII economic boom had begun to fade. Korean military needs revitalized the economy, and the boom times were back. Life was good in America if you weren't directly involved in the war and none of your loved ones were in the fight.

* * *

After stopping the North Koreans at Pusan in September 1950, a strengthened American force began the fierce job of driving them back. The breakthrough of the war was the Inchon landing—the brilliant but dangerous plan of General Douglas MacArthur, who commanded the American forces in Korea.

In what will probably be the world's last amphibious invasion, American forces landed at Inchon on September 15, 1950, on the eastern coast of South Korea, one hundred miles behind the North Korean forces who were fighting around the Pusan Perimeter. American forces eliminated the North Koreans who were trapped south of Inchon then quickly swept up the peninsula. My division, the First Marine Division, was at Inchon. By October, all of North Korea was overcome. The Americans were at the Yalu River, marking the border between China and North Korea. It appeared the war would be over by Christmas 1950.

That's not how it played out.

* * *

In November, without warning, a million Chinese troops entered the war. They flooded across the Yalu River into North Korea, taking the Americans by surprise, inflicting heavy casualties and driving our forces back in the longest fighting retreat in American history, finally stabilizing in July 1951 at the thirty-eighth parallel, back to where the North-South border was at the beginning of the war. Now the war dragged on. Heavy fighting and casualties continued for two years in what was increasingly being called a stalemate.

Dwight David Eisenhower was elected president in November 1952 on a promise to end the war. He got the fighting to stop in July 1953 with an armistice, not a peace treaty.

American soldiers, sailors, and airmen fought with the same heroism and skill in Korea as in WWII. In 1945, returning American servicemen were greeted as heroes. The Korean veterans, by contrast, returned to a country that hardly recognized them or their sacrifice. It was not only the Forgotten War; it was a useless war. The boundary between North and South was unchanged. The war established that the North cannot conquer the South because the US will protect the South, and the South cannot conquer the North or join North and South into a single country because China will not allow a South Korean-style democracy as its neighbor.

The Americans who died in Korea are just as dead as those who died on the beaches of Normandy in 1944. Where are the great annual memorial events? If indeed there are any, we don't see them.

As with all wars, technology leaped ahead thanks to Korea. At the start of the conflict, aircraft, warships, tanks, armored vehicles, and ordinance were all 1945 state of the art. By war's end, propeller-driven aircraft had been replaced by jets, and almost every other piece of WWII equipment was rapidly becoming obsolete.

The technology surge went beyond field weaponry, of course. Dunlaur was given orders and plans to build advanced electronic and communications components the Army had developed in rush time by specialized labs and teams of top engineers. It's indisputable that advancements in electronics and communications technology during the three-year Korean War would have taken at least three times that long in peacetime.

118

President Eisenhower

November 1952

THE 1952 US presidential election pitted Republican Eisenhower—Ike—against Democrat Adlai Stevenson. Both were notable men. Their histories and personalities could not have been more different.

Eisenhower was World War II's victorious Supreme Commander of Allied Forces in Europe—a father figure, loved and admired by the returned veterans he had commanded. He looked, behaved, and spoke like a man of the people. His language was simple and spare. His manner was direct. He had an unassuming air, yet it was one of authority.

Stevenson was a brilliant lawyer turned politician, former governor of Illinois. Everything about him said *scholar, gentleman, professor, aristocrat.* He was supremely articulate; his speeches were jewels, delivered with simple words and phrases yet with a touch of majesty. Complicated topics were unknotted and made easy to understand.

During the campaign, there were two occasions when I tuned into Stevenson's speeches. Each was close to an hour. They were mesmerizing. I was in awe of him as a draftsman of words. His delivery was mild. His words needed no bombast. Churchill could not have done better. This was the quintessential gentleman with greatness of mind. How had he become the governor of Illinois? How in those days, in a world of tough, secret, smoke-filled backrooms, had this quiet, cerebral man become the Democratic nominee for president? It seemed incongruous. But this pointed at the toughness of the man. Steel lay beneath the aristocratic charm.

Stevenson was a bachelor. Did that hurt him in the race? Probably.

There was no mystery about Ike's nomination. He was the anointed one. He could have been the nominee of either party. The choice was his, and he chose the Republicans. There was no contest. For the sake of good form, he acted as a reluctant candidate, as if the nomination had been forced on him, a soldier called to duty.

Both were reasonable, middle-of-the-road men. Their politics were similar, including how they would handle the biggest issues of the day—the A-bomb, the Soviet Union, China and Korea.

In the final days of the campaign, Stevenson gave a lengthy TV interview from his living room. As he relaxed on a sofa, legs crossed, the camera focused on the sole of his right shoe, which faced the camera. There was a hole in it! Did that hurt him? Who knows? There were many comments about it in the media, some of them scathing.

Essentially, the nation was Democratic. The economy was good. The Republicans were still brushed with the dark colors of the Great Depression. It was Hoover's Depression, a Republican Depression. Roosevelt and the Democrats saved the country. Truman beat Dewey because the country did not trust Republicans to keep the good times rolling for ordinary citizens. It was Korea and the Cold War with the Soviets that got Ike elected. He looked to have the toughness Americans wanted. Stevenson, who was plenty tough himself, simply did not look the part.

"I will go to Korea," Ike said. That clinched it.

<h1 style="text-align:center">119</h1>

<h1 style="text-align:center">Memorial Day</h1>

May 1953

WHEN I WAS a boy, Memorial Day was my favorite day of the year. It was a day of promise—the promise of summer, the end of school, the return of the tourists. Atlantic City celebrated the holiday with an extravagant parade on the Boardwalk. High schools from a dozen nearby towns brought their bands and drum and bugle corps. The Army, Navy, Marines, and Air Force sent small contingents to the parade. Local businesses joined in, as well as national companies like Coca-Cola, Lucky Strike, Heinz, Campbells Soup, and Texaco.

I went to the parade with Adam, Evie, Violet, Zena, and Mom. My father marched with the World War I veterans. Eddie marched with the World War II vets. I didn't march because I wanted to be with Adam.

We went early to get a good spot at the railing near the heart of the Boardwalk, near the Marlboro-Blenheim and Shelburne Hotels. I carried my son on my shoulders.

I expected the parade to be muted compared with those before Korea, but it was not. It was a joyous, fun-filled event that seemed to completely ignore that we were at war and casualties were continuing on the ground and in the air. *Will there even be Korean vets marching?* I wondered.

By the time the parade started, crowds were thick on both sides of the Boardwalk, three and four deep. Lots of spectators carried and waved American flags. All was colorful and cheerful. Bunting and banners were strung up along the entire line of march. Every hotel wore the colors this day.

A blast of bugles! Here comes the parade! First came the Atlantic City High School Drum and Bugle Corps. The snare drums rattled their message, *rat-a-tat, rat-a-tat.* The bugles spat out their tattoo from the opening bars of a WWII Glenn Miller march, *daaadadadadadadah!* The bass drum thumped. *Boom! Boom! Boom!* Then came the flag bearers, followed by the Atlantic City High School Marching Band led by twelve baton-twirling majorettes, lovelies raising their knees high, in their white patent-leather boots and prim blue and white military jackets; peaked officer's caps with red, white, and blue cockades; and short, pleated skirts, white with blue pleats peeking through.

The Armed Forces were represented by a Navy band, and a platoon of soldiers with their own drum and bugle corps and color guard, and a platoon of Marines. Slow-moving open convertible cars were scattered throughout the parade, some carrying dignitaries, some carrying advertising banners of the participating national companies, others carrying the banners of popular hotels, restaurants, stores, and so forth. Every car had a pretty girl perched on top of the rear seat, smiling and waving to the crowds on either side of the Boardwalk. Every car flew two American flags upright on their front fenders. The high school marching bands and the drum and bugle corps were spread throughout the parade. From the band just passed and the band that was passing to the band that hadn't yet reached us, the crowd was blanketed by the intermingling of loud, spirited band music.

Representatives of the wars were formed into marching platoons, each platoon carrying an American flag of its time and a number of regimental flags. First came three platoons of WWII veterans. These were men, and a few women, in their thirties and early forties. All were in uniform marching in good order: Army men, and Marines and Air Force and Navy. And three WACs in crisp khaki and two WAVES in those smart navy and white outfits that flattered every wearer.

Here was Eddie in his chief petty officer dress blues, looking sharp, marching briskly, his limp barely noticeable. We shouted and waved to catch his attention. He smiled and waved as he marched by.

These were the heroes. The war was only eight years past. These were the victors who fought in the Good War, who defeated mortal enemies and brought peace and good times to America. WWII and its absolute victory were still fresh in American minds.

The First World War was represented by two platoons of forty men each, also marching in good order. They wore their World War I doughboy uniforms, for the most part, with a sprinkling of sailors in Navy blues. World War I was only thirty-five years past. The veterans were men in their late fifties and sixties. Most were getting too big for their old uniforms. We spotted my father in the front platoon. We waved energetically and shouted. He saw us, gave us a salute and a smile as he marched by. In the second platoon, we spotted Alan Goren. He saw us and saluted. He looked out of place. As always, he was wearing a gray suit and hat, with a white shirt and gray necktie. He looked as though he should be sitting behind a desk in an office, not marching in a platoon of soldiers. He wore three military ribbons on his lapel. One of them, I knew, was for the Silver Star he received at Chateau Thierry in 1918. *Is there a Korea platoon?* I wondered again.

Next came the sentimental favorites: one squad of Spanish-American War veterans—fifteen men in their late seventies and eighties. They looked quite fit for the most part, though their marching was ragged. Several walked with canes. Only a few were in uniform; most wore suits. Only their American Legion caps and campaign ribbons hinted at their past military service. They received big cheers.

A few years earlier, there were still a handful of Civil War veterans, old frail men struggling to keep up. The last of them had been seen five years earlier, in 1948—a one-hundred-and-eight-year-old corporal in a faded blue coat and blue trousers and an old blue forage cap. He struggled, leaning heavily on a cane, supported by a young man. The *Atlantic City Press* wrote of him, "Aaron Stokesbury, Corporal, 18th Pennsylvania, wounded at Gettysburg, will be assisted by his twenty-five-year-old great, great grandson." On this day, there was no evidence of the Civil War.

Ah! Here comes a Korean platoon—a mere twenty-five men. The war and the killing were still going on, in spite of the so-called stalemate at the thirty-eighth parallel, and these marchers—all wounded servicemen— marched grimly, well aware there was no victory to celebrate. They had fought and been wounded in the Forgotten War and returned home unappreciated. Although the crowd cheered them, the cheers were subdued, as if the onlookers were embarrassed to have sent these young men to fight a far-off war with no purpose.

A line of six green Army jeeps were in the parade, each one towing a field artillery piece. A flight of four Sabre Jets buzzed the parade. They were painted with shark teeth on their fuselages, like the old Flying Tigers that flew for the Chinese against the Japanese during WWII.

The open cars went by with pretty girls waving from them. Many were models, hired for the day, but most were local girls—employees who had been selected for their beauty and charm from sponsors' Atlantic City offices.

When the parade ended, we met up with my father, Eddie, and Goren. We headed to the Knife and Fork Inn for dinner, with plenty of good conversation and laughter. Eddie and I struggled for the check, briefly, before Evie intervened firmly to say it was Dunlaur Retail's treat.

* * *

When I got home, I turned on the TV to watch a two-hour Memorial Day special entitled *Korea: The War Goes On*. It was all black-and-white footage with voice-over narration. It held my attention, viselike; I couldn't turn away for even a moment. One short segment, filmed in December 1950, showed my old company retreating from the 1950 Christmas onslaught by the Chinese, slogging through a heavy snowfall over a mix of frozen mud and snow, pushing mired-down trucks and jeeps. The journalist interviewed the company commander, a captain. I recognized him as Scott Jefferies, who hailed from a small town near Sante Fe, New Mexico. He was a second lieutenant on my staff when I left the company in 1945.

The journalist asked, "What can you tell us about what's happening, Captain?"

"You can see what's happening to us," he replied. He was wrapped in woolen scarves. Ice and frost covered his helmet and his overcoat. When speaking, he lowered a scarf from his nose and mouth.

"I'm wearing two pairs of thermal long johns," Jefferies continued, "and two pairs of woolen socks, and thermal glove liners . . . and it's not enough.

My men are exhausted and frozen, but we're pushing on. The Chinese are bearing down behind us. Division Headquarters says there may be a million of them. They're well-equipped. They have tanks and motorized artillery and rockets. Russian MIGs, flown by Russian pilots, are giving them air cover. My company is in retreat. We're a rifle company. There's nothing we can do *except* retreat. Our regiment has an artillery company back there, holding them up, to give us time to get out of here. I feel bad for those guys. They'll slow down the Chinese, but I don't see how they'll get out of there themselves."

"Are you getting any air cover?" asked the journalist.

"Yeah, the B-29 guys are great. They're coming over in waves, every couple hours. They're dropping a lot of stuff on the Chinese—bombs, napalm, incendiaries. But they're taking a terrible beating from the MIGs. We've got 1945 Mustangs and Corsairs and some Shooting Star jets. They're no match for the MIGs. I hear the Sabre Jet is coming. It's supposed to be superior to the MIG . . . but meanwhile, the B-29s are getting killed."

At the end of the program, the voice-over said, in that somber voice reserved for such news, "Some of the men you saw on this program have since been killed in action. Here are their names . . . to date . . . more are gone since this list was assembled."

To a background of "Taps" played very softly, a list of names scrolled down the screen. One was that of Scott Jefferies.

* * *

Two weeks later, the *Atlantic City Press* printed the obituary of Howard Gordon, USAF. The obit included a photo of Blinky and the brief story of how he had left behind a prosperous business career when he was called up. He'd been promoted from major to lieutenant colonel. His Superfortress was downed by a MIG on his fourth mission.

120

Peace and Adjustment

July 1953

THE KOREAN WAR ended in July 1953.

New defense contracts stopped being issued three months before the armistice. The military procurement people knew the war was ending. Contracts in progress were cancelled. The government had a complicated formula for renegotiating cancelled contracts to compensate for work in process and associated overheads and anticipated profits. Our accountants had to learn a new skill, one that involved heavy negotiating with the Army Audit Agency. A one-time skill; unlikely they would have use for it in the future.

Four months before the armistice, Eddie and I saw it coming and started to downsize the factory. The first contract cancellations arrived, and we knew more were coming. We needed a quick shrink-down to our prewar size. Downsizing is painful, involving letting people go, reducing work space, and canceling contracts with other companies.

Taking stock of our ongoing nondefense business, we knew we wouldn't return to prewar profitability. Too many added expenses would be hard to eliminate. The factory had idle space and idle machinery. And perhaps the worst of it was our wartime generosity in respect to salaries and hourly pay and benefits. Those were not going away with the staff and labor force that remained in our downsized business.

Our accountant told us that if we returned to our prewar sales level, we would be lucky just to break even due to the overhead that survived the downsizing.

On the retail side, Evie had demonstrated great foresight in introducing household appliances to our stores. Sales of refrigerators, washers, dryers, ovens, and small appliances had been brisk, easily outpacing sales of TVs and radios.

"What about the retail division?" I asked the accountant. "It appears retail sales are holding up."

"That's true," he said, "strong sales in the retail division absorbed the wartime salary increases. If sales stay where they are, the retail division will generate the same profits as before."

"So," I said to Eddie, "we're pretty lucky. I'm sure manufacturing division sales will increase. Our important customers like RCA and GE and Emerson and Motorola, their consumer business is not going to drop. I expect increased sales of TVs and radios. And we'll be seeing color TVs soon. That's a whole new industry. And our small business customers. They will be using more and more printed circuit boards. We are ahead of the game because we got in first with circuit boards, and our latest boards are designed for transistors. Vacuum tubes are history. And now we have the electrical components line: the switches and transformers and cable assemblies and all the other stuff that we didn't have before Korea. I just got an order for ten biomass generators, and I'm working on an order from the UN for fifty water purifiers. And I'm going after the electric utilities. We have at least twenty items in our catalog that they use every day."

My challenge would be sales. I needed to reinvigorate our distributors and sales reps. Working out plans to absorb more and more business—that had been my job for three years. Now it was back to work. Sales, sales. That would be my main effort. Eddie and our model shop had never slowed down on state-of-the-art developments. They were ready for post-Korea.

We mused about our wartime generosity with salaries and hourly rates. A return to prewar sales volume was not going to be enough. Wholesale reduction in personnel had to be done, but the workforce that remained was earning 25 percent more than at the start of the war, both at the retail division and in the factory. Were we too quick to share our swollen profits?

"Maybe we're not such great businessmen after all," Eddie said.

"Not to worry," I said. "We'll be okay. I'll bring in the business. You keep us at the front of the new stuff. We'll still earn more than we need. And look at all the money we have in the bank from those three war years. We'll be fine. Our business changed, that's all. But now it's healthier than before. The circuit boards got us going, but competition will be real tough. We're really an electronics manufacturer now. I say we don't give up any space. We'll fill it up again. We may lose money for a while. So what? The retail stores will cover it. And if that's not enough, the war chest will get us over the hump."

Eddie pursed his lips. "Here's what I been thinkin', Jack. First, we have to get serious with Evie." He paused. "She's ready for another store. Do we want it?" He paused. "Second, I'm for a big push into portable phones. It's the next big wave—that and relay towers. I need a strong R&D budget, and I'm ready to use a big chunk of that wartime money. Are you game?"

"I'll tell you what I think," I said, "but not here. C'mon, I'm draggin' you out for lunch."

121

Therapy for Eddie

I DROVE TO AN out-of-the-way restaurant on the mainland where it was unlikely we'd run into anyone we knew. We took a rear-corner table for extra privacy.

The big wind-down of work at the factory was mostly behind us, and after three years of the intensity of war production, the factory seemed eerily quiet. We talked briefly about how many jobs we had running and an extended sales trip I was planning.

Eddie was pensive. "Jack, I'm remembering that day back in '47. When you came with me to Spencer's place to install the antenna. Remember?"

"Do I remember?" I chuckled. "How could I ever forget? I thought you were going to get killed up on that flagpole, in the middle of the Pine Barrens, and the guy with the rifle—" I caught myself. I almost said the name . . . Charlie Norris. "Yeah, Eddie, that was quite a day. Was that really only six years ago?"

Eddie looked away as if studying the landscape through the passenger window. "That's right," he said quietly, "it's been six years. We've come a long way.

"Know what I'm feeling?" he continued. "A letdown. All that pressure and excitement over the last three years. And all the killing over there, for nothin'. And you and me safe at home and getting rich from it."

"That's why I dragged you out of the plant today," I said. "I'm worried about you, Eddie. You been working your ass off for too long without a break . . . without even taking off a day here or there. You're an amazing guy, a goddamn genius, and you've got more stamina than anyone I know. I don't kid myself, Eddie. You're the reason for Dunlaur's success. You and Evie. You in the plant and Evie with the stores. I'm just a salesman. You could find a thousand guys like me, but there's only one of you."

I continued. "Do you think about Evie and . . . your marriage? You gotta make room for that. She loves you, Eddie. She needs you. And I know you feel the same about her. Chrissake, Evie's and your life together are more important than Dunlaur. Now that the war frenzy is over, I know what you're going to do. I already see what you're doing. You're in the model shop all day and into the night. Eddie, it's—"

He interrupted. "Jack, big things are happening. We have to be there. It's a revolution coming in communications, and we need to build a portable phone." As he spoke, he grew animated. "I'm close now. I know how to make it work, but I gotta deal with some Bell Lab patents. Durell's office is working on that."

"Listen, Eddie," I said, leaning toward him. "I ain't gonna let you bury yourself in that model shop. Hire another engineer. Hell, hire two or three more engineers, if necessary. You gotta stop killin' yourself. You're destroying your marriage. Don't you realize that? I want you to save your marriage. If you slow down, so will Evie. You can enjoy each other.

"And what about children? You and Evie been putting it off, and putting it off, and waiting and waiting . . . until what? *Now*, Eddie. Now is the time. Go away on a cruise. Relax, have some fun together. Make love—I bet you hardly ever do it anymore."

Was he listening? Could he change? I would find out soon enough.

122

Sunday at the Beach

August 1953

Activity at the plant continued to diminish. The military business was done, and we were back to commercial products. Eddie had time to work on the mobile phones. In spite of my lecture, he was working as long and hard as ever.

Evie was completely absorbed in the retail division. She had a new store on the drawing board. It would be number five, out on the highway north of Wilmington, Delaware.

"That's where the action is," she said. "Convenient to get to, plenty of parking. The Center City shopping areas are going to be less and less important."

The retail division was making a lot of money. It covered for Dunlaur Electronics, which was barely breaking even.

Evie had become a dynamic, hard-driving business executive. The *Wall Street Journal* ran a piece on "the young, beautiful, tough-as-nails boss of a growing chain of electronics stores."

She and I never got around to talking about Blinky's death. I tried once, but she only had time for business.

* * *

An important attraction of living in Marven Gardens, New Jersey, is its closeness to the beach. It's only a block and a half away, and on a clear summer day, the beach is a paradise. Over breakfast, I told Violet I planned to leave work early and take Adam to the beach. I invited her to join us.

So that afternoon, we headed for the beach. I carried a beach umbrella and a folding chair, Adam on my shoulders. Violet was at my side, carrying another chair and a beach bag. The day was perfect. The sun was past its noon peak but still high in the southern sky, the sky a brilliant sapphire blue, glowing in the sunlight. The ocean was ideal, the waves rolling in smoothly, floating a hundred bathers up with the swell as each wave rolled in, lowering them as the swell passed before crashing onto the beach.

Laughter and shouting filled the air along with music from portable radios and the roar of the surf. Small children played at the water's edge. Tanned and bronzed teenage boys and girls with supple bodies frolicked and laughed among the waves and under the waves and into the waves, shaking the water out of their hair and ears. The sea was filled with human energy. Adults floated over waves in twosomes and small groups, holding conversations about anything and everything as they watched their children splashing happily in the surf.

Banner planes flew overhead, following the coastline, trailing their woven messages: *Steel Pier, A Mile Out to Sea; Captain Starn's for your Lobster; Tan with Coppertone; Fralinger's Salt Water Taffy.*

Motorboats sped by, some too close in. A few sailboats eased along in the distance, their sails full from the light breeze that added to the day's perfection.

Pretty girls flocked to the lifeguard stands where there was plenty of flirting and laughter. The hard-packed sand near the water was crowded with men, boys, children, women, girls, strolling, chatting, building sand-castles, picking up seashells. The beach was hopping that day.

I watched as Violet slipped off the light cotton sheath that covered her one-piece bathing suit. It was the first time I'd noticed her all grown up with few clothes on, and I was struck by her slender, long-legged grace. She wore a wide brim straw hat and sunglasses, her hair tied back in a ponytail. She smiled at me, noticing my approving glance.

"I'm going for a walk," she said and headed off toward the surf.

* * *

The beach was an artist's palette with the colors of the swimsuits and beach umbrellas and beach chairs: red ones and blue ones and green and orange and yellow ones and striped ones. Beach chairs were arranged to face the sun, sometimes two or three, side by side. And in semicircles of three, five, six, or more, open to the sun, each group a one-day resort community, filled with friends enjoying lighthearted conversation and laughter.

Near the water were children—clam diggers, hermit crab hunters, and sandcastle builders alike. As always, the ocean's roar was part of the experience, more than mere background noise, and the salty tang of the sea air filled our nostrils and lungs.

Men pitched quoits, pausing occasionally to admire a pretty girl or group of girls strolling lithely along the water's edge. Further up the beach, closer to the Boardwalk where it wasn't so crowded, boys were tossing footballs or having a baseball catch. An attractive girl among the baseballers let out a happy shriek as she sprinted barefoot after a pitch tossed well over her head.

Waist-deep in the water, a pair of middle-aged men were absorbed in conversation. They were almost mirror images: portly, with large, smooth, well-tanned bodies, their bellies overhanging their bathing suits. They might have been at a cocktail party. They did some arm-gesturing and finger-waving and shared an occasional laugh. Without stopping their discussion, they lifted themselves over each wave and came down in the same spot. When a particularly big wave came along, they ducked under, as if on command, and emerged again, wiping their eyes, but their conversation never stopped.

Adam was almost six and growing fast; he was smart and talkative. Happily, he was still small enough to sit on my shoulders as I made my way out to where the waves formed. It was only chest deep for me. I rode the swells, leaving the bottom for a moment until the swells passed and lowered me. Adam held on to the top of my head.

I spoke to him as I pointed to the horizon. "Look, Adam, out there. Do you see that sailboat?"

"Sure, Daddy." He pointed as he answered. "No motor. How come it's going that way? The wind is not blowing that way."

"Aha!" I answered. "That is complicated. I'll need to explain it to you with paper and a pencil. I'll draw it for you later."

"Comp—complicate—What is that?"

"It means *hard to understand*."

We rode the swells as we talked for a half hour, caressed by sun and water, warm and wet. It was a magical experience. I felt so much love for my son.

After a while, Adam twisted around to face the beach. "Violet," he said. "Where's Violet?" He called out to the beach, "Violet, come in the water!"

"I'll ask her to come in the water with us next time," I said as we emerged onto the beach.

I dried him with one of the thick white towels Violet had packed. He busied himself with his bucket and shovel while I reclined in my chair and read the Sunday *New York Times*.

* * *

Violet appeared. She removed her big hat. A young man, quite obviously tracking her, veered away as she plunked down in a beach chair next to me.

"So, Violet," I said, turning toward her, "how are things going at Dunlaur Retail?"

Smiling, her words tumbled out. "I love it!" she said. "Evie is studying three different locations for our next store, and when it's ready, whichever location she decides on, she says it will be my store to run. It's so exciting, but I'm also a little nervous. You and your mom and Eddie and Evie saved my life. I owe you everything. I'll never let you down. I just hope I'll be good enough."

I studied this beautiful young woman next to me. Her face was open, guileless, as her eyes roamed over my eyes—those strange violet eyes that narrowed and sparkled when she smiled.

"What about your free time?" I asked. "Your social life?"

A sober look, her eyebrows raised. "I really don't have much of a social life," she said. "There's no time for it. I have so much catching up to do. I read every evening. I visit Zena and Mr. Goren—he wants me to call him Alan—at their apartment. They were at my graduation. Did you know we'd become friends? Mr.—that is, Alan—selects my reading. He said he used to do the same for you."

"What has he given you?" I asked.

"Oh, a number of books. *A Tale of Two Cities, History of the French Revolution, Pygmalion, The Duty of Civil Disobedience, The Fall of the Roman Empire, Call of the Wild . . . War and Peace.*"

"All terrific," I smiled. "He gave them to me fourteen years ago. How about Joseph Conrad? Has he given you *Victory* or *Lord Jim*?"

"Oh, yes!" she said. "Conrad is my favorite. He writes like no one else. Sometimes I come across a sentence or a paragraph that's so good, it chills me. I read some phrases a few times. They are so . . . What's the right word? So beautiful. No, that's not enough . . . *crafted*, like a perfect piece of sculpture. Conrad is amazing."

"Did you know he was Polish?" I asked. "English was not even his native language. That's so hard to imagine. Did Goren tell you?"

"Yes, he did. He said he told you that when you were fifteen."

I laughed. "That Goren. Talk about one of a kind. How about Zena?" I asked. "How well do you know her?"

"Omigod!" she laughed. "I *love* Zena." She threw her head back and raised her arms to the sky. "I've adopted your mother as mine, and I adopted Zena as my special aunt. Alan and Zena, what a wonderful pair! You're blessed to have them as friends."

She was right, and I was suddenly angry at myself for not spending more time with them. I vowed to fix that.

"Violet," I said. "This is the most we've spoken together since that day I found you in my car. I'm very proud of the person you've become." I rose from my chair. "C'mon, let's take Adam into the surf."

The beach started to thin out around four in the afternoon, and by six, it was mostly deserted. That's the best time to be there, I've always thought.

The ocean calms. Its roar subsides, as if resting after the exertions of the day. The air becomes a little cooler, fresher, though still warm, with a sharpening tang and a light breeze. It's delicious. The sun lowers in the western sky, slipping behind the distant tree line on the mainland, a big, fat fireball turning the sky into an orange and gold work of art.

I would have stayed longer, but Adam was getting antsy. "Let's head home," I said. "Time for showers and cotton robes and dinner. I wonder what Mrs. Wilson has in store for us . . ."

It was the most relaxing day I'd had in a long time. A good kind of lazy sleepiness overtook me shortly after dinner. I went to bed early and slept well. I wasn't prepared for Violet's surprise the next morning.

123

Breakfast with Violet

I CAME DOWNSTAIRS FOR breakfast at five thirty, my usual time. Mrs. Wilson had everything prepared: a good breakfast, never the same two days in a row, and the *Atlantic City Press* neatly folded at my place.

Violet appeared. I looked at my watch. She never had breakfast this early. I was always long gone before she came down around seven.

"Good morning, Violet," I greeted her. "You're up early."

She wasted no time. "I can't stay here anymore. Your mom says I'm welcome to move in with them. I'm going to drop off a couple of pieces of luggage on my way to work."

Before I could ask why, she continued.

"This is why. It was all right when we didn't know about Alice, while we were hanging on to the hope she'd turn up and be all right. It made sense for me to be here to help you with Adam for a while. But it's different now," she said. "We know the truth."

"I don't understand," I said. "Why exactly are you leaving?"

She moved a step closer; she actually took my hand. "Because you're a widower." She choked up, her eyes filling with tears. "Now that we've accepted that Alice is not coming back, it's not right for me to continue living here. It isn't appropriate."

"I don't agree," I said quickly. "There's no reason you shouldn't stay here if you want to."

She withdrew her hand and looked at me intently. "Last week, I overheard two women from the neighborhood talking about us in the drug store. They were saying that you're a single man, I'm an unattached young woman—hardly more than a girl, one of them said—and it's scandalous we should be living under the same roof." She looked at me imploringly. "Don't you agree there's something to what they were saying—that it doesn't look right?"

I was angered by the revelation, though certainly not with her. "Listen, Violet," I said, "we are entirely proper, and I'll be damned if our lives are going to be ruled by busybodies who have nothing better to do than spread gossip and innuendo. Some people will find evil wherever they look—the devil with them!"

She wiped a tear from her eye. "I understand what you're saying, Jack, but my mind's made up. I'm moving in with your parents."

I thought about it for a moment, certain there was something else at work here that she wasn't saying. I needed a moment to frame my words.

124

Goodbye, Violet

V IOLET," I SAID, "is there something else? Something you're not telling
me?"

She appeared genuinely puzzled. "Of course not, Jack—what else could there
be? You know everything there is to know about me."

From our previous conversation about her social life, I knew I was about
to stick my neck out, but I had to try because I felt certain her decision was
related.

"I have a feeling that living here with me and Adam may be stifling your
social life. If that's the problem, we might find a way to work around it."

She slumped down in a chair, buried her head in her hands, and began
to sob. Her entire body shook.

"Violet," I said, alarmed. "What's wrong? What did I say?"

She looked up at me. He eyes were red and filled with tears. "You don't
understand, Jack," she sobbed. "When you talk about my social life, you
mean men, and I guess you didn't hear me the last time. I'm dirty, and I'll
never get clean. All the showers in the world won't do it. Dr. Stein can't do
it. He tells me I'm clean, but I know better."

I wanted to say something, but her words came out in a torrent.

"I'm sure I told you the day I stowed away in your car, Jack. Earl took
me when I was thirteen, and I wanted to die. He did it again, and again,
and again, then he gave me to a friend. Then he started trading me for
any stupid little thing that caught his eye, and I stopped counting the
times after fifty. I've been had *hundreds* of times from the time I was
thirteen until you saved me. It's a miracle I never got pregnant or had
a venereal disease.

"Did I tell you how I kept myself stuffed with rags or socks because I
never knew when someone might do me? There were times I wanted to kill

myself—the only reason I didn't was because I thought it might be a worse sin than the one I was already doing.

"Once, early on, I told Earl I wasn't going to do it anymore, and he whipped me bad. He said I'll do it whenever he says, or next time he'll beat me *for real.* For months, maybe even years, I prayed and hoped and planned how to get away, while all the time I don't think I ever went more than a few days without Earl or somebody doing me. The day I found you, he'd sold me for a shotgun shell and fifty cents."

After pausing for a moment to compose herself, she said, "I cannot imagine myself in a relationship with a man, Jack. I can deal with men at work—salesmen, customers, repairmen, and the rest—because it's business. But an intimate relationship with a man? That will never happen."

"You're wrong, Violet," I said, more sharply than I'd intended. "You're as clean as any woman I know and you have a wonderful future ahead of you. Marriage, friends and family—children, if you want them. Some lucky man, a *good* man, will come along one day and count himself blessed to have you as his wife. You've got to stop selling yourself short!"

"No," she said, standing up abruptly. "Thanks for the lecture, Jack, but it doesn't change anything. I know what I am. So do you and your folks, and Eddie and Evie. I love all of you for accepting me . . . for everything you've done for me. I'm not moving out so I can find a man. I'm moving out so *you* can find a woman."

125

Letter from Blinky

IT ARRIVED BY POST at the Dunlaur factory: an official Department of Defense envelope addressed to me and red-stamped "Personal and Confidential." Inside was a letter from the War Department saying that the enclosed piece of mail, also addressed to me, was among the personal effects of Major Howard Gordon, killed in action May 21, 1953.

Dear Jack:

This is one of those "I won't be coming back" letters. I wrote my first one when I was flying missions over Germany in 1943 but I tore it up on V-E Day. Did you write one when you were in the Pacific? I'm flying in a B-29 group. Our targets are not easy to spot—not like bombing a German factory. We are going after concentrations of military units on the move. Finding them is hard. Bombing them is hard. The terrain is mountainous. Troops move in the valleys between mountain ridges. Going in for a bombing run is tough. The enemy has plenty of time to see us coming and disperse. The bombing is not effective. We drop the bombs and fly away and the enemy reforms as if nothing happened.

Our planes were great planes in a propeller war, Superfortresses, vintage 1945. They were effective over Japan, with stationary targets and no fighter planes. Here we are attacked by MIG-15 jet fighters. They are flown by Russians. They are good and so damn fast. We don't stand a chance against them. We have some WWII Corsairs and Mustangs. They are sitting ducks for the MIGs. And we had some Shooting Star jets that were no match for the MIG. Now we have a new good jet fighter, the Sabre Jet. It is better than the MIG. But we don't have many. It is new. It is not like 1943 and 1944, when we built a thousand planes a week. The Sabre Jet is a good fighter but we do not have many. They are coming but not enough and not fast enough.

I just came back from my second mission. We were five B-29s that went out on the mission. Only two of us came back. It is real bad, Jack. In 1945, I was confident I would be okay. I even volunteered for extra missions when I could have stopped after 25. Here, I do not believe I will make it. We'll stop the B-29s soon. They are not effective. We are getting killed for nothing. I hope the brass will realize it soon. This whole war is for nothing.

Jack, I am writing to you because you are my only friend. That is sad to say because we hardly ever see each other. But I have no real friends, and I want to tell you how bad I feel over the Evie thing. You were right to stop me, even though my re-call was the end of it anyway.

I put on a great front when I came back in 1945. I made myself over and I changed my name and I bought those elevator shoes and I developed a real macho look and style. And I was successful with it. My insurance business did real good. Everybody thinks I am a great guy. Women think I am a real desirable man.

Truth is, I am still Blinky. I am no good with women.

Sometimes I start out to romance a woman, but I never push it past a flirtation or a quick affair. I do not follow through. I like women. I admire a good-looking woman. But I am not comfortable with the relationship that a woman wants. I know how to be glib and amusing. I can afford dinners, flowers, and gifts, but when a woman starts to want more of me, I end it. Did you know I tried to get something going with Violet? She had zero interest.

Nothing happened with Evie. Nothing. She may have enjoyed being with me, but it was too early on. If you and Korea did not stop it, it would have stopped anyway.

Was I afraid of you? Yes, Jack. I had it coming. I admire you, more than you know. You are tough. You are not afraid of anything. I never stop picturing that day in '39 when you and Eddie took on the Mackeys and you got beat up so bad and me and Bernie just stood by.

You and Eddie forgave us, but I never did. When you took revenge on the Mackeys with that iron pipe, I thought, Jack is the greatest person I know or ever will know.

I remember one day in '47 or maybe it was '48 when we bumped into each other at Gene's Diner. I told you how good I was doing—how much money I was making—how easy it was and I was making more than you. But I felt that you would do something important. Maybe you and Eddie together. Because you are smart and restless to have an important life. To do things. You were not afraid to get married. And to have a child. I admire that, and I admire the success you and Eddie have—not just the money, I made enough of that myself—but you guys DO things, you make things, you guys are fearless. I remain Blinky. You called it. I am still a coward. Always looking to be safe. How the hell did I end up here?

So, Jack, if you are reading this letter, I am gone. Tell Evie I adored her since I was fifteen and I still do. What a woman!

Please try to think kindly of me.

Blinky

126

Normalcy

MAKING DUNLAUR ELECTRONICS profitable again was not easy. We suffered losses for a year, bigger than anticipated, before we were able to stabilize, though on a more modest scale than at the outset of the war. From there, our business had to be reimagined to be regrown, with a sophisticated sales effort and constant improvement and additions to our product line. Building on wartime technology advances, we introduced a host of new gadgets for the electronics and communications industries.

Fortunately, Dunlaur Retail profits continued to cover steep losses in the electronics division. The retail division never stopped growing, even after the war ended. On the contrary, stores three, four, and five, in Trenton, Allentown, and Wilmington, respectively, saw improved traffic as highway stores became more popular.

By mid-1955, the electronics division was in the black again. With the burden of supporting that business eliminated, Evie started planning our sixth retail outlet in earnest.

My life fell into a comfortable routine. I spent as much time as possible with Adam. He was a happy, outgoing boy with an endless curiosity and a quick grasp of complex topics. By the age of nine, he was getting an education beyond his years through spending time with Eddie in Dunlaur Electronic's model shop after school and on weekends. He had all the marks of a future inventor, and I was as proud as any father could be.

Also in 1955, I observed that Eddie and Evie seemed to be growing closer, to the point where they had become true partners in virtually everything they took on. They were the beautiful businesswoman and the . . . How can I describe Eddie? Inventor, scientist, engineer, and savvy businessman all rolled up together and topped off with a caring, gentle persona. When the politicians took notice, he may have been surprised, but I wasn't. He was approached to run for US congressman serving New Jersey's Second District by both the Democratic and Republican parties, each promising that if he won, he'd be their next candidate for the US Senate.

Eddie politely declined. He suggested that either his business partner or his sister would be a better candidate, but the politicians wanted neither of us—me, a salesman, and Evie, a woman? You must be kidding.

127

The Model Shop

T HE MODEL SHOP is where our new products and modifications were designed and where we built our models and prototypes. Eddie had it constructed in 1950, soon after the Korean War started, near the far end of the factory. It was twenty feet by forty feet with a twelve-foot ceiling and resembled a laboratory clean room. Everything was white except the desktops and worktables, which were bleached, highly polished butcher block. Running the entire length of the rear wall was a counter, above which were white cabinets and a grid of square white cubbyholes for holding plans, drawings, blueprints, and related documentation.

Our engineers and draftsmen in white lab coats used the back counter, while the twenty-foot counter along the left wall was Eddie's personal work area. It was always covered with prototypes and drawings. Staff and visitors were required to remove their shoes and don slippers before entering. At the end of each work shift, the entire room was thoroughly swept and washed down.

Brightly lit, with its see-through wall, the model shop shone like a jewel. It was Eddie's favorite place. Adam's, too, from the time he entered elementary school.

I had Adam picked up after school and brought to the factory almost every weekday. Eddie gave him small mechanical and drawing tasks to work out at his own desk area. I noted with an occasional pang of jealousy that Eddie and Adam related more like father and son than uncle and nephew. At school, Adam was known to tell teachers and classmates, with no small amount of pride, "I work at Dunlaur Electronics."

128

A Favor for Bobo

WHEN I LEFT the Dunlaur plant that day, I found Frankie waiting for me in the parking lot, in a new, dark maroon Buick Roadmaster. He lowered his window as I approached.

"Hey, Frankie," I greeted him, leaning toward the open window. "What's up?"

"Hello, Jack," he answered, stone-faced as usual. "Bobo wants to see you. Climb in."

That was it—never a phone call. Never a reason. I climbed the rear steps to Bobo's second floor office above Trucci's. I always felt some apprehension when summoned by Bobo.

"Hi, Bobo. Hi, Georgie. What's up?" I tried for a cheery greeting. Was it going to be a pleasant meeting?

The scene was always the same. Georgie was relaxing on the sofa with a newspaper. Bobo was at his desk. He rose to greet me. "It's good to see you, Jack," he said, swallowing me in a bear hug. Then, turning his head, "Hey, Georgie, how's about a cuppa coffee for Jack?"

He released me from the bear hug and held me out at arm's length. "I'll come right to the point. I need a favor—and I'm gonna do you one at the same time."

He explained. "Loretta's got this niece, lives in Philly, not bad lookin'. She's down here for a few days. Take her out to dinner. Don't go to Trucci's. I'll pay for it."

"That's the favor for you," I said. "What's the favor for me? I'm not dating. You know that."

"It's time you was," he narrowed his eyes and brought his face a little closer to mine. "This is easy. She ain't a date. Just take her to dinner—some-place nice; like maybe the Knife and Fork or the Shelburne.

"Why is this good for you?" he added. "I'll tell you why. You been in mourning long enough. Gettin' back to livin' is hard, and it's easy to put off until tomorrow, or next month, or after you finish the big deal you're workin' on. So here's an easy way in—no pressure. You don't even have to make a good impression over here. And ya never know—you might like her. The worst what kin happen is—what? You'll waste a few hours."

"Okay, Bobo," I grinned. "You know I can't turn you down—and anyway, this has got to be easier than breaking into the chief's office."

He laughed and slapped my back. I took two steps forward to keep my balance.

"Good, good," he chortled. Her name is Elena Volpe. She's at the Claridge."

"Volpe," I repeated. "That's Italian for 'fox,' if I remember correctly."

She wasn't what I expected.

129

Elena Volpe

S HE WAS STAYING at the Claridge. We arranged to meet at the hotel bar. I was curious about how it would feel to be meeting a girl on sort of a date. Except for the one night in Louisville with Sally Carol the night before the Korean War started, I hadn't been with a woman since Alice. It had been four years.

I knew it wasn't right. A man needs a woman. Why did I not have the urge? Was there something wrong with me? Or was I just put off by the ritual of meeting and dating and seizing the right moment to bed her? Bobo made it easy by thrusting this girl on me. It didn't really matter what happened.

The place was dimly lit, but as my eyes adjusted, I spotted her at the bar, perched on a tall barstool. She wore a white cashmere turtleneck sweater and gray glen plaid trousers and high-heeled shoes. In the dim light, I saw that she had a thick mane of dirty-blonde hair.

"Elena?"

She turned. "Yes. Jack?" she said, slipping off the stool. She came toward me, smiling, her arm stretched out into a straight, firm handshake. My God!

In the clear light, she looked like Alice. I was speechless for a moment.

She looked at me curiously, wondering. "Jack?" she repeated, raising her eyebrows. "Is that you? Are you okay?"

I recovered. She really didn't look like Alice at all. Her features were fuller, but her smile was like Alice's: broad, generous, inviting. That, and her figure, and the way she carried herself as she came toward me—that was the resemblance.

"Excuse me, Elena." I moved toward her. "For a moment, I thought you were someone I knew. Shall we have a drink?"

She was an easy conversationalist, animated, always smiling. She appreciated Bobo looking after her. She was Loretta's niece, but she called him Uncle Bobo. She was a hostess at the Hunt Room at the Bellevue Stratford Hotel in Philadelphia. She was here in Atlantic City for a few days of vacation and self-indulgence. She knew quite a lot about me from Uncle Bobo and said she was really glad to meet me.

When I told her I'd made a reservation at the Shelburne, she said, "Let's have dinner here. This hotel has a good dining room, and we're here already."

The maître d' asked, "Where will you like to be seated?"

Before I could answer, Elena said, "We would like to sit over there," pointing to a table for two with the seats on an upholstered bench against the wall.

There was a small stage. The billboard featured three unknowns: an attractive young singer, a Jewish stand-up comic, and a piano player, all pretty good but not first-rate. Neither of us had heard of any of them.

Elena sat on my right. "This is nice, isn't it, Jack?" She smiled, leaning toward me. We raised our martinis. She shifted slightly. Her left leg touched me. The contact was slight. I moved my leg, but she inched closer. Just a small touch, but it was erotic.

The conversation continued. She told me about being a hostess at what was probably Philadelphia's most upscale restaurant. She had a regular stream of propositions coming from the city's leading citizens, most of them extremely wealthy and very married.

She was twenty-seven. No, never married—a few unimportant boyfriends along the way but nothing serious. She laughed. "I haven't found him yet," she said, invitingly.

Was I supposed to rise to that bait? As in, *Maybe I'm the one?* I didn't.

Aside from Philadelphia's beautiful people, her main interests seemed to be the movies and movie stars. She knew every popular movie of the last ten years and all the actors. She talked about some of her favorites—it was a long list. She knew everything there was to know about them. Had I seen *From Here to Eternity*? She was in love with Burt Lancaster. Deborah

Kerr wasn't good enough for him. How about *Roman Holiday*? She loved Gregory Peck, and did I think he and Audrey Hepburn were in love? And should Audrey Hepburn have run away with him? And how about Audrey in *Sabrina*? She should have married William Holden. Humphrey Bogart was too old for her. He must have been forty! Her all-time favorites were Clark Gable and Jimmy Stewart. Vivian Leigh, as Scarlett O'Hara, was a fool. Ava Gardner in *Mogambo* was the right woman for Gable. Grace Kelly in *Rear Window* was a good match for Jimmy, but she was pathetic in *Mogambo*. Marlon Brando? She got squirmy just thinking about him. Had I seen him in *On the Waterfront*?

I told her I liked the old black-and-white movies from the 1930s. Some of my favorites were *The Prisoner of Zenda*, *The Mark of Zorro*, *A Night at the Opera*, and *The Corsican Brothers*.

We were interrupted by a photographer. "Care for a remembrance photo?" she asked.

"Sure," I answered.

"How about sitting a little closer?" she suggested.

Elena shifted closer.

"You are a great-looking couple," the photographer said, raising and aiming her camera. "How about a little kiss to show how much you're enjoying yourself here in Atlantic City, at the famous Claridge Hotel?"

Elena turned to me. Our lips touched, briefly, but in that moment, her tongue darted between my lips, and at the same time, she rested the palm of her left hand on my leg.

I flushed with heat and a wave of passion. I took the inner side of her left thigh in my right hand and she didn't resist. She pushed closer, her breast pressing against me, firm inside that soft, white cashmere sweater. I felt the years of repression overtaking me.

"Let's get out of here," she whispered hoarsely. "Take care of the check then come to my room, four twenty-six. I'll be waiting." She rose and left.

130

Sex at the Claridge

Eⱼₑₙₐ OPENED THE door and drew me into the room. She was wearing a silk robe with nothing under it. She threw her arms around me and we kissed, passionately, open-mouthed. Her robe fell open. She pressed a knee into my groin. "Get out of those clothes," she murmured.

I tore off my clothes. I reached between her legs and found she was smooth-shaven. I lifted her off the ground and threw her on the bed.

Her body was marvelous. She was slender, firm, and soft at the same time. I grew enormous. She held me, writhing underneath me. She reached up and smothered my face with big, wet, open-mouthed kisses. She wrapped her legs around me. "Give it to me, Jack," she panted. "I want it—I want it!"

I slid in, just a little. She went wild. "Give it, give it, give it to me!" and then "Oooh!" as I plunged, deep, deep, hot, wet, writhing, writhing, writhing, until we both collapsed, spent.

After a half hour of lying together, exhausted, Elena rose, put on her robe, and reclined in an easy chair.

"I guess it's time to get dressed, Jack," she said.

"How 'bout I stay the night?" I said, leaning up on my arm as I admired her beauty.

"No, Jack," she said. "This was a gift from Bobo. We'll get together again. Next time, it's two fifty a pop—all night is a thousand dollars."

And I thought hookers never kissed.

* * *

I went to see Bobo the next morning. Before I could say anything, he gave me the big bear hug and a large smile.

"Welcome back to the living," he grinned. "You don't have to tell me how it was. She's really somethin', ain't she?"

"How do you know, Bobo?" I asked. "Are you a regular?"

"Me?" he laughed. "No, no, no," he shook his head. "She's Loretta's niece, for Chrissake. I'd be a dead man over here. This was my gift to you. You needed it, and you didn't even know how much. Remember how I got you broken-in back in '39, when you was fifteen, with that little blonde, Patty? And now, I brang you back to life with this one. You know how I feel about you, Jack. You're the son I never had, the son I wished I had. Now, get back in the groove. You ain't no holy man, so stop actin' like one!"

131

Women

ELENA WAS LIKE a blast of dynamite. She blew away my sexual logjam. I began dating at that point, continuously. At thirty-one, I was healthy, successful, reasonably good-looking, and apparently appealing to members of the opposite sex. But how could any woman have a serious chance? As much as I enjoyed female companionship, Alice was always with me. As to sex, no one could match Elena Volpe, the fox. The evening I'd spent in her bed was unforgettable.

Nevertheless, dating was good for me. I went to movies, concerts, and the theater. I had a social life again, which brought relief from the intensity of Dunlaur.

Every man needs a woman, and I realized just how much after shutting myself off for all those years. I entered into multiple relationships. Each woman knew she was not exclusive. Socially, the Atlantic City area is a small town, and each of my dates knew the others I was seeing. Some of them dropped me quickly when they realized there was no future with me. That was all right—there was no shortage of attractive replacements.

"It's no good," Eddie told me at lunch one day. "You gotta settle down. You need a wife, a mother for Adam. You need a *partner*, Jack."

"I know, Eddie," I said. "But where is she? There are no Alices out there."

He leaned forward. "That's the problem, Jack," he said, pointing a finger at me. "There is no Alice, but there must be someone else who can give you what you want . . . what you need. She won't be Alice. She'll be someone different, someone maybe as good, but in a different way. Stop looking for another Alice and start looking for a woman who is good in her own way."

"I'm keeping my eyes open, Eddie," I said, "but I ain't seen her yet."

132

A Shadow in Zena's Globe

Friday, September 23, 1955

E VIE HAD INVITED Violet and me to join her and Eddie for dinner at the Knife and Fork, saying she had a surprise for us. As I prepared to leave my office around six o'clock, Alan Goren called.

"This is puzzling, Jack," he said. "Zena opened her booth this morning at ten, as usual, and when she lit her globe, she saw something in it—something dark, like a cloud, swirling. She doesn't know what to make of it, but it frightened her. You and I know," he continued, "that Zena *sees* things. She says no, but you'll recall that she saw World War II a few days before it started."

That's right, I thought to myself, remembering a more recent instance. *She tried to stop Alice from going out that morning, but her warning was too late.*

Goren continued. "She knew I'd want to hear about it, but when she called our apartment, I was out. The parlor got busy, and it was after four by the time she reached me. So what could it mean, Jack, the dark cloud in the globe? A war, or something with the Russians? The Cold War is very much alive, but it seems calmer since Eisenhower. Maybe an earthquake, a volcano, or a forest fire? Who knows? Maybe her globe just needs a good cleaning.

"I couldn't imagine what this terrible thing might be," he contin-ued, "but it made me think about my exposure if something bad *does* happen. Jack, I'm short one hundred contracts of December wheat, and that could be a big exposure to some kind of shocking news. Remember how cocoa shot up to the limit when Hitler invaded Poland? You, me, and Benny—and Bobo. We made a killing. We were long cocoa. Today I am short wheat."

In the trader's parlance, being "short" is the opposite of owning something. It means you sold something you don't own. You'll have to buy it back in the open market in order to deliver it to the person you sold it to. If the price drops after you sold it "short," you'll buy it cheaper and make a profit. If the price goes up after you sold it "short," you'll have to pay more to cover your short position. You'll lose money. As Goren liked to say, *He who sells what isn't his'n, must buy it back or go to pris'n.*

Goren wasn't finished. "The market has been calm, Jack. I'm sure that wheat and all commodity prices are drifting lower. The wheat crop is big this year, but more important is that Eisenhower and the Republicans are determined to end high, rigid commodity price supports. Once they end the Farm Subsidy Act, commodity prices will fall to where they belong in a natural market, without price supports.

"So, although I couldn't see any reason to change my positions, I thought I may as well reduce the exposure. I called my broker to cover eighty contracts, reducing my exposure to only twenty contracts.

"I was ten minutes late. The commodity exchange closed at four thirty. Prices were mostly unchanged for the day. There was no significant news to affect the markets. I'm not alarmed, but as a precaution, I'm going to cover eighty contracts on Monday morning. But Jack, I want you to think about *your* potential exposure. Do you have any commodities? Stocks? Anything in your business that might be exposed?"

I thought for a minute. "No, Alan, I'm barely in the stock market, and I'm not trading commodity options. Not like our 1939 cocoa days. The closest thing I have to commodity positions are contracts for steel and wire purchases for future deliveries—to lock in prices. If prices fall, I'll be paying more than I might have, but it's nothing serious. Look, I guess anything could happen. The plant could have a fire, or a tornado could touch down. If there is something bad coming, I don't know what I might do to protect everything I have. It can't be done, to protect *everything* against anything that might happen. We carry insurance, all kinds of insurance. Don't know what else we could do. No, Alan, I can't worry every day about something bad happening, or else I wouldn't be able to work at all."

I started out for our dinner meeting at the Knife and Fork Inn. My concern about Goren's call slipped away when I climbed into my car and hurried to our meeting. Yes, I believed Zena could see into the future, but I had no idea of what this was about or what it might mean to me.

* * *

Goren was right to cover his wheat positions, I felt. Even if nothing disastrous happened, he was too heavily invested. It was a dangerous position. Every contract of wheat is five thousand bushels. He was short one hundred contracts; that's five hundred thousand bushels of wheat! I knew he was well fixed financially, but that is a huge exposure. Wheat was about $1.50 per bushel. If wheat prices moved up, he'd lose $50,000 for each $.10 increase. I didn't know him as such a wild speculator.

133

Dinner at the Knife and Fork Inn . . . and What Zena Saw in the Globe

SEPTEMBER IS ATLANTIC City's best month. The tourists are gone. The natives bask in an afterglow of ten weeks of good business. September to November is relaxing time before winter's hibernation and springtime's work to prepare for the next season. September weather is perfect. The days start to shorten, but they are still long. Morning and evening shadows grow longer. The evening air is delicious, fresh, with the tang of ocean and the scent of faraway lands. The Boardwalk is scrubbed clean from morning dew, stretching out toward the Arabian palaces in the distance. Those beautiful hotels are all gone now. But back then, they guarded the Boardwalk, splendid gold and ivory sentinels.

We met on the Boardwalk, relaxed, leaning against the railing, tasting the breeze. A pale early evening light touched the water with golden highlights. The sky was not yet dark, but Venus appeared, the evening star.

We talked of everything, enjoying our closeness away from business and the never-ending press of things to do.

Eddie studied his watch. "Okay, dinnertime." We left the Boardwalk and walked the short half block to the Knife and Fork.

"Dear ones," said Eddie, raising his glass with a broad smile. "Here we are, four lucky people. I toast our good fortune and wish for a good future for us and for Dunlaur."

"So, Evie," I turned to my sister after clinking our glasses. "What's the big surprise?"

She leaned forward, her forearms on the table, smiling. She turned her eyes, first to me and then to Violet. "First, let me say how much I love Eddie." She turned to Eddie and covered his hand with hers. "More than I can ever say. I treasure the moments we're together."

Eddie flushed. "I love you, Evie," he said, looking at her. He turned to me and then to Violet. "And I'm going to deliver the news—Evie is pregnant!"

I leaped from my chair and pulled him up from his. I gave him the biggest bear hug in memory. Evie and Violet were on their feet, hugging and kissing.

The baby was due next April.

Never was a dinner party more wonderful.

As we rose to leave the restaurant, the maître d' moved to the center of the dining room, raised his voice, and called out loudly for everyone's attention. There was a nine-inch TV on the cashier's desk. He had turned up the volume.

A newsman was talking about the president's heart attack. It happened in Denver, Colorado, where Eisenhower was visiting his in-laws. Vice President Richard Nixon would speak to the nation tomorrow; for now, he was acting president.

All of us in the room, staff and diners alike, stood silent and motionless as we absorbed the news. No one left the restaurant for an hour; our eyes remained fixed on the screen as reports came in from Fitzsimmons Veterans Hospital and from newsmen stationed near the White House.

"What does it mean?" Violet asked. "What should we be doing?"

"Don't know," I answered. "Zena said something bad is coming. She saw a shadow in her globe. Goren called me about it as I was leaving the office, but he couldn't foresee anything bad happening. I guess this is it. I'll ask him what it means."

134

Eisenhower's Heart Attack

T HE COUNTRY CAME to a halt, hanging on the medical releases. Eisenhower was a beloved president. There have been no beloved presidents since. Some have been admired, some merely accepted, but none have been beloved. What kind of president would Richard Nixon be if Eisenhower did not survive?

I saw Goren early the next morning; it was Saturday. We both knew he was going to lose a lot of money on Monday, but he seemed relaxed as usual. He drew on his pipe and leaned back on the sofa.

"What," he asked, "does Eisenhower's heart attack mean to the country and the markets? The reaction to his heart attack will be that he may die and Nixon will serve out his term. If he survives the heart attack, how likely is it that he'll run for a second term? It's quite possible that the Democrats will be in power starting in 1957.

"Among other things, high rigid agricultural price supports will continue. The possibility of that—no, indeed, the *likelihood* of that—will drive commodity prices up sharply. Commodity prices have been drifting lower because the Republicans are committed to lowering farm price supports. If the Democrats get in, price supports will be here to stay.

"Now," he said. "Let's talk about me. The commodity exchange will open on Monday. Wheat will go up the limit at the opening, fifteen cents a bushel. The wheat market will close immediately. So will the markets for corn, soybeans, barley—every crop that is presently subsidized. They will all go up to the limit. The threat of the Republican end to price supports will stop the downward drift of commodity prices.

"Yesterday, when Zena told me something bad was in her globe, I tried to cover my short positions, but I was too late. The market closed ten minutes before I called. There's no market today. There's no market tomorrow. I won't be able to buy in my shorts. On Monday, I'll lose seventy-five thousand dollars in the first minute. On Tuesday, the same thing will happen. I'll lose another seventy-five thousand on Tuesday. I guess the market will begin to stabilize on Wednesday. It will continue to go up but not so violently. I'll get a margin call on Wednesday for at least a hundred and fifty thousand dollars. I'll cover my short position. By noon on Wednesday, I will lose more than a hundred and fifty thousand. I'll sell stocks to raise the money to cover the loss.

"The rub is that just as the prospect for a Democratic administration means higher farm prices, the prospect of a Democratic administration is a negative for stocks. The stock market will not like Nixon for the remainder of Eisenhower's term. And the stock market will not like Democrats in 1956. So I'll get beat up both ways. I'll lose on commodities because I'm short, and I'll lose on stocks because I'm long."

"Alan," I said, "can you lose a hundred and fifty thousand dollars? Will you be okay? Listen, I'm here for you, and Eddie will be too. Anything you need, just say the word."

"Thanks, Jack," he said. "I'm wounded, that's all. I'm still good. I'm annoyed at myself for such an amateurish mistake at this stage of my life. I'll have to get more conservative moving forward, but Zena and I won't have to change our lifestyle. Besides," he grinned, pulling Zena to him, "Zena can support both of us from her reading parlor!"

Zena smiled at him. "I always knew you wanted to be a kept man, Alan."

Goren drew on his pipe, sipped at his coffee. Finally, he stood up and threw an arm around my shoulder. "Don't worry about me and Zena, Jack. We're okay. As for the country, I don't see any meaningful changes coming. Eisenhower may survive. He may even be able to run for another term next year. Meanwhile, nothing will be different. The country is in good shape. The general economy won't be affected—only some industries that could be affected by a Democratic administration coming in January 1957. I think Nixon will be the Republican candidate, and any Democrat can beat him. Eisenhower is loved. He is America's father figure. Nixon is feared. The country thinks he is unknowledgeable and untrustworthy. But he is not going to change anything during the remainder of Eisenhower's term. The election is only fourteen months away."

"What about the Russians?" I asked.

"Ah," Goren said, pointing his pipe at me. "*There* is a riddle. Who is the boss over there? Bulganin or Khrushchev? I think Khrushchev calls the shots. Curiously, Nixon may be better for us than Eisenhower, because Eisenhower is seen as a reasonable man, deliberate. He won't do anything rash. The Soviets can do something provocative and know that with Eisenhower, there is always opportunity to talk about it, reach a compromise, or undo it if necessary. But Nixon is an unknown. The Soviets suspect he's a little crazy. They can never predict his reaction to a provocation. They picture him with his finger on the red button, ready to push. They can't rely on him to be deliberate, seek counsel, talk things over. They regard him as dangerous and unpredictable."

He paused to draw on his pipe then continued. "We would like to think that Nixon has two faces when it comes to geopolitics. The face that foreign leaders see is the face of an unpredictable man who doesn't think things through. But we want to think, or hope, that the other Nixon face is careful and knows how to manage and cultivate his reputation as a dangerous nut to our advantage."

* * *

As it turned out, Eisenhower recovered after several weeks on the critical list. Some weeks later, I asked Goren how badly he got hurt from his wheat futures.

He answered with a dismissive wave. "More embarrassment at my foolishness than hurt, Jack. I'm worth a lot of money. It was a superficial wound."

Eisenhower ran for reelection and won in 1956. He took Nixon as his vice president again and functioned with no hint of disability for the next four years.

In 1960, Nixon was the Republican candidate for president. But he couldn't beat John F. Kennedy.

135

Young Edward

April 19, 1956

IF I COULD HAVE written the lead story for the *Atlantic City Press* that morning, it would have been headlined:

SON FOR EDDIE AND EVIE DUNAUSKAS, EDWARD JR.,
BORN TODAY AT ATLANTIC CITY GENERAL, 8 LBS, 7 OZS.
MOTHER AND CHILD FINE IN EVERY WAY. FATHER
OVERWHELMED WITH HAPPINESS!

Instead, the *Press* blared:

GRACE KELLY AND PRINCE RAINIER WED!

Stories and photos of the beautiful actress and her brilliant Hollywood career followed. The article described the handsome prince and offered a brief history of the fairy-tale principality of Monaco, famous for its glitzy, romantic capital, Monte Carlo.

Eddie was wild with joy over the birth of his son. He could not be still. He grinned, he laughed. He hugged everyone. At the end of the day, in a reflective mood, he took me aside.

"Jack," he said, "I can't express myself, but you know how it feels. It's incredible. It's also scary to find I have *everything* I ever wanted."

"I know," I answered. "A man doesn't understand what love is about until he has a son."

136

Sic Iter ad Astra:
From the Earth to the Stars

Friday, October 4, 1957

I WAS SEATED AT the breakfast table absorbed in the morning paper. I was reading about the second game of the World Series, in which the New York Yankees were pitted against the Milwaukee Braves. There were background stories about Hank Aaron, Red Schoendienst, Warren Spahn, Yogi Berra, Whitey Ford, and Mickey Mantle, among other baseball greats. The articles revealed that the average annual salary of the players was $15,000. Players on the winning team were expected to earn a bonus of about $8,000 each, the losers about $5,000.

Adam joined me for breakfast in what had become a favorite ritual.

"We're like two men getting ready to start the day, aren't we, Dad?" he said. "You're off to Dunlaur and I'm off to Atlantic City Elementary. In eight or nine years, I'll be going to Dunlaur, won't I, Dad? And you'll be able to stop working so hard!"

I set the paper aside. "Are you going to take over, son? So soon? Won't you want to go to college and study engineering, physics, electronics?"

"I don't see why," he said, chewing on Mrs. Wilson's home fries. "Uncle Eddie didn't go to college. You didn't go to college. Aunt Evie didn't go to college." He paused. "But Mom went to college, didn't she?"

Before I could answer, the phone rang. It was Eddie.

"Jack," he said breathlessly. "Did you hear the news? About Sputnik?"

"No, Eddie," I answered. "Who is he?"

"It's not a *he*," he answered. "It's a Russian satellite. They launched it last night, and it's in orbit. Unbelievable! Jack, they're way ahead of us. I been reading about how it would happen. We all thought the US would be first to launch, in three years or so."

I didn't know what to say.

"No matter," he continued. "My plan for a mobile phone is for transmission towers. But satellites—that's where all communications are headed. Communication satellites are still years away, but if we're gonna have a mobile phone, we don't have any time to waste."

137

The Mobile Phone

Sunday, December 20, 1959

I WATCHED CHARLES KURALT'S *Sunday Morning* TV show. In reviewing the news of the past week, Kuralt spoke briefly about the world's first communications satellite, SCORE, launched on Thursday atop an American Atlas rocket. It was only fourteen months since the Soviets had launched Sputnik.

It's as Eddie says, I thought. *The sciences are racing faster all the time.* This was stunning news—an orbiting satellite receiving and relaying a message from earth, something unimaginable only fifteen months ago.

I called him. "Eddie," I asked, "this communication satellite, SCORE? I never heard anything about it until today. Did you know about it? What does it mean? Does it mean anything to Dunlaur?"

"No," he answered, "at least not to Dunlaur's business or product line today. I emphasize *today* because electronics and communications are advancing at fantastic speed."

He paused then said, "Jack, can you come to my office? Now? I want to show you something."

* * *

A black suitcase sat on the conference table.

"This is it," Eddie said, pushing apart the buttons to release the clasps. The case popped open. "It's a mobile phone," he said. "Not a radio like our walkie-talkies—an actual telephone."

The instrument looked like a hybrid: part radio, part telephone, roughly ten by eight by twenty inches. It had a three-letter keyboard and a speaker and was housed in a black-enameled steel box.

"I'm going to demonstrate," he said. "Evie is in store number one holding the mate to this one. Each instrument has three dialing buttons. I assigned AAA to this one and AAB to the one Evie has. Watch, I'm going to call her."

He pressed a button marked *On/Off,* and a light appeared on the console. He pressed a *Call/Stop* button, and a dial tone began to hum. He pressed AAB. The hum of the dial tone changed to beeping, with the beeps coming at half-second intervals.

"I'm violating eight Bell Labs patents," he said, "but we'll deal with that later."

The beeping stopped, and I heard my sister say, "Hello, darling. How do I sound?"

"A little crinkly," Eddie said. "Can you hear me okay?"

"Yes, dear. Loud and clear. How far apart are we?"

"I'm at the plant, so we're only four miles apart. The signal is being relayed from the antenna we put on the Claridge. I think we could be about twenty miles apart with the same reception quality, but I want to test it. I'm going to get in my car and drive west on the White Horse Pike—let's see how far I can go without losing the signal."

I was stunned. He'd done it. All those nights in the model shop, all those Saturdays and Sundays. He'd told me he was working on a mobile telephone, but did I really believe he could do it? Eddie, alone, with no one to consult, while over at Bell Labs, a team of ten electrical and radio engineers had yet to produce a prototype. No doubt they'd have one soon. Motorola had a mobile phone project underway, with a radio engineer named Leonid Kupriyanovich working on it at a Russian company, ALTAI, in Moscow. And APC had a new Mobile Telephone Service, which worked by calling in to an APC operator who would then patch you into what amounted to a conference call with your party and operator. The APC mobile phone was double the size of Eddie's. It was an awkward system, and it was not phone to phone.

And now here was Eddie and Dunlaur with a working model! I was gripped with the kind of anxiety Eddie and I felt when we developed the printed circuit board and knew we had to be first to market. It would be the same with the mobile phone. Being second in the race would be the same as not being in it at all. We had to be first—and with ten numerical keys. Eddie's three-key ABC device could support only a twenty-seven-phone network, while ten numerical keys would allow ten billion combinations.

We drove out onto the White Horse Pike and found that reception was good up to twelve miles west of the Claridge. Evie left store number one, about a mile east of the Claridge, and drove north with her instrument, across the bridge into Brigantine then continued north. We were still communicating clearly when she was fifteen miles north of the Claridge. Beyond that, the reception grew poor, then poorer, and less than two miles later, there was nothing but static.

"So," Eddie said, "it works, as I knew it would. The key to a practical system is antenna towers. For openers, we have to install relays and boosters on top of available radio and TV towers. This is the future, and one day the country will be covered with relay towers. I'll build the relays so they can pick up from one relay to another, and then to another, just like TV."

He continued. "The next phone I build will be about thirty percent smaller, with ten keys. I still can't manage to dial like a telephone, but that will come. Transistors are the key. They get smaller every day. I keep redesigning our circuit boards to accommodate the smaller transistors. Each generation of these mobile phones will be smaller and more powerful. Someday, Jack, believe it or not, one will fit in a person's pocket or in his palm. And I'll tell you something that you'll really have trouble believing. Relay towers are necessary now, but in time, the phones won't connect through relay towers. Every spot on earth will be accessible through a system of satellites. Thousands of satellites will circle the earth, like tiny moons. Like SCORE, which just got put in orbit by a rocket—like our Atlas rocket, which is only one generation removed from the German V-2.

"You don't believe me, do you?" he continued, looking at me. "It's for real, Jack. I've been reading all about it for two years. Sputnik was the first satellite, but all it could do was beep a signal. Now comes SCORE, which can receive and relay back messages. In fifty or sixty years, you'll be able to speak to everyone in the world on one of these phones. Telephone lines will go the way of the horse and buggy."

We went to Eddie's house, where Evie was waiting with dinner. We talked into the evening and well into the night. It was one thing to develop a prototype, but negotiating and building hundreds of relay stations and negotiating for rights to use patent-protected systems?

Evie asked, "Are we financially strong enough to do it?"

"We should talk to Goren," I said.

"By the way, Eddie," Evie addressed her husband, "when was the last time you visited the Atlantic Avenue store?"

Eddie paused. "It's been awhile. Maybe three, four months. Why?"

"It's not our kind of store," she answered. "It's a TV and radio store. Do you realize we're still repairing radios in the back? I can't put appliances in there. There's no room. I want to sell it to the manager. He still goes out to install antennas and fix TV sets. He'll work it and make a living. I imagine he has a few thousand dollars . . . we'll carry him for the balance. He'll have to change the name of the store." She laughed. "Should we let him call it *Eddie's*?"

"It's still making money," Eddie said. "Not much, but it is profitable. I kinda like holding on to it. It's where we started."

"It's not for us," she replied soothingly, as one tells a child he can't have that particular toy. "There's a good location out on the White Horse Pike in Absecon. That's where the retail business is going—out on the highways, with plenty of off-street parking—like our stores in Trenton and Allentown and Wilmington. I'm going to have a traffic study. We'll do real well there. This store doesn't warrant our time and effort. Is that okay with you, dear? And how about you, Jack?"

"Sure," Eddie said. "The retail division is yours."

I nodded my agreement.

Truthfully, I would have kept the store out of nostalgia. Of the three of us, Evie was the one true merchant.

138

Goren, Mentor

THE GOREN APARTMENT was a place of warmth and friendship. It was a place where I could bring problems and confusion and know that Alan's opinions would be wise and honest. He was a man who had done it all: a West Pointer, decorated World War I veteran, infantry captain, commodities trader, real estate investor, student of national and international politics, economist, historian, and scholar. The man knew everything. That he was also a mystic added to his aura of being all wise, all knowing.

Eddie, Evie, and I gathered there, perplexed. How to make a go of Eddie's mobile phone system?

The living room was the same as always, strewn with newspapers, magazines, and open books. Delicious aromas drifted in from the dining room. Goren greeted us, dressed as always in a gray cardigan sweater over a white shirt, khaki pants, gray ragg socks, and loafers. Zena removed her apron as she as she came out of the kitchen to embrace us.

I apologized for not visiting more often. I said I felt like a *taker*—always coming to take his advice, without even the occasional gift of a visit unencumbered by the burden of a problem.

"Don't say that, Jack," Goren said. "Zena and I never forget what you and Benny brought us. You gave me a values system that changed my life. Zena and I owe our happiness to you and Benny. We can never repay you—but enough of that. Come. First, Zena's breakfast. Business later."

It is a hard thing to do—to set aside a pressing problem for an hour of friendship over an enjoyable meal. It was the Goren's special magic. After breakfast, we gathered in the living room.

"So, Jack, Eddie, Evie," Goren said, leaning back in his easy chair. "Tell me everything."

We did, and I ended the story by saying, "So what now, Alan?"

Goren sat quietly, collecting his thoughts. He drew on his pipe. He looked at each of us for several seconds. He raised his eyebrows. He studied us, but his words were addressed to Zena who was seated beside him.

"Zena," he said, "remember what I told you about these boys, that they will do big things. And they have. They built a big business and do groundbreaking work. And look at Evie, this pretty little girl. How is she such a remarkable businesswoman? Where did that come from? And now this—a mobile phone. It will change the world."

He paused, drew on his pipe again. "So what now, Alan?" he repeated my question. "What now? I can't predict where this technology is going, but remember: Tesla invented the incandescent bulb before Edison, but Edison got the patent, and the rest is history. You don't want to be Tesla, my friends, you want to be Edison. Ask your attorney to get you a patent specialist—fast! Eddie, you said you're using eight Bell Lab patents. Does your telephone have anything original in it that you can patent?"

"It sure does," Eddie said. "Two things I made myself are an automatic switch that activates a phone when a call is directed to it and a new kind of booster relay that goes on the tower—to pick up a signal, enhance it, and send it on to the nearest tower or to the targeted phone if it's closer than the next tower. Existing radio and TV towers have booster relays, but to compare theirs to mine is like comparing checkers to chess. Theirs broadcast to the world, to any and every receiver that can receive the signal. Mine directs the signal to a specific mobile phone. My relay is more than an improvement—it's a revolution in personal communication."

We talked for over five hours, exploring technical issues, marketing plans, and financial needs, before ending the meeting at two in the afternoon. We agreed to meet again the next morning, and each of us would propose his or her own plan.

139

A Plan

THE FOLLOWING MORNING, we met again at Goren's apartment. Eddie, Evie, and I brought our independent versions of a plan to develop a mobile phone business. After comparing and contrasting our ideas at length, our list of to-dos looked like this:

1. Our attorney, Larry Durells, will engage a patent lawyer.

2. Eddie will move quickly to convert the prototype into a ten-key instrument and reduce its size.

3. I will survey a circular area within a five-mile radius of Philadelphia City Hall. Within the circle, I will locate and rent space on enough radio towers to provide blanket coverage within that area. For any radio tower gaps in the circle, I will rent space on the tallest structure in the gap and, if necessary, erect a tower or a mast on its roof. The City Hall tower will need a ring of twelve relays. City Hall will be a tough deal to negotiate. But I have a good idea who can help us. Dunlaur Retail is a big advertiser. We're in the newspapers, TV, and radio. The editors of the *Inquirer*, the *Bulletin*, and the *Daily News*, along with the TV and radio producers, will help me. They have clout with City Hall, and what we're doing is an important news story.

4. Dunlaur's installation crew will mount our receivers, relays, and amplifiers on the towers and roofs and run the electric lines to the nearest power source for each relay. We need a ring of twelve relays. We divide the circle into twelve imaginary spokes radiating from City Hall, three in each of the four quadrants of the circle. Each spoke will have a receiver, relay, and amplifier at its end and another halfway

along its radial length, two and a half miles from City Hall. We'll have coverage for 75 to 80 percent of the city's population.

5. Eddie and his engineers will test the system throughout the circled area. If the system tests okay, we go into immediate production with a first run of five hundred units.

6. Evie will devote our entire regular Saturday newspaper advertisements in all the Philadelphia papers to the Dunlaur mobile phone. "EXPERIENCE THE MIRACLE!" will be our sales pitch, emphasizing the story of freedom from telephone lines and booths. Our price will be $400 for the unit and three months of access to our network—satisfaction guaranteed or your money back.

Goren asked how many mobile phones the network could handle, and Eddie said he thought each relay could accommodate five simultaneous calls. "But," Goren said, "that's only sixty calls going on in the entire network at one time. And you plan to sell five hundred units?"

"I agree," Eddie said. "We should limit the first wave—we'll sell one hundred and fifty units and see how it goes. If we've got a success, we immediately add two relays to each tower. That allows one hundred eighty simultaneous calls, but it's still only fifteen simultaneous calls per tower. I'm working on a new relay that can handle twenty simultaneous calls, and—this is the real key—automatically transfer to the nearby tower that can take on the call. That's the breakthrough. I know how to do it. I just have to put the pieces together."

"You remind me of Mozart," Goren smiled. "It's all in your head, just like the entire score of *Don Giovanni*. All you have to do is write it down."

Eddie laughed. "Not bad, Alan," he smiled. "Not as simple as writing it down, but that's the general idea."

"And what about money?" Goren asked.

140

Money

I ANSWERED GOREN'S QUESTION.

"We have enough cash in the company to do what we just described. The key to this is the number of simultaneous users. We can generate enough money to expand the network through the sales of units and the monthly service charges to be on the network. It's a question of how many users can be on the network at one time.

"Let's say the number is twenty-five hundred. We can sell twenty-five hundred units in Philadelphia in a few weeks. At four hundred dollars apiece, that's one million dollars. That's enough money to repeat the process in nearby markets. We have stores in Atlantic City, Allentown, Trenton, and Wilmington. Each of those is a market—smaller than Philadelphia, but if we're shooting for, let's say, only a thousand units in each of those markets, that's four hundred thousand dollars for each market, plus monthly service. I think we're going to charge ten dollars a month to be on the network. That will bring in twenty-five thousand dollars a month in Philadelphia from twenty-five hundred units, and ten thousand dollars a month from only a thousand units in each of the other three markets. The business will fund itself."

Goren did not respond at once. He drew on his pipe, looking directly at me, expressionless. After what felt like a long interval but was probably only thirty seconds, he lowered his pipe and spoke. "You know what your plan doesn't consider, don't you?"

"Yes, I do," I answered. "Competition from the big guys before we even finish the first network. If we commit financially to the Philadelphia network and it doesn't finish, or if we get stopped by a patent infringement suit, we'll be close to broke. And the legal cost of a patent suit could break us."

Goren frowned. "So what's your plan?"

Evie and Eddie and I had spent considerable time worrying over this. While we hadn't come up with a solution, we'd mapped a path we hoped would lead to one.

"The plan is this," I began. "We begin to do everything it takes to complete the Philadelphia program. If all goes well, that's nine to twelve months. In the beginning, I'll be locating the towers we need and identifying the tall buildings in or near the places where we'll need additional towers. I'll be negotiating leasing privileges to place relays on the towers and on top of City Hall. That's a big piece of work. It will take several months. I'll be working on the newspaper and radio and TV guys to help me with City Hall."

"But Jack, you'll be letting all these people in on it," Goren said. "Word will get out."

"We've thought about that, Alan," I responded. "I'll have a promotional booklet produced for what we'll be calling a *new communications network*—Dunlaur Broadcasting. The book will have a specimen application for a Federal Communications Commission license. The plan will be detailed, with drawings, specs, and editorial material. It will be printed on glossy magazine stock, very colorful. The introduction will be by me, vice president and director of marketing for Dunlaur Electronics. I'll explain that although Dunlaur has no commitment from the FCC yet, we're confident our application will be received favorably, and we have launched an exploratory phase."

"Hmm," Goren murmured. "Go on."

"While the booklet will appear comprehensive, the wording will be ambiguous. It will neither mention mobile phones nor contain information anyone could point to as ruling out mobile phones as part of the plan. The ambiguity will lead readers to assume our network will support an advanced kind of walkie-talkie, or citizens band network, whereby every communication goes out to every individual in the network. When we are ready to unveil the true character of the network, there will be nothing in the booklet that can be said to deny or misrepresent it.

"We'll consider carefully where we stand before we push the start button to begin implementation. Up to that point, we could abandon the project without a huge loss—no more than four months' profit. Once we push the start button, we'll be committed to big money . . . big for us, that is, not for APC or Motorola. But we will be hurt pretty bad if we have to abort after we've pushed that button."

I paused and turned to Eddie and Evie. "Did I miss anything?"

As one, they said no, I'd stated the case perfectly.

Goren studied each of us again. "Sort of like grabbing a knapsack and jumping out of a plane, hoping there's a parachute in it."

As usual, his metaphor was apt.

141

President John Fitzgerald Kennedy

January 1961

HE WAS YOUNG, handsome, clever, and an arresting speaker. He had a beautiful wife. He was rich, heir to a great fortune. His father, Joseph Kennedy, a Prohibition-era bootlegger, had parleyed illegal whiskey into a respectable motion picture and real estate fortune and climbed the political social ladder to a personal friendship with Franklin Roosevelt and the ambassadorship to England before his display of Nazi sympathies cost him his prestigious post and soured his reputation.

The young Kennedy ran against Eisenhower's vice president, Richard Nixon. It was grace and charm versus dark sullenness. The country had a love affair with the Kennedys—JFK and glamorous Jacqueline, known to all as "Jackie."

Just three months into his presidency, Kennedy got off to a bad start when, on April 17, 1961, he launched the disastrous Bay of Pigs invasion to overthrow Fidel Castro in Cuba. Fourteen hundred Cuban exiles, trained and equipped by the CIA, stormed onto the beach at the Bay of Pigs on Cuba's south shore without the US air support that had been promised. Every member of the attack force was killed or captured. It was a great humiliation to the United States, and it diminished Kennedy. It would also lead to the Cuban Missile Crisis two years later.

The lesson of the Bay of Pigs fiasco was not lost on Kennedy when he faced Khrushchev in August 1961 over the Berlin Wall and again in October 1962 over the Cuban Missile Crisis. Yet, somehow, he seemed to have forgotten that lesson when it came to Vietnam.

337

<h1 style="text-align:center">142</h1>

The World's First Wireless Phone Network

EDDIE SAID HE'D be ready in six months with a tested ten-digit phone, production-line ready, and enough units of his new recharger relays to cover the network.

Building the network became job one for me, occupying all my days and most evenings. I promoted one of our Dunlaur territorial salesmen to sales manager. He said, "I'll continue to cover my territory—no need to hire an additional salesman." I liked his eagerness and his willingness to take on two roles but suspected his goal was to preserve the sales job ... just in case. It was what I would have proposed in his situation; still, I felt compelled to hire someone to handle the sales territory.

My new role was different from anything I'd done previously. Instead of selling a Dunlaur product or a service, I was now the customer, asking to *buy* a service—namely the right to install on the other guy's tower or the right to erect a tower or a mast atop the other guy's building, and, with the help of the Philadelphia *Bulletin*, *Inquirer*, and *Daily News*, get rights to install our receivers and amplifier relays atop City Hall.

The City Hall task was neither selling nor buying, however. There would be little price negotiation. Price would be unimportant to the mayor and city council. It would be political—favor for favor—the pride and public relations value of being the center of the world's first wireless telephone network.

Every aspect of the job was new to me. I expected hard work, many meetings, and tough negotiations over prices and terms. All this would come to pass, but I had the confidence born of something good to offer, *and* I was ready to pay the price.

I wondered, every morning, if this would be the day APC filed for an injunction. The only plan if and when that happened was to fight for time to get our network running then to countersue for our right to license others' patents for a reasonable royalty. Or, as Durells suggested, "They might want to buy what we have."

I never devoted more than five minutes to those thoughts. I had work to do.

143

Small News

June 16, 1961

THERE WAS NOT much news that morning:

Walter Ulbricht, counsel chairman of East Germany, was quoted as saying that no wall will be built in Berlin. *(This would prove false, as construction of the Berlin Wall began less than two months later.)*

Rudolph Nureyev, world-renowned ballet dancer, defected to the West.

The Dow-Jones Industrials closed at 709.

The New York Yankees won at Cleveland, 11–4, with Whitey Ford pitching.

There was another small item on page three, just a short paragraph, like a pebble dropped into a pool before the ripples spread. It was reported that President Kennedy had sent four hundred Green Berets to Vietnam to train South Vietnamese troops.

Nothing of note.

144

Violet's News

V IOLET CALLED AND asked me to invite her to dinner. She had news to share with me—private, personal news.

"What kind of news?" I asked.

Her voice smiled but gave nothing away. "I want to tell you in person," she said. No hint of trouble, or of good news. No clue.

I hesitated. "Sure," I said, puzzled. "How's about a hint?"

"Please," she said, "be patient. I'll tell you when I see you."

* * *

It was six months into my new job of building the communications network. My secretary and I compiled a list of people who could grant leases to Dunlaur to mount receivers and relays on towers or atop high buildings. Some were owners; others were people who first had to approve then recommend to more senior persons. Just getting an appointment was difficult. These were all busy professionals. Fortunately, everyone on my target list knew the name Dunlaur from our electronics and retail businesses. That helped get me past the "Who are you?" hurdle.

By the time I met with Violet for dinner, I had tentative commitments to mount equipment on seven radio towers and to erect an antenna on two office buildings. The toughest job would be getting onto City Hall. I'd started the process. I had a tentative appointment with the head of city council and the deputy mayor, but the appointment kept getting changed. When I met with Violet, I had an appointment for two weeks later. Meanwhile, I went out daily on appointments with tower and office people.

* * *

She came straight from work, dressed in her usual style—a smart navy business suit and a mannish white shirt. I did not see much of her those days. Her life was dedicated to Dunlaur Retail in Evie's mold: intense, all business, all the time. She was now twenty-nine, a beautiful woman, wise beyond her years in the ways of business. I was thirty-seven. We had matured together in the thirteen years since she stowed away in the back of my car.

She walked toward me with long, handsome strides, high heels clicking across the marble lobby floor. Head held high, her smile brightening the room. Every man in the place turned his head. And most of the women. I never got used to her good looks. I studied her. She had developed her own fashion style. She did not coif her hair as did most women. It was dark, straight and long. She wore it pulled back, with a pony tail. She did not wear nylons. Her legs were bare but tan. They were smooth and silken. Nylons could not have improved them.

Some women wore corsets in those days, but not Violet. Her body had a loose fluidity, a suppleness. It occurred to me that Evie was emulating her, not the reverse. There was an aura of beauty about them when they were together. So it was Violet, the leader. How about that? For a moment, I had an image of her when I found her hiding in my car: dirty; discolored teeth with a front one missing; a wild tangle of drab, dirty hair; and the furtive look of a wild creature wary of danger. I was Pygmalion.

A wide smile as she lowered into the chair I drew out for her.

"So, Violet." I smiled back. "What's up?"

"Gee, it's good to see you, Jack," she said. She leaned forward and touched my hand. That was a surprise. She'd always acted shy and deferential toward me, although in recent years, as she took over managerial duties, I'd watched her grow more relaxed and outgoing with other people.

"How's the network coming?" she asked. She was a member of the small group who knew the network was not for radio transmissions but for mobile phones.

I brought her up to date quickly then asked again, "So, what's up? What's your news?"

"I've met a man," she said, looking up at me with a shy smile. "His name is Harry Chase Breckinger. I want you to meet him."

<h1 style="text-align:center">145</h1>

<h1 style="text-align:center">A Man for Violet</h1>

EALLY?" I SAID, feeling something strange instantly. Was it jealousy or the concerns of a big brother, or perhaps a quick imagining of her being taken away from me? Whatever it was, I tried not to let it show. I smiled, but the smile felt forced. I was hoping it didn't look forced.

"Tell me," I said, leaning toward her. "Tell me everything."

She had no difficulty looking at me directly. Her eyes wandered across my face.

"Harry is the sales rep for the Breckinger Corporation—his father's company. They're General Electric distributors: home appliances, radios, TVs, refrigerators, ovens, washing machines, and such. He calls on me as the GE rep. That's how we met. He's your age. He was in the War, like you. He's handsome and smart and good company. His family is wealthy. Harry's grandfather started the company. It's big. Harry's father inherited it. Harry will inherit it one day. Meanwhile, he earns a lot of money, and he has a lot of money."

She paused for a drink of water—and maybe to catch her breath as well. "The money doesn't attract me. It's him. He's modest about everything. He drives a Chevy. He lives alone in a small apartment on Rittenhouse Square. There's nothing about him to suggest he's rich.

"I've met his parents and his sister," she continued. "They're lovely people ... down-to-earth, friendly, interesting. They've been very welcoming to me. I think they're anxious for Harry to get married and raise a family. Apparently, I passed muster."

"What do they know about you, Violet?" I asked.

"That's delicate," she sighed. "I never lie, but I haven't told Harry everything."

"Meaning ... ?"

"I told him I was orphaned young and had a hard childhood, that you and your wife took me in and changed my life, that I live with your parents, who treat me as their own daughter. That Evie is like a sister—closer than any sister could be—and you've become my big brother."

"Is that all? Doesn't he want details?"

"He asked me once, about three weeks ago, *What's the mystery?* He wanted to know, and I told him there is nothing else to tell. He has to take me as I am—a poor farm girl with a bad past, really bad, until you and Alice and Eddie. I have nothing to be ashamed of. He'll have to let it go at that."

I studied her. I felt her struggle.

Her face became clouded. She was on the verge of tears.

Her voice broke. "It's as I told you—I'm so dirty. How can I ever be truthful with a man like Harry? His world is so clean and orderly."

I tried to speak soothingly. "If he's the one, your past won't matter at all. One day, he'll have to know, but it won't change how he feels about you."

We both knew the next question. There was an uncomfortable pause.

"What about sex?" I asked. I went all hot. I felt myself flush. I tried to shut out the image but only partially succeeded.

Her eyes filled. She dabbed at them with her napkin. She tried to get control.

"I have no urge," she said. "We do some stuff—nothing big. I think he thinks I'm a virgin, although he's never asked straight out. He respects that. His family is strong about that. Marriage, you know." Then she broke down. She sobbed quietly, trying not to make a scene.

"Oh, Jack, it's all so much trouble. What will I do? What will I ever do? I don't know what will happen when the time comes. I get along because I shut it out. I want a married life, but will he have me when he knows? Will I ever *do* it? The idea upsets me."

I rose from my chair and came around to take her shoulders. Other diners looked at us curiously. No matter.

"It's okay, Violet. I understand. It's okay. You're okay. It will be okay . . . don't worry. That's a long time away. Meanwhile, I'll call him. I want to meet him."

I really did want to see him. Did I hope I would approve, or ... What *did* I want to discover about the new man in Violet's life?

146

Harrison Chase Breckinger

W E MET FOR LUNCH.
She'd told me he was handsome. He was. He had masculine good looks. His smile came easily, full and outgoing. We were the same height. He was a bit broader. His handshake was firm, welcoming. There was no bravado about him. His manner was serious, friendly, self-assured, relaxed. I wondered whether he was submerging a low-level anxiety about presenting himself to me for examination. If so, it didn't show.

After a few moments of obligatory conversation on various news topics and opinions about which teams would be facing off in the World Series, I paused. "So, Harry, tell me about yourself. Violet says you're a great guy."

He laughed. "A great guy! Really, no such thing, but I know *you* are a great guy. I know all about you—and all about your war record. No, Jack, I'm very ordinary. And I've fallen for Violet. That's all."

"What's about you and Violet?" I asked.

He brightened, sat a bit more erect. "Jack, I'm crazy about her. She's everything good I could ever imagine in a woman. Beautiful, yes, but that's the least of it. She's *good*. She's honest. She's smart. She has so much personality. We talk for hours. She knows *everything*. I'm having trouble accepting that she's in my life . . . She's—"

"Yes, Harry, she's all that and more," I interrupted. "What do you have in mind for her?"

He was puzzled. "What do you mean, Jack? What do I have in mind? Marriage, of course, as soon as she says—but she says she's not ready to talk marriage. I am. I'd marry her this afternoon if I could."

"How 'bout your folks?" I said. "You know she came to us with nothing. She makes a good salary. She has some savings. She owes nothing. But she is dependent on her salary and career at Dunlaur Retail. I don't believe she'll give that up. She has a good future with Dunlaur."

His smile broadened. "My folks are plain people, Jack. They don't judge a person based on wealth; they go for character. Me, too, and Violet has it—she's straightforward, nothing phony, no artifice. I'll take her as she is, and of course she can stay with Dunlaur. Her job is the most important thing in her life, though I hope *I* will be, eventually. But I know Dunlaur is part of her—Dunlaur and you and Evie and Eddie and all the people she works with. I'd never ask her to give that up."

"What about children?" I asked.

"We'll have children, of course," he said. "More than one, I hope. We're in the twentieth century—women have careers *and* families." He laughed. "She'd have to take off an afternoon to give birth, I guess, but she'll have plenty of help to raise children and not give up Dunlaur. I think you know, Jack, that I earn good money. I have a lot of it, though it is not a source of pride. I don't know how I would be doing if I were on my own like you and Eddie. I admire what you've built from scratch. I try to get along on what I think I'd be making if I were working somewhere other than Breckinger's. Anyway, I hope you won't hold it against me that I have money and my family is rich."

I assured him I wouldn't, and we moved on to other subjects: what was new in technology, the Cold War, the future of telecommunications.

I think I wanted not to like Harry Breckinger—to find him shallow, spoiled, arrogant. He was none of those things. I liked him—no obvious faults, open, genuinely a friendly person. Was I disappointed that he seemed right for Violet? I suppose I was.

"What did you do in the War?" I asked.

"Not much," he answered. "I was drafted in June 1943. I was in Europe. I survived. That's about it."

His look said, *That's it. I don't want to talk about it.*

I respected that. I didn't press, but I knew I would be digging into his record. And I did.

* * *

Here is what I learned from official Army personnel records:

Breckinger was a ninety-day wonder, like me, but he was Army. I was Marines. He was a second lieutenant in the Twenty-Ninth Infantry Division, a platoon leader. His unit went ashore on Omaha Beach for Operation Overlord on June 6, 1944, the first day of the Normandy invasion. His unit fought across Europe. They lost half their men during the Battle of the Bulge. When the Germans surrendered, the Twenty-Ninth Infantry Division was the deepest unit into Germany. From D-Day until the surrender, his unit suffered 75 percent casualties. He survived the War with the rank of captain and a Silver Star for bravery.

Curiously, no one, even his own family, knew about his war record. As best I could learn, he never discussed it in detail with anyone.

147

The Berlin Wall

August 13, 1961

THE LEADING MORNING news story was the start of construction in Germany by the Soviets of a wall to divide East and West Berlin.

The Soviets established total control over the border between East and West Germany when it became apparent that a serious population loss was happening in East Germany. Millions of East Germans were leaving for West Germany in search of better living conditions, greater opportunity, and the types of personal freedoms that the East German government had been stripping away.

Berlin, however, in the heart of East Germany, was an escape hatch. Free travel existed between East Berlin and West Berlin. Once in West Berlin, an East Berliner could travel with little restraint from West Berlin into West Germany.

On June 3, 1961, JFK met with Khrushchev in Vienna. Khrushchev later confided to his diary that Kennedy seemed like an immature young man with no worldly experience. Kennedy tried to hold his own with the tough, seasoned veteran of a hundred battles, from the defense of Leningrad to the political infighting at the peak of power of the Soviet Union. Later, painfully aware of having been overmatched, JFK wept as he described the meeting to his brother, Bobby, his attorney general and closest confidant.

To plug the Berlin escape hole, emboldened by his meeting with Kennedy, Khrushchev surprised the Allies by starting construction on a wall to separate the two Berlins. Without announcement, construction began on August 13, 1961. It was one hundred miles of wall, completed in just a few weeks. Manned by armed guards at observation posts, the Berlin Wall shut down traffic between the divided portions of the city. Early on, there were several hundred killings of attempted escapees, resulting in a dramatic drop-off in attempts. Authoritarian rule had prevailed, and the Wall would stand for another twenty-eight years.

As was the case with the Berlin Blockade in Truman's time, there was no shortage of American tough-talkers who wanted US tanks to knock down the Wall. Fortunately, Kennedy ignored those voices. The Wall was an ugly fact of life that stood until Berliners tore it down, unopposed, in November 1989, presaging the collapse of the Soviet Union in December 1991.

148

Getting Deeper in Vietnam

352

NOVEMBER 18, 1961: Kennedy orders eighteen thousand "military advisors" sent to Vietnam.

* * *

December 11, 1961: Kennedy sends US military helicopters and crews to Vietnam.

149

Hard Work

PUTTING TOGETHER THE Dunlaur mobile telephone network was the hardest work I'd ever done. I had multiple appointments in Philadelphia each day to make deals for tower sites and rooftops. Building owners and operators wanted satisfactory answers to their questions. Among their typical questions and comments:

- *How high up do you need to go?*
- *What assurances do we have that your installation won't interfere with the tower's other receivers and relays?*
- *What about the Federal Communications Commission? You have to be licensed.*
- *Have you gotten an installation deal for City Hall yet?*
- *If we make a deal, I'll want serious up-front money. Don't want to take a chance that you'll abort or fail and I'll have to spend money to undo what you did. And I'll want a substantial deposit when we sign, even if you won't begin work until you've signed up all the other towers you need, including City Hall. So anything we may agree on today is subject to all of that.*
- *I'll have to talk to my lawyer.*

Fortunately, Dunlaur was well-known, with an excellent business reputation and an image of cutting-edge leadership. If it weren't for that, I wouldn't have had a prayer of getting the meetings. Our reputation got me in the door, but I wasn't going to get a contract without satisfying a host of concerns. I had to get agreements in place from the entire network, with deferred start dates until I had all—or almost all—of them signed.

From the beginning, we knew City Hall was a must. Without it, the rest wouldn't fall into place no matter how much effort I put in. Every day included a call by me or my secretary to Tom Malone, chairman of city council. His secretary continually inquired regarding the purpose of the requested appointment—our purpose was repeated when I called again the next day . . . and the next. Our calls were never returned. What to do?

On top of it all was the anxiety over a potential injunction from APC, Motorola, General Electric, or Westinghouse. We were infringing on patents held by these major players, as well as lesser-known companies and individuals with patents on various components. An injunction and lawsuit would stop us dead in our tracks. On the other hand, we worried that one of the big guys, say APC, might decide to wait until we were ready to do our first test before unleashing their attorneys. Either way, we would lose a lot of money; how much would depend on how far along we were when the axe fell.

Our plan was not to fight to win a lawsuit but, via countersuit, to compel the patent holders to accept reasonable royalties for use of their patents in the "national interest" of creating a revolutionary communication system. It was a fairly weak plan, endlessly discussed with Eddie and Durells and Goren. But it was a matter of going forward under that cloud or not going forward at all.

One by one, I asked for help from the editors and owners of Philadelphia's three major newspapers—the *Morning Inquirer, Evening Bulletin,* and *Daily News.* Dunlaur Retail was a big advertiser in all of them, and each promised support, albeit behind the scenes. General publicity was not what I wanted; it would bring on tough questions about what exactly our aims were. I did not solicit help from Philadelphia's leading radio stations, even though we were significant advertisers on radio, because we knew they would not welcome another station, which was our cover story.

When I failed to get an appointment with Chairman Malone after about a dozen attempts, the editor at the *Inquirer* tried to meet with him and struck out. Next, the *Bulletin* editor called me to say that he'd spoken with Malone, who was courteous and seemed receptive. Apparently, he'd said he would contact us. We were encouraged.

A few days later, my secretary reported that Malone's secretary had left a message:

Mr. Malone has no interest in the Dunlaur plan to place radio equipment on top of City Hall. There is nothing to discuss.

What now? Was this the end?

150

The Mayor

EDDIE AND I met with Durells. We discussed the possibility of reconfiguring the network using a ring of towers within a block or so around City Hall. That would add a lot of additional cost. More important, I'd made the mistake of showing our design with City Hall as the center of the network, assuring the tower owners the hub would be there. I would now have to go back to everyone with a plan that said City Hall was not a good choice, for technical reasons; a ring of twelve towers was a better, although more expensive, choice. That, I suggested, would be the official line.

Eddie made the Italian *bullshit* sign, pulling down the lower lid of his right eye with his right middle finger. "No one will believe it, Jack," he said flatly. "That should be our last resort—let's come up with something better."

Durells stood up. "Let's try the mayor," he said, animated. "He's forward-thinking. We will have to tell him the real plan. He should love it—to have the country's first mobile phone system in Philly. If he goes for it, he'll keep the secret until it's time."

"I like the idea," I nodded, raising my eyebrows, "but how do we get to him? I can't even crack city council."

"This is the most progressive mayor Philly's ever had," Durells said. "He's trying to revitalize the city. He'll get the old elevated *Chinese Wall* torn down from the north side of Market Street where the trains run into the Center City station. He'll open up Market Street. Someday, West Market will be lined with new high-rise office buildings and apartment houses."

Durells continued, "He's as straight as they come. If he wants it, nothing will stand in his way. We have to get him interested."

Eddie sounded skeptical. "And how's that going to happen?"

"Let me think about it," Durells said. "He is still the top man at his law firm—I may be able to reach him through a colleague. Or maybe one of Jack's newspaper guys can help. They should have better luck than with Malone. That guy's an old-time political hack. *What's in it for me?*—that's Malone."

"I could ask the *Daily News* editor," I said. "They haven't contacted anyone for us yet. All I need is an appointment with the mayor."

And that's what happened. The editor at the *Daily News* said, *Sure, I'll get him to see you. I know him real well. He's a great guy.*

* * *

The mayor was a stately, youthful-looking man with a warm and welcoming air. He was a veteran of both World Wars as a Marine. He'd served in World War I, receiving the Purple Heart for war wounds, then reenlisted when WWII began, at age forty-three. He was a combat officer on Guadalcanal, where his actions earned him a Silver Star for bravery. In 1962, when we met him, WWII had ended only seventeen years earlier. It was not a distant memory.

He had researched Eddie and me and, among other things, he knew our war records. There was a bond among combat veterans, and I sensed it right away with him. He knew how we started Dunlaur. He had complete dossiers on us.

We told him about the mobile phone system and how we improved the Korean War walkie-talkie. We hadn't been talking for more than twenty minutes when he pushed aside our drawings and said, "Okay, boys, you're on. Give me specs for what you want. You'll have it. All I want is to be the one to announce it when it's ready."

Elation!

* * *

I returned to my office invigorated, full of new plans and ideas. When I arrived, my secretary said there was a phone message for me.

"It's from a detective in Philadelphia," she said. "Something about Violet."

151

Abduction

IT COULD NOT BE happening . . . again.

The detective was telling me something. He was from some precinct in Philadelphia. He repeated himself, slowly, more than once, until I understood. It was not like Alice's disappearance. Violet had been abducted in broad daylight, on Chestnut Street. No mystery. There were witnesses.

The first witness was Violet's secretary. The detective had her statement.

My name is Anne Quinn. I am Violet's secretary. We arranged to meet for lunch at the Horn and Hardart on Chestnut Street, on the north side of the street between 10th and 11th.

I got there ahead of her. I found a table all the way over on the 11th Street side. The place was real busy. And noisy. I saw her come in. I hollered, "Violet! Violet!" I stood and waved. I had to call out loud for her to hear me over the noise. She waved back and came toward me.

I had to admire how she looked. She is so beautiful. She was wearing a navy business suit with a white blouse and a trim skirt. She carried a navy handbag on a leather shoulder strap. She was wearing navy shoes, plain high-heel pumps. They showed off her legs. Men looked at her.

Over her right shoulder, I saw this man who was at a counter all the way over on the other side of the restaurant. He stood up when I shouted her name. Violet didn't see him because her back was to him. I didn't think anything of it, but now I know he's the man who took her.

He had long tangled hair, and he looked dirty. He was wearing a dirty T-shirt, and he had a dirty beard and a dirty brown jacket—or maybe it was a vest. I thought he was probably a derelict, he was so filthy-looking.

Violet and I ate together, but I left before her. She said she wanted to go over some notes and have another coffee. That's the last I saw her.

A Horn and Hardart counter waitress also gave a statement.

He sat at my counter. He had a scruffy beard. His hair was long and unkempt. He was very tanned. Or maybe his face was just dirty. Everything was dirty. He was wearing a dirty white T-shirt and a brown jacket that was badly frayed at the sleeves.

I never saw him before. I would have remembered him. He smelled . . . horrible. When he sat down on the stool, the man next to him got up and moved to the next counter. Then the girl on the other side did the same.

I could hardly get close enough to serve him, he smelled so bad. He ordered mashed potatoes, peas, spinach, a roll with butter, and a cup of coffee. That's twenty-five cents.

In the middle of his meal, he jumped off the stool suddenly and looked around. I think he'd heard somebody call out a name—it was pretty noisy at the time, so I'm not sure of that. He was staring to the left, hard, toward the other end of the restaurant. He wolfed down his meal standing up then left. He left a quarter on the counter, no tip.

I didn't even want to touch the money, he was so dirty. I couldn't wait to finish my shift. I went straight home and took a bath.

The police interviewed seven people who'd witnessed the actual abduction. Each described a dirty, bearded man with long, unkempt hair and shabby clothes. One witness said she saw him as she was leaving the restaurant.

He was leaning against the light pole at the curb outside the restaurant.

He pushed off and sprang at the girl as she came out of the restaurant.

He hit her hard in the head with his right fist. He caught her as she fell. She looked unconscious. He lifted her easily. He must be strong. He carried her to a beat-up, rusty pickup truck that was parked maybe forty feet away, toward 10th Street. He threw her in the cab like a sack of potatoes and drove away. The whole thing took maybe ten or twenty seconds.

The six other witnesses were people walking by, each of whom had seen the man hit the girl and throw her into his truck. All described him the same way, and the truck—old, beat-up, so rusty and dirty that it was of no discernible color. Unfortunately, nobody had caught the license plate number, though two said it was a New Jersey plate, mud-splattered.

Dimly, as if the detective's voice was far away and hard to hear, I suddenly understood everything. It was Earl! He heard the name "Violet." He recognized her. She didn't look like the Violet he once knew—but he recognized her. He waited outside the restaurant. When she came out, he grabbed her, knocked her out, threw her in the pickup, and drove away.

I was convinced this is what had happened and that Earl had her. But where? I wasn't sure whether the village in the Pines that Violet had described still existed. I didn't know Earl's surname; I wasn't even sure of Violet's. The only place I could think to start was Rose's farm market on the Black Horse Pike, where Violet had stowed away in my car all those years ago.

* * *

It was unimaginable. It was unreal … this could not be happening. My head felt stuffed with cotton; I couldn't focus. I tried to pull myself together. I had to see Al Burns.

152

Al Burns on the Case

I ASKED MARGATE DETECTIVE Al Burns to make the abduction a Margate case. He said it belongs in Philadelphia or Ventnor—Philly because it occurred there or Ventnor because that's where Violet lives.

"No, Al," I said. "You have to take this case. I'm listed as guardian on Violet's high school enrollment records, plus her school transcript and driver's license list my address. Please don't leave me alone on this, Al. I'll go crazy."

Burns made it a Margate case. "For old times' sake," he said.

I gave him copies of the statements the Philadelphia detectives had taken. "I know who took her," I told him, "but I don't know his last name and I don't know where he lives, which I'm sure is where he has her. She told me he was a cousin but that his last name might not be the same as hers."

I related the story of how, unknowingly, I'd driven away from Rose's farm market with Violet in the back of my car. I told him her sad story of being abused by Earl from a young age, how Durells had created an identity for her and how she became part of our family—as Eddie Denauskas's cousin Violet from Ohio.

"She said her last name was either Moore or Moorer," I said. "Something like that. She'd never seen it spelled and wasn't sure."

"Get in the car," Burns said. "First thing we'll do is see if Rose can tell us anything about this Earl character."

* * *

Rose was of little help. She knew Earl, sure, but she didn't know his last name. She remembered the girl who used to come with him. She hadn't seen the girl for years, though Earl was still coming with blueberries and blackberries. She knew he lived in an abandoned Piney village, but there were so many of them. She assumed it was nearby. As to his pickup, Rose could neither identify the make and model nor hazard a guess at the year.

I was feeling deflated as Burns and I sat in his car and brainstormed ways to locate Earl's village. If it had a forge or a furnace, he said, that would cut down the possibilities, but I couldn't remember Violet describing the place in any detail. She'd mentioned a one-room schoolhouse she sometimes attended, and Burns made a note to see whether the school system had a record of her. She'd also spoken of a visiting doctor or nurse; Burns would check county health department records. We agreed it was unlikely Earl would show up at Rose's again, since he'd lost Violet here and investigators would want to check it out.

What was Earl doing in Philadelphia, assuming, as we did, that his finding Violet was a fluke? Something he couldn't get on the Black Horse Pike, in Atlantic City, or Camden. Medical attention? Special tools or equipment, maybe gun-related? Could he have been visiting someone?

"It's standard legwork," Burns said. "We'll need an artist's rendering of Earl and a recent photo of Violet. A lot of manpower."

"How many men can you put on it?" I asked.

"A pair of detectives, at best," he said, "but first I want to check the school and health records to see if we can narrow the field. This could be a long investigation, Jack, and a tough one. The one bright spot is that it doesn't look like a homicide, since the guy went to some trouble to take her alive."

When the detective dropped me off at the end of that first day of searching for Violet, I asked myself: *Do I want to bring this to Bobo?*

153

The Hunt Begins

I HAD A MEETING early the next day with Eddie, Evie, my secretary, and three of our engineers. I said I must concentrate on finding Violet. The network project would have to get along without me for a while.

My secretary knew my schedule and future appointments. She had taken notes of my ideas and the minutes of every meeting. She had the written tentative agreements with some of the tower people. She had the letter from the mayor confirming Dunlaur's lease for the circular base of the William Penn statue atop Philadelphia City Hall. Evie and Eddie knew everything I was planning to do. My work was divided up. All of them said I should put Dunlaur and the project out of my mind for as long as it takes. They would handle things.

I met with Bobo and Durells. Bobo was ready to assign two men—the same ones who found Charlie Norris. I said I wasn't ready for that. Not yet. Durells said he could ask the school districts for Atlantic, Gloucester, and Camden Counties to identify Violet Moore or Moorer. He was also willing to contact the county health departments, but ultimately we agreed to give the Margate detectives a chance before launching our own investigation.

"Thanks, Bobo," I said. "Thanks, Larry. I'll call on you if it becomes necessary."

154

Al Burns Takes Over

A L BURNS HAD a police artist make sketches of Earl and the truck. The artist drew portraits from each of the eyewitnesses and from me, though it had been almost fourteen years since I'd seen him. The portraits were eerily similar, and I thought any one of them could serve. Instead, Burns asked his artist to create a composite. The guy was very good: the portrait was Earl.

Next, the detective showed photos of old pickup trucks to me and the eyewitnesses. We settled on a 1935 Ford. The artist colored it and drew in some details.

The police poster shouted, "HAVE YOU SEEN THESE PEOPLE?" above the artist's color portrait of Earl, the truck illustration, and the most recent photo of Violet I could find. A line of bold type below the images—my doing—announced, "$10,000 Reward for Information Leading to the Capture of This Man." A dedicated phone number, manned around the clock by the Margate Police, was the finishing touch. We printed one thousand posters.

Harry Breckinger took a leave of absence from his firm and, with the help of several coworkers, we distributed the posters to every house, gas station, auto shop, hardware store, diner, and small business on the Black and White Horse Pikes, from Atlantic City to Camden. The merchants we visited were universally cooperative in posting them.

The Atlantic County school superintendent unearthed a record of Violet Moore, age seven, from 1949, when she had been on the student roll for the one-room schoolhouse in the village of Belcoville. The man told us the schoolhouse had closed in 1951 and the village was long gone—a ghost town, he said. He'd found no record at all of a village named "Arnold's Crossing," where Violet said she'd been living at the time I found the girl on my floorboard.

The county health department located a single medical report of an Atlantic City doctor who, in 1950, had treated Violet in Belcoville for an ear infection.

It wasn't a lot, but it was something to go on.

155

The Creation of the Pine Barrens

HISTORY OFFERS NUMEROUS examples of how jealously nature takes back her own when human civilizations abandon their edifices, among them the Mayans, the Incans, and remote central African cities that once flourished and dominated only to be quickly reclaimed by jungle once the inhabitants left for whatever reason.

The varied reasons for the abandonment of such places are often economic. The exhaustion of natural resources, shifting trade routes, and disease may all contribute. Rediscovered centuries later, concealed through nature's relentless creep, they instill a sense of mystery and awe. We marvel at what they must have been like: their public works, social structures, politics, languages, and technologies.

The lost towns of the New Jersey Pine Barrens are not such an example. Once thriving communities, most were never abandoned completely. Industry failed and people moved away, but a small remnant often remained rooted, devolving over generations into a primitive throwback of the advanced society they had once achieved.

The American colonies fought the Revolutionary War with bog iron forged in the Pine Barrens. At the height of the region's prosperity, in the late eighteenth and mid-nineteenth centuries, these pinelands were the industrial center of the Eastern Seaboard, with dozens of busy company towns, villages, and schools. The land barons who settled here became successful manufacturers of iron, paper, and glass and oversaw a booming agricultural base of cranberry bogs, blueberry farms, livestock, and cultivated fields. Long, sandy roads and railroad lines crisscrossed the pinelands, allowing the movement of goods in and out as dozens of towns grew and thrived.

As the Civil War ended, the region's activity and energy melted away with the invention of the blast furnace, the exploitation of iron ore further west, and the development of more efficient paper manufacturing processes. The overall Pine Barrens economy became obsolete and died, though glass-making continued on a limited basis thanks to the ready availability of fine "sugar sand." The towns that survived were greatly reduced in terms of productivity and population.

The Pine Barrens communities that Harry and I explored in search of "Arnold's Crossing" were the primitive remnants of a society from which structure, energy, and purpose had been drained generations earlier.

The area is not a tropical jungle by nature, and its civilization did not succumb to an encroaching forest. The ostensible collapse of the regional economy had occurred just eighty years earlier, and although nature's reclamation was well underway, it was far from complete. Remnants of villages remained, notable for dilapidated houses and barns, overgrown roads and trails, and cloistered family groups eking out meager lives through rudimentary scratch farming and the sale of handcrafted goods, firewood, charcoal, and sphagnum moss—popular with florists—to more affluent communities. There were no telephones, electricity, or running water, and there was very little in the way of public education. In the 1960s, technological advances that made the United States the most powerful nation on earth had passed the Pine Barrens by.

156

The Search for Arnold's Crossing

FTER LOCATING THE spot where the Piney village of Belcoville had once stood, I identified four schoolhouses where most of its children were likely to have been taught. I mapped an approximately sixty-square-mile area served by these schools that I believed, based on what Violet had told me years earlier, must have included Arnold's Crossing.

I hired a pilot and a small three-seater plane, a Piper Cub, to crisscross the target area. My idea was to mark a map with all the roads, clearings, and buildings we were able to see from the air. As Harry and I prepared to board, I asked whether he'd flown before. He said he'd taken dozens of commercial flights, mostly business trips. I shared with him that during the War, I'd been transported on troopships, trains, trucks, and buses and that for Dunlaur, I almost always traveled by car. This was my first flight.

We took off from a small airfield on the outskirts of Atlantic City. Before heading west to our search area, the pilot did a quick flyover of the town. It was quite an experience seeing it from the air—the Boardwalk with its huge hotels and the beaches as we flew low along the water's edge. Momentarily, I set aside the reason I was in an airplane. I recalled Blinky, that day in Gene's Diner, telling me about his days in the Eighth Air Force, about how it felt being "up there" in his B-17.

I'll do this again, I promised myself. *Someday when life returns to normal.*

It was summertime, and the trees were in full foliage. From the air, the Pine Barrens were a solid green blanket, punctuated here and there by a lake, by a river or dirt road weaving among the canopy, by an occasional clearing with buildings and vehicles, by a cranberry bog. Harry and I each had a thirty-by-thirty-inch map and red felt-tip pens to mark up every road, clearing, house, or farm we could discern. When we compared our maps later, we'd find them very similar. We didn't expect them to be identical; they were close enough to help us with starting points.

We went up again that night, this time looking for lights. There was no electricity in use out there as far as we could tell; nighttime illumination in the pinelands was mostly supplied by kerosene lamps. We identified additional settlements by spots of light penetrating the canopy of trees. More sites to investigate.

I knew what Harry and I were in for. We were going to be explorers, pushing into thick brush, cutting away tree branches, bushes, and tangles of vines to reach a given house or clearing.

I was pessimistic when I returned home that night. Adam greeted me. He was almost fifteen, no longer a child. He carried himself as a young man.

"Let me come with you next time," he said. "I can help. I can carry stuff. I want to help."

I embraced him. "It's okay, Adam," I said a bit emotionally. "You tend to the home fires while I'm away, please. Or spend time at Dunlaur, if you like. Harry and I will find Violet—whatever it takes."

Everything a man hopes for in a son—it would all be Adam.

The hunt began the next day.

157

Carlyle Langton,
Our White Hunter

I HAD ASKED AL Burns to find a man who lived in or close to the Pine Barrens of southern New Jersey. Harry and I needed a guide, someone who knew the forest and the sandy roads that traversed it, someone who would keep us from getting lost. I hired a four-wheel-drive GMC pickup, a brute of a truck that could push through narrow, unimproved roads and go off-road into thick underbrush when necessary.

From my research, I knew many of the old Piney villages were located along lakeshores or near navigable rivers, so I bought a canoe. I thought getting out on the water would provide a useful and quite different perspective than we'd get from roads and trails.

Al Burns knew a guy. His name was Carlyle "jes' call me Carl" Langton. Carl was a retired cop who had grown up in Batsto, now basically a ghost town, where he'd lived for twenty-three years until he decided there must be a better life out there somewhere. He entered the Atlantic City Police Training Academy and graduated into the Margate Police. He was about sixty, small and wiry, with a full gray beard and a mane of uncontrollable hair. His Piney speech pattern had never left him.

Burns described him as an excellent cop who'd retired at fifty-five as a detective sergeant.

"He's your man," Burns said.

When we met Carl for the first time, I explained Violet was listed in the county school and health records as living in Arnold's Crossing and she sometimes attended the one-room schoolhouse in Belcoville. Using that information, I had circled the logical area where Arnold's Crossing was located.

Carl studied the aerial photos and our maps. "I know there was a town at Belcoville," he said. "Never heard of Arnold's Crossing; prob'ly a handful of shacks and nothin' else. I imagine you checked the post office for Arnold's Crossing?"

I nodded. "There hasn't been mail delivered to the area on my map since 1910, other than Belcoville, which had postal service until 1935. There's no record ever of Arnold's Crossing according to the main branch."

Carl paused. He pursed his lips. He stared at our maps and photos for a long time.

"It's a needle in a haystack," he said finally. "Worse, we're not sure if the needle is in this particular haystack. Ya did a good job mapping out the area. It's what I'da done, but we ain't sure that's it. Tell ya what," he continued. "I'll work for you. Twenty-five dollars a day. Can't guarantee we'll find yer Violet, but if she's in there, I'll find her. When do we start?"

158

Terror in the Bush

HARRY, CARL, AND I divided our target area into sixty-one square-mile sections. We hoped to explore two or three sections every day. We drove into areas where it was possible, or at least to the edge of an area. We hiked into the most heavily wooded areas along the remnants of roads or footpaths, where one could be found; where trails were nonexistent, the underbrush was often thick and unforgiving. Knowing what we would encounter, Carl had me buy three machetes to hack through the heaviest tangles of weeds, bushes, and vines. A large, dark snake slithered out of our way.

"Most ain't dangerous," Carl said, "but watch out fer rattlesnakes. They's the ones can kill ya."

There's a wild, colorful beauty in the heart of the Pine Barrens. There are scores of bird species, in addition to snakes, turtles, and other reptiles. Long vines hang from tall, straight cedar trees, and the underbrush glistens with every shade of green, red, yellow, and brown. Summer days are hot and dry in the pine forest, though surprisingly cool when you set foot in a cedar bog.

The first day in the woods, we encountered not a living soul, though we did come across a few collapsed, abandoned skeletons of old frame houses and shacks and the overgrown remnants of what might once have been a village.

Carl had a compass. He traced our movements on our map. He mapped out a route that took us through and around the day's section. Our route was always crisscrossed; no point retracing a route, Carl declared. Without him, Harry and I would have been walking in circles, or worse, become hopelessly lost.

Near the end of the first day, Carl stopped. "That's it for today," he said. "It's near dusk—skeeter time. Time to git outta here."

I studied my watch, and the sun through the trees. "Looks to me like we have another good hour, hour and a half," I said.

"Jack, you don't wanna be here when the skeeters come out," he shook his head. "If you fellas ain't ready to quit yet, I'll wait for you in the truck." He turned and walked away.

"We'll be along in a half hour," Harry called to Carl's retreating back.

"Okay," I said to Harry, studying the map. "We can push along this path for, let's say, twenty minutes and circle around here"—I drew an arc on the map—"back to where the truck is. We can cover the section before we quit for the day."

Harry nodded, and we pushed on.

Twelve minutes later, a solid wall of mosquitoes appeared from out of nowhere. We were in the midst of a humming, whining cloud that penetrated our ears, our brains. We turned and ran as fast as we could, waving our arms and slapping at them as they covered every inch of exposed skin.

When we jumped into the truck, Carl gave us a sharp look. "Thanks, boys," he said facetiously. "Ya must've brought a couple hunnerd inside with ya."

Lesson learned: listen to Carl.

159

Pineys

ON OUR EIGHTH DAY in the brush, a footpath ended abruptly at a clearing to a settlement. There were five inhabited houses among a rectangle of twenty that must have once framed a town square. The inhabited ones were rundown, shabby; the others were mostly collapsed. Wire-fenced yards held chickens and henhouses, while on the far side of the settlement, a field had been cultivated for crops.

We counted four beat-up pickup trucks, three men, two boys, a half dozen women, and three girls. A baby cried from inside one of the houses. The men were all bearded. They wore overalls over bare chests. The women, mostly barefoot, wore thin cotton dresses similar to the one Violet was wearing when I found her. They eyed us curiously, suspiciously. Two of the men, sitting in chairs on porches, reached for shotguns. *Who are ya and whatcha doin' here?*

Carl raised his hands. He explained, unfolding a poster. "We's lookin' for this here girl and this here man. This here's his truck. Anybody seen 'em? His name's Earl, don't know a last name; she's called Violet Moore. They's a big reward." He pointed to the poster. "Ten thousand dollars."

Men and women crowded around to study the poster. "Ten thousand dollars!" they echoed.

But, no. Nobody recalled seeing either of these people.

A boy, no more than Adam's age, spoke up. "Kin I come with ya? I'll find 'em for ya."

"Well, thanks everybody," Carl said. "Here's fer your trouble." He nodded to me, and I handed a dollar bill to each of the nine folks who had gathered.

"I'll leave a few of these posters," I said. "Show them around. Maybe somebody you know knows Earl or Violet. If they do, there's a number to call."

We turned to trudge back through the bush, hot, tired, disappointed.

After twelve days, we hadn't developed a single credible lead. Each day, we went out searching only to return home exhausted, empty-handed, and demoralized. I wondered if we might do better when the weather turned cold. The underbrush would be thinner, and we might begin to see chimney smoke.

* * *

She is in here somewhere. The thought never left me. *In here. With him . . . What is he doing to her?* The rage rose up in me.

The thoughts were going to make me crazy. Her life with Earl—before she escaped. I heard her voice, trembling, that day, when I found her, hiding in my car.

"He lends me out, fer a quarter, or a couple of fish hooks . . . a piece of rope, or a beer."

What is he was doing to her now? I had to find her. I would kill him.

Most days, we never encountered a person. When we did, we were usually met with suspicion and often with hostility. These were people living outside society, as if in a bygone era, and I guessed they wanted to keep it that way.

* * *

On the drive home, we heard the announcement that Marilyn Monroe was dead, at age thirty-six, from an overdose of sleeping pills. Desired by men, romantically involved with President Kennedy, admired by women, but beneath the beauty and glamor was a troubled, insecure human being. It was a sad end to a light that had glowed so brightly.

We were all too weary to talk about it. We rode the rest of the way in silence.

* * *

When I returned home after two fruitless weeks of searching, the sky was dark. As I came inside, Mrs. Wilson told me Eddie had called and would I please call him back right away.

Adam greeted me with a worried look. "Dad," he said as we shared a hug, "you're all beat up. Please let me go with you next time—I can help."

"It's okay, son," I said. "I'll take a shower, put on a robe, and sit down to dinner with you. I'll be fine. Thanks for waiting to eat with me."

First, I called Eddie. He wanted to know whether I'd had any luck on the hunt then asked me to come to the factory the next day. "It's kind of important," he said. "Can you come tomorrow evening before you head home? I only need a half hour of your time."

"Sure, Eddie," I said. "I'll be there."

160

Catching Up with Eddie— Big Surprise

I ARRIVED AT THE Dunlaur factory around seven thirty at night. It was mid-August and I'd just spent a ninety-something-degree day in the Pine Barrens with no hint of a breeze. The woods had been an oven, and I was grimy and drenched with perspiration. Eddie's air-conditioned office felt good, but I wanted to get home.

Eddie was waiting for me along with two of our engineers, Evie . . . and Adam! Why Adam?

"Hi, Dad." He hugged me. "Anything?"

"No, son," I said. "But we're narrowing the field. What brings you here this evening? Just like that?"

"Well, Jack," Eddie said, "we'll get to that."

We'll get to what? I wondered.

Eddie gave me a brief progress update on the network. He hoped to give a private demonstration to the mayor in a month. Our City Hall installation was complete, including two relays on high rooftops five miles to the north and south. Eddie and two engineers had tested it, with Eddie located at the airport in South Philadelphia. One engineer drove north, the other northwest. For a distance of almost fourteen miles, Eddie could communicate privately with each engineer, as if on a direct telephone line. The engineers were able to call each other or Eddie by punching in their "phone numbers." I wasn't surprised by the success of the test; we knew we had the right technology.

"I'm pushing ahead, hard," Eddie said. "We've applied for six patents. Tomorrow, we're going to apply for another one. Here it is—a study in elegance."

I was stunned by what he showed me.

161

Elegance

EDDIE MOVED TO a nearby tabletop. On it were two relays, open to reveal their insides. The first I had seen many times; I called it "Eddie's relay." We were patenting a microprocessor switch in it, Eddie's design. The relay's cavity was crowded with silicon transistors and other components. Twenty-two components, to be precise.

The second relay had the same framework, but I counted only ten components, with unused space in the central cavity. It had a simple, uncrowded appearance compared to what I thought of as Eddie's relay.

"What am I looking at here?" I asked.

"It's a study in what engineers call *elegance*, Jack," he flashed me a smile. "It refers to the simplest, shortest, most direct configuration to achieve a task. This relay is elegant in its simplicity."

I listened intently as he continued.

"When I am designing a piece of equipment, I add a component at every point where I have to make something happen. I add a switch or a booster or a relay or a transmitter or a receiver, and then maybe I need to transmit here and here and here and here and here. When I'm done, I have something that works. Good. Then I try to simplify it. I get it down to the fewest number of components. I might reduce thirty components to twenty-five, or if I am especially imaginative that day, maybe to twenty-two. A truly great design is beautiful in its simplicity—in its elegance.

"But look here . . ." he handed me a pair of his distinctive telescoping glasses. "Go ahead, put them on."

As I complied, he gestured with his slender twelve-inch pointer to the second relay. "This is the Dunlaur-Adam 101 relay. Yep, you heard right—it's Adam's design. It does everything my original can do but faster."

"What—what are you saying?" I stammered. "What does Adam have to do with it?"

"It's his work, Jack. He's been poking around in the model shop for two years now, studying everything we do." Eddie unfolded a blueprint and flattened it out on the table. "A couple of weeks ago, he showed me this diagram."

Eddie continued, moving his pointer from the diagram to the Adam 101. "See these four transistors? They're new Texas Instrument products. They are a major step forward. Adam read about them. He had me buy a dozen. He said he could program these to be the receiver and also send to the transmitters, each one doing the job of three of these." He pointed to the four new transistors in the Adam 101 and then to the twelve transistors they replaced in the older relay.

"This unit replaces five different relays in our catalog—I'm scrapping our inventory of those five relays immediately. They're obsolete. We'll issue a flyer for the Dunlaur-Adam 101 tomorrow.

"This is what's so amazing about the electronics field, Jack!" He was practically shouting now as he motioned to the relay. "The technology that goes into a television set, radio, telephone, or relay tower is moving ahead so fast that what's state of the art today is obsolete tomorrow."

He looked to confirm he had my attention before continuing. "My friend, before our network is finished, there will be breakthroughs galore. If we can get it up and running, we'll have the advantage of simply replacing components—the network itself won't be obsolete for maybe twenty or thirty years."

"What will make the network obsolete?"

"*Satellites*, Jack!" He raised his arms over his head. "Since Sputnik, more than fifty of them have been put into orbit, and now we can put a satellite into an orbit geosynchronous with the rotation of earth. At approximately twenty-one thousand miles above earth, a radar signal can reach it in less than one-ninth of a second and relay back down to the intended receiver in another one-ninth of a second. Forget about towers—we'll be putting our relays on satellites."

As he finished, my eyes were glued to the Adam 101.

"Adam did this, you say? On his own?" I raised my eyebrows and looked Eddie straight in the eye. "C'mon, he's not even fifteen—you must've had a part in it."

"Jack, I swear I didn't even know he was working on it until he showed me the plans. When the model shop built the prototype, they only had a couple of minor questions, and Adam addressed them immediately. Honestly, Jack, I'll be happy if my little boy grows up with half your son's brainpower."

"Not to worry," I laughed. "Between you and Evie, Junior will be a *wunderkind!*"

162

Carrying On

A T THE END of each day's hunt, I brought the truck home and washed it down to remove most of the dirt and debris that clung to it after a day in the bush. Then a hot shower, then dinner with Adam. He always greeted me with the same question: "Anything, Dad?" and my tired answer, "No, son, nothing today."

I looked forward to the time spent with him. We discussed all the usual subjects, but it was as if I were only half awake. My head was filled with thoughts of Violet, all conversation filtered through a screen of frustration and anxiety.

In the morning, it was back on the truck; pick up Harry and Carl at six thirty and head for the day's hunting area. We went out every day, including weekends, except when it rained. On rainy days, I went to the Dunlaur plant and tried to do something productive.

* * *

Days slipped away. Frustration deepened. *Mustn't lose heart,* I thought. *Mustn't give up.* The physical effort was intense. We were like tired soldiers, pressing on, pushing on, trying to stay hopeful that our objective was just ahead in the forest.

When we started out in the morning, the truck radio told us the day's news. Once in the Pine Barrens, we lost communication with the world. We carried walkie-talkies, but their range was extremely limited.

I spoke to Eddie every evening. He kept me up to date, especially on progress with the network. So far, there did not appear to be a breach of security. He'd planted a few lines in the *Philadelphia Inquirer* every few days about the radio station Dunlaur was building. As far as we could determine, the only person outside the company who knew our real objective was the mayor.

Eddie was aiming for a first demonstration in September. At that point, we would have only the City Hall relay and three towers—an incomplete network but sufficient for demonstration purposes. Our own people tested each relay station as it was installed, and there were no problems. The risk of a security leak would come when we demonstrated the network to the mayor. He would want two or three of his own people there, understandably. Eddie agreed with my proposal to personally drive them from one location to the next, communicating only with our own people and not revealing the true nature of the network to anyone until we were ready to go public.

163

Eddie Is Ready

ARRIVING HOME AT the end of another fruitless day of searching, I was surprised to find Eddie and Alex Perskie, Dunlaur's chief engineer, waiting inside for me.

"What's up, guys?" I asked, dropping my gear in the foyer.

"Go ahead, wash up," Eddie said. "We'll talk over supper. You'll want to be fresh and alert for this."

"C'mon, Eddie," I said. "Tell me. I'm too worn out for games."

He hesitated. "Okay, Jack," he said. "I'll say this—but no more until you shower and eat something." Eddie said he'd agreed on a demonstration with the mayor, something he'd been working on for a week.

"He called me this afternoon," Eddie said. "It's tomorrow at one thirty. It's going to be me and you with him in his office. After that, I'll drive him around North Philadelphia. We'll communicate with you while you drive around South Philly."

I was surprised at the suddenness of this announcement. I shook my head as he continued.

"Please, Jack, I need you tomorrow. Can you put off the search for just one day? The mayor is way out on a limb for Dunlaur, and I don't want to disappoint him. He wants both of us."

I had to think about it. Adam and I and our two visitors shared a cold supper in silence. It was a big day for our venture, but I hadn't taken off a day from the search except in heavy rain, and there was no rain in tomorrow's forecast.

"By the way, Jack," Eddie said, "here are your phone messages." He handed them to me, only three. Two were matters my secretary could deal with, but the third was from Al Burns. *Please call me early tomorrow morning. I'll be at the station by 7:00 a.m.*

383

"Eddie," I said, "please let me find out what Burns wants before I decide about tomorrow. I'll call him right away, at home."

I let the phone ring at least a dozen times, but the detective didn't pick up.

"No answer, Eddie," I said. "But you're right—I've got to be part of the demonstration. I'll ask Harry to cover for me tomorrow with Carl."

164

Harry Will Carry On

I CALLED HARRY AND explained the situation. He understood, as we hoped everyone did, that we were creating a new "radio" network. Harry wasn't in the inner circle.

"It's no problem, Jack," he said. "You've taken the lead in all of this, which is great, but after all, I'm going to marry her. You take care of business. I'll go out with Carl."

A wave of possessiveness washed over me. "Harry," I said uncomfortably, "if you find Arnold's Crossing, how about not going in until the next day—with me?"

There was a moment's silence on the line, then, "Jack, if we can just reconnoiter, okay, but if I have to act, I will. You understand."

"Yeah, sure," I said. "You'll do what you have to. Tell you what—pick up Carl and be here at six forty-five. We'll call Burns. If there's been some sort of breakthrough, I'll come with you."

I told myself the most likely scenario was that tomorrow's search would be as fruitless as every other day we'd gone out.

* * *

Harry and Carl were at my house before seven in the morning. They were ready to take the truck and be on their way if I wasn't going to join them.

At seven sharp, I called Burns.

"Come to the station," he said in a short, clipped tone. "Be here by eight. Maybe a break in the case—maybe nothing. Tell you about it when you get here." He hung up before I could get a word in.

I called Eddie. "Harry and Carl are here. We're heading over to the police station. Unless it's really something, Harry and Carl will bring me home and go on. I'll be at your house by nine. I'll call you from the station."

165

Lennie Short

BURNS WAVED US into his office. He wasted no time. "I'm expecting a gentleman any minute who's looking to claim the reward. He says he knows our man and where he lives. According to this guy—"

Burns was interrupted by a voice over the intercom. "Al, there's a man out here says he has an appointment with you."

"Put him in room five," Burns said. He turned to us. "He phoned in yesterday, clearly motivated by the ten grand. Let's go."

The man looked like other Pineys I'd met, though I suspected he'd cleaned up for the meeting. His face, arms, and hands had the appearance of brown, well-weathered leather, but his age was hard to judge—maybe about fifty, I thought, but grizzled beyond his years. His graying hair was slicked back with pomade into a tangled twist above a pair of bushy eyebrows, his short beard crudely trimmed. He wore a frayed black T-shirt under a pair of stained but relatively clean denim overalls. His ankle-high work boots, loosely laced with brown twine, were scuffed and paint-stained, the heels and soles badly worn.

Holding up one of the flyers we'd distributed, the man announced, "My name is Lennie Short. I knows this man and where he lives. How's 'bout the re-ward?"

The detective spoke. "Have a seat, Mr. Short. Here's how this works. We'll give you five hundred dollars to lead us to him. If we find him and catch him, you'll get the rest, ninety-five hundred dollars."

"Who's gonna give me the money?" he asked, eyebrows raised. "You? You?" He looked from Burns to Harry and then to me.

"That would be me," said Burns.

For a Piney like Mr. Short, $9,500 was an unimaginable sum of money; he was probably lucky to handle all of $200 in the course of a year.

"Well, I knows him all right. I'll take ya there."

166

Locating Arnold's Crossing

Y EAH," LENNY SHORT continued. "I kin take ya there—but not all the way. Maybe a half mile away. I ain't gonna get no closer. Name's Earl Collier. He usta have a niece. Ain't seen her for a long time. She ain't the woman in the poster. She's a Piney gal—has a missin' front tooth. Earl is mean, and he's got a big mean dog. Carries a shotgun. I ain't gonna get too close. But I'll take ya there. You'll hafta go the last half mile yerselfs."

Short shot each of us a look to be sure we understood then said, "It's a place usta be Arnold's Crossin' but ain't hardly nuthin' no more. I ain't been there fer a long time, but I knows Earl's still there. I bumped into him 'bout a year ago, and he ast me to come huntin' wit him. So when ya wanna go?"

"Right now," said Burns. "Here, show me where we're going."

I spread our maps across the table and pointed out the area of our search. I explained to Short that we believe Arnold's Crossing was in the area serviced by the Belcoville school house.

Short studied our map, tracing the outline of our target area with a gnarled index finger.

"Earl ain't in there," he snorted, stroking his chin. "You been wastin' yer time. I see what ya did, and it makes sense. You figured Arnold's Crossin' has t'be in that circle what ya drew, 'round Belcoville, 'cause the girl was goin' t' the school at Belcoville. But that ain't so—she was goin' to Belcoville 'cause they was a *road* from Arnold's Crossin' to Belcoville, 'bout four miles. See this town here? That's Whitesbog. Usta be a school there, and *that's* where the girl shoulda gone, but they ain't no road from Arnold's Crossin' to Whitesbog."

Short chuckled. "You bin lookin' in the wrong place," he said. "Arnold's Crossin', what's left of it, ain't in this here circle you drew 'round Belcoville. It's over here." He pointed to a spot on the map east of our search area. "It's closer to Whitesbog, as the crow flies. What fooled ya was the road. Earl could drive 'er to Belcoville in ten minutes er so. Whitesbog woulda been a longer drive fer 'im."

He looked up from the map and flashed a wide, gap-toothed grin. "I knows where's Arnold's Crossin' usta be," he said. "I think they's just the one house left, Earl's house—maybe one more. All the res' collapsed a long, long time ago."

167

I Miss the Demonstration

I CALLED EDDIE. "Eddie, it's for real. There's a guy here who can take us to Earl. We can find her today. I have to go."

Eddie was quiet. What could he say?

"The mayor must know about Violet, with all the publicity," I broke the silence. "If you explain the situation, I'm sure he'll understand."

There was another short silence before he spoke with a positive energy. "I know what to do, Jack—I'll bring Adam! I'll explain the situation with Violet to the mayor and say, *You, sir, would do the same thing in Jack's situation. I'm bringing his son, Adam, instead. He's only a boy, but he knows every inch of our network—in fact, he designed our new relay. Please forgive my partner; the timing is unfortunate, but there's no way around it.*"

"Eddie—" I started to protest but he cut me short.

"Jack, let me do this. I have a feeling about the mayor—what kind of man he is—and I'm sure we'll be just fine. After all, it's Adam. You're a salesman, but Adam—he's the future of communications technology!"

"Okay, Eddie," I said apprehensively. "God bless this enterprise."

168

Finding Violet

WE CLIMBED INTO THE truck. Me and Harry and Burns in the cab, me at the wheel. Carl and Short in the back, in the open cargo area.

The road into Belcoville was almost fully concealed from the Black Horse Pike, but we found it and drove in. It was badly rutted and heavily overgrown. The truck could bull its way over bushes and small trees, but we had to get out several times to hack through tangles of shrubs and vines and once to move a fallen tree.

"He's 'bout a half mile further," Short said as the rest of us climbed back into the truck. "I ain't goin' no closer. He's dangerous, and so's the dog. I'll wait here. Good luck to yas."

After nearly twenty minutes more of bumping and rocking over the rutted road and pushing through brush, we broke through a particularly dense hundred-foot stretch of vine-covered undergrowth and into a clearing. An area of about two acres, what I assumed was once a town square, was ringed by the broken remains of houses. Only partly visible through the trees behind the buildings were the collapsed remains of an iron forge. A rust-covered pickup was parked near a derelict house that appeared habitable, its roof and porch sagging. It had to be Earl's place, his truck. Where is Violet? She has to be here.

Suddenly, at the end of the clearing I saw movement. It was Violet, standing up in the bushes.

I shouted to Harry, and we raced toward her. She started toward us, her arms reaching out as she cried, "Harry . . . Jack . . . I'm here!" then fell back into the bushes.

I stopped and let Harry run ahead. I wanted to study the clearing. Where is Earl? He wasn't in the truck. I approached the house, gripping my service pistol. "Earl! Come on out!" I hollered at the top of my lungs.

Violet's voice answered my call from the bushes, haltingly, "He's . . . not there, Jack. He's out hunting . . . but he'll be back . . . soon. Him . . . and the dog. Please . . . take me away from here!"

Behind me, Carl and Al Burns were walking toward us cautiously, one on either side of the clearing, like infantrymen looking for any sign of an ambush.

Harry reached Violet and lifted her into his arms. He carried her out of the bushes and over to the sagging front porch of the house, setting her down on a rickety rocking chair.

It was hard to believe it was Violet. She was sobbing uncontrollably, and she was filthy. She was wearing one of those thin cotton dresses that seemed to be the standard female uniform out here in the Pines. The fabric was so thin, it was almost transparent but for the dirt it was covered in.

Violet's tears streaked the dirt on her cheeks, and I noticed that her front tooth was missing—the same one we'd replaced all those years ago. There was a slash on her left cheek—a two-inch cut, swollen, festering. Her hair was a dirty tangle drooping below her shoulders. Her face, arms, and legs were brown from exposure to the sun and by the dirt that caked every visible inch of her.

She was barefoot. Her left calf was wrapped in a thick dirty rag, tied with a piece of brown twine that circled a half dozen times around the wrapping. Her eyes were rheumy, her lips cracked and swollen.

Harry kneeled beside her, holding her hand. "Violet, Violet . . ." he said softly. "I'm here. Everything's okay. I'm going to take care of you now."

Violet threw her arms around him. He lurched back slightly—an involuntary movement, no more than an inch or two. I saw it, but doubted she'd noticed.

"Oh, Harry," she cried. "He cut me." Her voice was weak, trembling. "Here . . . on my cheek. He said he marked me . . . so he could find me easier the next time."

"What happened to your leg, Violet?" I said from the porch steps.

She looked vaguely in my direction, eyes unfocused. "He broke it . . . maybe a week ago, maybe longer. I tried to run away but he'd taken my shoes. I didn't get far. He hit my leg, hard . . . with a shovel. He said I wasn't . . . going to do . . . any more running away." She paused, stifling a sob before continuing.

"I can't stand on it. I tried to clean it and . . . twist the bone back into place, but I couldn't. He made me a crutch . . . it's over there"—she pointed—"in the blueberry patch. I was picking them just now. I don't . . . know where he goes to . . . sell them. I'm sure he . . . doesn't go to Rose. She probably knows he took me. He brought home . . . a poster about me, and the reward . . . that he saw at a gas station."

"I'll bring the truck over," I said.

I was about halfway across the clearing when I heard rustling from the woods to my left. Pulling my gun, I sprinted toward the tree line, keeping low, certain it was Earl in the bush, ready to shoot me down.

As I reached the edge of the clearing, the bushes parted and a huge, dark-colored dog was charging toward me. It was on me in a second, powerful teeth bared, growling. I had no time to aim carefully as I pulled the trigger.

169

Earl

I'D SHOT THE DOG in the neck or chest, killing it immediately. I ran quickly to the edge of the clearing, about ten yards to the right of where the dog had come charging out of the woods. Earl would not be far behind. I expected him to emerge from the same bushes at any moment.

I stood with my gun drawn, waiting for Earl to appear, only briefly turning to look for Al Burns. He was in a crouch, moving slowly toward me, about forty yards away. I saw that Carl, who had been on the other side of the clearing, had crossed over and fallen in about five yards behind Burns. Both had their handguns drawn.

The silence in the bush was eerie. I knew Earl had to be in there, following his dog to the clearing. Where was he? Why so quiet?

I looked toward the house and saw Harry carrying Violet around the side of the building, opposite of where we now crouched, where they'd be shielded from any gunfire emanating from our side of the clearing. The silence was intense as seconds passed; it could have been a minute.

Suddenly, Burns shouted, "Jack! Behind you!"

I turned as Earl rushed out of the bush, not from where the dog had emerged but about twenty feet behind me, where he now stood, the barrel of his shotgun aimed straight at me.

170

A Good Kill

I DROPPED TO THE ground and rolled into the bush in one motion as Earl fired. The blast sent the cluster above me, where my head and torso had been a moment earlier.

Immediately, I heard another shot—no, two shots in quick succession, pistol shots, from Burns's .38. Earl was down. As we approached cautiously to examine him, I could see he'd been struck in the chest, under his left arm. The other shot had blown off the left side of his face.

I slumped to the ground, my heart racing. I closed my eyes as I sat there with my arms wrapped around my knees, memories of the War flooding my mind. Diving into the bush, rolling in mud, running, in the infantryman's bent-over crouch, moving warily along the edge of a dirt road, dropping. The sounds of war: rifles, senses sharpened to the utmost, firefight, men dropping, mortars, grenades, carbines, cannon—a tank column moving up, aircraft, bomb blasts . . . screams. I hadn't dredged up those memories in years.

"It was a good kill," Burns said. "His next shot would've killed you."

Harry came around from the side of the house, carrying Violet. "Jack, you okay?" he called out.

"I'm fine, Harry," I hollered back. "Earl is dead. Stay there—I'll bring the truck over."

Harry and I sat with Violet between us in the cab of the truck. Carl and Burns wrapped Earl in a sheet they'd found in the house and placed the body in the cargo area. As we drove slowly out of the woods, we soon came upon Lennie Short, who was standing in the middle of the road. As he climbed into the back, he nodded toward the shrouded corpse.

"Earl, eh?" he said. "So when do I get my money?"

171

In the Truck

RELAX, VIOLET, YOU'RE safe now," I said. "We're going to Atlantic City General for some medical attention."

She held her face in her hands and sobbed. Several times she tried to speak then broke down again. Harry had his arm around her shoulders. She leaned tightly into him, as if she wanted to get to safety, inside of him.

"You're okay, dear, you're okay," he said.

Violet's left thigh, pressed against my right leg, felt warm. I reached over to touch her forehead, and it was burning with fever. Meantime, the press of her thigh was erotic. *What's wrong with me?* I thought, disgusted with myself. *She's sick and injured, and I'm getting a hard-on?*

After a while, the sobbing stopped and she tried to sit up. She wiped the tears away with the bottom of her dress. Her face was a sepia palette of tearstained dirt, the wild tangle of dirty hair half covering her face and the nasty, suppurating cut on her left cheek.

As if reading my mind, she pointed to her cheek and whispered, "He cut me here . . . so he'll recognize me . . . next time I run away." She gasped for air then coughed several times before continuing, "After he broke my leg, he said he's sorry—not that he broke it but that I wouldn't be able to work as hard now. *It will be like it usta be,* he said. *I'll take care of you,* he said. *You'll take care of the house . . . look after the chickens and the garden,* he said. *And you won't be running away no more.*

She began to cry again, "I told him I need a doctor for my cheek and my leg. He said, *Sure, I'll get you a doc. But not today.*"

Her voice strengthened with anger. "A few days after we got here, he brought a man to the house. He was going to sell me for a dozen shotgun shells. I said if he forced me to do it, I'd kill him. I said I'd find a way—maybe poison or maybe a knife in his sleep. He looked at me strangely, and I said it again, quietly. I thought quietly would scare him more than screaming. *I swear I'll kill you, Earl.* He never brought anybody after that, and he didn't try to do me himself."

The strength left her, and she leaned back into Harry. "I'm so tired . . . I hurt all over, especially the leg . . . I'm worried about gangrene."

A few seconds later, she was asleep, her chin buried in Harry's chest.

172

Atlantic City General

T HE DOCTOR CAME to us in the waiting room. His face was filled with the gravity of bad news. A nurse was with him.

"I'm Dr. Elgin," he said. "This is Nurse Sharon Shelly, head of intensive care nursing. Violet is very sick. She's running a fever of one hundred three. The cut on her cheek is infected. The left leg is badly fractured, and there is gangrene. Infection has spread throughout the leg, as well as in the left side of her face and neck. We're going to X-ray her chest to see what's going on there and in her lungs. We had to shave her head; her scalp was covered with lice."

"What can you do for her?" I asked.

The doctor pursed his lips. He looked at me through narrowed eyes without speaking. Then he took a deep breath. "Antibiotics, for one," he said. "We've come a long way since penicillin and erythromycin and tetracycline. The one we're using now, methicillin, is an advance over demeclocycline, which was the best we had until this year. The drug will reduce infection, but there's more than one infection in her. Her cheek is being cleaned out right now.

"It's the gangrene we have to address immediately," he said. "The accepted protocol is amputation. In her case, probably below the knee. But I can't tell yet how far up the leg the infection has spread. I should know soon, then we'll have to act quickly."

"Doctor," I said. "Please—no amputations. I saw enough of them in the Pacific. Half the guys died anyway. There has to be something else."

"It's possible," he said. "I intend to reach out to Dr. Dhiraj Mehdi at Mt. Sinai Hospital in New York. I just recently read about him and his research. He has twenty years of experience at Safdarjung Memorial Hospital in New Delhi, India, with a PhD in infectious diseases—he's only been in the US a year." The doctor paused, looking from me to Harry then back again before continuing.

"This may sound strange, but Dr. Mehdi has had success treating gangrene with maggots. As you may know, maggots eat decaying flesh—some primitive societies have used them for hundreds or even thousands of years to treat infection, but typically these have been topical applications. Violet's infection is deep inside the leg, which reduces the chances for success . . . though possibly not for Dr. Mehdi. He breeds a special kind of maggots in the lab using his own formula and method, with some remarkable results. New medical techniques are slow to be accepted, but Mehdi's treatment appears to be a breakthrough."

Dr. Elgin sighed. "I don't want to give you false hope—Violet's gangrene appears to be two, maybe three weeks along, and it's deep. At this point of infection, there's really no time to lose."

"Get Dr. Mehdi," I said. "I'm Violet's legal guardian, and I'll take full responsibility. I'll pay whatever it costs—whatever he wants, beginning with a driver to bring him from New York." I turned to Harry. "Harry, do you agree with what I'm saying?"

"Sure, Jack," he mumbled, wiping away tears. "Whatever you think."

173

Time Slipping Away

D R. ELGIN DID NOT hesitate. "You fellows come with me to my office. I'll put a call in to Dr. Mehdi right now."

A woman's voice came through the phone. "Mt. Sinai, can I help you?"

"This is Dr. Elgin calling from Atlantic City General. Please connect me with Dr. Mehdi in Infectious Diseases. It's urgent."

The receptionist put the doctor on hold for a minute or two, returning to say, "I'm sorry, Doctor, but Dr. Mehdi is away this week. I can connect you with Dr. Mehdi's intern, Dr. Daniel Presser."

Dr. Presser came on the line. "How may I help you?"

After Dr. Elgin explained the situation, Dr. Presser said, "I'm truly sorry, but Dr. Mehdi is in England, delivering a paper at Cambridge University Hospital. We don't expect him back in New York until next week."

"Is there anyone else who can do it?" Dr. Elgin asked.

"I know of only one other physician who uses Dr. Mehdi's method—James Kerner at Houston Methodist. Shall I try Dr. Kerner for you?"

"Houston?" Dr. Elgin said it like a curse. "He could never get here in time . . . but yes, Dr. Presser, please do get me on the line with him. I'd like to have his opinion."

A conference call, which is what Dr. Presser now suggested, wasn't a great option in 1961—at least not for anyone in a hurry. The state of the art required an operator to place two separate calls and connect the parties through a switchboard. It was a slow, unreliable process, and more often than not, the sound quality was terrible.

"Rather than a conference call, Dr. Presser," I said, "why don't you call Dr. Kerner on another phone, then place the two phones together, speaker to receiver?"

The doctor was willing to try, and within a few minutes, a connection was made and the situation was being discussed among the three doctors. Dr. Kerner in Houston said, "I couldn't get there in less than fifteen hours, with a lot of luck, and I don't know anyone else who uses the treatment." Kerner was silent for a moment before adding, "Dr. Presser, you're aware, of course, that Dr. Mehdi might not even advise it in this case. The gangrene is advanced. It could kill her before the maggots even begin to work."

"Point well taken," said Dr. Presser, "and I'm sorry to say, Dr. Elgin, that you may have no choice but to amputate."

Dr. Elgin hesitated. Then, "Thank you, doctors. It was worth a try, but I'm going to amputate while there's still a chance of saving the knee."

Hanging up the phone, Dr. Elgin turned to me. "Violet is under heavy sedation and won't be awake for another five hours. Mr. Laurel, as her guardian, you'll have to make the decision regarding amputation. And I want to be sure you understand that if the gangrene is in the bloodstream, amputation may not save her life."

I turned to Harry. "I don't see any choice, Harry. What do you think?"

Harry was slumped in his chair, asleep. I put my hand on his shoulder and gave it a shake. He opened his eyes. "What's happening?" he asked, sitting up.

I explained that Dr. Elgin was going to amputate and why, that I was going to authorize it, and asked if he agreed.

"I'll back you up," he said.

Dr. Elgin spoke to Nurse Shelly. "Get the patient ready, Nurse. We'll operate immediately."

I closed my eyes. I prayed. "God help us," I said under my breath.

174

Desperation

Hᴀʀʀʏ ᴡᴇʀᴇ ꜱᴇᴀᴛᴇᴅ quietly in the waiting room when Eddie and Evie arrived. For a split second, the question flashed in my head: What happened with the demonstration? But I erased it. We all sat in silence.

If only . . . I thought. How life can turn in an instant. Alice, now Violet; all those guys in my company during the War; and Blinky. Poor guy. I think he welcomed death. Does any of it make sense? The minutes passed. The wall clock ticked off the seconds, the only sound in the room, bringing the outcome closer.

Suddenly I was struck by an urgent impulse. I jumped out of my chair and raced down the corridor to the nurse's station. "Stop the amputation!" I shouted. "I'll get Dr. Presser to do the treatment!"

Dr. Elgin appeared behind the nurses, dressed and scrubbed for surgery. "What is it, Jack?"

"Get me Dr. Presser, please, Dr. Elgin! *He'll* have to do it!"

Dr. Presser came on the phone, and I begged him to come at once. Only he could do it—the maggot treatment. He hesitated. "You have to understand, Mr. Laurel," he said. "I've assisted Dr. Mehdi many times, and I know how to apply the culture . . . but only topically. In this case, the gangrene is inside the leg, requiring a surgical application. I've watched Dr. Mehdi do it, but I'm not a surgeon, and I've never done it myself."

"You're Violet's only chance," I said. "Please . . . *come!*"

Dr. Elgin spoke. "Dr. Presser, amputation may be our most reliable option, but Mr. Laurel is the young lady's guardian, and he's determined to save the leg. I'm not going to override him. If your treatment doesn't stop the gangrene, it's possible we could still amputate above the knee—assuming you're willing to try and can get here quickly."

"I'll be there in four hours max," Dr. Presser said unhesitatingly. "Mr. Laurel will have to sign a release. Keep the patient prepped for surgery and have a surgeon ready to go."

175

Dr. Presser and the Maggots

A T TEN FORTY-FIVE that night, I saw the flashing lights of an ambulance approach the hospital then heard its sirens as it pulled into the entrance of the emergency ward. Dr. Presser emerged. "We got here in under an hour and a half," he said, climbing out of the ambulance, "sirens screaming all the way."

Dr. Presser was young. He appeared boyish: owllike with large round steel-rimmed glasses under an unruly shock of sandy hair. He had brought his nurse and a lab technician with him. The technician carried a steel container. Inside was a glass box with two rubber gloves built into one side, so that arms and hands could reach into the box without exposing the interior to any contamination from outside it. The special lab-grown maggots and unhatched maggot eggs were in hermetically sealed glass flasks with Petri dishes inside.

With a hospital administrator leading the way, I followed as Dr. Presser's team raced through the ER. At the door to the operating room, the doctor said, "Okay, we need to get washed and scrubbed. Mr. Laurel, I'll see you in a few hours."

It was now eleven o'clock.

176

Waiting

I ASKED EDDIE AND Evie to go home. I said I would phone as soon as I knew anything.

"No," they said. "We'll stay."

I dozed off, waking at one o'clock in the morning.

It took a moment for me to recognize where I was . . . before consciousness of the past twenty hours flooded into my brain. Harry, Eddie, and Evie were awake, slumped in their chairs.

"Anything yet?" I asked.

"No news," Harry murmured.

I studied him, thinking his fatigue was worse than mine. His eyes were vacant, his body limp. I said, "Harry, take the truck to my house. I'll call ahead. Mrs. Wilson will let you in and give you a pair of my pajamas. Take a hot shower. Eat something then try to get some sleep. Come back in the morning. No sense all of us being here. I'll call the house if there's anything that can't wait."

Harry protested, but with additional encouragement from Eddie, he reluctantly agreed.

"Are you okay to drive, Harry?" Evie asked.

"I'll grab a coffee," he said. "I'll be fine."

Once he'd left, I asked Eddie, "How did it go with the demonstration?"

"It can keep, Jack," he said. "There's a lot to tell, especially about Adam. But it will keep. Try to catch some sleep."

"Eddie, I'll tell you something. The whole day—the truck ride, finding her, the shoot-out—the demonstration was on my mind. Not up front but in the back somewhere, asleep. Does that make any sense? I didn't think about it, but I knew it was there. I'm wide awake now, so tell. It will help. This waiting is torture."

"All right, Jack," he said. "I guess it's better than just sitting here."

Evie said, "I'll find us some coffee. I don't have to hear about it. I was there."

"Really?" I shook my head. "You were there?"

"Eddie will tell you all about it," she said and left the room.

Dr. Elgin came in moments later, just missing Evie. Eddie and I rose to hear his news.

"I have very little to tell you," he said. "Dr. Presser and his team just finished sprinkling two thousand maggots on and inside the infected area of the leg—maggots and eggs. It will be several hours before he can say it's working."

He continued. "I suggest you all go home and get some sleep. I'll be here—I'm not going off duty until we know something. Plan to come back around seven in the morning unless I call you first."

177

Eddie's Story

I'M STAYING, EDDIE," I said after Dr. Elgin had left. "I won't sleep if I go home. You and Evie should go, but please fill me in on the demonstration first."

"I'm sorry you weren't there," he said, "but I knew you had to go after her. I had to think it through—how to handle the demonstration without you. I drafted Evie to come with me and Adam. It was a good idea."

He continued, "First, I got hold of Adam. I told him you were in the search for Violet. He had to stand in for you. He said, *Uncle Eddie. I'm just a kid. What can I do? You expect me to take Dad's place with the mayor?*

"I said, *You won't be alone, Adam. You'll be with me and Evie when we meet the mayor.* The idea of Evie had just come to me. I'd been thinking about security. Outside of Dunlaur, only the mayor knew our real plan for the network. Should we take a chance introducing the plan to three of his people? I didn't like the idea, even knowing he'd vouch for them.

"I realized I needed a script. First, I had to talk to the mayor, explain to him about you and Violet, then convince him it would be dangerous to reveal the plan to *anyone* until we were ready for a general announcement. We don't have to complete the network for that—we just have to demonstrate that the mayor can communicate anywhere from North Philadelphia to South Philadelphia, within ten miles of a tower.

"So I figured Adam, Evie, and I will go to his office. I'll explain that Evie knows everything and she's the one who'll be introducing the product in the Dunlaur stores. Dunlaur is a major advertiser in the newspapers and radio. Getting the word out and selling the devices—that's Evie's job.

"So Evie will drive to ten different locations in Southwest Philadelphia, with the rest of us in the mayor's office communicating with her. Alex Perskie will do the same thing in the Northeast. Then me, Adam, and the mayor will get in my car. We'll drive in a big circle and communicate with Evie and Alex in their cars. The mayor will understand that only the skeleton of the network is in place. The added towers will improve reception.

"Now, about Adam. He's a great Dunlaur asset. The relay is his invention—and his property. He knows the network configuration as well as I do, probably as well as you do—maybe even better.

"I know the mayor will like Adam, so I'll have him answer the mayor's technical questions. What Adam can't answer, I will—though there's nothing about this project that Adam can't handle himself.

"So I asked Adam, *Do you have a good suit, Adam?* He turned red and said he has a sport jacket and a nice pair of chinos and a sweater and new loafers. *Well,* I said, *it's not even nine o'clock, Adam. We have time to drive downtown and buy you a suit.* But Evie made a good point. She quoted Henry Thoreau, who said, *Beware of enterprises that require new clothes.* She said, *Adam doesn't need a new suit any more than you do. You guys are what you are. You won't even look right in new clothes. And the mayor will take you as you are. I think he knows quality when he sees it.*"

Eddie went on. "Your Adam. What a guy. I knew he was building a catalog of the network. The engineers knew it, but I never saw it. He calls the current implementation 'Philadelphia, Region I.' Every tower is assigned a number. The City Hall installation is '1001.' Going north, the masthead we built on top of the Majestic Hotel is '1002.' Going south, the masthead we built on the building roof on Washington Avenue, that's '1003.' They are all that's up and operating. Our next one is the masthead we're putting on top of the Garden Court Plaza at 18th and Pine.

"For every relay, he has all there is to know about it: a photo; the height above mean sea level; the height of the masthead; a drawing; the date of the installation; the model number and serial number of every relay, booster, transmitter; the signal strength. He has the financial story—who is our landlord—lease digest; how much rent we pay; basic lease terms; names of our contacts; then he has the testing history. When we finish with Philadelphia, Region I, assuming we get to finish it, he'll have the data on every relay station in the network.

"While we were in the mayor's office with the mayor, Adam recorded every communication, starting with Evie. She drove around Southwest Philadelphia. She stopped ten times: on South 63rd Street, at 70th and Woodland, on Grays Ferry Avenue, and seven other places. She spoke with the mayor for several minutes at each stop. Adam recorded each connection on a one to ten scale, with ten being the best, based on clarity, volume, static, and consistency.

"Then Alex did the same thing in his car up in the northeast, with Adam recording everything. Then we—me, Adam, and the mayor—got in my car and drove in a big circle around the city. We spoke to Evie at her same ten locations, moving from one location to another while Adam recorded them. Then we repeated the process with Alex.

"The demonstration went off perfect, *and* the mayor had a good time. He was like a kid with a new toy! He must have said at least ten times, *Adam, you created all this? Amazing!* He also called the network *amazing*. He said Dunlaur is an *amazing* company. He knew something about how you and me got started, which he called *amazing*. That's his favorite word, *amazing*.

"Jack, the mayor is a wonderful man. I never had to say how critical it is that there's no leaks about what we're really building. He said it for me.

"Afterward, he asked me to bring Adam to his office. He talked to Adam for an hour. He wanted to know everything about him. When we were about to leave, the mayor came from around his desk and he shook Adam's hand and said almost word for word what Bobo told you in 1939, when you were sixteen: *If I had a son, I'd want him to be just like you.*

"Remember, Jack? Well, the mayor said, *Adam, you are a fine young man. I have a daughter and I have a granddaughter, but I don't have a son or a grandson. If I had one, I'd want him to be just like you.*

"Honest, Jack, that's exactly what the mayor said. He was more impressed with Adam then he was with our revolutionary mobile phones and network."

I was speechless as I turned to hide the tears in my eyes.

Update on Violet

D R. ELGIN CAME INTO the waiting room around four o'clock. We all stood, groggily.

"Violet will live," he said, "but may still require an amputation." He paused. "We can see the maggots working, but it's too soon to know how much they'll clean up. Her tibia—that's the larger bone in the lower leg, below the kneecap—is compromised. The smaller bone, the fibula, is okay. The maggots can't eliminate the infection inside the bone; that will require surgery. If we save enough of the bone, it can be reinforced with a steel plate and screws. If not, we'll have to amputate the leg—as things stand, below the knee.

"Violet's other issues are not life-threatening. The general infection in her body is responding well to the methicillin we gave her last night. We cleaned out and stitched the cut on her cheek; there will be a scar. As to the missing tooth, there's a nasty cut at the gum line, and an adjacent tooth will have to be removed. It's a straightforward dental procedure, nothing to worry about.

"So, people, you should go home. There's nothing you can do here. Figure on coming back around eight in the morning, which is the soonest we'll have any news. The entire surgical team will remain until she's been completely stabilized, with or without an amputation. Go home."

Updating the Family

W HEN I GOT HOME around five in the morning., every light in the house was on. I found Adam sleeping on one sofa, my mom and dad on another, and Mrs. Wilson snoring away in an easy chair. They all woke as I shut the door behind me. *How is Violet?* they wanted to know, and I brought them up to date quickly. I explained I had just enough time to shower, grab an hour's sleep, and put on clean clothes before heading back to the hospital.

They all wanted to come with me, but I said it was better they stay home. I would call from the hospital with updates. They could be more helpful from home.

"Of course, Mr. Laurel," Mrs. Wilson said. "I'll look after things here, so you needn't worry." She handed me a slip of paper with a name and number scrawled on it. "A gentleman called last night at seven, wishing to speak with you."

It took me a second or two to recognize the name: Fred Walsh. It was my old staff sergeant who'd become an APC regional operations manager. The same *never-ending friend* who hired me in December 1945 and had me fired in 1947 on the day Adam was born.

What could Walsh want? I wasn't about to call him. Not now, anyway.

Yet, as I slipped the note into my pocket, I had a chilling thought: *Could APC be on to us?*

180

Progress Report

WHEN I RETURNED TO the hospital, I found Evie in the post-op waiting room. She'd arrived a few minutes earlier, she said, giving me a hug and a peck on the cheek.

"Where's Eddie?" I asked. "And where's Harry?"

"I haven't heard anything from Harry, but Eddie should be along soon," she said. "Something happened to a relay on the Majestic Hotel; he and Alex are there checking it out. He said a bird could have hit it or it might be that someone was up there examining it."

It's not a bird, I thought, thinking about the missed call from Fred Walsh. I tried to shake away the thought, but it lurked in my head until Dr. Elgin entered the room.

"It's still too soon to call the treatment a complete success," he said. "The maggots have consumed most of the gangrenous flesh, but they're still working on the tibia. Come, I'll show you the X-rays."

We followed the doctor into another room where four X-ray films were mounted on a large backlit panel. Using a pointer, he drew our attention to the third X-ray.

"This dark spot on the tibia is where the bone was eaten away. The other three views are clean. If this is the full extent of the damage, one or two metal plates screwed into the bone may be enough to support her. When the surgeon goes in, he'll make that decision. If the bone can be saved, he'll anchor the plates and, in time, she should be able to walk.

"The even better news is that the gangrene is not going to kill her. Even if she loses the leg, she is not going to die from infection. This X-ray is an hour old, from seven o'clock. We'll take pictures again at two o'clock. Hopefully, what we see is the extent of the damage. If there is a little more when the surgeon goes in, he may be able to clean up what's left with an antibiotic, or, if Dr. Presser advises, by applying maggots directly into the bone."

"When will we be able to see her?" Evie asked.

"Probably not until midafternoon," he answered. "By then, we'll know everything."

"We'll wait here," I said.

181

The Secret Is Out

EDDIE ARRIVED AT noon. He was agitated.

"What did you find?" I asked.

"First, tell me about Violet," he answered, slumping into a chair.

I told him the situation, summing it up by saying, "So, Eddie, she could still lose the leg, but she's not going to die."

I told him about the call from Fred Walsh.

"So that's it," he said. "They know what we're doing. Someone opened an Adam 101 relay and removed one of the new Texas Instruments transistors—that's what set off the relay malfunction signal."

Eddie said he'd told Alex to suspend all work on the network until we had a better grasp of what was happening.

"So they know," I said. "Before I return Walsh's call, we should talk to Durells."

"I wonder who gave us away," Evie said quietly, almost to herself.

"Doesn't matter who, dear," Eddie said. "The fat is in the fire."

* * *

I called Larry Durells. I filled him in on Violet then told him about Fred Walsh's call and the vandalized relay at the Majestic.

"I'd like you to call Walsh from my office," the attorney said. "I'll have a stenographer on an extension. You won't say anything that matters—you'll just let him talk. I'll be on another extension right beside you."

"I'm not leaving the hospital until Violet is out of danger," I said. "Eddie and Evie are here too."

"That's all right, Jack," he said. "This will keep for a little while. Call me when you're ready to come over."

*　*　*

We waited, the three of us, mostly in silence.

"I wonder where's Harry?" I said at one o'clock. "I guess he drove back to Philly. I should have taken him home with me."

He showed up less than an hour later, all cleaned up but looking drawn and unsettled.

"I'm sorry I took so long," he said. "I wanted to catch a couple hours sleep."

"I'm the one who should apologize," I said. "I don't know where was my head—I shoulda brought you home with me." I filled him in on Dr. Elgin's latest report. "So you really didn't miss anything. Hopefully we'll know more once he's looked at the two o'clock X-rays."

Harry said, "I told my folks and my sister how we found her and about her condition. They want her to come there to recuperate. They'll take good care of her."

"That's so sweet," Evie said. "I figured she'd stay with me and Eddie—but she'll make that decision."

Again, we sat in silence. My thoughts shifted back and forth rapidly, from Violet to the Fred Walsh call. There was nothing to do about Violet but to wait. As for Walsh, I wanted to act—to do something . . . to confront the situation. Being discovered had once seemed a reasonable risk; now it seemed like foolish, wishful thinking. And arrogance.

I felt reckless and stupid. We'd convinced ourselves that the downside of exposure would be the negotiated cost of buying some patent rights, or, at worst, dropping the project and abandoning several hundred thousand dollars. But now, facing the actuality, it occurred to me that APC might prefer to ruin us by forcing us into a litigation war. Even if they didn't win the case, the litigation costs would likely bankrupt us.

Sometimes a person can convince himself that the downside of a risky project is manageable, that the risk of loss is manageable, or that the chance of something going awry is remote. When the plan blows up, he can't imagine how he convinced himself to expose himself to ruin—hubris, hubris—magical thinking.

I realized with sudden clarity how Eddie, Evie, and I had reinforced one other's recklessness to the degree that each of us became comfortable with the amount of risk we were taking, jeopardizing the future of the company we'd worked so hard to build.

I wanted to share my thoughts with my two business partners, but it wasn't anything Harry should hear, so we kept our voices low.

Harry noticed. From the other side of the waiting room, he said, "If you guys need to talk shop privately, I understand. I think I'll take a walk."

"Please stay, Harry," Evie said. "Yes, we're a bit preoccupied with Dunlaur business, but please don't let that drive you away."

"Thanks, Evie," he said, standing, "but I'm going to grab an early dinner and leave you guys to talk freely. I'll see you in a couple of hours."

182

The Verdict on Violet

AT FIVE O'CLOCK, Dr. Elgin returned to the waiting room, accompanied by Dr. Presser and another doctor we didn't know.

"This is Dr. Ridgely," Dr. Elgin said, "the hospital's head of surgery. He's going to explain the situation with Violet's leg."

The surgeon led us to another room where five X-rays were mounted on backlit display panels. "In observing Violet's progress," he said, "it's clear the spread of the infection has stopped. The X-rays for the last fifteen hours are unchanged. Here . . ." he said, using a pointer, "are the first pictures, taken right after she came in. This dark area is infection, and here it is again, four hours later—somewhat larger. Now, here it is after the maggots have been at work, and these last two show no change."

He continued, pointing to the dark area. "I propose to go in here, clean out the debris, and flood the area with an antibiotic solution, several times, to make certain there is no further infection. Then I'll anchor two five-inch plates, one on either side of the bone, reaching from above to below the damaged area—here and here. If it goes well, she'll have good use of the leg."

"What can go wrong?" Evie asked.

"If the damage is confined to what I can see on the film, probably nothing. The danger is if there is damage inside the bone that I can't see on the film, damage that I'll find only while I'm in there. If there is significant damage . . ."

"What then?" I asked.

"Maybe a graft. Maybe a steel leg brace. I can't really say until I'm in there. Or maybe the lower leg has to come off. The damage is below the knee."

Dr. Elgin spoke to me. "Jack," he said, "Dr. Ridgely will have to decide what to do once he's in there. Will you give him authority to make the decision on the spot?"

I stared at the surgeon. He returned my look, silently, unwavering.

"Is there anything you want to add, Doctor?" I asked.

"No," he said. "I've told you everything there is to tell."

"Eddie, Evie . . ." I said, "I think we should leave it to Dr. Ridgely. You?"

They nodded in unison.

"Okay," I said to the surgeon. "You make the call."

"Sign here, Jack," said Dr. Elgin. "We'll begin within the hour."

183

The Surgeon Reports

WE DIDN'T LEAVE THE hospital that evening. Evie brought sandwiches and coffee from the cafeteria. We ate solemnly, our thoughts focused alternatively between Violet and APC. Harry arrived at eight o'clock. I told him the surgery had started around six; no news expected until nine. He joined the silent waiting.

At nine thirty, the three doctors entered the waiting room. The surgeon, Dr. Ridgely, addressed us.

"It's a good result," he said. "The leg is sound; there's no more infection. The maggots did what they were supposed to, but the infection had already done its damage. It ate away an irregular, sort of oval-shaped section of the tibia, about an inch and a half long and a half inch wide. I put in a plate and two screws. She'll be fine, though she'll probably have a serious limp. That should improve as her leg muscles recover from the trauma."

I choked. Evie cried. Eddie closed his eyes. Harry wiped away a tear.

Dr. Presser spoke. "I'm so happy how this turned out—better even than I'd hoped for. Wait until Dr. Mehdi hears about this—he'll either fire me or promote me." He grinned and shook our hands vigorously.

Dr. Elgin answered my question before I could ask. "You can see her now but only for a few minutes. She needs to rest.

* * *

Violet was lying on her back, her head resting on a flat pillow. Her head had been shaved to deal with the lice. A bandage covered the left side of her face.

Her eyes were open, staring at the ceiling. When she saw us, she tried to raise her head. A low cry escaped her lips. Tears emerged and began to stream down her face.

"Jack, Harry, Evie, Eddie . . ." she sobbed. "Oh," she whispered weakly. "You're all here. I wondered whether I'd ever see you again. Do you know everything? At first, they told me I might not survive. The gangrene could kill me. Then they said I will live, but I might lose my left leg. Now they say I'll be all right except for a limp. I'll have a scar on my left cheek. I'll say I used to be a duelist." She smiled.

I had thought I'd never see her smile again.

Calling Fred Walsh

EDDIE AND I WENT to Durells's office to make the call to Fred Walsh. As I dialed, they sat close eough to listen in.

"Fred, it's Jack Laurel, returning your call."

"Jack!" Walsh sounded thrilled to hear my voice. "Before I say anything else, I want to tell you how hard it was for me to let you go—What was it? Thirteen years ago, I guess. The way I handled it has been an embarrassment for me to this day. I reached for the phone a few times to call and apologize, but I was too ashamed.

"Believe me, Jack, the firing was not my doing. I had a call from the northeast area director to create an opening in Camden—a congressman wanted a job for his nephew. My orders were to can the biggest commission earner in Camden and give the new guy his book. That was you.

"I shoulda told you myself, but I didn't have the balls, so I passed it on to Bill Kane. He was your champion—told me over and over how good you were and that your wife just had a baby. He said, *It stinks,* and he was right, but there was nothing I could do about it."

"I'm sure that's not why you called," I said flatly when he'd finished talking.

"Sure, Jack, but I wanted to get it off my chest. After everything we went through together, I'm sorry I didn't handle it myself instead of laying it on Bill."

"Fred, you're not calling to say you're sorry for something that happened fifteen years ago. It was fifteen years ago, Fred, not thirteen. So what can I do for you?"

"You and your partner have done pretty well for yourselves, Jack. I'm glad for you—really..."

"Yeah, we're doing okay," I said, waiting for him to come to the point.

There was a pause—a silence I wouldn't break. Walsh would have to. And he did.

"So, Jack, I'll tell you why I called. It's about the Dunlaur radio network."

"What about it?"

"APC wants to talk to you about it. We're headed for a conflict, and we want to head it off. Will you and your partner meet with us to discuss it?"

"What exactly do you want to discuss?"

After an audible sigh, Walsh said, "We want you to stop, Jack. APC has a good relationship with you. Dunlaur is a good customer and a good vendor. We're looking to defuse a situation that could spoil a good relationship. Can we meet?"

"How about expanding on what you just said?" I responded. "About stopping?"

Another long pause. "Jack, APC has information that Dunlaur is building a wireless telephone network, and they want it stopped."

He continued. "Headquarters picked me and Bill to meet with you because they know about you and me in the War, and because Bill was your district manager and you had a good relationship. We want to handle this quietly, in a businesslike manner."

Nervousness crept into his voice. "But Jack, I have to tell you: my job is to get Dunlaur to give up the wireless phone. Bill and I already talked it through . . . how to work it out easy for you."

"Do I hear a threat?" I asked.

"Not at all!" His voice went up a notch. "But to avoid any trouble, the company would like me and Bill to meet with you and your partner to start a conversation."

"Fred," I said, "do you know my partner's name? I'll tell you—it's Eddie Dunauskas."

"I'm sorry, Jack," he said. "Yes, I do know that—Dunauskas has made quite a name for himself in electronics and telecommunications."

"Fred," I said. "I'll get back to you on this."

"Okay, Jack," he said with disappointment in his voice. "I'll expect your call. And I hope we'll be friends again. No two men could be closer than we once were. You saved my life more times than I can count."

And you saved mine, I thought, but wouldn't say it. "You'll hear from me," I said. "Goodbye."

I turned to Eddie and Durells. "Now what?"

We spent the next three hours developing various scenarios. After running out of ideas, Eddie and I agreed to return to Durells's office the next day and continue. Maybe one of us would have a brainstorm overnight.

As we rose to leave, Durells asked us to stay a bit longer. He had something to tell us on another matter.

"What's it about, Larry?" Eddie asked.

It was a stunner.

185

A Favor for Bobo

I'LL COME STRAIGHT to the point," Durells said. "It's Bobo. He asked me to tell you that he needs to borrow some money from you. He said to tell you he wouldn't ask if it weren't critical. He said he has no way to get it, that you two are the only ones he can turn to. He said you won't even ask what it's for."

"Sure, Larry," I said. "How much does he need?"

His answer took my breath away: "Five hundred grand."

As if on cue, Eddie and I jolted back in our chairs. This was 1962, when a new Chevy sedan cost under $3,000 and average family income was $5,700. A half million dollars then was the equivalent of seven million today.

I took a deep breath before responding. "C'mon, Larry," I said. "Is it a joke? A half million and he doesn't think we'll ask why? You gotta give us more than that."

"How about if I tell you it's nothing illegal—not even off-color."

I was agitated. "Larry, you know how much trouble we may be in with APC. They could break us. Sure, Bobo saved us with the Traymore job, and we owe him big time, but Dunlaur can't part with a half million."

The room fell silent, and before anyone could respond, I said, "Okay, if it's legitimate, I'll raise two fifty myself. Between my stock portfolio and CDs, I can just about scrape it together, but it can't come from Dunlaur." I turned to Eddie. "Whattaya think, Eddie? We owe him a lot but not to jeopardize the future of the company."

Eddie was ready with his answer. "We'll give it to him, Larry. Me and Evie have close to a half million in assets. If Jack can't quite manage it, we'll make up the difference."

My partner turned to me. "I almost feel I gotta apologize for having more than you, Jack. But me and Evie been earning two salaries all along." He turned back to Durells. "Just a couple questions, Larry. What's the chances of our getting it back? And we gotta know what it's about."

Durells was silent for what seemed like minutes but was probably just ten or fifteen seconds. "Okay," he said, looking at us through half-closed eyes, "to the first part, I'd say there's less than a fifty percent chance you'll be repaid. As to the other part, I'll have to talk to Bobo. He said you wouldn't ask. I told him that's too much to expect, but he said there is something very special between him and you two. I'll get back to you tomorrow."

186

The Feds Have Him

EDDIE AND I RETURNED to Lawrence Durells's office the next day. Durells said, "Bobo said to tell you, *Sure you have to know, and forgive him for thinking you wouldn't ask.* He is in deep trouble. He's been indicted by a secret grand jury on multiple counts, including bribery and extortion. I got my information from my friend, the New Jersey prosecutor for Atlantic County. This is federal, not state, but my friend knows what's happening.

"The Philadelphia mob has had their eye on Atlantic City for a long time," the attorney continued. "But Bobo kept them out. The locals—the police, the mayor, and the prosecutor's office—regard Bobo as a relatively benign criminal who helps to maintain a certain order in Atlantic City. He keeps out and often *eliminates* bad actors and even keeps our police chief under control. I'm not sure how, but he does. All of us prefer Bobo, and the way he runs things, to the alternative: the Philadelphia mob. They're bad news.

"The feds are in this because some Philadelphia businessmen filed charges against Bobo over the supposedly illegal measures he uses to keep them out of Atlantic City. That makes it an interstate commerce matter and thus a federal matter. The Philadelphia to Atlantic City Bus Company, for instance, is saying that part of their route license fee ends up with Bobo. An association of Philadelphia wholesale food distributors says they can't get into our hotels unless they contribute to a local school welfare fund, where most of the money ends up with Bobo.

"Anyway, Jack, it's a bad situation for Bobo. I know what's coming. He'll be arraigned within the next three weeks, and it will be front-page news. The federal prosecutor will ask for immediate incarceration pending trial. That's probably ten months. One of the lawyers in my firm will defend him. He'll get him out on bail. But the amount of bail will set a record—seven hundred fifty thousand dollars. He can only come up with two hundred and fifty thousand.

"That's the story. Bobo said the two of you would loan him the five hundred grand he's short. And he said—and I agree—that you shouldn't make any effort to communicate with him. He's protecting you in saying that, because he knows anybody close to him will get dragged into the investigation. Dunlaur may already be on the list, since Bobo got a commission from you in '48 for the Traymore contract—the job that saved you from going under. *Perfectly legitimate,* he said, *but you know . . .*

"Anyway, you must stay away from him. If you're going to come up with the money, do it with wire transfers into the law firm's escrow account."

Eddie spoke for both of us. "Understood," he said. "We'll have it for you in a week."

* * *

I remembered something Bobo said to me a long time ago when I was a teenager—just fifteen. We'd *exchanged favors.* What I'd done for him was a small favor. What he did for me was a *big* one. That was in 1939, when he saved me from prison for beating the Mackey boys with an eighteen-inch length of iron pipe after they molested Evie. She was only thirteen.

"Jack, we are friends," he said. "Friends don't measure what they do for each other over here. It ain't like sayin' my last favor for you was a fifty over here and what you done for me was a thirty, so I got a twenty comin'. No, Jack, friends do what needs to be done—get it? I won't forget what you done for me when you hardly knew me. So you'll do for me if I need you over here, and I'll always do for you. That's how it works. You got it?"

I was completely intimidated by him in those days. "Yes sir, Mr. Truck," I said. "I got it."

"Jack," he said with a half-smile, "when you gonna start calling me *Bobo*? Go 'head, try it—*Bobo.*"

"Sure . . ." I stammered, looking at the floor, a wet-behind-the-ears kid in the presence of a giant. *"Bobo."*

He put his powerful right arm around my shoulder and drew me to him. "Atta boy," he said. "You're mine and I am yours. And another thing over here, when you need something, you don't have to tell me why. That's how it works."

187

From Eisenhower to Kennedy to Vietnam

ISENHOWER UNDERSTOOD WAR. He understood that American power, short of war, could not change the natural equilibrium that, for better or worse, a country settles into from its own dynamics. Trying to change regimes from the outside, through the use or threat of military power, doesn't work.

Truman also understood the limits of American power. In 1948, he did not confront the West Berlin blockade by the Soviets. He held on to West Berlin with the Berlin Airlift. Nor did Kennedy confront the Soviets in 1961 when they built the Berlin Wall. In both instances, Truman and Kennedy would not be stampeded into war by Washington war hawks who thumped for "Action—let's teach the Soviets a lesson!" Kennedy was still reeling from the Cuban debacle; he seemed to have forgotten the lesson when it came to Vietnam.

The Cold War lasted forty-four years until the collapse of the Soviet Union and the repudiation of communism. Along the way, there were plenty of opportunities for it to turn into a shooting war. Fortunately, there were cool heads in control, on both sides, despite Soviet bluster.

In 1954, in a remarkable display of patient, sober statesmanship, Eisenhower refused a French appeal for US military help to save thirty thousand French troops trapped at Dien Bien Phu in Vietnam, facing annihilation and surrounded, improbably, by Ho Chi Min's ragtag army. That French army, well-trained, well-equipped—mostly Foreign Legionnaires—were the cream of the French military. Yet they were completely outmaneuvered by a patriot army that possessed neither aircraft nor armored vehicles.

Eisenhower saved those French soldiers in 1954 through dialogue with Ho Chi Min. No Americans were sent to Vietnam. The French were given safe passage out of the country. Eisenhower, the warrior, understood that Vietnamese patriotism was a force whose time had come. It would not be thwarted by armies.

Overcoming a tidal force of nationalism worked in the age of colonialism when well-armed and well-trained regiments could conquer an entire civilization that fought with stones, clubs, and spears. The myth of western war-making dominance over former colonies died at Dien Bien Phu. Eisenhower understood. Kennedy did not.

Apparently Kennedy forgot the lesson of the disastrous Bay of Pigs Invasion, when, on June 16, 1961, he opened the door in Vietnam that Eisenhower had so deftly closed. Kennedy ordered four hundred Green Berets to Vietnam to train South Vietnamese soldiers. Later that year, he sent sixteen hundred more, then more later. It was the snare that eventually led to the US forces that fought in Vietnam, peaking at five hundred forty-three thousand troops in April 1969.

By the time the Vietnam War ended with the humiliating defeat of the US in April 1975, a total of 2.7 million US servicemen had served in Vietnam. Ninety thousand died during those fourteen years, with more than one hundred thousand wounded. Vietnam changed, forever, Americans' faith in our government. There was no patriotism about Vietnam. It was a war fought by draftees: a dirty, endless killing machine, unsupported by most of the country, especially the young. A war without purpose and without hope.

History says Vietnam was Lyndon Johnson's war, and Richard Nixon's—the two presidents who followed Kennedy. An argument might be made, given that the great escalation occurred after Kennedy's assassination, but Johnson always said he was committed to honoring Kennedy's legacy—to taking the country in the direction Kennedy had envisioned and fulfilling his vision for America. As for Nixon, by the time he took office, the war was already very much out of control.

* * *

Adam was fourteen when Kennedy sent those first four hundred Green Berets to Vietnam in 1961. By 1962, there were more than ten thousand American troops in Vietnam. Adam turned fifteen in September, and I began to worry that if the war escalated, he could be called to serve overseas.

* * *

In October 1962, the Soviets, under Khrushchev's leadership, began moving nuclear missiles to Cuba, threatening the possibility of a nuclear attack on the United States. President Kennedy's reaction was swift but deliberate. The crisis threatened nuclear warfare. Unthinkable but possible. A thirteen-day standoff ended with an agreement with Khrushchev that the nuclear missiles would be removed from Cuba. They were.

Kennedy is praised for his patient, deliberate, and successful defusing of the crisis. The reality is that it was his inattention to the festering issue of US missiles in Turkey that caused the Cuban Missile Crisis. It ended it in a secret deal with Khrushchev that removed the missiles from Turkey quietly, almost secretly. That's really what ended the crisis.

188

Planning to Meet APC

WE ASKED GOREN to join us, and Durells had invited one of his partners who understood patent law. Durells introduced him: "This is my partner, Jeremy Grossman. He does patent work."

Jeremy spoke up immediately. "Larry has explained your situation, and, first things first, I have to tell you I am not on par with the attorneys representing APC on patent issues. They are among the best in the world, not only for their legal knowledge and their experience negotiating patent disputes but at destroying their opponents through costly, drawn-out litigation.

"Not only that," Jeremy went on, "but every major patent firm has done work for APC. If you try to engage the best patent lawyer, you'll find they can't represent you because APC is or has been a client. You'll have to settle for someone like me. I know the law, but if it comes to litigation, I will be facing a team of ten or twelve lawyers, each with a staff of researchers and paralegals. They will drown me with motions in several jurisdictions and simultaneous hearings in several courtrooms. Since I lack the manpower to handle that, I'll have to round up a team of attorneys from other law firms. Very costly and inefficient. Meantime,"—he looked from Eddie to me and back again—"you two won't have time for anything besides dealing with the litigation.

"That's how APC plays the patent game." He shook his head. "And it's not only the APC way. It's all the big players—the auto companies and DuPont and Pfizer and GE and all the other biggies." Jeremy leaned back in his chair, put his hands behind his head, and thought for a moment.

"I understand you are using eight of their patents in your mobile phones. I'll help you draft a proposal to license them. You need to tell me how much you can afford to pay in royalties for each, depending on how many phones you either produce or sell. It's easier to track sales than production.

I'll develop a sliding scale *per patent* rather than for all eight collectively, because over time you'll develop improved phones that will drop one or more of their patented components.

"That's the obvious approach," he continued. "But you may want to propose something radical, like a joint venture with them—a partnership, or a new company where you and APC develop the mobile phone jointly. Maybe fifty-fifty, sixty-forty, or whatever. With them as a partner—well, I don't have to tell you what that would do to expand the use of your phones."

We labored three long days and well into the nights. On the morning of the fourth day, we agreed to offer two proposals: the royalty plan, with detailed charts of royalty payments; and an APC-Dunlaur partnership plan at fifty-fifty, complete with details of funding, management, regions for development, satellite offices, and more. The royalty plan was five pages. The partnership plan was fifteen pages, and it was only an outline.

"Okay," I said. "Let's leave it alone for two days. If we're ready to go, I'll have them printed up and bound—a dozen copies of each, and I'll call Fred Walsh to arrange a meeting."

* * *

After I'd reached Walsh, Durells reserved a business suite at the Bellevue Stratford Hotel in Philadelphia for the morning of Friday, November 9. Walsh said his side would consist of himself, Bill Kane, and Bradford Wister—a lawyer from APC headquarters in Chicago.

Goren declined to join us. Best, he said, that it be just the principals and their lawyers.

189

Friday, November 9, 1962

IT WAS SIXTEEN YEARS since I'd seen Fred Walsh. That would make him forty-seven or forty-eight. He'd moved up at APC and was now executive director of its northeast region, a big job. He looked the part. He'd put on a dozen easy pounds, and his complexion was smooth and pink, his hair stylishly cut. His fingernails were perfectly manicured, clean and lightly polished. He wore the APC executive uniform: a finely pinstriped black suit and a brilliant white-on-white, straight-collared shirt. Black silk socks, gleaming black Blucher shoes, silver cufflinks, and a red and silver striped necktie completed the image. Everything about him spoke to his position near the top of the APC pyramid.

Bill Kane, my old boss, was now the company's regional operations manager for eastern Pennsylvania and southern New Jersey. About the same age as Walsh, and in the job that Walsh had two years earlier, Bill was clearly working his way up the ranks. He conveyed the same successful APC executive persona: impressive job, friends in high places, swank country club, beautiful wife, and perfect children enrolled in perfect private schools. I knew him to be smart and focused, a strong leader, open to new ideas, admired by his employees, respected by his customers and the APC hierarchy alike. I'd always liked Bill, and we greeted each other warmly. Fred Walsh approached me with a kind of hesitancy. No surprise, given how he'd handled my sacking fifteen years ago.

In the interest of making everyone comfortable, I stepped forward to greet him. I shook his hand and smiled broadly. "Hello, Sarge," I said.

Walsh immediately relaxed. "Captain," he said with a grin, clamping his left hand over our handshake. "God, Jack, it's good to see you." I thought I saw a hint of moisture in his eye.

Introductions all around. Lots of smiling, belying the tense seriousness of why we were together.

"Where's your lawyer?" I asked. "Bradford Wister?"

"He's stuck in Chicago," Fred explained. "He missed the flight yesterday, and nothing is flying out of Midway today."

"The good news," Bill said, "is that we've got breakfast set up in the conference room. What say we get at it?"

There is ritual about such meetings. First, there has to be an atmosphere that this is just a friendly get-together. There has to be talk of everyday things. We talked about baseball—always a safe topic: Roger Maris, Mickey Mantle, Ernie Banks, Hank Aaron, Willie Mays, Warren Spahn, Stan Musial, Ted Williams, Sandy Koufax—the current greats. And talk about the Cold War and the stock market. The Dow-Jones Industrials were hovering in the middle 600s. Walsh wanted to bet me it would break 700 before year-end. Jeremy Grossman said he thought we'd see it break 1,000 within a few years. That drew polite derision. "That's as likely as a World Series this year between the Kansas City A's and the Philadelphia Phillies." Both were comfortably stuck in last place.

"Hey, Jack," Walsh said. "Did you know today is nineteen years since I took over your second platoon after Peleliu? I keep a diary. Peleliu was my first invasion. I was so raw and so scared. But you, you were a real veteran. You were at Cape Gloucester. At Peleliu, you knew how to command. I decided to stick close to you."

A sobering moment. My thoughts flew back to that day at Peleliu. I survived three of those amphibious assaults: Cape Gloucester, Peleliu, Okinawa. It all seemed like a dream now.

The five of us in that room were all combat veterans of the War, and for a minute, silence reigned.

Finally, Bill broke the spell. "How about talking some business, guys?"

"Okay," Eddie said. "Let's get to it."

"If I may begin . . ." Jeremy said pulling one of our proposals from his briefcase. "I have two proposals here. I'll start with a proposal to head off any dispute, through a royalties arrangement." He began to distribute copies of the five-page proposal.

"Please, Jeremy, may I interrupt?" Walsh said. "I don't want to be impolite, but Bill and I have a plan that might save us all a lot of time. Can I give it to you in twenty seconds?"

190

1XL12MOS+180SEBPx5

FRED WALSH STOOD. Broad smile. "Here it is guys," he said. He handed three-by-five cards to me, Eddie, and Jeremy. He was electrified, a man bringing exciting good news.

There was only this cryptic message on our cards: "1xL12MOS+180SEBPx5." I studied it carefully—what did it mean?

Jeremy was the first to speak up. "What is it?" he asked.

"It's in-house shorthand for a purchase," Walsh said. "It means we'll buy Dunlaur for the equivalent of your last twelve months' sales—a cash deal, and we offer Jack and Eddie each a five-year employment contract at one hundred eighty thousand dollars annually plus our standard executive benefit package. The offer is for your industrial division. It doesn't include the retail business. The purchase offer is fourteen million, equal to your sales for the last twelve months. You'll be rich men."

Walsh paused to let the offer sink in for a moment then continued. "We know a lot about Dunlaur. We like everything about the company and especially you two guys. We've been able to pretty much create your financials for the past three years. We know what new products you're working on. We're particularly aware of your mobile phone. It puts where *we* are to shame. We want to be in it with you. Whattaya say?"

While I was trying to assemble my thoughts, Eddie spoke up. He addressed me, not Walsh. "Jack," he said calmly, quietly, "how about we find a place to talk about this? You, too, Jeremy."

As the three of us headed to an adjacent meeting room, I turned back to ask, "Fred, how did you guys get to know as much about us as you say?"

"We have the best due diligence operation in the business," he said. "We have to, because we're investing in companies all the time. Those DD guys get stuff out of your bank, out of your vendors, your customers, your foremen, your accountants, your model shop people—sometimes even out of your trash. Before we make an offer, we know what we're getting. In your case, we know it, we like it, we want it. Do the deal. You won't regret it."

Eddie, Jeremy, and I talked for almost fifteen minutes. We were nothing if not stunned by the direction the discussion had taken. In an instant, fears of total destruction at the hands of a predatorial giant had given way to heady thoughts of great wealth and long, wonderful careers with a benevolent employer that would provide us with all the tools necessary to pursue our ideas. That's not to say we didn't have questions; we had plenty of them.

Returning to the meeting, the next few hours were filled with our questions and what-ifs. One that hadn't come up in the other room was posed to Fred by Jeremy: "What is your authority to make this deal?"

There was no hesitancy in Fred's answer. "My authority comes from Arthur Brandt, director of mergers and acquisitions at APC. Brandt knows everything about you and your mobile phone system, and he's pushing hard for this."

"Does Mr. Brandt have to get final approval from anyone above him?" Jeremy pressed.

"Technically, a deal this size needs Martin Dunlap, our CEO, to sign off on it," Walsh said. "I suppose Brandt also needs an okay from the board chairman, but that's a rubber stamp."

"Anyone else?"

"Well, there's Bradford Wister. He's the lawyer we're expecting later today."

"And what's his role?" Jeremy asked.

"He's your opposite number," said Walsh. "He knows the deal; he's on Dunlap's staff. He has the same deal memo we have here." He reached into his briefcase and held up a bound book, about three inches thick. Imprinted on the cover were the words "Dunlaur Communications."

"This book," he said, "covers everything we know about Dunlaur and its mobile system, plus sales projections for the next five years. It outlines the development and marketing of the mobile phone and"—he stroked the cover with his palm—"improvements to five other Dunlaur products and the manner of manufacture. We've had Dunlaur under the microscope for two years, but we went into full-court press acquisition mode the day you negotiated for your first rooftop relay mast."

He paused to be sure we were all following. We were.

"This book has been read and reported on by at least a dozen different men in the APC system: market guys and economists and production managers and electrophysicists and patent lawyers and accountants. We like Dunlaur. We like Eddie and Jack. We want them on our team. APC is the best. We want them 'cause *they're* the best."

"Can we read the book?" Eddie asked.

"You bet. I have three copies right here," he said, pulling them out of his briefcase.

"What's the latest on Wister?" Jeremy asked.

"He was scheduled for an eight o'clock flight out of Chicago." Walsh looked at his watch. "That should get him here in the next couple of hours. He has a first draft of an acquisition agreement. We're hoping we can work on it later today and tomorrow. If we don't finish on Saturday, we'd like to take the day off on Sunday and come back to it Monday. I think you'll like Bradford. I know him a little bit, and he's a good guy."

"Well, Fred," I said, "you certainly got our attention. While we're waiting for your man, how about we break for a little reading?" I chuckled at my copy of the Dunlaur book. "I'm interested in learning something about my company."

The suite was extensive and well-appointed, with a luxuriously furnished library in addition to several meeting rooms. Eddie, Jeremy, and I adjourned to the library to review APC's research on us.

At four o'clock, Walsh walked over to tell us Bradford Wister had phoned. He was about to get in a cab at the Philadelphia Airport and expected to be with us in less than an hour. There was something in Walsh's tone that told me Wister was more than a lawyer charged with finalizing an agreement.

191

Bradford Wister

H E WAS ONE OF the best-looking men I'd ever seen—handsome the way every man would like to be handsome, with chiseled features and bold eyebrows and thick black hair. Central casting could have sent him to play the strong, smart executive on the way up. He had a marvelous smile. Perfect teeth, a smile that drew you in. You wanted to look at him; you wanted him to know you and like you. He laughed occasionally, a laugh that made you want to join, but it didn't invite you. There was no foolishness about him. There could be laughter but not frivolity.

He stood six feet tall, taller than most men in those days. He had a good physique. You could see that through the navy pinstriped suit, clearly custom-tailored. The shoulders had a slight slope, unlike most men's suits of the day which favored broad horizontal ones. There was not a wrinkle anywhere. The creases in his trousers were knife-sharp. He wore silver cufflinks stamped with gold initials: BRW. An altogether impressive package. I guessed him to be a few years older than me, early forties.

Wister was attentive during the introductions, an outstretched arm, a firm handshake. His eyes fixed on yours—a half smile, a nod, and he repeated your name.

"So, Jack Laurel," he said, looking at me straight on. "I know who you are. The twenty-one-year-old Marine captain, three missions, decorated. You are quite the guy. You and Eddie—what a pair. You built a great company from zero. Jack, it's an honor to know you."

He moved to Eddie with the same enveloping manner. He knew all about Eddie. He even knew about Eddie climbing the mast on the Wichita to check out the antenna, and his leg wound, and Eddie's improvements to the walkie-talkie. Even with all APC's research, remembering so many details was no small feat.

"What about you, Bradford?" Eddie asked. "I feel at a disadvantage. All I know is your name and that you're a lawyer."

Bradford laughed. His eyes sparkled. "I'll give you the highlights," he grinned. "I was drafted in 1942 out of Duquesne Law School into the Army military justice system. My good fortune was to become a clerk for a full colonel who got drafted by APC. After the War, he recruited me to APC and got the company to fund me to finish law school. I owe him and APC a lot. When I graduated, I was assigned to Mr. Dunlap.

"What else . . . ?" he mused. "Oh, yes—I married Mr. Dunlap's daughter. Good career move, yeah? That's what everybody says." He laughed. "We have two children and a perfect marriage, and Mr. Dunlap thinks I'm real smart." Again the good-natured laugh. You could not help but like the man.

"Tell you what," Wister said. "I've been up since four thirty in the morning. How about we call it quits for today and have dinner sent up?" He nodded to his copy of the Dunlaur book. "I'd like to refresh myself on the details in the morning and pick up here at noon."

Dinner was pleasant, although I felt a low-level uneasiness that Wister seemed to be still reviewing rather than pushing forward to lock up the deal. We broke up at seven thirty, leaving Wister behind, his necktie off, yawning, anxious to get to bed.

Jeremy used a phone in the hotel lobby to report to Durells, after which the three of us had a nightcap at the bar. We needed to decompress.

I arrived home around eleven thirty that night, happy to find that Adam was asleep. I didn't want to be pumped for information about the meeting, mainly because something about Wister was bothering me. I fixed myself a bourbon and soda and went to my room.

I lay awake in bed, reviewing the day's events for at least three hours. So much going on. Grave trouble and unimaginable success lurking, both flirting with me. I watched through my window as the moon emerged from a cloud bank; moonlight flooded my room. Drowsily, I realized it was the first day since I'd brought Violet to Atlantic City General that I hadn't visited her.

First thing tomorrow, I promised the moonlight.

192

Bobo Indicted!

ADAM WAS WAITING for me at the breakfast table. I was surprised to see him up this early on a Saturday, but he was eager to hear about our meeting with APC.

"Mornin', Dad," he said cheerfully. "Wanna tell me all about it?"

For the past two years, I'd been discussing Dunlaur's business activities freely with Adam. He knew the proposals Eddie and I had prepared for the meeting. He grew excited when I told him the APC proposition to buy Dunlaur.

"Wow!" he exclaimed, standing up from the table. "We'll blanket the country in a couple of years, Dad. We're gonna change the way people communicate. With APC, the money will be unlimited. Wow!" he repeated. "Wow!"

I told him that the third member of the APC team showed up late and never commented on the APC plan, just said he was going to review it again before we meet again today. Adam's jubilation subsided. "What's his role in the deal?" he asked.

"I don't know, son. Our guess is he wants to toughen up the deal—maybe lower the purchase price or give us less authority or salary or a shorter contract. Anyway, we'll know soon enough." I looked at my watch. Six thirty. Eddie and I planned to spend a few minutes with Violet before stopping at Durells's office en route to our meeting. With fifteen minutes to spare, I took another sip of my coffee and unfolded the morning paper.

The headlines shouted at me in thick one-inch-tall type:

BOBO TRUCK INDICTED!

According to the article, the secret grand jury indicted my friend on five counts:

Corrupting public officials

Extorting money from Atlantic City businesses
Illegal gambling and operating a criminal enterprise
Income tax evasion
Conspiracy to commit murder

That last one was for the three men from the Philadelphia mob who disappeared in October 1951 on their way to meet with the police chief.

The article went on to say that Bobo Truck—real name Benno Trucci—had been arraigned then released on the largest bail posting in New Jersey history: $750,000. It was a remarkable sum, equivalent to $20 million today.

The fact that he'd made bail was proof, according to the article, of the immense wealth Bobo had accumulated through the criminal activities charged in the indictment. "Who else in America could post seven hundred and fifty thousand dollars virtually overnight?" the reporter asked rhetorically.

Only Eddie, Larry Durells, and I knew how the money was assembled. I flushed and my body went hot. Making the loan was traumatic because it compromised our financial security, but now, reading the newspaper story, I shuddered at being linked to Bobo by an aggressive investigation. I wondered how well Eddie and I had covered our trail and decided we hadn't been nearly careful enough.

But what of it? I asked myself. *We loaned Bobo some money. So what?* Even my most optimistic view sounded lame. Not only was it likely Eddie and I were never going to see that money again, we were going to be targeted by the FBI for collusion with Bobo. But what kind of collusion? The only instance of financial help from him was the Traymore job that saved Dunlaur. What I did was 100 percent legitimate: I quoted the job, we delivered, we were paid, and the Traymore saved a lot of money.

True, but we were clumsy in the way we paid the commission to Bobo, and I didn't know what, if anything, Bobo had gotten from the Traymore. Still, that was in 1948—fourteen years ago. What's the statute of limitations on something like this?

What a mess, I thought. *If APC gets wind of it . . .*

"What's it about, Dad?" Adam asked, noticing how the newspaper story had affected me.

"Nothing, son, nothing at all," I lied.

The phone rang as I headed for the door. It was Eddie.

"I'm leaving for the hospital now," I told him. "I'll pick you up."

"Hey, Dad," Adam called out. "It's Saturday—no school. Can't I come with?"

"No, Adam," I called back over my shoulder. "Not today. Shoot over to the plant. There's plenty of work that needs you."

Leaving the house that morning, it felt like I was headed into a whirlwind.

193

Heading to the Bellevue

THERE WAS LITTLE to say as Eddie and I drove to the hospital. He had absorbed the news of Bobo's indictment and reacted the same as I did. Our main point of concern was the $250,000 each we'd given Durells at Bobo's request. We talked about crisis control but couldn't think of any action we might take to avert the problem.

"Durells is our lawyer, after all," I said. "If anyone questions the money, he's holding it in escrow for the APC issue—in case we need it to reach a patent infringement settlement."

Eddie wasn't crazy about how that sounded but agreed our best approach for now was to keep a low profile. We hadn't done anything illegal, so charges seemed unlikely, but news of a financial entanglement with Bobo would be very damaging. The mayor would have to disown us, and the APC offer would be withdrawn, but what could we do?

We were in a hurry, and we agreed to keep our visit with Violet brief. We entered her room to find her lying flat on her back in the bed. Her left leg was heavily bandaged and elevated in a suspended sling. Hard to believe they were about to release her, but that's what we'd been told. She smiled as we came through the door, revealing the gap where her two front teeth had been. It gave her a comical air.

"Jack, Eddie, I'm so glad you're here," she said, reaching out to take our hands. "I tried smiling with my lips closed, but I couldn't do it. I must look terrible, but I'm too happy to worry about it."

"Apparently they're going to discharge you today or tomorrow," Eddie told her. "Where do you plan to go?"

"We all want you," I said. "Mom, Eddie and Evie, me and Adam. It's your decision."

* * *

Eddie and I stopped at Durells's office before heading to Philadelphia for our meeting. The attorney was waiting for us. The first thing I asked him was, "How easy is it to trace my and Eddie's money to you—and from you to Bobo's bail?"

"It all went into my escrow account," he answered. "I'm not required to explain it coming in or going out. It's privileged. But"—he paused—"I won't kid you. A good investigator will start with the bail clerk. He'll see the seven hundred and fifty thousand dollars coming in from me as Bobo's counsel. He'll ask me how it came to me. I needn't tell him anything. The weak link is the deposits into my escrow—your banks and brokers, and then tracing them back to you.

"However . . ." He pursed his lips. "I don't think you need to worry. Posting bail is routine, and although this is a big number, everyone believes Bobo has that kind of money and more. The most likely link to you will come from the IRS indictment. When they examine Bobo, they're the ones who will trace the money."

He paused. "Anything the IRS knows is absolutely confidential. They may look you fellows over, but there's no wrongdoing. Besides, they won't get into the case for at least a year, and by then, things should have quieted down. So the IRS discovers you put up some money—there's nothing illegal in that."

He was trying to be reassuring, but neither I nor Eddie were reassured.

* * *

Durells started moving papers around on his desk, and I could see him weighing what he was about to say. The silence grew uncomfortable. He took a deep breath as if he were about to dive into a pool then finally began quietly and slowly. "You know," he said, "APC is fully unionized, and so is every one of their subsidiaries. You will be too." Another pause, then, "Did you ever wonder why there's never been an attempt to organize at Dunlaur—either the electronics or retail divisions?"

Eddie and I looked at each other, and it was Eddie who answered. "Yes, Larry," he said. "We've talked about that. We're good employers. We pay our people above union scale, and we offer a solid benefits package. We like to think maybe there were attempts, but our people weren't interested."

"Not to burst your balloon," Durells said with a slight head shake, "but the Communications Workers *and* the Retail Clerks wanted you. Bobo told them to lay off, that they couldn't have you. Bobo told me I'm never to tell you that. But I'm breaking my promise because maybe you'll feel better about the five hundred grand you loaned him."

* * *

We were on the way to Philly by nine thirty. As we pulled onto road, I told Eddie I felt like we were convening to hear Bradford Wister pass judgment on the APC plan to buy Dunlaur. He shot me a grim look.

194

Thoughts in a Moving Vehicle

THOSE DAYS, BEFORE the expressway had been built, it was at least a two-and-a-half-hour drive from Atlantic City to midtown Philadelphia. Eddie and I had plenty of time to talk. I was doing the driving.

"The APC offer came as such a surprise that you and I never really talked about it, Jack," he said. "I'd like to do that now."

He paused, staring out his window into the Pine Barrens. The two-lane road was crowded by walls of dark green trees and foliage, an occasional small opening giving a glimpse of the bleakness within. He turned back to look at me. "When I came out of the Navy, I promised myself I'd never work for anybody but me. I never wanted to take another order. Eddie's TV and Radio was a tough business to run, but I managed to make a living at it, and I was my own boss. Do I want a guy like Bradford Wister looking over my shoulder since the money is real big? We'll be rich men. And most likely we'll do with APC a hundred times what we can do alone. But"—he paused again—"maybe screw the money. How's about Adam? I know you think he'll be running Dunlaur someday. And Eddie Jr. will be his partner—just like you and me.

"APC will make them over, Jack. No matter how high up a man gets in a company like that, in the end, he's an employee, and some guy he's never even met is his boss—I'm thinking about when you were with APC and Fred Walsh canned you on the order of some higher-up who didn't even know your name. That's life in the golden APC cage. Is it what we want?

"Don't get me wrong, the big money is a real, real, *real* big thing. It's *Fuck you* money—enough to do anything, or do nothing, to buy anything, and to say *Fuck you* or *Fuck off* to anybody. Pretty terrific, hey, Jack? Is that what we been working for? Is that what we want for Adam and Eddie Jr.?

For me, the worst thing that could happen would be if Eddie Jr. turned into someone who doesn't do anything, because he doesn't have to."

"Eddie, I got a low-level feeling we won't have to make that decision," I said. "I'm thinking this guy Wister will try to water down the deal—and not just a little bit. I don't think we should decide anything until we've heard him out and taken some time to digest it."

I took my attention off the road for a quick second to look at him. "My guess is Wister will tell us he wants to modify the deal and he needs a few days. If he does, I'd like to say, *Sure, meanwhile, here's our proposal for a royalties deal.* We'll give copies to him and Walsh and Kane and ask them to study it. Not the partnership deal, though—I think we should keep that under our hat for now. If I'm wrong, and he's ready to sign a deal, let's hear him out but not accept it then and there. We're gonna have to do some heavy-duty thinking.

"In the meantime," I continued, "we're in a precarious position if APC wants to get tough—if our loans to Bobo leak out and we're kept from building the network for two or three years while APC kills us with lawsuits." I sighed. "Those worries had sort of evaporated with the plan Walsh laid out, but now..."

"You're right." Eddie shook his head. "Here I am worrying about a deal that's too good for us, when there's a mountain of bad shit ready to come down on us."

Wister Speaks

W E ASSEMBLED IN THE suite's conference room, where the table was set for a meal: fresh linens, glossy silverware, hot coffee, sweating silver pitchers of fresh-squeezed orange juice, baskets of warm rolls, butter and jam, and platters of eggs, ham, and home fries.

"C'mon, fellows," Bradford Wister welcomed us with a warm smile. "Breakfast is served."

Once we were all seated, Fred Walsh said, "So, are we ready to sign a contract, Bradford?"

Wister frowned as he buttered his roll. "Not quite, Fred." He drew out the words. "I'm not happy with the deal."

A collective sharp inhale was followed by a moment of stunned silence, then Walsh said, "What's wrong with the deal, Bradford?"

The attorney smiled, as if about to deliver good news, before suddenly sitting up straight in his chair and planting his palms on the table. It was an aggressive gesture.

"I'm going to recommend against the deal," he said. "I don't like it as a solution to the problem we're dealing with." He scanned all our faces before continuing. "I'll be blunt, gentlemen. Dunlaur is promoting an import-ant new business based on eight patented APC components. You see the problem?"

The Dream Ends

WAIT A SECOND, Bradford," Walsh said. "I understand your responsibility is to tighten up the terms of the deal, as our attorney, but it sounds like you want to make policy. The deal was approved by Arthur Brandt. The only authority above Brandt is Martin Dunlap, and Brandt told me Dunlap okayed it. What gives?"

The Wister smile was friendly, but the words were not. "Well, Fred, I think you know that I'm pretty close to Mr. Dunlap. He doesn't care to read detailed reports, as everyone at APC knows. Let me tell you a story." The attorney paused, smiling at the story he was about to tell.

"The first time I reported to Mr. Dunlap, he handed me a twenty-page report from the Army Signal Corps. Across the front page, he had written in big red letters, one word: CONDENSE. He said, 'What's your name, son?' and I told him. He nodded. 'Wister, take this. I haven't read it. Bring it back to me tomorrow morning.'

"So I took it and labored over it for the rest of the day and most of the night. In the morning, I had a four-page condensation. I gave it to his secretary. I hadn't gotten halfway to the elevator bank when she called me back and handed me the report. Mr. Dunlap had printed in red, across the first page, CONDENSE.

"I groped for words. 'I don't get it,' I said to the secretary. 'This was twenty pages. How much more can it be condensed?'

"She said, 'Let me give you some advice. Mr. Dunlap is a brilliant and busy man who trusts his staff to give him the essence. Make it one page, or less—three-quarters of a page. Capture the essence.'

"And that's what I did," Wister said. "And you know, the secretary was right. If Mr. Dunlap wants more than the essence, he'll give it to you with EXPAND written on it."

Wister stood. He leaned forward. His smile disappeared. He spoke flatly.

"I'm recommending the withdrawal of the purchase proposal. Mr. Dunlap will back me. I'm sorry for you, fellows," he said, looking first at me and then at Eddie and Jeremy. "This deal is not in APC's best interests. That phone is eighty percent APC. It's an APC phone. You built your unit with *stolen patents*, and the proposed deal would reward you for it. No deal."

Eddie shot up from his chair. A snort escaped his lips. *"Stolen?"* He took two steps toward Wister and leaned toward him. His lips were a grim slash across his thrust-forward chin. He was shorter than Bradford but broader, and he suddenly appeared much bigger, seeming to tower over the lawyer.

The faintest shadow of fear passed quickly across Wister's good looks. He took a step back.

I knew that Eddie look. The first time I'd seen it, we were only fifteen. Eddie jumped off the railing on the Boardwalk during the Memorial Day parade and flattened a hulking seventeen-year-old bully who was being fresh with Evie, thirteen. One punch and the bully went down, bleeding, his nose broken. I told Eddie I'd learned a valuable lesson from him that day—that some situations require immediate action. Hit! Strike out! Don't waste time on talk or analysis. In a moment, I feared Wister would be flattened. I jumped out of my chair and put my hand on Eddie's shoulder.

"It's okay, Eddie," I said. "Relax."

Turning to Wister, I said, "You should choose your words more carefully."

I felt Eddie relax, then I watched as he stepped back and gave Wister a tight-lipped smile.

"Listen, Bradford," Eddie said evenly. "Lots of people have tried to build that phone, including APC and Bell Labs. You're saying the lightbulb doesn't belong to Edison because he didn't invent glass and tungsten? The phone is mine—nobody else's."

Fred Walsh appeared crushed and perhaps a little frightened. Wister was obviously a force to be reckoned with at APC, and in that moment, I suspected my old boss was wondering about his future with the company.

"Well, Bradford . . ." Walsh said a bit meekly. "The Dunlaur team has its own proposals. Will you look at them?"

"Of course." The big smile returned. Wister studied his watch. "Tell you what," he said. "I'm headed back to Chicago in the morning, but I'll read this and call you Monday."

"All right, Bradford," I said. "Until Monday, then."

After icy handshakes all around, Eddie, Jeremy, and I departed the suite.

As Jeremy left us at the curb, he said he would update Durells on the situation.

Disaster.

197

Licking Our Wounds

WHAT CAN YOU DO when catastrophe is coming, and you know it, but you can't stop it? There must be a way to head it off, you think. You concentrate all your energy and imagination, but you can't think of anything to do. Nothing. As time passes, uselessly, the ancient joke comes to mind about the man who fell off the roof of a twenty-story building: as he passed the twelfth floor he was heard to say, "So far, I'm okay."

Fred Walsh called me at home a couple hours later. "Jack," he said dolefully. "I'm so sorry. Our plan was studied by at least ten senior guys—even space satellite guys, because we want to know when space satellites will take over from relay towers. The plan is good. Rather than us working to catch up with you, we will already be in business. And do you know what fourteen or fifteen or eighteen million dollars means to APC? It's peanuts, and look what comes with it—a plant, already in production and making money. Sometimes we buy a company and pump money into it for years before we even have a product to sell. With you, we'll be profitable from day one while we develop the phone."

He went on, "I thought Wister might say it's too rich for you and Eddie, and maybe tweak some of the management things—but this? I can hardly believe it."

"Thanks for calling, Fred, I appreciate your effort," I said. "I caught a hint that maybe you and Bill are in for some trouble. Just how strong is this guy Wister?"

"He's got sway, all right," Walsh said. "Guys who know say he's in the running to be the next CEO. Look, Jack, we all know that mobile phones are the future. Over at Bell Labs, we've been poking around at it for years, but you and Eddie *have it.*

"It was one of our Philadelphia area salesmen who found out what you were doing. He told his boss and the news got to Bill and he told me about it right away. We got on it fast, and we had the go-ahead less than a few days later. I can't understand Bradford, that he wants to nix it. All I can get outta this is that he's gonna break you with litigation and end up getting it for free and it will be *his.* Bill and I put it together on a fast track right away, but we never thought of it as *ours.*"

"Is there any chance Dunlap won't accept Wister's decision?"

"Probably not," Walsh said. "He believes in Bradford. The reality is that anything Bradford recommends turns out okay in the end, because APC, as a monopoly, is so big and so strong. And in the end, APC will make the mobile phone turn out okay. Dunlaur may get ruined, but APC will be the winner. Who else can do it? Not Motorola, or GE or Ericsson or Nippon. There's no contest. APC will be the first, with or without Dunlaur."

"Okay, Fred," I said. "I appreciate your honesty, and I'm sorry I held a grudge about being canned—I probably should have thanked you for getting me into the telecommunications business in the first place. I hope you and Bill don't end up on Wister's shit list, because guys like that have a long memory of those who oppose them."

Eddie and I drove to the Dunlaur plant that afternoon. We hardly spoke, each of us trying to collect our thoughts. *What now?* was the hovering question.

I called Durells from my desk. "Push ahead with the network," he said. "Expect a lawsuit that starts with a petition for an injunction. That will take a few days—maybe as much as two weeks. Push ahead until a judge stops us. Litigation is on the way. I'll start drafting our response."

198

Violet Returns

MOM CALLED ME at seven thirty Sunday morning. "Jack, I hope you don't mind me calling so early, but the hospital discharged Violet late yesterday. Dad and I know you and Eddie have been tied up with important business, so we went and got her and brought her here. She's in Evie's room."

"How is she?" I asked. "I'll come over right away."

"Take your time, son," she said. "There's a long routine to get her ready. When you get here, I'll make breakfast."

* * *

Violet was sitting up, eating from a breakfast tray when I arrived. I noticed her hair had started to grow back; for me it recalled Ingrid Bergman's look in *For Whom the Bell Tolls*. The bandage was gone from her left cheek, and the once-fiery red scar was starting to fade. The cast had been removed from her left leg, but it was still heavily bandaged, resting on two pillows to keep it elevated.

"Jack!" she exclaimed, smiling broadly. It was that same comedian's smile, I thought, with the two missing front teeth, but she looked adorable. She reached out her hand, and I took it. I kissed her hand. I kissed her forehead. She squeezed my hand.

"Oh, Jack, it's so good to see you. Here. With Mom and Dad. You're my family. I'm so filled with love. I . . ." She choked up, and I saw tears welling in her eyes. She turned away.

I was silent as she composed herself and turned back to face me. Brightening, she sat up more erect. "Dr. Elgin said the bandages can come off in a week. I'll need physical therapy. I have to learn to walk again, but I'll be all right. Just a bit of a limp. Or maybe not even that. I'll get the teeth replaced. The scar on my cheek will fade, but it will always be there. So what? It won't affect my life.

"I'm so happy," she continued, animated, smiling. "And I'll be back at work soon"—she laughed—"before Evie finds out she can get along without me."

We shared a laugh over that one, then I asked about Harry. "I haven't seen him for a while," I said. "Is he okay?"

"Sure, he was here early this morning. He left just before you got here. He's fine, just very busy at work. The company's distribution contract with GE is coming up for renewal, but he said he'll break away and come again tomorrow, no matter what."

"But tell me, Jack," she said with a concerned frown. "What's happening with APC and our network? I've been out of touch with what's going on. Eddie and Evie say *all's well*, but I know better. Eddie seems distracted—worried, maybe. Are we okay?"

"We've got problems," I said, "but we'll work it out."

"Tell me," she said, squeezing my wrist.

"No, Violet, it's not something you need to worry about right now. We'll be fine, and there'll be plenty of time for you to get involved once you're back at work."

"I'll need my teeth fixed first, but it shouldn't be more than three weeks." She tossed her head back and laughed. "Dunlaur Retail!" She held up both arms in a victory salute. "I miss it. I want it. I love it!"

* * *

Later that day, Eddie, Evie, and I met at the plant; I'd brought Adam along too. There was a lot to talk about. We couldn't decide which was the greater potential threat: a lawsuit by APC or a news story exposing our $500,000 contribution to Bobo's bail bond.

Durells was already planning our response to a lawsuit. There was nothing to be done about the bail bond. So, we concluded, it's back to work until we're stopped. I said I'd try to see the mayor the next day.

199

Business as Usual

Monday, November 12, 1962

T HE MAYOR WAS KIND enough to see me on short notice—and on a Monday. He seemed sympathetic when I told him about APC and my concerns about a lawsuit.

"My law firm handles patent infringement suits," he said. "We usually settle them before or during trial. If APC does sue, your trial will be in federal court in Philadelphia. It will be expensive. In the end, I believe you'll be paying royalties, probably a lot of money, but I don't see APC taking over your invention. This is America. This country encourages new technology and companies like yours that bring positive change to people's lives.

"As to the network," he added, "tell me what I can do to help."

There was no point in trying to maintain secrecy about our network any longer. We decided to push hard for a ten-digit phone. It had to be top priority. Eddie said he knew how to build it, but that it would violate four more patents.

Evie said, "Let's go. Let's get the towers up. I'll arrange a public demonstration. Give me a date. And I'll want four hundred phones to sell in the Philadelphia store the day after the demonstrations. We'll take a full-page ad, and they'll sell out in a day. We want to be in business while any lawsuit is going on."

Our work was cut out for us.

* * *

At six o'clock that night, I called Jeremy Grossman—five o'clock Chicago time. Was there any word from Wister?

459

"Surprisingly, no," he said, "so I called his office a half hour ago. His secretary told me he's staying over in Philadelphia, doing research at the Penn law library. *Out of touch,* she said, *no way to reach him. He'll call you Tuesday afternoon or Wednesday morning.*"

"What do you make of it?" I asked.

"My guess is he's doing patent law research, although I don't know why he can't do that in Chicago. Their university law library is as good as they come."

"So it doesn't quite add up," I offered. "I wonder if he's actually in Philly."

"I called the Bellevue Stratford and he's still registered there, so I guess he's in town at least until tomorrow."

"Is there anything more we should be doing?" I asked.

"Not that I can think of," he said. "If he is preparing a brief, it will take several days at least. He'll have it reviewed by staffers, then back to him, back to staff, etc. No telling what he's planning. Will he call to talk settlement, or will he just hit us with a complaint? I wish I knew."

He continued. "Try to go about your business, Jack, rather than driving yourself nuts. Durells has engaged a patent lawyer from one of the big New York firms, and I'm having my own patent research done. And because APC stole a Dunlaur relay and disabled a tower, when Wister files, we'll countersue for malicious interference, vandalism, and theft."

200

In Suspense

IT'S HARD TO WORK normally when your head is full of a problem that dominates everything you do. Nevertheless, on Tuesday morning I picked up where I'd left off and headed out to sign up more tower locations. Eddie and his team were focused on building a ten-key prototype.

Adam's school day ended at two o'clock. Eddie arranged to have him picked up and driven to Dunlaur every day. "He's as good at this as any of us," Eddie told me, "but he's got something the rest of us don't—a completely open mind. We know too much about the way it's *always been done*, but for him, each problem is pristine. I think he could be another Philo Farnsworth—you know, the guy who invented television in 1927 when he was fourteen? Adam's only a year older."

The day was productive. I signed up two locations and had promising talks with two others. The rumor mill was running. My prospects all knew something was going on between Dunlaur and APC. They'd heard Dunlaur wasn't building just another radio station but something new, possibly TV-connected. One of the new accounts wondered whether we were building wrist radios—the famous Dick Tracy futuristic comic book invention. One of the building owners I approached that day said, "I'm in your corner, Jack, but my lawyer has to okay the contract because we don't need any trouble with APC."

My last appointment ended a little after five o'clock. I called Jeremy, but he had nothing to report.

The drive to Atlantic City took more than two hours. I headed to see Violet, arriving just as Mom and Dad were leaving to catch *Lawrence of Arabia* at the Warren Theatre.

"I'm glad you're here, Jack," Mom said. "Harry just left. I think he upset her, but she said she's all right and ordered us to get going."

I found her propped up on three pillows, staring at the ceiling. An open book was lying on her stomach, the radio playing "The Third Man Theme" from the Orson Welles movie. I could tell she'd been crying, but she brightened as I entered the room. There was no blanket on the bed. Her left leg was still bandaged, but the bandages now started below the knee. Her right leg was bent up slightly and her light cotton nightgown had risen to expose most of her thigh. As she reached to pull it down, I was struck with an erotic jab.

"So, Violet," I said, slipping into her outstretched arms, "how are you feeling?" It was upsetting to see her eyes so red and swollen. "Is everything okay?"

"No, Jack," she answered, squeezing my hands. "No," she repeated as her eyes welled up with tears.

"What is it?" I asked, sitting up on the edge of the bed. "Would you like to talk about it?"

She reached for a tissue and dabbed at her eyes. "It's Harry," she said hoarsely.

"What about him?" I asked. "Trouble with the GE contract?"

"No, Jack," she said, searching my face. "He was here earlier to tell me it's over . . . between us." The tears were back now, and she dabbed at them angrily. "It took less than two minutes for him to speak his piece, standing at the foot of the bed. He talked about my past, about Earl and all the other men who'd had me before you rescued me the first time. His family insists he break it off. His mother wanted him to write a letter, but he wanted to tell me face-to-face. Then he said goodbye and left. Just like that."

Bursting into tears, she sobbed, "He made me feel filthy all over again."

"It's okay, Violet," I said. "Believe me, there is nothing dirty about you." As I leaned over to kiss her forehead, she threw her arms around me and pulled me to her.

"Take me, Jack," she said. "*Please*. Take me, love me." She pulled my face to hers and kissed me, a big, teary, open-mouthed kiss, all the while murmuring "Take me . . . love me."

I became aroused mightily. It was awkward with her bandaged leg, but I managed somehow. She opened to me, warm and moist. When I entered her, she whimpered, *Oh my god, oh my god.* She responded to my thrusts, rising up to me, covering my face with big wet kisses. She was wild, pulling me to her with fresh strength, her entire body trembling. She threw her head back and screamed—"Fuck me, Jack! Fuck me!"—pushing against me as she came, and then collapsed.

"Oh, Jack," she cried softly. "I wanted to do this from the minute you found me. I love you. I love you. I love you so! I never made love before, Jack, not to anyone. You are my first, my last, my everything!"

201

Jeremy Grossman's Surprise

THE LOVEMAKING WITH Violet shook me to the core, but not in the way I might have hoped. Before our limbs had even untangled, confusion started to set in. Confusion and a sense of panic over the suddenness of my conversion from surrogate big brother—maybe even father figure—to lover and confusion regarding Alice, who had taken Violet in without a moment's hesitation and showered her with love like only mothers give.

As gently as I could with my mind raging, I told Violet I cared for her deeply but needed a little time to sort out what had just happened. How much time I couldn't say, because it was a situation I'd never been in before. The words did not come easily; I thought they sounded harsh.

She sat still and silent in the bed, looking at me with watery eyes. I knew I'd hurt her. She accepted my declaration with a sad smile that tore at my heart.

After I'd put on my coat and turned toward the door she said, again, "I love you, Jack."

I left without a word.

* * *

Eddie and his team were working all day and well into the night, almost every night, on the ten-key prototype. We had patents pending on our three-key model and Adam's relay and the system itself. Meantime, Evie was developing the marketing program that would introduce the mobile phone and the network. Was it to be the introduction of our three-key model, or could we achieve the ten?

We fixed on a date by which we believed the network would cover 80 percent of our target area. It would be the three-key model unless we completed the new prototype in time. The latter seemed unlikely, but we were shooting for the stars.

* * *

Jeremy Grossman called me a week after my wild encounter with Violet, which I'd been thinking about with deeply mixed feelings every day. It had been almost two weeks since the Bradford Wister disaster, and we were all on tenterhooks over the lawsuit we knew was coming. It loomed over everything we did. Eddie said it was like trying to build a sea wall with a hurricane set to make landfall but you have no idea when it will hit.

"What is it, Jeremy?" I asked. "Did Wister file?"

"No, Jack. I've been expecting it, but that's not why I'm calling."

"Tell," I said, bracing for the worst.

"It's very odd," Jeremy said, "but Wister's taken himself out of the picture. He's turned the matter over to another lawyer—a young guy named Ted Gaither who's only been with Wister's group for a few months. Gaither called me to say Wister had given him the three proposals—the APC purchase proposal and the two Dunlaur proposals—and said any one of them is acceptable to APC. That comes straight from top. Gaither says they lean toward Fred Walsh's purchase proposal, but they'll accept the deal Dunlaur prefers."

I was speechless.

"Jack?" Jeremy prompted after a long silence. "Did you hear what I said?"

"Yeah, I heard you, Jeremy, but I don't get it. It must be some sort of trick."

"Maybe not, Jack," he said. "Durells thinks it could be on the level. Should we go along with it?"

"Why?" I said. "Wister is out to destroy us, so it must be a trick. Is Durells in the office? Can I speak with him?"

After a short hold, Durells came on the line. "C'mon over, Jack," he said. "We'll talk."

"I'll pick up Eddie," I said. "See you in thirty minutes."

202

Mystery

L ARRY AND JEREMY were waiting for us.

I didn't waste time on pleasantries. "What kinda game is Wister playing?" I asked.

Durells stroked his chin and hesitated before responding. "I don't think it *is* a game," he said finally. "What would he stand to gain? I think it could be on the level."

"C'mon, Larry," I said. "The guy is out to destroy us. Let's back up and think about those days. We had a deal with Walsh and Kane on the Friday, but Wister was delayed. He arrived that evening and didn't want to talk about the deal. He said he'd review it and meet with us the next day at noon."

I paused to think through the events before continuing. "He killed the deal on Saturday, and Eddie almost decked him for a nasty remark about stolen patents. We gave him our proposals and left the hotel. He was supposed to call Jeremy on Monday morning. He didn't. His secretary said he'd stayed over in Philadelphia to do research at the Penn law library. We don't know when he left Philly, and he never did call Jeremy. So what's he been doing all this time? It's eleven days since he shot down the Walsh plan. Jeremy thought he was preparing a lawsuit. Now this. Out of the blue. What happened? He wants us to relax—to start concentrating on putting a deal together with this new guy, Gaither, then one day, boom—he'll hit us with an injunction and a giant lawsuit."

Eddie asked, "Larry, what makes you think he's on the level?"

"I think he's probably moved on to something else," Durells said. "And the litigation could be a factor. It's long, hard work and maybe he doesn't have the stomach for it. Anyway, we lose nothing by trying to make a deal with Gaither.

"If they *are* trying to put one over on us," Durells continued, "I should be able to flush them out real quick. I can start with a letter of intent stating that both parties intend to work in good faith to reach agreement on one of the three proposals presented at the Bellevue meetings. If they're willing to sign the document, it will have impact even though it's not binding. For APC not to deal honestly then turn around and sue us . . . that would not be good strategy for them.

"Yet, their game might be just that—that while negotiating, maybe they discover we've done something egregious. Bottom line, yes, it *could* be a trick, but if it is, we'll know in two or three weeks. I say move ahead."

"Can I call Walsh?" I asked. Durells said okay.

I dialed the number. "Fred," I said, "what's happening?"

"Nothing new," Walsh answered. "Last I heard, Bradford was putting his lawsuit together. He told me I'm out of it. Like I said, Jack, I'm a little scared. If he wants, he can get me fired, demoted, or transferred to New Mexico."

I didn't tell Fred the latest. I thanked him and ended the call.

Eddie spoke up. "Okay, guys, let's try to do the royalty deal. We won't go into business in any way with APC. We'll pay them royalties, and that's it. Meanwhile, me and my team are pushing ahead with the network."

Durells said we should postpone a response for a couple of days. For one thing, he wanted to consult a friend who was a top litigator in Washington regarding the value of a letter of intent in our situation.

* * *

Evie and Adam asked the same question. "Is it for real?"

Eddie and I had no answer. "We're going to play it that way, but we'll be keeping our eyes and options open."

203

December 7, 1962

IT WAS PEARL HARBOR Day, the twenty-first anniversary of the surprise Japanese attack on Hawaii. I reflected on the memory of that day. It and the War shaped my life. Now, seventeen years after it ended, the War was still fresh in the country's consciousness. The typical veteran was in his late thirties to midforties, a civilian soldier, returned to civilian life. It was the generation of Americans that built America into the most successful and powerful country that ever was.

Veterans dominated the government. Veterans ran the construction industry. They created new products. Veterans were the CEOs of the country's most dynamic businesses. Veterans spearheaded the entry into foreign markets.

In 1998, popular newscaster Tom Brokaw wrote a book about World War II veterans, calling us *The Greatest Generation*.

204

Closing the Deal—
Christmas with Violet

NEGOTIATIONS ON OUR royalty proposal began immediately between Jeremy Grossman and Ted Gaither. Gaither asked for small increases in the royalties, linked to increased sales of our phones, and he wanted the royalties paid per phone as built, while our plan was to pay per phone as sold. Nevertheless, the negotiations were quiet and remarkably friendly. A deal was signed in less than a month.

"Some kind of a record," Gaither said. "APC deals usually drag on and on while department heads and their own legal staffs pick flyshit out of pepper."

* * *

The signing took place the day before Christmas 1962 in the mayor's office, a Monday. The *Philadelphia Inquirer* ran a front-page story under the headline: BIG WIN FOR PHILADELPHIA—HISTORIC DEAL BETWEEN APC AND UPSTART DUNLAUR ELECTRONICS TOUTS MAJOR MOBILE TELEPHONE NETWORK WITHIN SIX MONTHS

A photo accompanying the story included Gaither, Walsh, Kane, me, Eddie, Jeremy, and the mayor. The mayor and Eddie appeared to be speaking to each other on Dunlaur mobile phones.

There was another story on the front page that day, this one somewhat less conspicuous. The first day of Benno "Bobo" Trucci's trial had been set for the second Monday in July 1963. The article reported on a press conference a day earlier, where the feds announced that "the Crime Boss of Atlantic City" had been brought down by diligent FBI investigators and the tireless efforts of the district attorney's office.

* * *

We celebrated Christmas at Eddie's home. It was a happy gathering attended by my parents, Eddie's folks, Mrs. Wilson, Adam, Evie, Eddie, and little Eddie Jr.

And Violet. I hadn't seen her since the day of our lovemaking, and there was an awkward moment when we came face-to-face. Having been to the dentist for a new bridge, her smile had lost the gap-toothed look. She walked with a limp, using a cane to support her left leg. She was dressed in a soft white blouse and silky dark pants, slightly flared and closely fitted at the waist, showing off her hips to good advantage. Her hair had grown in but was still quite short—very stylish, I thought. Her eyes were bright, her face clear and lovely, marred only by the scar on her left cheek.

As I struggled to find words, she reached out and touched my arm. "Hi, Jack," she said, smiling. She seemed completely at ease, which surprised me considering how hard my heart was beating. I felt like the world's biggest cad and its biggest fool to boot. This lady was one in a million, and she'd cared for me before I messed everything up. What a dope.

"Hello, Violet," I stammered then mumbled something about how sorry I was not to have been in touch; things had been so busy lately.

"It's okay, Jack," she said, giving my arm a gentle squeeze. "I know how hectic things have been. It's great to see you."

In that moment it was obvious to me that I'd been in love with Violet for years but had lacked the maturity to see it. I stood tongue-tied as she excused herself and walked briskly off to see if she could help the other ladies in the kitchen.

205

Evie's Story

A FEW DAYS INTO the New Year, Evie walked into my office at Dunlaur unannounced. "It's personal, Jack," she said.

I waved her into a chair.

Our lives were so filled with business that I rarely saw my sister except during company meetings and family holidays. She'd been working harder than ever with Violet out of commission, but with her good right hand back at work, it seemed the pressure had eased. I studied her in her well-tailored dark blue business suit and thought how terrific she looked. Not only terrific but well-rested for a change.

"It was a wonderful Christmas, Evie, but I can't remember the last time you and I spent any time together, just the two of us," I said. "What's up?"

"It's about Violet," she said. "I have a story to tell you."

"Tell," I said.

* * *

"Violet has been back to work for almost a month now. She's supposed to be putting in half days, but she's working full time—no, make that more than full time. At first, I had a driver picking her up and taking her home, but her leg has healed to the point where she's now driving herself. When she's in her office, she can move around with very little trouble. I hardly ever see her using the cane anymore. She amazes me.

"The other day, I was in the supply closet in the conference room when she came in with Harry Breckinger, and they're talking. I should have let them know I was there, but it was a highly personal conversation, and within a few seconds, I lost the opportunity. And I must confess, Jack, that I *wanted* to eavesdrop. Is that terrible? I guess so, but since I did, I have to tell you.

"So Harry says he wants to clear the air. He wants to establish what their relationship is going to be moving forward. He says Dunlaur will continue to carry GE products, and since Breckinger is the distributor for the area, the two of them will be in regular contact like before. He says he wants to forget about what he said that day ... when they broke up. He couldn't help it—the shock—learning the truth about her past and seeing her in that horrible place in the woods. And that guy, Earl ... the revelations about her past. Until that moment, Harry says, he thought of her as so pure—that's the word he used, *pure*. He was devastated.

"Then he says he's been thinking about her ever since, and he knows he can get over it—that, in fact, he already has. He wants to get back together.

"Violet says something like, *I suppose I should be grateful you want me back*. Her tone was scathing.

"*C'mon, Violet,* he says. *Don't say it like that, like I think I'm doing you a favor. I want you back, and I want us to be together on New Year's Eve.*

"*Thanks, Harry,* she says. *You're a good sport to overlook my sordid past and try to forget I'm soiled merchandise.*

"*That's unfair, Violet,* he says. *I want to put all that behind us. I know it will be awkward for a while—but remember how good we were together! And I know what Earl did to you wasn't your fault. I know we can be happy together, and we won't ever have to talk about the past.*

"So then Violet said something like, *Thanks so much, Harry. I suppose you're even thinking that now you know about all the men who fucked me, you and me will be able to go at it. No, Harry, nothing doing. I don't want to be with you. I don't want to know you. I'll do business with your company, but you'll have to assign another rep to our account. And believe me, if there was another way to carry the GE line, I'd drop Breckinger in a heartbeat. In fact, I think I'll contact GE and see if they'll deal with us direct. We're a pretty big customer.*"

"Evie," I said. "I'm surprised at you, eavesdropping like that. But I'm glad you did."

"That's not all, Jack," Evie said. "When Harry left, I came out of the supply closet. I had to let her know I overheard everything. I told her I was ashamed I'd listened in, but that I was really proud of how she handled the jerk.

"Then I said to her, since I know how Harry broke off with you and how you iced him, you have to tell me what's up with Jack. I know something's going on, because neither of you ever mentions the other.

"She starts to well up on me. She's going to cry. *Don't cry,* I say. *Tell me about you and Jack.*

"Of course this isn't word-for-word, but she said, *I love him so, Evie. I can't describe how much. I threw myself at him the day Harry dumped me. I thought I could never make love to anyone. But when Harry broke things off, I realized he was really just a defense screen. I didn't love him. I love Jack. I always have. He ruined me for any other man, and not because we had sex that day. I've loved him with all my heart, all my soul, almost from the minute he found me hiding in his car. When Harry dumped me, the dam broke, and I couldn't hold it back any longer. I let myself go. Jack didn't have a chance. I was all over him. It was almost like I raped him, and it was glorious.*

All those men in the past, it was like they were sticking it into a scarecrow—I wasn't even there. With Jack, I had an orgasm for the first time ever. It was incredible, like I'd floated out of my body and left the room, but I completely overwhelmed him, and now he avoids me. When I saw him at Christmas, he hardly spoke to me. I try to keep my cool, but it's so hard, Evie. I'm crazy about him. What can I do?

"I think you love her, too, Jack," Evie said. "You have probably been holding back for years, just like she has. You should talk to her."

206

Eddie Wants to Talk

IN THE DAYS THAT soon turned into months after hearing Evie's story, my unspoken feelings for Violet and especially the knowledge that she was in love with me were like a lead weight across my shoulders. My sister was right, and I knew it. I loved Violet as I'd loved no woman since Alice. Why was I helpless to act?

Trying to work it out in my mind analytically as I would a business problem, I concluded that *fear* was what kept me from confronting and confessing my feelings for Violet. A fear of commitment that was rooted in the loss of Alice. Somehow, rather than freeing me to act, getting a handle on my fear seemed to further my inaction. It was maddening.

The fear, which I never spoke of to anyone, seemed to tighten its grip as each day I ignored the urge to call or just drop in on Violet. There were times when I felt desperate to hear her voice, to bask in her smile, but my thoughts always turned to Alice, and cold fear neutralized my will.

* * *

Dunlaur was growing more quickly than any of us could have anticipated, and the challenges of expanding our sales and distribution networks helped me put Violet out of my mind as the weeks flew by. One late summer day in '63, Eddie stopped by my desk and announced he was taking me out to lunch. He said we needed some quiet time to talk, best outside the office. He had an agenda handwritten on a three-by-five-inch card. He didn't read it to me. He studied the card.

"First item," he said. "Report on Dunlaur. The company is growing. The retail division gets better every day. Evie and Violet are planning to open up in Harrisburg. It's a reach geographically because the Philly papers and radio are not very strong in Harrisburg. But it's their division to run and their decision. You'll hear more about it tomorrow."

He studied the card again. "The manufacturing division is profitable, but unfortunately, the mobile phone project eats it all up and we're not expanding the network fast enough. Got to face it, Jack, we're not big enough. We need a budget maybe four to ten times what we've got, *and* we need more manpower—a recruiting system and a team system and team managers. My own time is almost entirely dedicated to the network. Right now, I got a serious problem with our new printed circuit line. We're investing a lot of money in it, and I'm starting to think we should be putting the money into a new technology. We're making the boards faster and better all the time, but we're using the same technology as when we started, just with more efficient equipment. We're the biggest in the industry, and we keep lowering our prices because we're so good at what we do. So, an idea came to me for a new way to make the boards. I have to work it out—and fast, because no doubt a couple kids in a garage somewhere are working on it right now.

"I gotta get on it, Jack," he continued. "We're building the world's best Model T Ford, but somebody is going to introduce a brand new Chevy. That somebody has to be us."

"What do we need most?" I asked. "More help? More R&D money? *What?*"

He hesitated before responding. He studied the card intently, as if the answer were on it. Then he stared at me for a few seconds. "This is a biggie, Jack," he said. Another pause. "I'm for selling the mobile network."

It was a stunner, and I hesitated to respond. I studied Eddie's face.

He did not appear in the least agitated. He had spoken calmly, as usual, his thoughts clear and fully formed.

"How long you been carryin' this around?" I asked him.

"Maybe a month," he said, "but you know I don't like to air a problem until I've thought of a solution. It hit me a couple days ago."

"You're not thinking of selling to APC?"

"C'mon, Jack," he chuckled. "*Never.* We're good with APC the way we are. It's a good contract. They get their royalties, and they don't bother us. No, it's

Motorola. They're a big customer. They've been buying just about everything in our catalog, not just printed circuit boards, and they share their design ideas with us. It's almost as if their engineers are part of Dunlaur."

He took a deep breath. "Motorola wants to buy the phone and network, and the offer is four million. Unlike the APC offer, we'll keep Dunlaur Electronics."

He sipped at his coffee. "This deal does it all, Jack. It's enough money for us to do whatever we want at the plant and it means lifetime financial security for both of us. But I ain't about to retire, and neither are you. Hell, we're not even forty. Dunlaur will keep growing, and we'll be supplying Motorola with most of the components for the network."

I was dumbfounded, and he knew it. He reached across the table, put a hand on my arm, and looked me straight in the eye. "I don't expect you to make an immediate decision, Jack. Motorola can wait. Take whatever time you need to think about it. We'll talk when you're ready."

"Eddie," I said, "I'm stunned. All this going on around me and I don't see it? Am I so out of touch?"

"Not at all, Jack," he said. "You've been busy with appointments, running your sales force, dealing with distributors, putting out fires . . . you're focused on the daily priorities, and that's as it should be—it's why you're the very best at what you do. Give you the product to sell and you'll sell it, whether it's a two-dollar-and-fifty-cent printed circuit board or a multimillion-dollar mobile phone network. Me, I couldn't sell a dollar for ninety cents."

He picked up the three-by-five card and stared at it then back at me. "There's something else, Jack. Bradford Wister. I never was one hundred percent convinced his turnaround was on the level. It didn't make sense then, and it doesn't make sense now, even though we closed the royalty deal with APC. I think I understand human nature . . . a little bit. The network was a chance for him to catapult to the top. With APC behind the proj-ect, he would have a network up and running across the country in two years—three, tops. He could be the top industrialist in the country. I still can't believe he just walked away from it. It doesn't fit."

He continued. "I think he's still plotting, and if we sell to Motorola, we're rid of him. He won't fuck around with Motorola."

He turned his attention to the card again. "One more thing, Jack. I want to talk about Adam."

What about Adam?

WHAT WE JUST talked about, Jack"—Eddie held up the three-by-five card—"isn't the most important thing on this card. The most important one is what's with Adam?"

"What about Adam?" I asked, my gut suddenly tight with worry. "What's going on with Adam?"

"That's it exactly. You're so busy working, you've lost touch with your own son. Do you ever talk with him? Do you know how he spends his time? Do you know his friends? Do you know if he even *has* any friends? Forget about Dunlaur, Jack. The main reason I dragged you out today is Adam. Your boy is the most important thing in your life, and you need to get the relationship on track before it's too late."

Adam Plans a Party

WHAT EDDIE HAD said about me and Adam was a body blow. He was right, of course, and I knew I had to fix it. I pondered how to go about it. There would be no instant makeover. Adam was perceptive, and if I pushed too hard and fast, he would suspect something phony.

Propitiously, the opportunity came from Adam himself.

"Hey, Dad," he said when the Dunlaur driver brought him home at six that evening, "can I have a bunch of kids over Sunday afternoon?"

"Sure, Adam," I answered, a bit surprised. I knew of only one friend, Billy Davis, a schoolmate whose father was a longtime employee in charge of our press room. That's where the shears and slitters and brake presses and punch presses did their work. Billy loved cars and was always tinkering with them; he had an after-school job at an auto repair shop. He reminded me of Eddie when we were that age.

"I'll get Mrs. Wilson to prepare the eats," I said. "How many kids?"

"We'll be twelve," he said, "six boys, six girls. I want to move the furniture in the living room against the walls so we can have a dance floor. We'll need to use your record player; a friend is bringing the music. Snacks and sodas are all we need."

"Good deal, son," I said. "Do you mind if I'm in the house? I'll stay out of your way, but I'd like to meet your friends."

"Sure, Dad," he said, cheerfully and without hesitation. "You'll like these kids."

I didn't want to be alone that day with a houseful of teenagers, so I asked Evie to come by and keep me company.

Sure, she said. It'll be fun.

Bobo's Trial

THE NEXT MORNING, Durells brought me the news that Bobo's lawyers had again successfully petitioned the court to delay the start of his trial. The initial postponement had been from July 1963 to the Tuesday after Labor Day; the trial date had now been moved to February 1964.

Durells reminded me that contact with Bobo could be disastrous for Dunlaur, adding that there was nothing Eddie or I could do to help him anyway. "Just keep your distance," he said.

Selling the Mobile Phone System

EDDIE AND I CONTINUED to discuss a possible sale of our mobile phone system to Motorola but only superficially. Evie asked good questions while expressing her trust in us to make the right decision. We set down the thirty-first of October as "Decision Day."

The way we were looking at it, selling would be more a lifestyle choice than a financial decision. The network was a demanding master. It demanded all our money and time and denied our attention to other issues. To do the network properly, we would have to raise three to five million dollars, which meant taking on big debt or selling an interest in the company. Why not sell and relax? We could continue to build Dunlaur Retail and keep the plant at the leading edge of every new development in our product lines. With our personal financial security assured, our business lives would be relatively free of stress. Motorola would be a major customer for our relays, boosters, transmitters, and all the other components that went into the network, apart from the phones themselves. And although Motorola would be building the phones, they would purchase from us a number of components we'd patented.

A sale now would also reduce the chance that a really big company would enter the field and leap ahead of Dunlaur. Motorola might even decide to do it. That, I thought, would be a battle in which I wouldn't bet against Motorola, not to mention that losing them as a customer would be a major setback.

So really, what was there to decide? Why were we hesitating? It was hubris, we agreed—the urge to be not only pioneers but leaders in the new world of wireless communication. Let's be realistic.

211

Adam's Party

ONE OF THE SUNDAY morning talk shows focused on segregation in the United States. There was a clip of George Wallace's January 1963 inauguration as governor of Alabama. The highlight of his speech was *segregation now, segregation tomorrow, segregation forever.*

Walter Cronkite spoke of the country's deepening involvement in Vietnam.

"Whattaya think about Vietnam, Dad?" Adam asked.

"I don't like it," was my reply. I carried the dread that Vietnam might become a long war that brought back the draft. Adam was going on sixteen—less than three years separating him from military age—and while thinking about it filled me with anxiety, it wasn't something I wanted him worrying about.

"C'mon," I said, "let's give Mrs. Wilson a hand setting up for the party."

"Sure, Dad," he said.

I believe he understood why Vietnam was not a topic I wanted to discuss. At least not yet.

* * *

About an hour before the party, Adam came downstairs sporting a crisp pair of khakis, loafers, and a well-pressed oxford button-down shirt with a necktie. No, you don't find teenage boys dressing like that today, not without adult intervention. As I admired his appearance, I reflected how much he was like me at that age. *But he's better looking than I was,* I thought.

Adam was tall, blue-eyed, and fair-haired, slender but well-built, with an engaging smile. I had been skinny and freckle-faced with unruly straw hair. I have a photo of Alice and me in the summer of 1939, leaning against a railing on the Atlantic City Boardwalk. She's wearing a light cotton dress, slightly lifted by an ocean breeze, her face illuminated with her great smile. I have my arm around her, holding her close. Alice looks like a young woman; I'm an ungainly boy. Hard to imagine that skinny youngster becoming a Marine combat officer just four years later.

At two o'clock, the doorbell rang.

"That will be Evie," I said, going to the door. I was wrong. It was Violet.

"Violet . . ." I said in surprise. "I was expecting Evie."

"Well, Jack," she said with a quick smile, "something came up, and Evie asked me to fill in. I hope you don't mind."

Did I mind? The sight of her took my breath away. As usual, she wore slacks to conceal her scarred left leg. The scar on her left cheek was barely noticeable, just a narrow line—as she said, like a dueling scar. I stood immobile in the doorway for several seconds, at a complete loss for words.

Fortunately, and in spite of the months that had passed since I'd last seen her, Violet didn't miss a beat.

212

Party Time

S HE'D BROUGHT SEVERAL items for the party. Flowers; two tall candelabras; rolls of red, yellow, and green ribbon; a red strobe light; and a camera.

"This is a party, Jack," she said. "Let's make it look like one. Help me drape these ribbons across the ceiling. The candles go on the dining room table. We'll light them once the guests arrive. A good place for the strobe light is right here . . . the kids will love it when they're dancing. And here, Jack," she said, handing me the camera, "you'll be the *Candid Camera* man. Turn on all the lights in the house and the outdoor ones too. *Festive* is what we want—the guests should see the house from a block away."

First to arrive was Billy Davis with two girls I hadn't met. "Hi, Adam," he said. "Hi, Mr. Laurel. Meet Laura and Thelma. I picked them up on my way over."

Billy smiled as he shook my hand, looking at me directly—nothing bashful about him. I'd found that most boys of his age were uncomfortable around grownup males, especially their friends' fathers. And me, his father's employer for many years. I really liked this kid.

The other guests began arriving minutes later. The boys were similarly dressed in khakis, loafers, oxford shirts; some wore crewneck sweaters. All wore neckties. The girls wore skirts and blouses; a few wore sweaters.

Mrs. Wilson appeared in her regular cooking attire, a starched white dress and a white apron. "Food is served," she announced cheerfully. "Come and get it!"

The dining room sparkled with light and Violet's ribbons. As Mrs. Wilson lit the tall candles, the kids attacked the food.

Adam introduced Violet and me to each guest, and I realized that except for Billy Davis, I was meeting all of them for the first time. How had I let that happen?

I was surprised when the dancing started to the swing music of yesteryear rather than the rock and roll that was all the rage. The speakers reverberated with the irresistible sounds of the Big Bands: Benny Goodman, Glenn Miller, Tommy Dorsey, Duke Ellington, Harry James, Woody Herman, Lionel Hampton, Count Basie.

"A String of Pearls," "Sing, Sing, Sing," "Take the A Train," "Pennsylvania 6-5000," "Song of India," "And the Angels Sing," "One O'Clock Jump," "Moonglow," "In the Mood." I was impressed and appreciative and couldn't have kept my toes from tapping if I'd wanted to.

Violet's strobe light was an inspiration. She turned off all the other lights, and the living-room-turned-dance-hall became a place of magic, filled with the throbbing beat of the Big Bands. The strobe caught the dancers in motion, froze them momentarily, then released them back to the darkness. There were smiles on every face.

I was unprepared when Violet took my arm. "C'mon, Jack," she urged, tugging me onto the dance floor, "dance with me!"

"I'll try," I said, "but I have two left feet."

"You'll do fine, Jack," she said. "It's not really dancing, it's jitterbug—you just bend your knees and shake a little. I'll do the rest." And that's what she did. Holding my hand, she circled me, hips and shoulders in motion, rolling, dipping; coming closer, backing away; smiling, laughing, shaking her head, leaning into me.

As the music ended, she wrapped herself into my arm, turning her back to me. My arm was around her waist, holding her deliciously close against me.

She turned and kissed my cheek. "So you *can* dance," she whispered. "Liar!"

I held her tight for two seconds longer than necessary. A vision of Alice flashed in front of me. That hadn't happened for a long time. I took a step back into safety.

The kids were laughing and applauding us. "Good show, Dad!" Adam cheered.

213

Loosening Up

THAT FLASH OF ALICE in my mind's eye came to me less and less as the years passed. The image was of that moment in the morning . . . the last time I would ever see her.

I had just finished breakfast and was getting ready to leave for work. She called from the top of the stairs. "Come up," she said. She had something for me. I took the stairs two at a time and entered the bedroom. "What is it you have for me?" I asked.

"Me!" she said, laughing, as she threw herself onto the bed. Her hair spread out on the pillow, framing her head, her arms reaching out to me. We made love. Then I left the house, never to see her again.

I relived that moment unexpectedly, randomly, the image flashing for a fraction of a second. It had happened a thousand times. Lately, not so often.

* * *

Adam's party was a big success. Music and laughter filled the house. It enveloped me in a glow of good feeling but left a tinge of melancholy. This should have been Alice's joy.

I took Violet's hand and led her to the den. "Let's take a powder," I said. "We're inhibiting them."

I turned on the TV. *The Ed Sullivan Show* was on, and we sat on the sofa to watch it. Violet smiled at me. She began to say something but was interrupted by a couple of girls peeking around the corner.

"Can I ask you something?" one of them asked shyly.

"Of course," Violet said, waving them in. "Ask me anything."

The girl gathered her confidence. "Shall I call you Miss Dunauskas?"

"No, dear. Please call me Violet. And what are your names?"

"I'm Laura, and this is Thelma. We read about you . . . how you run a business . . . about everything you've been through. You're *so* beautiful . . . and the way you dress—so stylish!"

The girl blushed before continuing. "I want to be a doctor, like my dad. I think that's a great thing to be, and my dad says there should be more women doctors. But it's scary to think about sometimes, and when I see you, I wonder how you got so strong and confident."

From Violet's own blush, I could see the admiration had caught her by surprise. "You are a flatterer!" She patted the sofa. "Here, come sit with me, both of you."

Perhaps not wanting to crowd me out, the two girls sat on the floor beside us. They looked up at Violet worshipfully, and soon the three of them were engrossed in animated conversation, smiling faces, frequent laughter. Violet drew them out effortlessly and put them at ease, as if she did it all the time.

I found my way to an easy chair across the room and had no sooner sat back when Billy and another boy came into the den to see me. "Mr. Laurel," Billy said. "Would you tell us about the invasion on Port Gloucester? I'm reading a history of the War in the Pacific, and it makes the Port Gloucester landing sound like an easy one—but real important because it stopped the Japanese. Seems like they never advanced anywhere after that. I know you were there, leading an infantry platoon—your first engagement?"

I had never told anyone the details of my war service. Like most who served in combat, we said where we served and little else. How could anyone really describe the feelings, the fear, the prayer, the horror of a combat engagement? That was for writers and poets.

"Not much to tell, Billy," I said. "We landed on December twenty-fourth, 1942. I'll never forget the date. The fighting was over by New Year's Day. My platoon was forty men. I lost seven of them. I was scared. We all were scared."

Billy had another question on his mind. "Mr. Laurel, what's gonna be in Vietnam? My older brother told me there are over twelve thousand American soldiers there, and the president says we're there to stay. He's sending helicopters, and my brother thinks he's going to send a lot more troops. In a couple of years, kids my age might have to go."

I answered him as frankly as I could, aware that Vietnam was becoming a more sensitive situation for American families every day. As we talked about it, Adam wandered in. Then another boy. Then another. Soon they were all on the floor at my feet. The conversation drifted from Vietnam to WWII and back to Vietnam before shifting to the new football season—talk about Chuck Bednarik of the Eagles, Fran Tarkenton, Mike Ditka. And talk about baseball: Mickey Mantle, Willie Mays, Hank Aaron, Yogi Berra, and the great pitchers, Sandy Koufax and Whitey Ford. As we talked, I noticed Adam stealing quick looks at the girl, Laura—Violet's new friend who wanted to be a doctor. She didn't seem to notice him, so focused was her attention on Violet.

Suddenly, I couldn't take my own eyes off Violet. Six teenaged girls now sat at her feet, laughing, smiling, pushing forward, all talking at once as Violet alternated as moderator, listener, instructor, storyteller. She was lovely. She looked over at me and smiled.

I loved her.

The Party's Over

AT NINE O'CLOCK, I announced that we had to wrap the party up because tomorrow was a school day.

The kids groaned collectively. "Can't we have another hour, Mr. Laurel? Another half hour, please?"

"No, kids, it's time to go home, but we'll do it again soon." I turned to Billy. "Billy, would you please call your folks and ask if Adam can stay overnight at your place?"

Adam looked at me, a question on his lips, but Billy broke in. "I don't have to call, Mr. Laurel. My parents say Adam is always welcome anytime."

The kids assembled in the foyer, put on their coats, and filed out, each one stopping to tell me and Violet it was the best party ever.

As Billy and Adam walked out the door, I overheard Adam say, "Billy, what's this all about? Why is my dad sending me to your house?"

And I heard Billy's answer, as they walked away. "You're asking me that? Whatsamatta with you, Adam? You stupid or somethin'?"

215

The Day After

I KNEW DINNER THE next day would be uncomfortable. And so it was. Adam was at the table when I arrived home, and Mrs. Wilson was looking at me differently. "Good evening, Mr. Laurel," she said and retreated quickly to the serenity of her kitchen.

"Hi, Dad," Adam said. He raised his eyebrows expectantly, waiting for me to open the conversation.

"Good evening, son," I said cheerily. "Great party, wasn't it? We'll have to do it again."

He came straight to the point. "What's with you and Violet, Dad?"

I forgot to have a prepared answer. Instead, I responded lamely, "What do you mean, son?"

"It's okay, Dad," he said. "I've known her all my life. You couldn't do better."

Kennedy Assassinated!

November 22, 1963

W E ALL REMEMBER where we were that afternoon.

Lyndon Baines Johnson became president and promised to honor Kennedy's memory by pursuing his programs and policy objectives. A shrewd, coercive politician, "LBJ" was a master at getting what he wanted out of Congress, and it was he who coined the phrase Great Society, recalling Roosevelt's New Deal and Truman's Fair Deal. Under that slogan, Johnson created Medicare, passed meaningful civil rights legislation including the Voting Rights Act, banned racial discrimination in public places and interstate commerce, and fulfilled a half dozen other goals that Kennedy, for all his charm and charisma, could have only dreamed of making into law.

Sadly, one of Kennedy's aims was to defeat the North Vietnamese. In honoring that particular Kennedy initiative, Vietnam became Johnson's war. It destroyed his reputation. It ruined his legacy. The country never recovered from Vietnam. It was wrong on so many levels.

* * *

The war divided the country. It unleashed a flood of national debt. It created a class of young people who regarded their government with anger and distrust. Two million seven hundred thousand Americans served in the war, which left fifty-eight thousand dead and three hundred four thousand wounded. Vietnam was a poor man's war. The soldiers who fought it were disproportionately poor, black, and undereducated. It was not a people's army, as had been the case in World War II. And it was not crowned with victory. After fourteen years of struggle, America snuck out of Vietnam ignominiously, our tail between our legs.

Kennedy's rationale was that it was a war to arrest the spread of Chinese communism throughout Southeast Asia. So it was really a surrogate war, just as Korea had been a surrogate war against the Soviets.

The war destroyed Johnson, a man with the capacity to be one of our truly great presidents. He was smart, tough, a forceful and effective leader, a man with a vision and the energy to build an equal and just society—a *Great Society*. All that talent, all that ability laid to waste by one colossal, defining mistake. Vietnam. Johnson's life and legacy disintegrated in the crucible of that hideous war.

It was Vietnam that brought Richard Nixon to the presidency. The unfinished war, dragging on murderously, unwinnable, killing Americans daily, the evening TV news bringing its horror into our living rooms every day.

If you study America during the Vietnam War, even at the height of it, you find a nation that was walled off from the conflict. Americans at home made no sacrifices. There were no clothing drives, no blood drives. There was no Hollywood Canteen for Vietnam servicemen. Unlike WWII, the country was not at war. The troops in Vietnam were at war, inside a capsule that didn't touch the everyday life of Americans other than the families of the warriors inside that capsule—like a glass globe you shake to create a snow shower over a tiny scene.

We Americans knew the war was going on. We saw it on TV. We read about it in the paper. But unless a loved one was in the capsule, it was not part of our life. It was some nasty, distant thing. There was some talk about a draft, and in a couple of years, Adam would be of draft age. That concerned me, but I felt sure the war would not last that long. After all, we were in WWI for less than two years, in WWII less than four years, and in Korea for three.

The country paid attention to the stock market, to professional baseball, to the NFL and the NBA, and to the movies and the movie stars and Washington gossip. The lobbyists plied their trade. Corporate CEOs raised their salaries. The spread between incomes of management and workers widened. The American economy was drifting toward marketing and finance and banking and corporate dealmaking while our emblematic penchant for *making things* was in decline.

The country had little concern about the future. We were dominant everywhere. Although there were always cycles of boom times followed by corrections or recessions, our basic economic health was strong. Our only clear threat was the Soviet Union, but that contest had become a standoff. Mutual Assured Destruction—MAD—was the bond that kept our relationship with the Soviets in cold equilibrium.

The bad things creeping in were still too small to be noticed except by a few astute scholars, economists, and sociologists. But dangerous times lay ahead.

Shadowed

A T THE END of a clear December day, I left the Dunlaur plant for home. I quickly realized I was being followed by a dark green Buick.

I went off my regular route and detoured through small side streets. The Buick followed. I continued on until I reached Wellington Avenue, a main road with plenty of traffic. I pulled into the parking lot of a busy shopping center. The car pulled up alongside me; a man got out and approached my window.

"Jack Laurel?" he said. "Leave your car here. I'm taking you to Bobo. He wants to see you."

I'd been warned by my attorney and others to avoid the man, but old habits die hard. I'd never once refused a summons from Bobo. Instinctively, I got out of my car and got into his.

Bobo's Man

W HO ARE YOU?" I asked. "I don't recognize you."

"You wouldn't," the man said. "Bobo had me get you because I'm a nobody here. I work the uptown district, above Arctic Avenue. Ain't nobody watchin' me. They got Bobo under twenty-four-hour surveillance, but he give 'em the slip. We gonna drive around till dark, then I'm takin' you to him."

We drove north for a while before finally crossing the bridge to Long Beach Island. Bobo's man killed his headlights as he made a turn and pulled over. "Here we are," he said.

We walked in the dark to a small inlet where a fifteen-foot outboard runabout with a windshield and a canvas top was moored.

"Get in," he said, and I complied. He unmoored the boat, climbed in, and pushed off.

"Where we headed?" I asked.

"He's out there," he gestured out to sea. "It'll take 'bout forty minutes."

219

Bobo

I T WAS A CLEAR night, no clouds, a quarter-moon rising in the east. There were stars, but only the brightest could compete with the surface lights from the Atlantic City shoreline. They spread a weak, milky light over the ocean.

A 171-foot-tall lighthouse marked the entrance to the Atlantic City Inlet. Its beacon is now extinguished because the Trump Taj Mahal and the Revel are three times higher than the old lighthouse. Their lights are visible thirty miles out to sea; the old lighthouse beam was only good for ten.

With each mile we covered, the fading lights of shore let a thousand more stars come into view. When we reached the rendezvous, the sky was a white canopy of a billion stars, set in a pitch black sky.

We pulled abreast of a sixty-foot motorsailor, a black silhouette drifting in a calm black sea. The boat displayed running lights, a masthead light, and a stern light. No other lights were visible. A dark figure leaned over and extended his arm to me. My hand disappeared in his, half again bigger than mine. He lifted me easily up a rope ladder with wooden treads. It was Georgie.

"Jack," he grunted, pulling me into a bear hug. "Good t'see ya."

Frankie, man of few words, stood beside him. "Jack," was all he said, but he embraced me no less tightly.

We went below. The boat was spacious and luxurious, its saloon outfitted as a comfortable living room. Blackout curtains were on all the windows. I had seen no light from outside, but the space was well-lit. And there was Bobo. I hadn't seen him for two years. I studied him. The years were making their mark. He was pushing seventy but still big, powerful. His slicked-back hair was mostly gray, but little else showed the passage of years.

"Hi, Jack," he smiled, gathering me into his powerful chest. "My boy," he said, "I've missed ya. Here, have something to eat." He nodded to an array of plates and platters on the ship's bar.

"I'll probably never see ya again," he said, "'cause I ain't gonna stand trial. I ain't gonna let them pick me over like a jackal havin' a long meal."

"Whatcha gonna do, Bobo?" I asked, but I already knew.

"I'm takin' off. This here boat has a captain and a crew of three. It's a motorsailor. It can sail anywhere. It's gonna take us to a place where nobody will ever find me."

"Whose boat is it?" I asked. "Yours? And the crew? This is an expensive business."

"It's this way," Bobo said. "I sold out to the Philly organization. They been tryin' to take over Atlantic City for a long time. You know that. *Why fight me?* I told 'em. You can have it all—easy—everything in good order—and Georgie and Frankie to keep it tight. Just buy me out. And they did. Me and Loretta gonna get paid—good money—as long as either of us is alive. We'll be real well off."

Bobo continued, "The boat belongs to a big Philadelphia real estate developer. He's loanin' it to me."

He sipped at his drink. "Jack," he said, "I never knew really big money. This gang—this real estate developer—the kinda money he makes, the kinda money he has, you can't imagine. The Philly organization thinks they got him in their pocket, but I think it's the other way. I think he's got the organization under his thumb. I met him for five minutes. He wanted to get a look at me before he approved the buyout. *Ya need to get away?* he said. *Take my boat. And my captain and the crew. They'll take ya anywhere ya wanna go. Be my guest.*"

Bobo snorted, stifling a laugh. "Then the guy says, *But, Bobo, don't forget to send the boat back!*"

"This guy is big time over here. He owns a whole fuckin' island with its own hotel, a mansion, and a landing strip. He has his own jet, maybe two. He's got a yacht makes this boat look like a toy—it's like a cruise ship.

And he's got seven, maybe eight security guys. They're like a small army. He makes me and my organization look like pikers."

"So, Bobo," I asked, "where will you go?"

"Jack," he smiled, "ya don't wanna know. Georgie and Frankie don't even know. It's better that way. You can't tell what you don't know."

As he spoke, Loretta entered the cabin. Still the black-haired beauty, fifty-something, a handsome woman. "Jack," she said as she approached me. "So good, so good, *so good* to see you!" She wrapped her arms around me and kissed my cheek. "This is a goodbye party, Jack, but don't be sad. Bobo and I had a grand time here for so many years. The good times are not over—we're going to have a comfortable life where it will be warm and beautiful and no stress."

I was grasping for words when Bobo said, "Son, I'm jumpin' bail, and that means you and Eddie will lose your five-hunnert thou. I kinda think you knew it might happen. But I'll have somethin' goin' on, and I aim to pay you back. As long as it takes."

"We're headin' out tonight," he said, "and I had to see you one more time."

There was a knock on the door before it opened partway and the captain leaned in. "Time to get going, Mr. Truck," he said.

Bobo took Georgie in a bear hug. It was a sight to behold. Two giants in close embrace. I saw moist eyes. They choked out words of farewell. Then Frankie. The eyes turned teary. And then, my turn.

"Goodbye, son," he whispered then pushed me away and turned his back to me.

We all came on deck. Georgie and Frankie climbed down into the runabout. I followed.

"So long, Bobo. So long, Loretta," I called out. "God bless you!"

The big boat hoisted sail and slipped away. Bobo's voice boomed in the darkness. "Goodbye, fellas. I love you."

A wave of sadness came over me. I was never going to see him again. Somehow, he was my dear friend, my security, my harbor in a storm. I cupped my hands and shouted into the night, "I love you, Bobo!"

220

An Imperfect Tranquility

WHEN WE CLOSED the deal with Motorola, Eddie and I were suddenly multimillionaires. Dunlaur prospered. Evie and Violet opened stores in Harrisburg and Pittsburgh. The manufacturing division continued to add to its product line. Our profits grew embarrassingly large.

Laura, Adam's friend who wanted to be a doctor, became his girlfriend and a regular visitor at the house. I was reminded of myself with Alice at their age. I remembered how it was those days, coming home to find Alice at the dining room table, helping my mother stuff envelopes. But Laura was not like Alice. Alice had been effervescent, always talking, always in motion. Laura was shy and reserved, though Adam could bring her out of her shell. He made her laugh, a pretty sound. I liked Laura, and I liked her and Adam together.

Violet moved in with us in the spring of '64. We were in love, inseparable. It was a blessed time. It was the best of times.

221

Bobo's Favor That I Didn't Know

August 1965

U NDERLYING THE TRANQUILITY of my new life with Violet was the gnaw-ing, growing worry over Vietnam. In March 1965, the US had sent two battalions of Marines on shore at China Beach north of Da Nang, and now there was talk of additional troops. Adam would be eighteen in September, and it made me crazy to think he might be called to serve. It was a helpless feeling that didn't leave me alone. Violet and I talked about it often.

I drove to a meeting with Larry Durells about a revision in the Dunlaur retirement program, nothing important. On the way, I listened to the morn-ing newscaster discussing recent events. The war had been a background story for a long time, but the potential escalation was getting some airplay. The newscaster mentioned Medicare, which Kennedy had pushed and Johnson had just signed into law. He remarked, as an aside, that the cost of a NYC transit ride was about to jump from fifteen to twenty cents.

A lot of attention was paid to the $130,000 salary that Willie Mays was rumored to receive for the 1966 baseball season. It would be the highest salary ever paid to a ballplayer.

Along with the news, I listened to a few of the top songs of the day: *I Got You Babe* by Sonny & Cher, *Henry the VII, I Am* by Herman's Hermits, and *Help!* by the Beatles.

My business with Durells was completed quickly. As I prepared to leave, he asked me to wait a moment. He had something for me from Bobo.

"I hope he and Loretta are okay," I said, and Durells assured me they were doing fine.

"So, what've you got, Larry?" I asked. "Any money? Eddie and I wrote off the five hundred thousand dollars we gave him, but you never know—maybe..."

"Wishful thinking, Jack," he said with a slight smile. "Bobo said I could tell you something though. About the APC lawyer, Wister. I'm sure you remember him."

"I sure do," I said. "You know, we never understood what happened with that guy. We thought we were going down—the whole company—and then, suddenly . . . well, you know. So what is it you want to tell me?"

"All right, Jack," Durells said. "This is the story. Bobo knew about your trouble with APC. I gave him the news on you every day after they got wind of you and Eddie building the mobile phone network. He knew about the meetings at the Bellevue.

"Bobo sent Georgie and Frankie to Chicago that Friday, a week after Wister told you *no deal* and that he would sue you for patent infringement. Anyhow," he said, "This is Georgie's story about the trip to Chicago.

"Georgie and Frankie showed up Friday morning in Chicago at Wister's office suite. They were well-dressed, like business executives. You know how they look when they get dressed like that—brute power stuffed into navy blue suits. They told the receptionist they're here to see Mr. Wister. *Do you have an appointment?* No, says Georgie. *Sorry, you need an appointment. Mr. Wister doesn't see anyone without an appointment.* I know that but this is real important. Mr. Wister will want to see us. Georgie hands the receptionist a nine-by-twelve-inch flat mailer envelope with Wister's name and address on it. He says please give this to Mr. Wister. He repeats, I'm sure he will want to see us. Georgie looks like a man you don't want to disappoint.

"The receptionist says, *I'll give this to Mr. Wister's secretary. Please have a seat.* A few minutes later, Wister's secretary comes to the receptionist area, carrying the manila envelope. *Who is the gentleman who wants this delivered to Mr. Wister?*

"Georgie stands up and says very politely that *Mr. Wister wants to receive that. It is very important. Please just hand it to him. He will want to see us right away.*

"The secretary says, *He's in a meeting with a number of his associates, and I can't disturb him. The meeting might last for hours.*

"*Just excuse yourself and hand it to him.* There is something very authoritative in Georgie's manner, a sense of power concealed in the business suit and behind the quiet words.

"She says, *I'll try.*

Only a few minutes have passed when four men file out of Wister's office, followed by Wister. *Who delivered this?* Wister wants to know.

"Georgie and Frankie stand up. Wister motions them to follow him to his office.

* * *

"Here," Durells said, handing me a manila envelope. "It's a copy of what Georgie delivered to Wister."

I opened the envelope and pulled out perhaps twenty eight-by-ten-inch glossy prints: photographs of Bradford Wister and a great-looking girl. The girl was completely nude in half the pictures. *My god!* I knew her—Elena Volpe! And then I remembered that the Bellevue was her territory. She'd been Bobo's gift to me at that same hotel a few years ago. He'd sent her to me to burst open the dam that was keeping me from dating, and it had worked wonders.

Some of the photos showed Elena and Wister sexually engaged, naked, and in an array of positions. There were a few shots of them seated at restaurant tables, and several of them walking and sitting in a park, holding hands. I flipped back to the sex shots, They were salacious, especially the two or three showing Elena's lips and cheeks working Wister's engorged penis as he looked down approvingly, smiling broadly, his hands on her breasts. Wow!

Durells continued.

"Georgie told Wister that the pictures were taken the week before, in Philadelphia, on Friday night, on Saturday night, and on Sunday, Monday, and Tuesday. Georgie said, in a kindly tone, that Wister was supposed to return to Chicago on Sunday morning, but Georgie thought it must have been too wonderful to give up, so Wister made up a story about staying over a few days to do research at the University of Pennsylvania law library."

"These here pictures ain't gonna' to sit well with Martin Dunlap or your wife, Georgie said. *Your wife is Dunlap's daughter, ain't she?*

"Georgie said Wister turned bright red then all the color drained out of his face. He went white. *What do you want?* he asked.

"Not much, Georgie said. *Just lay off those Dunlaur boys—that's all. Nobody else will ever see these pictures.*

"Wister could not compose himself. *All right, all right. How about the negatives? How about all the copies? Do I get them?* Georgie stood up and leaned on the desk toward Wister, a hint of menace in his face. *You get nothin',* he said. *You'll do what I said or the world will see these pictures.*

"C'mon, Georgie said to Frankie. *We're done with this piece of shit. He'll do the smart thing.*

"They left."

* * *

It took me a few seconds to process what I'd just heard and seen.

"I don't get it, Larry," I said finally. "Elena Volpe? It can't be a coincidence—or an accident. How does she come to Bradford Wister?"

"I'll tell you, Jack . . ." Durells said. "You and Bobo and me—we've been through a lot of shit together, haven't we?"

I nodded and he continued, "I had a feeling that Wister character could be trouble, so I did some research on him. It's the reason I set up the meetings at the Bellevue—because it's Elena's territory. I suggested to Bobo that he get her on Wister."

"How did she get to him?" I asked. "And who took the pictures?"

"That's her business, Jack," Durells answered. "She's the best. She uses a photographer when she's on a case. They know what to do and how to do it so the mark never knows."

"You mean to say that Bobo has pictures of *me* and Elena?"

Durells laughed. "No, Jack. For you, she was a favor—a gift from Bobo. Wister was an assignment. What do you think it cost for her and the photographer for that job? My guess is five grand. She doesn't work cheap.

"And Jack, as Bobo would say, this is *appena fra noi*. Only between us. Not a word—not even to Eddie or your sister. Understood?"

I was musing on my relationship with Bobo as I left Durell's office, about everything he'd done for me. He got me the Traymore job, which saved Dunlaur and put us on the road to success. He found and levied justice on Charlie Norris, Alice's killer. Then he saved Dunlaur again—this time from Bradford Wister at APC. Remarkable. What had I done to deserve such a friendship? A few small errands when I was fifteen, and an introduction to Alan Goren and Benny James, which, while a lucrative partnership, almost ended in disaster for all of us. Bobo had come through for me then too.

Until I left for the Marines in 1942, my feelings for Bobo were always a combination of admiration and fear. When I returned from the War, I was no longer a boy. I related to him as men do when mutual respect overlays a deep reservoir of trust and friendship. Eddie and I did one favor for him when we bugged the police chief's office; another when we removed the bug. And we gave him a half-million dollars for the bail bond. Viewed in this light, I had no better friend in the world than Bobo.

* * *

It was that very evening, after we'd climbed into bed, that Violet told me she was pregnant. She had been so certain that her reproductive system was destroyed in her youth that we'd never bothered with contraception.

"So," she said, matter-of-factly, "shall I abort?"

"Are you crazy?" I said, holding her close. "It's a blessing! We're getting married on Sunday!"

"You know people will count the months," she smiled.

"Let 'em count," I said smothering her with kisses.

She cried, fumbling for the words. "I'll be a good wife to you, Jack," she said. "And I'll be a good mother. You won't be sorry." Then she cried some more.

222

Adam at Eighteen, Vietnam, and the Draft

A DAM GRADUATED ATLANTIC City High in June 1965 and started classes at MIT two months later. His eighteenth birthday was on September 15; he came home from school to celebrate it with a formal Saturday night dinner-dance that Violet and I had arranged at the Traymore.

The Traymore ballroom was a study in elegance. All was light, silver and gleaming that evening, with flowers everywhere. Twenty-two tables for eight were arranged in a semicircle around a polished hardwood dance floor facing the stage, which held a popular eight-piece band featuring two talented vocalists. The intermission rock group, consisting of five Atlantic City High students billing themselves as "The Facts of Life," was energetic, loud, and, to my ear, a bit rough around the edges. Yet the younger guests clearly preferred their music to the smooth sounds of the professionals. They danced up a storm.

Adam's closest friend, Billy Davis, had come with a date. Thirty other boys and girls from the graduating class were there, many with dates. Violet was pregnant, in her third month and beginning to show. She was radiant. She and Laura shared hostess duties. Laura's parents had accepted Violet's personal invitation, and we met for the first time.

Goren and Zena arrived. I hardly recognized him in the tuxedo; Zena was striking in a flowing burgundy gown. Larry Durells and his wife came, as did some fifty Dunlaur employees, their spouses and dates. Eddie and Evie were a handsome couple. I was surprised how relaxed he appeared in his starched white shirt and black bowtie. He must have gone for one neck size larger than usual, I thought, as he wasn't constantly tugging at his collar—a longtime habit I'd always observed with covert amusement.

The party was full of life, and the dance floor was crowded. High spirits and laughter overflowed. A reporter from the *Atlantic City Press* crashed the party along with a photographer. He described it to me as an important social event—this party for the son of one of Atlantic City's most illustrious industrialists. I told him he could stay if he promised to keep the story short and sweet—and no pictures. He didn't keep his promise. A big story ran in the Sunday edition, with photos.

The *Press* story described the festivities as not only celebrating a gifted young man's birthday but also the Laurel family's great good fortune, which included the success of Dunlaur and my recent marriage to Violet. The reporter profiled Violet as one half of a dynamic team, with Evie, that was leading the way in retail innovation. He described Adam as a prodigy who, along with his young cousin, Eddie Dunauskas Jr., was heir apparent to the Dunlaur business empire. One remarkable family, he concluded.

The article made me feel proud, of course, and I could hardly have disagreed. *But…* What was the *But?* It overhung everything. I tried to shut it out, as though not thinking about it would make it go away. The *But* was Vietnam.

The WWII draft had never been discontinued, just set aside. It was reactivated for Korea and was now being enforced for Vietnam. Eighteen-year-olds were required to register. The call-ups were small in number so far, but the number was growing. You could get a deferment if you had a medical condition or if you were a father, conscientious objector, college student, or essential civilian personnel. I had prayed the war would be over before Adam was eligible, in part because I knew he had honorable ideas about duty in wartime.

Not just because of the war, though it was certainly a factor, I'd encouraged Adam to attend MIT after high school. His initial reaction had been, *No way, Dad.* He wanted to work at Dunlaur, like Eddie and me. Who needs college? After much consideration and further cajoling—not only from me, but from Eddie and Laura—he came to accept that technology was moving too fast, that there just wasn't enough time to learn everything on the job. He would be of greater value to Dunlaur after four years of engineering studies.

The night after the party, Adam asked whether we could meet for breakfast before he headed back to Cambridge. Not at home, though—maybe the diner? He wanted to talk privately.

"Count me in, son," I said.

This spelled trouble.

223

Not a Patriot

WE WENT OUT FOR breakfast. What he had to talk about was what I feared.

"Dad," he said, "I'll come right to the point. I'm going to enlist. Either the war will get worse and I'll end up being drafted before I graduate, or the war will be over by the time I graduate and I'll feel that I dodged it while guys like Billy Davis serve. He could get drafted. He could go to college, but he doesn't want to. He wants to work for Dunlaur like his father—like I want to do. But he's going to enlist rather than start a job and hope he doesn't get called up. Guys that enlist can choose their service."

"Adam—" I started to protest, but he didn't let me.

"Dad, this is the first tough thing I've ever had to do. You and Uncle Eddie, Grandpop and Alan Goren and Major Gordon and Billy's dad and Mr. Durells—you all served. I'm sure all of you could've got out of it, but you didn't. I'm like you, Dad. It's not that I'm some great patriot. It's that I owe... to go. I owe more than you did when you went. Look what I have. You were a kid with nothing waiting for you. It's because I have so much—like I have to deserve it—that's why I have to go. Does that make sense?"

* * *

It was a small victory when I convinced Adam to complete his freshman year before enlisting. It was less than nine months off, and his college deferment would allow it. Meanwhile, I thought, maybe the war will end. That didn't seem likely.

224

America's Golden
Quarter-Century

L OOKING BACK, I'VE come to realize that the twenty-five-year period from the end of World War II in 1945 to the end of 1969 was America's Golden Quarter Century. Some historians have begun calling it that.

It is always that way with history. The significance of events shaping the future, and what motivates them, are not considered in their own time, only much later.

That quarter century saw living standards rising; incomes rising; men with factory jobs enjoying middle-class incomes and pensions and medical insurance; terrible diseases being wiped out; college enrollments swelling; a new network of highways and bridges binding the country, making travel easier and more affordable; air-conditioning making life bearable in hot, humid climes, with places like Florida, Mississippi, and New Mexico becoming habitable year round.

Television brought free entertainment into the home. Air travel shrunk distances and travel prices dropped. Ordinary people became world travelers. Enjoyment of distant and exotic places was no longer reserved for the extremely wealthy. Americans were special—citizens of a magical land where anything was possible.

Above all, there was a sense of American Greatness. We believed in our institutions. We trusted in our government. We knew our economy was powerful. We endured recessions, confident they would end quickly.

America was envied and admired the world over. American businessmen could solve every problem. American business and industry were the incubators for an endless stream of inventions and new products and new ways to make life better.

I don't dismiss the overhang and dangers of the Cold War and the struggle to contain communism, and the fear of nuclear war. Maybe it's because we survived the communist challenge and witnessed the collapse of the Soviet Union that I can look back on those years and feel positive about them, in spite of the Cold War.

225

Endgame

* * *

JUST NOW, ALICE'S death scene flashed in my head. It unnerved me. I hadn't seen it for years. But here it was, sharp, devastating as ever. I suppose it will never leave me.

* * *

Violet and I have a daughter, born in 1966. We named her Alice. A perfect child.

When I told Violet we were going to get married, Violet said she would be a good wife and mother. She was—there could be none better.

* * *

Adam enlisted in the Marines in June 1966, one week after completing his freshman year at MIT. Thanks to his skills in communications, he was offered his choice of assignments and chose to head up a forward area communications unit. The Marines promised him a commission. They sent him through the same officers training program I'd gone through in 1942. He came out a captain.

He and Laura announced their engagement the day he received his commission. They had the same anxieties Alice and I had in 1942, deciding to defer their marriage until Adam returned home from the war.

* * *

In the summer of 1972, Larry Durells asked me to pay him a visit.

"What's up, Larry?" I asked.

"Come by tomorrow," was his answer.

When I arrived, Durells took me into his office and closed the door.

"I have something for you from Bobo," he said. He opened his desk drawer and took out two stacks of hundred dollar bills. "Bobo sent this," he said. "Five thousand dollars—for you and Eddie, on account of your loan. He hopes to send more soon."

"How did he send it?" I asked.

"That's a complicated story." Durells smiled. "But it's not important. There's a letter though. It's addressed to you."

Jack:

Me and Loretta are okay. I will try to send you and Eddie what I can whenever I can. The Philly Guys are holding to the deal. Me and Loretta are good for money. We are both healthy and feeling good. But lonely. We live quiet. This here is a fine place to live quiet. Nothing ever happens. It's beautiful. Good weather. Good scenery. We do not socialize. Only a little with some neighbors. But they do not know anything about us. We do not talk about ourselves. One day this neighbor, he is from Milan, he asks me do me and Loretta have any children. I did not want me and Loretta to look like just some old people all alone with no friends and no family, so I said yes, we have a son. He lives in America. His name is Jack. I hope that is okay with you.

Your friend,

Bobo

The End

About the Author

J. LOUIS "JACK" YAMPOLSKY (1928–2017) was a graduate of the Wharton School of the University of Pennsylvania who found career success as an accountant, business owner, restaurateur, and real estate investor. A lifelong Philadelphia-area resident, he built and ran two leading accounting firms in the city, retiring from public accounting after almost fifty years to become a financial manager of trusts and investment partnerships and to write.

During World War II and throughout his life, Jack was an active supporter of Jewish causes. As a teenager, he worked alongside his Russian-born parents and many other dedicated people in helping thousands of Jews escape from the Nazis, and after the war, he was involved in humanitarian efforts to resettle Holocaust survivors in the United States. In later years, his contributions to Israel and the Jewish people evolved in different ways, but his commitment never waned.

Jack's enduring interest in history, literature, and the complexities of human nature inspired a remarkable first novel, *A Boardwalk Story*. It was published in 2009 while he was a resident of Wynnewood, Pennsylvania, and Margate, New Jersey, with his wife, Judith; readers' enthusiasm for the novel encouraged him to write a sequel. He completed the manuscript for *The Best of Times* shortly before his death from cancer at age eighty-nine.